BOOK BELONGS TO
AMELIA KATE FLESHMAN

"FORD THE PACHOLET is a meticulously researched and beautifully illustrated history of the stirring events leading up to the pivotal Battle of Cowpens, told through the eyes of a local boy simply trying to survive and protect those he holds dear. Richly evocative of the time when the patriots of South Carolina—the site of more Revolutionary War battles and skirmishes than any of the other thirteen colonies—stood up to Bloody Banastre Tarleton and set our nation on the road to liberty. Not to be missed!"

~ K.G. McAbee, award-winning author of *Cabbages and Kings, Gilbert and the Clockwork Pirates*, and co-author with J.A. Johnson of *The Nereus Project* trilogy.

"Meehan's unique take on the Battle of Cowpens and the events leading up to it benefit from the perspective of both a young lad and an Indian 'lassie' thrown together by chance and circumstance. Highly readable and brimming with a palpable love of South Carolina and Revolutionary War history, this is a book for anyone who has ever wondered how our great country first came to fruition."

~ Jon Kirsch, best-selling author of the *Princess Who Defied Kings.*

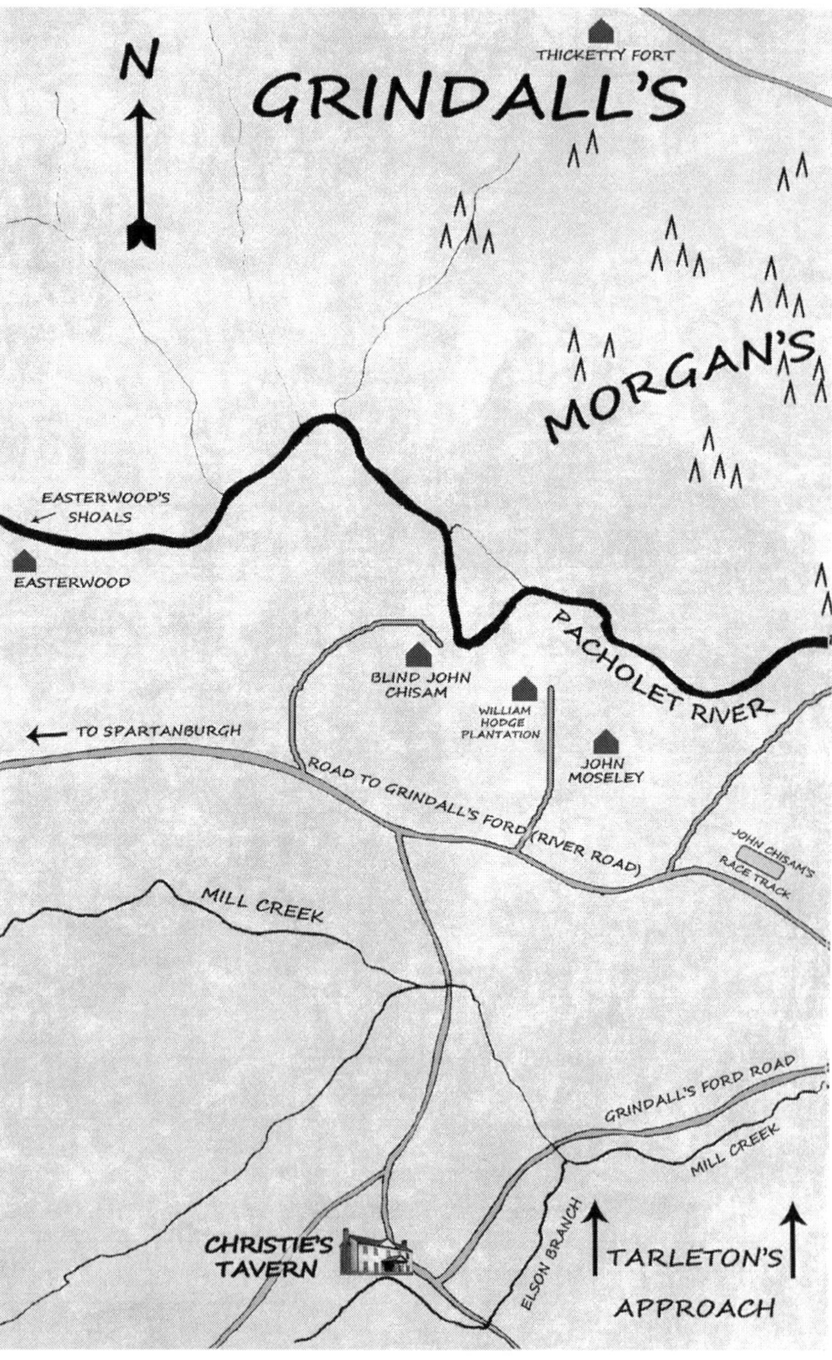
THICKETTY FORT
N
GRINDALL'S
MORGAN'S
EASTERWOOD'S
SHOALS
EASTERWOOD
PACHOLET RIVER
BLIND JOHN
CHISAM
WILLIAM
HODGE
PLANTATION
JOHN
MOSELEY
TO SPARTANBURGH
ROAD TO GRINDALL'S FORD (RIVER ROAD)
JOHN CHISAM'S
RACE TRACK
MILL CREEK
GRINDALL'S FORD ROAD
MILL CREEK
ELSON BRANCH
CHRISTIE'S
TAVERN
TARLETON'S
APPROACH

SIMS-MARCHBANKS MEETINGHOUSE
FORD
ASBURY
GREEN RIVER ROAD
ENCAMPMENT
GOUDELOCK CABIN
TO LOVE'S FORD
TO ASBURY
GRINDALL'S FORD ROAD
FARNANDIS MILL
MORGAN'S TENT
MOSELEY'S OAK
ALEXANDER CHESNEY
LITTLEJOHN MILL
SWAMP
FARNANDIS FEED, SEED, AND FLOUR
GRINDALL'S FORD
MILL CREEK
PACHOLET RIVER
FARNANDIS HOME
JASPER
FOSTER
BECKHAM
HAMES
SANDY RUN CREEK
MITCHELL
WILLIAMS
MOSELEY

FORD THE PACHOLET

FORD THE PACHOLET

AN AMERICAN REVOLUTIONARY WAR NOVEL CULMINATING IN THE PIVOTAL BATTLE OF COWPENS

Richard C. Meehan, Jr.

Noggin Universe
Press

Library of Congress Control Number: 2021925097

"Lem's House" illustration by Renee Meehan.
Cover art and all other interior artwork by the author.
Some image elements by Liz Crawley Photography
Images of General Daniel Morgan and Colonel Banastre Tarleton are public domain.

Printed in the United States of America.
First Edition

ISBN: 978-1-7372975-3-6 (hardcover)
ISBN: 978-1-7372975-4-3 (paperback)
ISBN: 978-1-7372975-5-0 (e-book)

Published by Noggin Universe Press, LLC.
Spartanburg, South Carolina.
www.nogginuniverse.com
info@nogginuinverse.com

Visit https://www.rcmeehan.com for more information about the author.

To all those who gave up everything to free America from
an oppressive government and set in place
The Constitutional Republic

Contents

*Acknowledgments*

To John Robertson, historian, cartographer, and former Park Ranger, Cowpens National Battleground, for checking the accuracy of this book, and for the use of his "Captain Benson's 1786 Map of Spartan County."

To Will Graves, for tracing and transcribing Robertson's "Captain Benson's 1786 Map of Spartan County."

To the staff of the Cowpens National Battlefield of South Carolina for their assistance with details described herein.

To my friend, Larry Shull, for hours of hashing it all out.

To my wife, Renee, for her artwork assistance, editing, and listening ad nauseam as the story developed.

To my cadre of beta readers: David Atherton, Sara Falls, Jim Johnson, Jon Kirsch, Gail McAbee, Trace Miller, Janice Pack, Marty Rammy, and Susan Shealy. Your comments were much appreciated.

Foreword

This story is a work of historical fiction based on Revolutionary War events that swirled around Grindall's Ford, a South Carolina pioneer settlement, from December 25, 1780, until January 16, 1781. Both Brigadier General Daniel Morgan's "flying army" of American Patriots and Colonel Banastre Tarleton's British Legion used this ford on the way to the pivotal Battle of Cowpens on January 17, 1781.

The characters described were real people who lived around the ford during the latter part of the eighteenth century. Local legends tell of exciting events that occurred in this Colonial American community. Any portrayals that resemble living descendants are purely coincidental.

Today, Grindal Shoals (Grindall's Ford) is no more than map coordinates near the township of Jonesville. Adjacent to the ancient crossing is the hunting preserve known as Grindal Shoals Sportsman's Club. The club's founders were Richard Carl Meehan Sr., Dr. Alva S. Pack III, James Anderson, and Richard Carl Meehan, Jr. Leading down to the shoals is a rutted dirt lane, Meehan Road, named in honor of Richard Sr. Along this old roadbed are the foundations of ancient buildings, broken chimneys, swamps, hills, trails, wildlife, and artifacts. Perhaps Grindal Shoals is a forgotten byway, but the land retains the natural beauty and richness that lured the native Cherokees.

The narrative is written in period English, so some words and phrases may be unfamiliar. The Appendix contains a glossary of terms and other helpful information, including biographical descriptions of the real and fictitious characters.

1

Wagon, Mule, and Boy

"Now remember, Lemuel," said Mamma, using his given name, "we'll be having your favorites for your birthday celebration this eventide. We'll also finish the apple cider from last season toasting your good health, so don't dawdle!" Her Scot Irish accent always grew heavier when she was in a temper. "When you're passing the store, stop by and remind your father. You know how busy he gets, what with everybody putting off their errands till Saturday!"

"Aye, Mamma," said Lem, his mouth watering over the upcoming feast in his honor—roasted wild turkey, corn-and-potato chowder, and Mamma's apple pie. The pleasant odor of sourdough bread baking on the hearth added to his expectations of a fine repast after a long day's labor.

"And don't forget to tell Sukey that I'll be wanting her help with the cooking this afternoon. Let her know she can bring Big Tom and Little Tom, especially if Big Tom would grace us with some of his fiddling after the meal. How that negro can play! Little

Tom ought to be capable of turning the spit at six years old, surely. Fill a jug at the well and take it up to the mill. Walter and Sukey will both be thirsty. Stay on track today, young man. I don't want dinner getting overcooked because you show up tardy. You need to earn those new breeches and high-tops you got this morn!"

"Aye, Mamma."

"Five other entire days, they could make their trades without infringing upon Saturdays, but do they? Nay! I hold to Mr. Franklin's view: 'Don't put off until tomorrow what you can do today!' 'Tis a common shame more folks hereabouts can't abide by his wise words. Why, if it wasn't for him and a handful of other honorable men, nary a one of us would have a choice about our daily labors. We'd all be slaving to pay King George's taxes! Thanks be to God for the Continentals!"

Lem's attention strayed as Mamma continued to rant about taxes on sugar, paper, tea, and many other staples in Papa's store. His thoughts fell to the objects upon the walnut mantle beside his hand. A large tome and five smaller booklets were held upright between heavy iron horse-head bookends. Lem had learned to read from the black leather-bound family Bible at his father's knee. He could recite the Farnandis generations, recorded in India ink on the inside cover, and many verses throughout the sacred script. However, Mamma held the highest regard for Statesman Franklin, author of the five brittle tanned copies of *Poor Richard's Almanack*. While Lem respected the Bible as the Word of God, he fondly recalled the witticisms, poems, puzzles, and amusing stories authored by Mr. Franklin under the guise of Poor Richard Saunders.

"Lemuel! Have you been a-hearing me? When you arrive at the tavern this afternoon, be sure to inquire of Mr. Coleman if he could spare a jug of cider. I'm afeared we may run short. Tell him your father will reckon the charge against Mr. Coleman's balance at the store same as always."

"I will, Mamma."

"Don't be talking to his Mistress about it neither. She's a devout Tory and would sooner spit in your eye than sell ye a drink."

"I won't, Mamma." His mother's yammering made Lem's head feel ready to burst. Rather than letting her have another go, he launched away from the hearth, bracing for the chill outside. At times Mamma made silence seem like a woolen blanket on a cold night. No wonder it was called *blessed silence.*

Treading as lightly as he could in his new knee boots, he made for the side door in hopes of escaping before Mamma could add further tasks to his already lengthy list. Her broad backside was to him as she diced potatoes at the counter. Lem retrieved his shapeless felt hat from the nob of the nearest dining chair and absently pulled it down over his ears. Sallie and Jane, arms and aprons dusted with flour, both looked up from their kneading as he skirted the long plank table. They knew he was trying to sneak away and started giggling and pulling faces as he passed. Little Caroline held the folds of Mamma's gown and gazed at him with large blue eyes.

Lem felt heat rise in his cheeks. The most *they* would have to do the rest of the day would be peeling apples and feeding the chickens. Once done with those chores, it would be jackstones and Scotch hoppers for them. He lifted the latch and stole his way out the heavy plank door, shutting it as lightly as he could manage. In his ire, he slapped the latch home. It made an unexpectedly loud clack. A wail arose from Henry II, who had been sleeping in his cradle near the hearth. Lem's heart sank over the unwise way he handled his anger.

Mamma, her voice barely muffled by the wood between them,

yelled, "Lemuel Alston Farnandis! Just look what you've done! You've awoken Baby Henry! Now, what am I supposed to do? I'm covered head to toe in work for your special day, and now I'll have to drop everything to calm your brother! Don't you ever slam that latch again!"

"Aye, Mamma." Hand still resting on the offending latch, a tinge of guilt settled in Lem's chest at having been the cause of her tirade and his brother's yowling. Then, his sisters broke into howls of laughter over Mamma's parting remark about men not thinking with their brains! This vanquished his feelings of guilt in the matter. He spun away, tromped down the stairs, and plodded across the side yard toward the back of the house. The frozen mud of the driveway, covered in tiny quartz-like crystals of ice, crunched satisfactorily beneath his heels.

Lem breathed deeply to calm his head, expelling white fog into the crisp air. After the stuffy kitchen, getting to his chores was a respite. Although the sun filtered ruddily through the bare limbs of the water oaks that sprawled about the yard, it was still too early to offer warmth. Icy frost sparkled on every stem, fence post, blade of grass, and stone. His eyes followed a lazy ribbon of bluish smoke trailing from the chimney, past the barn, and up through the bare sweetgum forest behind the house.

His approach to the chicken coop vexed Hotspur. He could see the rooster's silhouette strutting to and fro across the shed roof, tail puffed in agitation. Upon realizing that Lem was not deterred from his course, the shape paused and seemed to swell even more. Hotspur let off a most indignant *cock-a-doodle-do*, which awoke the hens. Soft clucks began to emanate from deep inside their nesting boxes.

"Sorry, girls," Lem said as he passed. "You'll have to wait a while. Sallie and Jane are busy helping Mamma." In protest of his statement, one of the hens let out a loud *pee-kaack!* "That must have been one big egg you just laid! *Huzzah!*"

Another forty paces brought Lem to the front of the weathered gray two-story barn. The buckboard was already parked to the side, so Papa, John, and Walter must have drawn it out by hand before they left for work. It would have made it easier to saddle their horses without the wagon sitting in the aisle, but it also saved some effort on Lem's part. He was grateful for that kindness.

Throwing the latch to the massive central doors, Lem pushed them inward to send a shaft of sunlight streaming down the main corridor. He could see that the two stalls on the right were empty, and for a moment, he thought the two on the left were also, but then a barely discernible puff of white fog lifted from behind the last door post. Old Bo must have pressed his rump against the very back of his stall to be able to draw his head in that far.

"You don't want to go to work either, do you, boy?" The mule snorted in disgust, knowing he'd been found out. Lem shook his head. Sometimes the mule's larks amazed him.

It didn't take long to get Bo hitched to the buckboard. The gray animal stood sullenly, breath steaming, his left rear haunch drooping as if lame. Lem smiled at this new ploy to get out of work and gave the beast a solid slap on the flank. Slowly the mule stood up straight so Lem could finish cinching the traces properly.

Lem then retrieved an empty water jug from the rack inside the barn door, slung it over his shoulder, and headed across the barnyard toward the well. Papa had smartly positioned the water source halfway between the house and the barn, making it convenient to both. Or perhaps Mamma had made Papa do it that way for her practicality.

As he trudged along, eyes fixed on his destination, recollections of one hot day two seasons ago sprang to mind. Papa had brought from the nearby township of Unionsville an ancient woman he called the Water Witch. She crawled off the wagon carrying a forked hickory limb. It looked smooth from wear. As soon as her buckled shoes hit the ground, she held the stick out by the forks and commenced to creeping around the yard, humming a ditty through toothless gums.

Walter had asked Papa what was going on and Papa had said the woman was dowsing for water. Once or twice, the dowsing stick pointed to the ground, but the woman shrugged it off. When she had walked all around the house without success, she headed off behind the barn with the whole family in tow. Suddenly, her arms began to tremble as if the dowsing stick was growing too heavy. She started to moan and weave and turn in a tight circle. Just then, the tip of the stick dove straight down to the ground.

"Dig heeaah!" she cackled.

Mamma was furious. She grabbed the rod from the older woman's hand and marched right back around toward the house. When she got to the middle of the backyard between the house and barn, she jammed the stick into the dirt so that it stood up like a *Y*. She turned on her heel and told Papa to "Dig heeaah!" And that was that.

Lem arrived at the well and gently set the heavy crockery jug down beside a coil of hemp laying on the capstone. He then drew the wooden cover from the center hole to protect his knees as he crawled onto the burred surface. Papa had set the spent granite millstone atop the mortared wraparound at the start of the winter to protect the well from dirt, bugs, small rodents, debris, and leaves. The cap had truly helped keep the water sweet, as the neighbors had discovered soon enough. Since then, folks had been dropping by to fill a jug or two because they "happened to be passing." Mamma was pleased for the attention, never begrudging anyone a fresh drink of Adam's Ale. Thus, the coiled hemp rope awaited the next person to draw water.

Lem grabbed the end of the rope and deftly tied it to the jug's handle. With a tight grip on the rope's other end, he shoved the pottery through the hole in the capstone. The crock plummeted down the fifteen-foot shaft where it splashed, sank, and gurgled as it filled. Lem waited until the gurgling stopped, then gently drew the now thirty-pound pitcher back up the shaft. Mainly it was shoulder work. The handle was almost within his grasp when the rope broke. There was a loud *kerplunk*, and more gurgling arose from the well.

"Gol dern!" Lem exclaimed, peering down into the black depths. Alas, he could see nothing.

Mamma threw open the kitchen shutters and hollered, "Heed me now! If I ever hear blasphemy from your mouth again, I'll wash it out with lye soap!"

"Aye, Mamma!" Fuming, he retrieved another jug from the shed, got it filled, corked, and stowed under the wagon's bench. At last, climbing aboard, he shook the reins, "Get up now. Haw Bo, haw! That's a good boy. Haw, Big Bo. Haw!" The wagon slung dirt as it rolled to the left, gathered speed up the drive, and clattered onto the riverside lane. Dark thoughts of having obtained the unlucky age of thirteen this very thirteenth day of January, in the Year of our Lord seventeen eighty-one, stewed in his belly

Lem's House
by Renee Meehan

Farnandis Mill

2

Maidens and Catamounts

Old Bo required little guidance, having traveled the route many times through the narrow valley to the ford. The sun crested the ridge along the river's east bank, its golden rays washing the tops of the tall pines and leafless poplars to the left side of the lane. Frost began to melt from twigs and needles, sprinkling the loamy forest floor. This set a few crows and sparrows to flitting amongst the high boughs. Riverside foliage flickered between shafts of light as the wagon trundled along. The chill in the air kept Lem alert despite the gentle rocking of the bench upon its springs and the beat of Bo's hooves on the packed dirt.

A squeal off toward the river gave Bo a start. Lem tightened the reins and added a few words of encouragement, "All's well, Bo. Naught around of which to be afeared. Just take it easy." Squinting against the glare, Lem espied a large boar at about forty paces, rooting beside a stand of cane by the river. "See. It's just a wild hog."

Lem recalled his last taste of pork this past fall. Mr. James Moseley and several of his hunting friends had shot an enormous boar on a Friday eve. The men had stayed up all night smoking and seasoning the meat. The following morning, they sent runners to invite the whole church congregation up to the Sims-Marchbanks Meeting House for a pig picking that afternoon. By then, the meat was falling off the bone. Papa had sent Lem ahead to help with the preparations. Womenfolk came laden with platters of boiled vegetables such as new potatoes, onions, and corn on the cob. There were heaps of biscuits and fresh butter. Tables were thrown up and set. A barrel of ale was tapped for the pouring. Torches were posted and readied for sunset. From up and down the river, folks began to arrive in their best livery, by carriage, horseback, or afoot.

No plates or utensils were needed. Like the kings of old, Lem and the others enjoyed delving fingers into the moist, warm, hickory-smoked boar. He remembered licking his fingers clean of the savory juices, then digging into the trays of vegetables. Ale flowed, and there was music and dancing. A bonfire was laid once bellies were full, and several veteran Indian fighters began to talk about old times.

The high-pitched voice of Mr. James "High-Key" Moseley plied even the dullest of listeners with tales of daring-do against the red heathens. Lem heard how the Cherokees had been pushed from Grindall Shoals down to Tugaloo near Georgia. The Cawtawbaws were driven up to Rock Hill. He had never seen an Indian at Grindall's, but many elders had.

Unfortunately, mulling over the pig picking had set his stomach to rumbling and brought him out of his reverie. It had been hours since he had broken the fast. Surely Papa would let him at the pickle barrel once he got to the store. Lem cast around for something to draw his attention, trying not to think about food. He noticed a few crows and sparrows that had remained for the winter darting amongst the pine boughs. Several fat brown rabbits in heavy fur coats caught his eye. They were squatting next to a withered blackberry thicket on the left at the upcoming bend of the road. Long ears pricked up, and, in a blink, they launched into the mass of thorny brown stalks. Lem and his siblings had spent many seasons picking fruit at that blackberry stand for Mamma's cobblers and preserves. His mouth began to water, which brought him around to feeling jealous of his sisters again.

Lem wished he didn't have to work all the time, but Papa had warned him to be mindful of what he sought lest he received it. "To die is a way to shirk one's obligations," Papa had pointed out. Still, it would be nice to play as he did when he was younger—like his sisters were probably doing now. But Papa wouldn't allow it. Papa said he was well-nigh a man and should put away childish things. He needed to learn to earn his keep at a trade, milling, or farming.

Now the wagon rounded the bend. Lem was shaken from his thoughts as four maidens in homespun caps, woolen cloaks, gloves, and gowns came into view. Their garb ranged in color from a dirty tan to mushroom to off-white. All wore hand-me-downs full of patches. Their shoes were in various stages of decline, probably once belonging to brothers, sisters, or cousins. They were skipping arm-in-arm up the middle of the road, going in the same direction as he. Their voluminous apparel swayed gracefully with their gait. The girls on each end of the row were swinging covered baskets.

Old Bo plodded right along, taking no notice of these obstacles in his path. Lem called out, "Make way! Make way!" Instead of moving off to the side as expected, the girls turned around to watch the oncoming wagon. He hastily reined in the mule. "Whoa, boy! Whoa!" The wagon jangled to a halt. He stood up and shouted, "Why are you blocking the road? I've got to get this wagon up to the store before midmorning!" He knew all four maidens, as they were neighbors from Sandy Run, a little creek not far beyond his home. The oldest was Phoebe Jasper, at fourteen. The rest were within a few months of Lem's own age. It wouldn't be long before their fathers married them off to get them out of the house.

"Why, if it isn't Lemmy Farnandis," slurred Lily-Beth Beckham, stretching the surname to sound like "Fernandez." This was accompanied by a sassy swish of her gown. Her brown hair flowed from beneath her cap to drape lazily across one shoulder. In Lem's opinion, that was a mite unseemly, but Lily-Beth had always been precocious. "Lemmy, would you please let us ride with you? My daddy's expecting us at the store too. We've brought baskets of food for a picnic, and he's going to take us all over to Mr. Chisam's race track this midday. You know how Papa loves to train horses for Mr. Chisam and Captain Hampton. He said we might even get to watch a *breeding*." At that, all the girls erupted in laughter, gloved hands streaking to cover their mouths. If Lily-Beth had been playing for a tone of mortification over the bold statement, it was a failed attempt—except to Lem.

Flustered, Lem managed, "I wish you would call me by my proper name, Lily-Beth. You know I don't like *Lemmy*. I haven't been called that since I was little."

"Oh, so you're *big* now, are you? I heard tell that today's your birthday." This came from a smirking Angelica Mitchell, Lily-Beth's fiery-tongued cousin. "I suppose you don't want to play hide-n-seek anymore unless you get a finder's fee." This set all the girls to tittering again.

Lem felt a rise in his bile. "You'd better stop all this vulgar chatter, or I'll leave you behind so you can walk it out of your systems!"

Apparently, this threat was on target, for the effect of his statement was immediate. Various forms of pleading met his ears. "Please don't...oh, my...you just can't... we'll be good... we'll share a chicken leg...You mustn't, or we'll simply die of exhaustion!" They were so pitiful in their dithering that Lem felt his honor sufficiently restored. "Awwwww. Climb on and be quick about it!" He sat back down on the bench, holding tight to the reins to keep Bo still while the girls crawled onto the wagon.

The girls were grateful, and the promised chicken leg was handed to him by Phoebe. He had just stripped the meat and tossed away the bone when something soft and moist brushed against his cheek. He spun around to find Angelica's puckered lips withdrawing as she sat down. Lem's face grew hot, much to his chagrin. He tried to ignore the burning sensation where the kiss had landed and pretended to check that his charges were safely seated. The maidens were backed against the side rails, dresses tucked beneath their bottoms on the floorboard. They were all looking elsewhere, faces composed, yet Lem knew that some secret message flashed between them. Holding onto as much dignity as possible, he turned back to the task of driving and clucked up Old Bo. It was a good thing the maidens wore lots of fabric. They were going to need the padding for their backsides, as he figured Old Bo would hit almost every pothole in the road between here and the store. He smiled to himself.

Between the commotion of the wagon and Bo's plodding, the shrill chatter coming from the girls was muted, so Lem's thoughts began to fall into their former track. The lewd remarks of earlier and the laughter that followed were quite a bit to take. Still, Papa had recently told him that staying his tongue in favor of his ears was a sign of coming into manhood. A glimmer of pride caused him to sit straighter on the bench.

Suddenly, a high-pitched scream erupted from directly beside the wagon! It sounded as if a woman was being stabbed. The hairs on the back of Lem's neck rose at the unholy din.

Old Bo brayed and bolted!

All Lem could do was chock his feet against the footboard, hold to the reins, and pray he didn't fall from the jolting bench. Glancing back, he saw a massive tyger at the edge of the road. Even as he watched, the feline used the claws of one skillet-sized paw to snag its prey—a large doe. Still shrieking, the catamount began to draw the carcass from the roadside into the forest as if it weighed no more than a feather. The buckboard rumbled away from the gory scene. He was safe! Then, he realized the tyger was still yowling close at hand. Lem looked back again to see what was happening. All four of the maidens were huddled together, keening in fear. He had forgotten about their safety while fighting for his own. Shamefully, he turned back to the task of driving.

Now that they were well clear of the devilish wildcat, he tried to slow the mule. "Whoa, Bo. *WHOA*!" But no amount of bellowing or tugging on the reins did any good. He knew the beast would eventually tire, but how long would that take? The turn to the ford was approaching, and he was unsure whether the wagon could make it without flipping over, even with the extra weight of the maidens to keep it down.

"HOLD ON!" he yelled.

The wagon rose onto two wheels as it swung into the turn. Lem struggled to keep his seat; the girls screeched; a breath or two later, the wagon righted itself. Now its weight became a push engine on the downhill slope to the ford, spurring the mule to even greater speed. Lem chanced a look to see all four girls were still aboard. Straining until every sinew in his body was about to pop, he managed to tug the stubborn mule's nose down to its chest. Old Bo thundered on, moments from plunging them all into the Pacholet River. No wagon wheel, axle, or hoof could withstand river rocks at this pace. Realizing that what was about to happen was beyond his power to prevent, a strange calm settled over Lem.

Time slowed.

He saw iron-rimmed wheels joggling violently over ruts, mud clods flying from hooves, the mule plunging into chest-deep water. The frigid dowsing quenched the fire in Old Bo as abruptly as the tyger had stoked it.

Lem was nearly thrown from his seat by the abrupt halt. There was no sound except for the babble of water against the wagon wheels. The mule calmly dipped his head for a drink.

"S-spared by the H-hand of P-providence!" Lem stammered. "Don't ever scare me like that again, Bo!" The mule looked back and snorted.

Sounds of anguish broke across Lem's relief. He had yet again forgotten his responsibilities to his passengers. He forced his hands to relax their painful grip on the reins with conscious effort. Turning in the seat, for he didn't yet trust his quaking legs to hold him, Lem took stock of the maidens. They were all crying, their clothes in various stages of dishevelment. They, too, had been drenched in muddy water and lay sprawled in disarray across the bottom of the buckboard.

"Is anyone hurt?" he asked. His voice sounded shaky.

"N-no, L-Lem," managed Angelica. She was trembling. In fact, they all were.

"Let's get to the store so we can dry by the fire," said Lily-Beth.

Her brown jacket was splattered with globs of mud and seemed to have shrunk as she tried unsuccessfully to stretch it over her chest. Her eyes met Lem's, and her cheeks reddened. She turned away.

Nancy Foster, golden braids falling from under her straw hat, which itself resembled a wilted sunflower from the soaking, nodded vigorous approval of the idea. Though shaking from head to toe, her blue eyes were afire with excitement, and her smile was bright. Lem marveled at her cheerful disposition after such a trying experience.

Black-haired Phoebe Jasper, almond eyes filled with tears, attempted to wring out her bonnet. She seemed unaware that one of her pale legs lay exposed to the thigh on the floorboard. Lem tried to avert his gaze, but fighting his own eyes was like trying to wrest control of the panicked mule. Despite his best efforts to the contrary, they slid along the pleasing curves that tapered into the top of her buckled black shoe.

She caught him looking.

His ears seemed to blister.

Phoebe's tears miraculously disappeared as she boldly held his gaze. Was she awaiting confirmation that he liked what he saw? Another instant passed, then she flipped her gown to hide her flesh once again. An almost imperceptible upturn of the lips told Lem that she was far from angry. He noticed a distinct silence in the air, and then suddenly, all the maidens erupted in laughter. Their mirth seemed to feed off the terror of the earlier experience. He joined in despite his embarrassment. Once the merrymaking finally spent itself, he was ready to drive onward.

Reins back in hand, Lem encouraged the mule, "Get up, Bo! Get on up there!" The sun had crested the treetops of the east ridge, but despite the encounter with the tyger, they had made good time.

Maidens of Sandy Run Creek

Tyger Encounter

3

Feed, Seed, and Flour

Bo picked his way across the sixty paces of axle-deep river without further mishap. Reaching the ford's easterly bank, Lem was impressed that the mule plodded uphill at a steady gate without slowing. After the heavy exertion used escaping from the tyger, he wondered if Bo would be capable of maintaining the pace once Walter and Sukey filled the wagon at the mill. Lem pondered the same thing of himself. Perhaps he would feel less drained after food and rest at the store. At least the maidens seemed to be of good cheer. Their chatter had increased since leaving Grindall's Ford.

Banks grew higher on either side as the road dug deeper into the rutted ocher soil. As always along this stretch, his teeth set to rattling in his head. He was not the only one relieved when Bo finally crested the hill onto a smoother patch of the roadway. Thankful murmurs came from the back of the wagon.

Before them, nestled in a glade among tall white pines, sprawled Farnandis Feed, Seed, and Flour Mercantile. The familiar log structure's wraparound porch was studded with a dozen empty spindle chairs. Smoke poured invitingly from the river rock chimney. It was evident that Papa's customers were inside where it was warm.

He noticed half a dozen horses tied side-along to the iron porch rings. A spry bay gelding in a worn saddle with a pistol bucket was nudging a magnificent tan mare also leathered in English tack. Next to them was a sleek black stallion sporting a matched racing saddle. In comparison, the other beasts in the line were mere nags decked in sawbucks for hauling.

The bay belonged to Mr. John Chisam, a frequent customer. He had fifteen children to feed. Lem didn't recognize the stallion, but the animal must belong to a wealthy man. The tan mare was unmistakably Maw. She belonged to Lily-Beth's father. At seventeen hands high, she was equal of Old Bo in mass but splendid of equine lineage.

Mr. Jack Beckham trained some of the finest horses around, and he too had a large family, to date nine daughters and one son. Lem tried to put himself in Jack Junior's place and shuddered to think of dealing each day with that many females. Perhaps that's why Mr. Beckham was gone from home frequently on scouts for the Old Wagoner, General Daniel Morgan. It was said that Mr. Beckham kept the general well-informed and constantly moving to prevent Loyalist spies from capturing him. The Beckhams and their relatives were all known to be solid Whigs.

It occurred to Lem that the black stallion probably belonged to Captain Wade Hampton. The captain served with the Second South Carolina Regiment, and he was known to be fast friends with Mr. Beckham. Hampton was a renowned breeder of fine horses. Mr. Chisam had recently built a racetrack on his property, and he, too, bred fine animals. Both Hampton and Chisam always had Beckham coach their horses, as Beckham was highly regarded as the best trainer in these parts. Breeders, trainers, racers—a cooperative triangle based on a shared interest in horses. It made sense. The idea settled, and Lem's attention was drawn back to driving.

There was a flurry of activity in the back of the wagon. Lem checked over his shoulder to see the girls straightening their gowns as best they could. Apparently, they had also noticed the row of horses parked at the store. They began to chatter nonsensically about the type of men that perhaps they might meet besides their Uncle Jack.

"I wonder if that beautiful black belongs to Captain Hampton," mused Lily-Beth. "You all know how he dearly loves for Pa to guide him on hunting expeditions. He's such a handsome man for one so captivated with tracking bears in the backwoods. He always comes to stay a few days when he's in the mood to shoot something, and Pa always accommodates him."

Angelica said, "You've told us that time and again, Lily-Beth! Haven't you better things to do than moon over someone you can't have? You'd do better to set your sights on my brother Joab. He's much prettier to look at than old Hawknose Hampton, and he's a private in the militia with good prospects for promotion. Besides, Captain Hampton is rich beyond account, what with all the land and slaves he owns. What would he want with the likes of any of us? Just look at us!" She flipped the grimy bottom of her gown for emphasis.

"You're just jealous that my Pa's bosom friends with the captain. Been so for simply years, you know."

"Of course, Lily-Beth! We all know! You never let it lie," said Angelica. She added waspishly, "For *simply years*, Uncle Jack has wandered all over Creation, leaving the raising of all of us to

Auntie Betsy. Besides a little blacksmithing and teeth-pulling with those homemade tooth pinchers of his, the best one can say of Uncle Jack is he knows how to pull a cork. Why just last week, Uncle Jack yanked a perfectly healthy canine out of old Mr. Haymes' mouth and then had to pull the offending molar to boot! If Mr. Haymes hadn't gotten into the Water of Life himself on the pretense of dulling the pain, he would have had a good case against Uncle Jack. As it was, he didn't know a thing about it until the next day. By then, Uncle Jack and Captain Hampton were out hunting."

Lily-Beth's voice raised in pitch, "Too bad Auntie Mary left you on our doorstep when your family packed up and went back to Boonesborough last April!"

Angelica spat, "At least my pa died a hero fighting the Indians! He helped save a lot of settlers at Big Creek Fort without pulling a cork!"

Phoebe interrupted the squabble. "Stop it! You are speaking pure meanness, Angelica! And you too, Lily-Beth! Just you wait! I'll tell Auntie Anna when we get back this eve! She'll fix both of you!"

Lem spun around, "Hear now! Let's not come to blows, seeing as we're about to arrive. You might be overheard putting your kinfolk in a bad light! Is that your hankering?"

Little Nancy Foster looked like she wished to crawl in a hole. Her hands were covering her face, and she was peeking through her fingers. Angelica and Lily-Beth glared at each other but fell silent, apparently realizing they had made fools of themselves in front of Lem.

Lem shook his head in wonder. It seemed he wasn't the only one with a want for controlling his tongue. Sometimes, with the way they needled each other, he nearly forgot that these four maidens were cousins by blood or marriage. "Gee, Bo. Gee! That's a good mule."

Old Bo trundled up next to the loading dock on the near end of the building and stopped. A big brown eye turned to watch Lem as he set the hand brake and leaped down. He knew Bo was waiting for his payment—a small taste of Papa's molasses sweet feed. The maidens spilled out of the backend in a flurry of fabric and chatter, heading for the front entrance. There were a few calls over their shoulders of "Thanks, Lemmy…thank you so much…and we'll do it again soon." He deflated to realize that they would have told the stirring tale of the tyger before he could join them, although he knew better than to ignore the mule's needs. Mamma's redhaired temper was *nothing* compared to Papa's Spanish disposition. "Care for the beast foremost, lest he fails you when needed most!" If necessary, Papa would back up his words with a hickory switch.

Lem reached for the water jug and Bo's wooden bucket beside it. Filling the bucket by one-third to not overwater the hot animal, he returned the pitcher to its place under the bench. He then put the bucket on the ground before the mule. Old Bo dipped his nose down to loudly slake his thirst while Lem headed for the sweet-feed barrel just inside the wide-open dock door.

Above the barrel, hanging from wooden pegs were a tin scoop and Bo's nose bag. When he opened the barrel, the smell of molasses mixed with corn and oats filled Lem's nose. He knew if he fed Bo too much of the rich mixture, the mule would get colicky and refuse to work. He measured four pounds into the nose bag, hung the scoop back on the peg, and replaced the barrel lid. Papa would skin him if he didn't keep the place tidy. Rodents and insects were already problems enough without leaving easy access to foodstuffs.

As Lem was about to step foot outside with the sweet-feed,

loud voices erupted from the storefront. The maidens were recounting the tale of the tyger. Although he knew it was wrong to listen uninvited, his ears strained to hear what was said on the other side of the central door.

"It was as big as a barn," came the sweet voice of Little Nancy, "maybe even bigger!"

The rumble of Jack Beckham asked, "Was it now? As big as all that. Sounds like we need to go a-hunting again, Wade. Maybe get us a catamount rug out 'o the bargain, eh?"

"T' would that I could, Jack. I'm afraid I've spent too long in the woods with you already these past few days. Dan's militiamen were glad to have the meat, and I certainly have no complaint about my new bearskin. A pleasure hunting with ye, as always, good Jack." The words were spoken in the refined tones of Captain Hampton that Lem knew well. "To that end, I must excuse myself and return to my duty post. Heed my words, Henry, and look to your holdings. Ladies, I am so glad to have made your acquaintance."

There was a round of goodbyes, tittering from the girls, and the tromp of boots crossing the floor.

"Hold up, Wade," boomed Mr. Beckham. "I'll be a-joining ye for a short way. Come on all ye lasses, iffen you still want to see them horses trained down at the track. Captain Chisam, I'll be down yonder to yer place with Maw and the girls as fast as our legs will carry us. Henry, toss that bag 'o flour to me shoulder. If I showed up tonight without it, Betsy'd skin me alive."

"Seems a shame to use Maw as a draft animal," said Lemuel's father.

Mr. Beckham replied, "Maw's tough as nails. She carries me own bulk, don't she?"

"Be that as it may, you're a paying customer. John, carry the sack out for Mr. Beckham and cinch it down behind the saddle for him. He's already got his hands full with all these young ladies."

"Aye, sir," came the response from Lem's brother John.

Figuring the conversation had turned away from the morning's excitement, Lem went back to feeding the mule. He paused when Captain Chisam's voice rose above the girls and the remaining customers. "Jack, I'll finish up here with Henry, and I'll be on down to see to Maw's mating with Black Thunder."

Mr. Beckham's retreating voice said, "Sounds like a date, Cap'n. Let's go, girls!" The feminine prattle died away.

Mr. Chisam said, "Henry, things are heating up around these parts, what with that band of thieving Tories hiding out around Fair Forest Creek. They've been raiding every good Whig family up and down the Pacholet. What good did it do to run the naves out of Thicketty Fort last summer only to have them hole up so close?"

"Remember what they did to poor Master John Nuckolls these two weeks past—murthered by treachery up yonder at McKown's mill by Mckown his self! Lured in with kindness and betrayed in his sleep with his little son right there beside him! The master of Wagstop Plantation would have been better served to come to you for his grinding, that's for sure. I hear tell folks have begun calling the place Whig Hill since he got buried there." There were murmurs of agreement. That was the raspy voice of Mr. Adam Goudelock, Lem thought.

Mr. Gouldlock lived at the fork to Asbury barely half an hour north by foot. Lem had delivered many a bag of salt, sugar, flour, and cornmeal to the Mistress Goudelock. She always fed Lem several of her molasses cookies as a reward for his service.

"You're one to talk, Adam," said Henry, "considering how you straddle the fence yourself. Word has it that British regulars,

Morgan's men, Tories, and Whigs frequent your cabin, situated on the main road from Love's Ford to Thicketty Fort as you are. Not saying I blame you for welcoming all comers, considering your lameness. You gave valuable service against the Cherokees ten years back and paid the price. Nay, sir. I suppose that's the best stance for a cripple with two beautiful daughters in the prime of life. Why shouldn't I be allowed the same consideration?"

"Henry," said Mr. Chisam, "till now, the Loyalists have left your properties alone. That's not to say your luck can last forever. We must stand together and put an end to the Tory looters hereabouts once and for all. If we don't, more stalwart Whigs like Nuckolls will die!"

"Aye, Henry," said a new, treble voice that could only be Private James "High Key" Moseley. "Why, it was a week ago today that a band of them ruffians came by me place and kilt all me chickens whilst I was out scouting around for General Dan. They dragged me poor wife Nancy Anna into the yard by the hair, they did! Suppose that party of stalwart Second Regiment lads hadn't passed by. There's no telling the mischief them Tory scalawags would've done. My wife's only fifteen, you know."

"You have my sympathy, High Key, but times being what they are, I can't afford to pick and choose my customers. How can I do otherwise?"

A low English rumble said, "That's sticking your head in a hole, Henry, and you know it. One of these days, your luck is going to change, and you're going to have to choose your side. Me, I would suggest falling in with the Patriots. Our Continental script is good tender, backed by Patriot blood, whereas Loyalist currency—"

"William, if you're saying I should mind with whom I do business, then the Devil take you!" Lem could tell that Papa's back was up. His father's heavy Latin accent punctuated each word.

"Times are hard, and I've got my responsibilities just like all of you. So long as a man pays in pounds and shillings, or even beaver pelts, he is welcome in my store! At least I can turn furs at the hatters for spendable money! But most certainly, I need no more kindling for the hearth! Fie, I say, to anyone wishing to gainsay my right to turn a profit these dark days!"

Lem now realized the deep English voice belonged to Master William Hodge of Hodge Plantation. "Nay, Henry. We are not suggesting you should stop doing business altogether." There were murmurs of agreement from several listeners. "What we're saying is you might be biting off more than you can chew in letting just any political persuasion come in here. Some might accuse you of Loyalist sympathy, then where would you be? Jailed perchance? Planted in your eternity box? God forbid!"

"I say again, William. Pounds are pounds. That Continental script isn't worth the paper it's printed on, and you know it! I hear it makes a good arse wipe when you visit the muck pile. Let people rumor what they will about me, but I'll not be bit by idle gossip!"

"Henry, calm yourself," said a cultured voice. Lem had heard it before during church meetings. It belonged to Gentleman Thompson from up Thicketty Creek way. "All we're saying is that winds of change are about to blow through Grindall's. A man may have to make hard choices. We hear Bloody Ban's dragoons may be swinging this way soon, and you, sir, have one of the finest farms in these parts—this store, a grist mill, house —"

"Enough of your covetous tone, Bill Thompson! I've got work to do. John, go see to your brother Lemuel. I haven't heard a peep out of him since the wagon arrived."

"Aye, Papa."

Lem hastily crossed the storage room floor with the feed bag, trying to get out to Old Bo before his brother caught him eavesdropping.

"Safe travels, gentlemen," continued Papa's voice. "Your advice is well taken, even if not heeded. Good day to you!" A variety of goodbyes were said, and footsteps went in different directions.

The large door swung inward, and John, his lean form ducking through the frame, exclaimed, "Lem! You should have been ready to leave for the mill by now! If you don't get a move on, you won't make Christie's delivery before dusk. Don't you want to be home in time for your birthday supper?"

"Guess what happened to Bo and me –" Lem began.

"We heard all about the tyger and the splashing you gave the maidens. They looked like an assortment of dirty mops, thanks to your driving!" John attempted to steer Lem onto the dock by the elbow.

"Unhand me! I must give Bo his treat. You know he won't budge unless he gets it." Lem pulled his jacket sleeve from his brother's grasp and stepped out the door.

"What took you so long to get here, anyway?" John planted his fists on his hips just like Papa. "I'll wager you stopped down at the ford all in a dither over that catamount and let those maidens swoon over you for saving their lives."

Lem's tongue unlimbered of itself, "Leave me be you *chamber pot!*"

John's mouth shut with a snap.

Tromping sounded from the front of the store. Lem's knees turned to jelly. In the doorway appeared his father, rage blazing from under his tufty eyebrows. His long, twisted black mustache quivered above thin lips. Hairy forearms capable of much toil hung from rolled-up sleeves straining against upper muscle. Lem watched his father's fists clenching and unclenching. The boom was about to be lowered.

In a deadly quiet voice, Papa spoke. "Lemuel, calling your brother names will not be tolerated. I'll warrant you heard those words from some foul bird over at the tavern. There's no undoing that, as the orders must be delivered. However, I am vigorously *disappointed* that you choose to carry such filth in your heart. It goes against God's commandments!"

Lem hung his head. "Aye, sir."

"I am truly concerned about the trust I have laid upon your shoulders." Papa drew a deep breath and let it out slowly. His hands fell still. "Today is a celebration of your birth and the coming of manhood, yet you still have the ways of a boy. Punishment shall come on the morrow. For now, finish your work in a manly fashion. I want no more grief from you. Come, John. Let's leave him to mull and to grind about what he has done." So much alike in stature and ways, the two men turned heel and repaired to the storefront. John closed the door behind them.

Lem forced his legs to bring him out to Bo. He slipped the feed bag over the mule's nose and pushed the support strap behind his ears to hold it in place. The mule gratefully munched the feed. Lem's stomach growled, but he didn't have the fortitude to go back inside to the pickle barrel. Before anger could unlimber his tongue again, he sat on the edge of the dock to wait for the mule to finish eating, a hand clamped firmly over his mouth.

Lem had known all the men behind the voices that had spoken. They were acquaintances from church, the store, and the mill—all supporters of the Patriot cause. It sounded as if some of them were urging Papa not to trade with the Tories. Lem was aware that Captain Hampton was a cavalry commander in the Second South Carolina Regiment. Gentleman Thompson, a refined upper-class fellow, had served with the famous Patrick Henry. Lem had once heard Thompson quoting Governor Henry from the pulpit at the meeting house. "Give me liberty or give me death!" Thompson would follow up with tales of how he had fought with Henry to run Lord Dunmore out of the Virginia Commonwealth and back to England. That had happened fifteen years ago, and still, Gentleman Thompson spun a good yarn for eager ears. Master Hodge, Captain Chisam, Jack Beckham, Adam Goudelock, and Old High Key Moseley were rugged frontiersmen who had driven the Cherokees out of Grindall. Now they were urging the community to stand together against their Tory neighbors.

Lem had heard all the arguments concerning the cause of Liberty. It was the main topic at any gathering. The whole mess was confusing, especially since Papa and the other men still looked upon him as a child and refused to answer his questions about the politics of the situation. All Lem knew was that King George III wielded power over the Colonies. And the Colonies resisted his laws and protested his taxes.

Realizing Bo had finished eating, Lem stood with a yawn and a stretch, then walked over to remove the feed bag. He gave the mule a reassuring pat on the neck and quickly returned the bag to its peg. Then, he stalked out and sprang aboard the wagon.

"Git up, Bo." Lem snapped the reins, perhaps too firmly. The beast's head flipped in defiance as the iron snaffle dug into his upper pallet. "Sorry, boy. Gitty up now! Haw, Bo. *HAW!*"

Wagon, mule, and boy pulled away from the dock and onto the lane. From this point, it was called Asbury Road, and it went out of sight through the woods to the north, but Bo took the upcoming left turn onto Ridge Road without guidance. The wagon would now snake westerly above the river for about four furlongs until reaching the mill. Forests on both sides were silent except for the rattling of the buckboard. The sun was nearly overhead. Lem fell into dark thoughts of injustice at being treated partly like a man and partly as a nursling. Papa expected him to provide a man's toil, learn a man's ways, yet still receive treatment as if he were a child. Could a child have saved the maidens and the wagon from the tyger?

Farnandis Feed Seed and Flour

4

Millworks

After passing through some of Papa's cornfields, the wagon rounded the final bend to the mill. Dry stalks resembling pickets stood on each side of the road. A hawk darted unexpectedly into the midst of the field on the right, just as quickly returning to a nearby treetop with a gray squirrel dangling from its talons. The rodent screeched pitifully as the hawk thrust its beak into the prey's chest. The cry slashed through the racket of the buckboard, jolting Lem from his private reflections. He had never heard a squirrel make a sound like that, and if he had not been passing at this moment, the ending of the squirrel's story would have gone unheeded.

Life seemed unjust all around.

"Hey day-uh!"

Startled, Lem reined in Big Bo. From the shadows of the cornstalks rose two figures, one thin and short, the other tall and broad.

"Tom! Thank the Lord it's only you and Little Tom! You gave

me such a fright! You're so black I couldn't see you sitting in the shadows there. Methought I was about to be attacked by those Tory raiders I've heard so much about lately." Lem mopped his forehead with the sleeve of his jacket.

"Heav'n forbid, Massah Lem. We uns didn't mean to cause no strife. We wuz jus taken a sit-down rest. Them Tory boys ain't on this sheer side o' dee riva nohows. Massah Walter and Mammy done tolt me and da boy they's done with our heppin at da mill, so we's gwine down to the fishery foe a bit. Say 'halloo' ta Massah Lem, boy."

"Halloo, Massah Lem!" cried the little negro. Like his father beside him, his fluffy black hair was sprinkled with flour, his feet were bare, and his clothes were mainly patched rags. Both emanated the same pleasant attitude with toothy smiles and laughing brown eyes. Their skin was so black it seemed almost bluish.

Lem smiled. "My mamma said for me to tell your mamma that you all are invited to my birthday celebration this evening. She was wondering if you could bring your fiddle and Little Tom could come early to turn the spit?"

"Show we kin. Mighty proud to. Soons me an' Lit'l Tom checks them catfish traps and skint up some meat, we'll tote 'em ta yo house, and the Mis'ress kin adds 'em to the pot. Then I'll git mah fiddle from our place."

"Thanks, Tom. The way you play is like magic to the ears. See you both this evening. Let's go to the mill, Big Bo! Git up, there!" Lem waved as the wagon pulled away. He noticed how relaxed Tom and Little Tom seemed as they turned toward the ford.

Papa had never taken time to go fishing, Lem mused. Except in sleep, he never relaxed either. Papa oversaw a five-hundred-acre plantation, a one-burr grist mill, a store, a household of five sons, three daughters, Mamma, Sukey, and nine negro families. There was precious little time for leisure. It seemed a heavy responsibility to Lem, born of a desire for power and control. In a small way, Papa must be like the King.

The wagon turned down a westerly trench off the ridge road. Both sides were ruddy embankments sparkling with quartz and mica in the overhead sun. Over the pines off to the left, Lem could see the mill's smutter trap belching chaff into the morning air. Walt and Sukey must still be grinding. Through his feet and backside, Lem could feel the thrum of the mill. The mule's whole bearing perked up. Bo would welcome another water break and a few more mouthfuls of fresh grain. Lem's own thoughts were on the food pail Sukey would have for him to take along when he left for Christie's.

Bo drew the buckboard up to the wide-open doors of the Farnandis Grist Mill. Pale dust issued from the edifice, born on a breeze set up by all the moving levers, gears, and rotating waterwheel. Lem again set the brake and eased to the ground. Stretching, he welcomed the feel of raw energy vibrating up his legs. It was a compelling demonstration of the river's force.

Power.

Control.

Everything Lem had witnessed this day bespoke of these two concepts. The tyger overpowered the deer, Papa overpowered Lem, the hawk overpowered the squirrel, and King George III's taxation overpowered the Colonials. Power meant Control. Lem had neither. In that sense, he was like Tom and Sukey—enslaved.

He patted Bo affectionately on the rump. Animals didn't care about right, wrong, good, evil, power, or control. They just lived. Although Tom and Little Tom were not animals, as enslaved people, they perhaps didn't care either. They, too, lived their lives doing someone else's bidding. Like farm animals, they were fed and housed.

Were the Colonists slaves in the King's eyes? Papa was fair to his workers, never abusive. He called it *responsibility*. From what Lem understood, the King himself was not only vicious to his subjects but irresponsible in his arbitrary taxation policies. Because of that, his Colonies were rebelling.

Bo swung his head around and goaded Lem in the hip. It served as a reminder of his own small responsibility. Lifting the water jug from under the seat, he took Bo's bucket down from the hitching post and filled it. The mule dipped its muzzle and took a long pull.

"Laws a-mercy young un," Sukey exclaimed in her heavy Gullah accent, ample form plugging the doorway, "when did you get in? We didn't hear you a-coming." Yellowish powder caked her round, black face. She removed her bonnet and used it to beat the flour from her apron and worn buckled shoes.

Despite his dark mood, Lem gave a hearty laugh. "Sukey, you look like a ghost!"

Sukey wiggled her finger. "You's a-going to git yourself a whooping if you don't wipe that smirk offin your face! You knows better'n to call on no spirits."

"Sukey! You'd better watch to your position!" Walt's baritone cut clearly over the rumbling of the mill. "Papa doesn't take kindly to those who know not their place."

The negress fired back over her shoulder, "You's just a-begging for Bedlam! I'm gwine to turn you over my knee liken I used to if you don't hush up!" Lem knew that Walt was only pretending to poke the hornet's nest. He and Sukey were always matching wits.

Sure enough, Sukey wiped a dirty homespun sleeve across her forehead, which left a black streak showing through the yellow mask and lumbered back inside the mill. "Young'un, I done raised you since you was knee-high to a toad frog! I's seed you necked, I's seed you sick, an I's seed you bruised n' broken! I's tended you through thick n' thin, hot n' cold, sin n' sorrow! Outta all that, yo mamma and papa's been right pleased with my helping around here. Asides, I works for your papa, not for you young-uns, and I's doing what he wants!"

Lem saw Walt in the dimness next to the millstones holding out his hands as if to plead. "Whoa, Sukey. You know my affection for you goes beyond all reason. I have ruminated upon the situation and deem I don't measure up! A pox on me, O' African Queen." He bowed to the waist.

Sukey laughed from the belly, her whole body shaking. It didn't last, though. As quick as a snap, she changed tack. "Lemmy, if you don't gits loaded up an outta here, you ain't gonna make it home for dinner."

"Mamma said to remind you to come home and help her in the kitchen," said Lem.

"Laws a-mercy. I plum forgot." Sukey bustled over to the sacks of cracked maize and threw a forty-pounder over her broad shoulder as if it weighed no more than a goose feather. "You boys get them sacks on the wagon!"

The three worked together to load the buckboard with just over half a ton of flaked maize the next quarter-hour. Walt and Sukey kept up a vulgar banter the whole time. It was nearing midday, judging by the sun's height in the sky.

Once loaded, Lem stepped up to the bench to take his leave.

Sukey handed him the promised food pail, a red-checked cloth wrapped around the edibles inside. "I's done put you a loaf, a hunk o' cheese, a slice o' salt pork, and a small crock of pickled eggs in dare for you."

Gratefully, Lem took the pail by the handle and placed it

beneath the bench. "You are a true pippin, Sukey." The negress swelled pridefully at the compliment, which made her all the more imposing.

"Heed me now, young 'un, your Papa don't truck with you'uns getting mixed up wiff them militiamen up yonder ways," Sukey pointed to the north. "Nor wiff them Tories they say's creeping up on us from down yonder below the river crossing." She pointed south. "I's been hearing strange noises in these woods the past couple o' days, that is, after shutting down the mill at night and before starting up in the mornings. Now mind your business so's you can get home safe afore dark." She patted Lem on the knee. "Go careful, now." She turned back into the mill, starting to hum a corn ditty. It was a worshipful song that Lem and the other children had drifted to sleep by all their lives, "All they pretty gals will be there, Shuck that corn before you eat; They will fix it for us rare, Shuck that corn before you eat…."

Just as Lem was about to shake Bo up to leave, brother Walt began to rail. "Brother! I expect you're thinking to fiddle your way to Christie's. It's already half past midday, and the drive's no ball—near three miles south as the crow flies—and then two more back home. Don't traffic with anyone on the road, and don't suffer to stop along the way to break your fast. Eat on the wagon!" He paused long enough to unlimber his gourd. "I see you've forgotten your canteen again. Take mine. I'll tote the water flagon home for ye this eve."

Black bile rose in Lem's vitals, but he held his tongue. It had gotten him in enough trouble for one day. He said meekly, "Aye, Walt." Then, a whim came over him. "Why don't you spark for Sukey and leave me be, you—you *mechanic.* Zounds!" He whipped up Bo. "Gee, Bo. Gee, Big Fella. That's it. *GEE.*" The mule circled to the right and headed back toward the ford. When Lem looked rearmost, Walt was shaking his fist and yelling. He couldn't make out the words over the racket of the now loaded buckboard.

Everywhere he turned, it seemed someone wanted to run his life.

Sukey

5

Fall

Lem sat on a gunnysack of corn flake at the edge of the outcrop. He shoved the last pickled egg in his mouth and washed it down with a swig from his canteen. This ridge overlooked the boggy areas that paralleled the river. It was his favorite spot for taking a break from the pummeling of the wagon's hardwood bench. He held his face to the warming rays of the afternoon sun, wishing there was more time to enjoy the respite from the humdrum. Ancient water oaks along the riverbanks clutched at the wintery blue heavens, as tired as he over biting days and dreary landscapes. Only the pitch pines held any color. Their dark green needles seemed to yearn for springtime. Bo, tied off yonder to Moseley's Tree, snorted in pleasure while calmly munching a handful of corn. If the mule had heard the tale of the wolves that chased Mr. Moseley up that oak last fall, he wouldn't be so content.

With a sigh, Lem stood and stretched. It was time he got back on the road to Christie's. As he bent to retrieve his makeshift throne, a silvery flash stayed his hand. Pushing up his hat, Lem squinted against the glare of the sun reflecting off the swampy waterway below. Shadows were moving through the trees across the river. Just then, a flock of crows, uprooted from their perches, came winging towards him, cawing raucously. People must be creeping along the old logging road near Captain Chisam's racetrack.

There was another flash of silver, and Lem realized it was probably the sun glinting from someone's belt knife. A chill crawled up his spine, and questions flooded his thoughts. What if the moving shadows below proved to be a band of Tory ruffians? Should he try to beat it for home or continue to Christie's? Once he crossed the ford, he'd be halfway between.

Last week, he had overheard a discussion between Mamma and Papa. Papa said that much of his trade in the previous few weeks came from some six or seven hundred of General Morgan's militia. Since Christmas Day, they had been bivouacked, scattered over five square miles from here to Asbury. Mamma supplied that Christie's Tavern benefited from Patriot's mouths though Mr. Christopher Coleman himself was a lukewarm Tory. Of course, Christie's was the only nearby place to wet a whistle. Mamma warned Papa that Mrs. Coleman was scalding for the King, and if she got a hint of Whig sympathy about Papa, she'd find a way to cheat him on the cracked corn!

A few hours ago, at the store, Papa spoke plainly that he would do business with anyone who could pay so long as it wasn't with worthless Continental paper. Lem had caught Mr. Coleman a month back telling his patrons that he wasn't too particular whether Tories or Whigs came to eat and drink. He, too, would accept Whig patrons so long as they paid up in coin of the Realm. That meant pence, shillings, and pounds of the King.

Recently, Lem had found humor in Christie's methods. If Tories were spotted coming to the tavern, the Whigs would run for the nearby ditches to hide until they left. What if Tories were heading for Christie's right now? What would Papa say if Lem went straight home, and his misgivings turned out to be a false alarm? The mill would lose the tavern's grain contract. It took Papa a year to get that business. Major Jack Littlejohn's new mill was closer to Christie's—the same side of the river—and the major was a Tory. Papa didn't like a trepan competitor nearby. He had stood on the roof of his mill cursing the laborers installing the major's new waterwheel. Lem never again wanted to see such fury in Papa. He decided to make the delivery first and then bolt for home.

Lem felt an almost overwhelming desire to flee, but people might think him chicken-hearted if he did. Was Mr. Moseley a coward for letting those wolves chase him up the tree? Certainly not! The hunter was saving his own skin. These and other dispiriting thoughts plagued Lem as he lifted the flake sack to make his way back to Bo.

Without warning, the edge of the outcrop collapsed beneath his boots.

Clutching the heavy sack ambitiously, Lem followed it down the rough embankment on his belly. Suddenly, his face smashed into the coarse bag, silt filling his mouth and nostrils. Murky water rose around his arms and waistcoat. He floundered onto his side and saw a sharp bayonet pointing at the tip of his nose. Spluttering the effluvia from his mouth, he tried to speak. A dirty finger pressed against his lips.

"No sar, nary a peep from ye, or I'll gut ye like a boar," hissed the bayonet owner.

Lem cowered. A bracing gust whipped black hair into his eyes, which he automatically shoved behind his ear. His hat was missing. A sense of defeat stole through him, for he saw no way out of this situation.

"T'aint no reason to feel peevish, boy. Just a tetch of ill luck for ye. I ain't gonna kill ye outright, lessen ye gives me treble." The man tossed his own queue of salt-and-pepper hair tied with what appeared to be a bloody rag back over his shoulder with some annoyance. Lem agreed in his heart that the hairstyle was ridiculous, avowing never to wear one. "Now, how's aboot you get on up thar and let's make the best of a trying circumstance, aye?"

"What are you going to do with me?" Lem felt he at least deserved to know that much.

"Well, methinks we'll just mosey on over to Christie's since that's apparently where you was a headed anyhoo." The man reached down in a fluid motion to grasp the collar of Lem's coat and yanked him straight out of the muck as if he were a mere child.

"Let me down!" Lem flung his arms about, disturbed that anyone could so easily restrain him. "How'd you know I was headed for Christie's?"

"Take heed to me words, ye little ratbag," the man growled, rattling Lem's teeth in his head, "ye clamp down on yer mouth an ye just might live through this. But try to escape an I'll be forced to run ye through dah mill." The man dropped Lem in the mud and poked his chest with the tip of the bayonet. "Gimme yer oath o' honor, boy, that ye ain't gonna scarper on me, an' I'll let ye navigate under yer own power. I don't rightly wish to carry yer dead weight. Twig me?"

Lem choked out, "I do, sir. You have my word."

The unsavory man let his bayonet drop to Lem's chest, so the full length of the deadly flintlock fell under Lem's eye. "Why ye's right blue at dah mizzen. Landed gentry fer a daddy, I take it?"

Lem nodded.

"Gimme his name."

"Farnandis. H-Henry. I'm L-Lem. His son." Lem knew the weapon with the bayonet was a Brown Bess rifle, but that wasn't telling much. The gun was the firearm of choice in both the British and the Colonial forces. Papa sold them to hunters without the bayonet. Only soldiers used the 'sticker'—to poke holes in people.

"Ye kin call me Tyger if ye got to call me. Figured ye for one of the upstarts hereabouts. Scoop up that hat o' yorn an' let's make tracks."

Lem discovered his hat sprawled at his feet like a dead animal. He bent to retrieve it but did not immediately place it back on his head. Askance, he eyed Tyger while slapping the hat against his thigh. From the bottom of the ruffian's spatterdashes to the top of his waistcoat collar, filth wore the man. His rotundity spilled over a rusty belt buckle, barely contained by a dirty green hunting shirt.

Tyger chuckled. "You purse-proud uns are all the same. Can't take a bit 'o grime. Nary ye mind, 'cause we'll be follering the edge of this slough till we git to the ford. Thar's goner be lots more sludge ta fill yer boots. Now, move on and keep quiet."

Lem frantically considered his position while he slogged through the swamp. Bo and the wagon were still up there, sure to be discovered by Sukey as she walked back to the house. Judging by the sun's height, that should be very soon. Sukey would drive to the store and tell Papa. Then, a search would be mounted. If only some time could be bought. A sharp object dug into the small of his back, obliging him to freshen his step.

They were heading due east toward Grindall's Ford. Leafless poplars, stunted oaks, islands of dead grasses, and brambles drowned their roots in the wetlands. On the left, an embankment of red mud thirty feet or higher held the Pacholet river and its swamps at bay. Along the ridge stood the dark forest lining a portion of the mill road. Ribbons of gray vines hung over the edge all the way down to the water. Lem marveled at how lucky he was to have received only a few scrapes to the belly after falling all that way.

Tromping through the mire in his new boots dispelled some of the chill settling into his bones. Every step held some small hazard—sunken logs, roots, hidden potholes. Over and again, he had to tug the bootstraps to extract himself from the clinging mire. The thought of water dank with stagnation and rotting vegetation spilling into his boots was revolting. The unusually tall brigand fared no better, muttering curses each time he stumbled. Glancing back, Lem noticed the so-called *Tyger* scowling down at the conspicuous trail they were leaving. His hopes grew that someone would soon take note and choose to discover who or what had made such a forthright passage along the swamp.

As it neared teatime, clouds began to roll in with a promise of rain. Lem had spent many dawns and sunsets water-fowling in this swamp, so he was confident in his navigation. Sure enough, they started to ease through saplings perfectly shorn by beavers' sharp teeth. Flotsam, woven expertly into a dam, appeared just ahead. It held nearly an acre of water up against a cove in the embankment. As they clambered over this mess of sticks plugged with debris, a raft of wood ducks took sudden flight, their wings whistling. Lem yelped in surprise and fell back against Tyger.

"Hesh yer mouth, boy!" He seized Lem's shoulders and shoved him away. "If anybody spots us, ye'll be the first ta go, I swear it!"

Lem retorted, "It would have been easier if you'd taken us by way of the ridge trail. We'd have already been to the ford and gone by now!"

"Ye got spunk boy, speckin' to me like that! But if ye tip them Whigs that we're a-goin' along down here, I'll do ye in. Now, move!"

Lem fell silent. He reached for his brother's gourd in hopes of sloshing out his mouth, but it wasn't there. It must have come off when he took his spill. He supposed there was nothing for it but to suffer his thirst and the remnants of muck still clinging to his teeth. Another quarter-hour would bring them to the ford anyway. There he could dip his hand.

No further mishap occurred until they reached the base of the slope where the road cut down to Grindall's. They angled along the side through shale and scrub brush, still hidden from travelers. Lem's captor was breathing heavily, his bloated face flushed from exertion. The day's warmth began to wane, mainly because rain clouds were now blotting the sun. A chill breeze started blowing up from the river. Lem shivered; he was wet and muddy to the bone. Mamma would be upset that his new boots and breeches had met ruination.

A filthy hand with broken yellow nails grasped Lem's shoulder, forcing him to a crouch. "Heed me now," Tyger said. "We're goin' to be out in the open as we cross the ford. Don't think ye kin turn tables on me. Best just do as yer told!" He shoved Lem toward the river and, at the same time, unlimbered a canteen that had been hidden among his bulky garbs. Taking a swig, he offered the canteen to Lem, "Here then, but don't be guzzlin' it all."

"Thank you, sir," said Lem, taking the canteen. He uncorked

the tin and wet his parched throat. It was then a wit came to him. Grasping the leather strap of the weighty canteen, he swung it in a high arc with all his might. The canteen thunked solidly against Tyger's jaw, staggering the man. Lem dropped the strap and sprinted for the river, legs pumping faster than ever in his life. Scrambling up the short bank onto the ford road, he dared not look back. He careened downhill over treacherous wagon ruts until his boots splashed into the Pacholet.

For a dozen steps, it seemed he would easily cross the ford, then the water deepened. Lem found himself floundering up to his waist in midstream, feet slipping on smooth underwater stones. It took all his strength to plow forward against the crosscurrent and remain upright. Now his garments bore their fill of the river, weighing him down. He paused to gulp air into his burning lungs, hoping to recover enough strength to keep going. There was a splash behind him. He twisted to see if Tyger had caught him up, and a boot got lodged between rocks. Down he went, and try as he might, Lem could not get his feet back under him, nor his head above water.

A meaty hand caught him by the collar and wrenched him up. Tyger, full of bile, shook his hatchet over Lem's head as he fumed, "I suffered ye a bit o' freedom, and this is how ye repay me? Ye gave me yer oath! Iffin I had any scruples about killin' a bantling, I ain't got none now!" He rubbed a welt on his jaw that looked as if it would make a purple goose egg by morning. "I profess I ain't gonna murther ye jus' yet, but don't push me." He started dragging Lem by the arm toward the south shore.

Swagging through muddy tracks to exit the ford, it was clear that Tyger was winded. He propelled Lem off the right side of the road onto what amounted to a game trail, then plunged in behind him. Lem tripped over the roots of an ancient oak tree and sprawled into the loam at its feet. Rolling over, he took the opportunity to hold his legs up so his boots could drain. That didn't relieve the chill seeping into his skin, but at least he would be able to walk the remaining mile or so to the tavern without lugging the extra weight.

"Get offin' yer hinds, boy! We got a ways to go, an' I wanna arrive before dark."

"Aye, sir." Lem stood and began to climb the familiar trail. He had used it many times while hunting squirrels and such. It was no more than a deer path that meandered uphill through a pine forest littered with small glades. There would be a rivulet to jump somewhere ahead. Eventually, the trace would empty out at the tavern.

Last year, a new road had been cut through from Christie's to the river. He had heard papa fuming some months back over how Major Littlejohn had contracted that logging. The result was quicker access from the major's new millworks to the tavern. The deer trail ran alongside it in places. Perhaps he could hail someone before Tyger could stop him.

It started to rain. Tired, worried, and afraid, Lem began to tremble. Fear for himself and for his family overtook his thoughts.

This day he had learned much about power. Power was control, authority—in short—bending people to one's will. It didn't matter what one knew or what one could do. Those with power, like the King, could trample those without.

The stock of Tyger's rifle prodded Lem in the back. "Boy, stop draggin'. We need to git whar we're goin'. I'm soaked plum through an' thar's a mug up to the tavern with me name to it. Look lively now, an' don't think of opening that mouth o' yorn to call out iffin ye hear someone a-coming along that road yonder. Ye don't want to know what a lead ball will do to your skinny little gullet."

Grimly, Lem answered, "Aye." His feet were cold, blistered, and sore. Dark thoughts on the evils of corrupt authority plagued him as he stepped up the pace.

It began to rain in earnest.

Tyger's Anger

6

Christie's Tavern

There came a sudden crashing of undergrowth from up ahead. Tyger shoved Lem against the trunk of the nearest tree, a white pine of great girth. A grubby hand clamped Lem's mouth, and he felt the point of the old villain's bayonet under his chin.

Tyger breathed, "Narry a peep, my little cockerel."

His captor was pressed so close Lem could map every spidery red vein on his bulbous, greasy nose. Worse was the foulness emanating from between those cracked, rotten teeth. Lem nearly retched. To distract himself from the woe of his situation, his ears strained for the possibility of an approaching friend. From the sound of it, several horses were picking their way down the trail. Tyger's gray orbs were fairly sparking in concentration. The riders drew closer. Just as it seemed Tyger would let the riders pass, he gave a whoop like an Indian warrior and sprang into the path before the muzzle of the lead horse.

"WHO BE YE, FRIEND 'ER FOE?"

The horses reared and whinnied, nearly unseating their riders.

Lem, rooted in fright, chanced to watch the proceedings from around the rough bark of his tree. It took a few moments for the riders to get their mounts under control.

"Lord God in Heaven!" exclaimed the man on the lead horse. He wore a British dragoon's kit—a wooled leather helmet with plume, deep green waistcoat, tan knee-breeches, Wellingtons, and a sword. He replaced the sword in its scabbard with a practiced stroke and saluted smartly. "We've been searching for you this long day, Captain Moore!"

"Shesh yer mouth, ye witless wonder," screamed Tyger. "How many times do I half to tell ye, Peppercorn? No salutin', no calling by true names, no mentionin' o' ranks. I got me a pris'ner!" Tyger reached over to pull Lem forward by the coat sleeve. "This sheer's Lem Farnandis. He's the son of that bigwig farmer we heard 'bout yesterdee. We got to keep 'im now since he's seed an' heard too much." He looked at the lead soldier in disgust.

Embarrassed, the so-called Peppercorn said, "Aye, sir! My apologies for the lapse. It won't happen again!" With a flourish, he thrust a wax-sealed letter down to Tyger, "Urgent dispatch from Colonel T., sir!" Tyger hastily stuffed the document in the outer waist pocket of his coat. Then Peppercorn looked down squarely at Lem from atop his bay gelding. "Perhaps we should dispose of him?"

"Nay!" said Tyger. "He might work out as bait. I'm too wore down now to think it through. Budge up thar an' give us a lift. Whatever ye do, don't be lettin' that boy out of yer sight. He's slick as a snake. Don't keep his word, neither. We're gonna haft ter poke him somewhar's for the duration."

Peppercorn, a smile spreading over his handsome face, said, "I know just the place, sir."

The sound of that didn't sit well with Lem. He was about to be jailed. What he'd heard so far was spinning in his head. Tyger's real name was Moore, a captain in disguise, working for Colonel T., and his men were under orders not to act like soldiers. These had to be the ruffians his father had heard were coming—the ones known to be pillagers. Colonel T. might be that Tarleton fellow Mr. Chisam had bespoken of this morn. Tyger got a hand up behind Peppercorn, which took some doing. Tyger was rotund, so he had to use his flintlock as a counterbalance. While the captain's attention was driven toward seating the horse's rump, Lem snatched the document from his coat pocket. None of the three blackguards took notice. Lem stuffed the pouch inside his shirt.

"Git up here, Scarlet," waved Tyger, "an' hoist the boy."

Lem was careful to hide his glee over nipping the dispatch as the rearmost horse, another bay gelding, thrust forward. It was ridden by a grim man with an unsightly red scar from chin to ear, just above his lamb chops in plain sight. His cap had a buck-tale set in the back. A rough homespun coat lay across deer-skin pantaloons. Moccasins, a large knife in a leather sheaf, and another Brown Bess rifle stuffed in the saddle holster finished the appearance of a rustic woodsman. The man caught Lem staring and leered, the scar folding into ugly purple welts. He thrust out a knarred hand to help Lem up.

"Move out!" Tyger looked back to pierce Lem with an eye that could not be misread. Behave or die.

It was growing dark. Rain pelted the forest mat. The laden horses struggled uphill, hoofs slipping in the wet peat, scraping across occasional rocks. No one spoke.

Lem sat miserably on the rump of the wet horse, grasping the edges of the drenched saddle blanket for support. Now and again, his head would bump against Scarlet's back when the horse stumbled. The man smelled of sweat and swine.

Lem realized that his birthday dinner was likely set out waiting for him unless Sukey had indeed raised the alarm. The comforts of home seemed far away.

Raucous laughter and specks of yellow light began to filter through the trees. As the riders broke out into the road in front of Christie's, Lem realized there were a dozen thugs loafing around the tavern's porch. Several began yelling and whooping.

"It's the Captain!

"Tyger's arrived."

"Hurrah for Captain Tyger!"

The door flew open, and more ruffians poured from the tavern, all yelling, singing, and drinking. Some held lanterns aloft. The lot was dressed in a mix of uniform parts, homespun, and leather. All were grubby and unshaven. Each had knives, sabers, or pistols strapped on their persons—a few carried all three.

The cheering was taken up by all but the silent horseman, Scarlet. He shifted to indicate that Lem should slide off the horse, then dismounted himself.

"Who's that you got, Scarlet?"

"Naught but a scrawny rooster."

"COCK-a-doodle-DO." This last was yelled by a man whose nose was fiery red, with a countenance to match. He raised a mug to his lips but sloshed most of its contents over his own canvas jacket.

Tyger dismounted heavily. He strode with confidence to stand before all his men, feet spread, hands posted at the hip. "Moon Face. Am I to take it that ye and these diabolical scoundrels have completed yer mission?"

"Aye, Captain Tyger." Moon Face's round face smiled whitely in the lantern beams. "We've set the snare for the morrow, and soon you'll have your quarry, sir."

"Then, I'm supposing the time for celebrating has not yet arrived," said Tyger. He glared around at all those who were drinking. Instantly, mugs were emptied on the ground, if reluctantly. "Leftenant Moon Face, we'll be staying here a day or three. Take a handful of these Devil's sons an' forage us some deer meat tonight. Peppercorn, Red Snoot, Clap Claw, Hoot Owl—you're to join me inside for some schemin'. Mind me now, Mr. Fussy's to take charge an' see to it that the rest of ye layabouts get camp set up. By the blood o' yer hearts, git movin'!"

Lem realized the strange nicknames were part of a deception. These men, by their organization, must be more than simply a gang of thieves. It was evident that Major "Tyger" Moore was well-minded, respected, even loved. Tyger was lumbering toward the tavern door, issuing orders as he went.

At once, the pack scattered to their tasks. Hunters fired up some pitch pine faggots, grabbed muskets, and headed into the woods after deer. Another bunch was hanging canvas between trees to act as makeshift tents. Yet another group led off the horses to get them fed and settled, probably in Mr. Coleman's barn around the back of the tavern. That's where Lem would have unloaded the wagon. The thought made him sick for home.

Peppercorn, who still had not dismounted, sidled his horse up to Scarlet. "Scarlet, feed this boy, see to his necessaries, then toss him in the cellar for safekeeping. Post yourself at the door, so he can't sneak out." The arrogant man swung from his saddle and tossed the reins over to a ramshackle youth about Lem's age, whereupon the boy led the horse away. The dragoon marched ahead into the tavern.

Scarlet nodded assent to Peppercorn's rigid back without a word. He clamped Lem's shoulder with one large hand and steered him toward the open front door. There was raucous noise and flickering yellow light issuing from the edifice.

The inside was lit by brass candlesticks scattered about on rough plank tables and several large wagon wheel chandeliers. Warmth radiated from the massive stone fireplace. An extended counter ran in front of a wall of corked bottles and wooden kegs. Lem saw that Master Christopher Coleman himself stood polishing a pewter mug behind it. The owner of Christie's was a stocky, medium build man with a close-cropped white beard. He was wearing a greasy apron over a heavy woolen shirt.

"Why bless my soul if it isn't young Lemuel Farnandis," began Coleman, "Are you all right, boy? I wondered what happened when you didn't bring in my cornflake earlier. Can't make liquor without it." He set the mug down and leaned forward over the counter for a better look at Lem.

"Aye, sir. I got a little wet, sir. The wagon –" Scarlet popped him in the back of the head, causing him to bite his tongue. He tasted blood and turned to glare at his attacker.

Master Coleman exclaimed, "Hear now, there's no call for that, Scarlet! I can bloody well see with me own eyes that poor Lem has been dragged through the swamps, and a mite more than that, I'm supposing."

Scarlet slammed his fist on the counter and pointed to a tripod holding a cauldron over the fire. Lem had not noticed the vessel when they came in. A pile of embers smoldered beneath it, keeping the contents warm. Now that Lem's attention had been drawn to it, his stomach rumbled.

"Scarlet—I understand," said Master Coleman. "You wish me to stop jabbering and feed Lem. I take it that you'll be putting him down in the cellar too?"

Scarlet nodded.

"Very well. I'll see if the mistress can scare up a couple of extra blankets. We can't have Lemuel catching his death down there, now, can we?" Mr. Coleman reached under the counter and brought out a wooden bowl and spoon. He sat them on the bar. "Go fill your belly, lad, and dry yourself by the fire. I'll pour you a cider and leave it here while I go scrounge up the goods." Mr. Coleman turned away and disappeared up the stairs beside the far end of the bar.

Scarlet roughly shoved the bowl and spoon over to Lem. Lem gratefully picked them up and crossed the room to the pot. He took down the tin dipper hanging from the mantle and drew a generous helping of venison stew. Ladling the steaming brown liquid into his bowl, Lem was delighted to see lots of meat, corn, potatoes, and even a few mushrooms. The whole time he stood by the pot, he could feel Scarlet's eyes on his back. He replaced the ladle on its hook and sat at the slab table next to the fire. While bringing a spoonful of stew to his lips, Lem discovered Scarlet still glowering at him from the shadows beside the bar. It made him uneasy.

Tyger stood up from the sizable middlemost trestle table and clomped over to the fire with his own bowl. He was closely followed by a handful of scruffy men. They filled plates and mugs and returned to their seats. A serious discussion commenced over swigs of ale and slurps of stew. Lem itched to hear what they were saying. Tyger turned and yelled to Scarlet, who was now drinking Lem's cider over at the bar, "Plug that little cockerel down in the cellar now, so's we can get to plottin' without long ears."

Lem hurriedly scooped the last of his stew into his mouth and returned the bowl and spoon to the counter. Mr. Coleman was coming down the stairs, arms laden with heavy woolen blankets. The middle-aged man draped the blankets over Lem's shoulder in passing and took note of Scarlet holding Lem's mug of cider. He stepped behind the bar, reached under for another cup, filled it from the barrel spigot behind him, and held it out for Lem to take. Lem noticed that Mr. Coleman's lip was puffed. His salt-and-pepper hair hung in limp strands to his shoulders and his beard barely covered a bloody welt on his jaw. Apparently, Mr. Coleman had not fared well by these ruffians either.

"Sleep tight, Lem, don't let the bedbugs bite!" Mr. Coleman gave a strained smile. Most of his front teeth were missing. It seemed that being a lukewarm Tory was not acceptable to the real thing any more than being a Whig.

"Thank you, sir." Lem wondered if the tavern master had any idea what was happening.

Scarlet steered him to the left of the counter and prodded him through the door leading down to the cellar. There was a sole candle burning on a table at the foot of the wooden stairs. Lem's eyes could barely make out each step as he descended. He stumbled on the next to last when it bent and creaked underfoot; cider sloshed down his hand. There was a chuckle from above as the door slammed. A bolt slid in place.

Christie's Tavern

7

The Cellar

The cellar was dank. Cold. It reeked of stale beer. Lem was dreadfully weary. What would his family be thinking by now? Might they be looking for him? What was to become of him? Placing the blanket and cup on the table, he took up the candlestick by its brass finger hook and peered around to find a suitable spot to relieve himself. He could use a chamber pot if there was one. If not, he supposed a far corner would have to do. The floor was dirt, at least.

Barrels were lined up in neat rows with aisles between, probably rum and beer. Lem moved deeper into the darkness, the candlelight flickering. There was a short ramp leading to exterior double-doors set at an angle. He walked up and tested them with his shoulder but found them bolted from the outside. He descended again and continued to explore. Finally, setting the candlestick on the nearest barrelhead, he unbuttoned his breeches and relieved himself against the stone foundation.

A cough made him jump. Quickly he rebuttoned. "Who goes

there?" There was a shuffling of feet, then a delicate face came out of the dark. Involuntarily, he stepped back. "Who are you?"

"I Amadahy." The girl's eyes were wide, black. Twin flames reflected from them. The candlelight revealed that she was dressed in doeskin and a rough shawl.

An Indian. Should he be afraid? She seemed tame.

"What are you doing here?" Lem's voice sounded harsh.

"I thirsty."

"There is drink. On the table. Come with me." Lem retrieved the candlestick from the barrelhead and edged his way back toward the stairs. He wasn't going to take his eyes off the Indian girl. She stepped out of her aisle and followed just at the verge of the light.

Lem pointed to the cup of cider on the table. The Indian moved forward in a flurry of fabric and leather and took it in both hands. She drank greedily.

"They forgot I." Amadahy placed the now empty cup back on the table. "I alone until you came."

Lem stepped forward and put the candlestick beside the cup. Amadahy stood an arm's length away. She was perhaps a year or so younger than he, although nearly his height. Only recently had he begun to note female qualities other than those of his three sisters and mother. It was plain that this girl was beautiful. Her long charcoal hair was carefully braided and tied near the ends with colorful yarn. One braid had fallen behind her back while the other draped to the front. Her shawl was heavily decorated in rows of shells from a faraway sea, and her flawless skin shone as of polished brass in the candlelight. High cheekbones tapered to a round chin. Full lips hung beneath a thin, straight nose. Dark, intelligent eyes were accentuated by thin brows. It was then that Lem realized he was being appraised as well.

Amadahy smiled.

It felt to Lem as if the chill cellar had suddenly become flooded with warmth and sunshine. His knees quivered of themselves. Never had he laid eyes upon a creature so stunning.

With much effort, he managed to ask, "How did you learn to speak English?"

"When I was small, my village was often visited by two Presbyterian missionaries, a husband and wife. They were the Reverend and Mrs. Sims, who lived near Cawtawbaw Town. They would hold school during the winters for the children. Having no children of their own, they were kind to us and always brought good things to trade. My people would let them stay until it came time to visit our relatives in Tugaloo Town. We would travel the Trader's Trail. This is how I came to be taken."

Lem stared. The girl had just spoken unflawed King's English. Astonished, he asked, "Why were you taken?"

Amadahy's face clouded. "I know not! My family hauled goods to trade—pelts, leather, salt, shells, cloth—and the bad men came. Those above. Three days passed. They took our horse and travois. My family ran into the woods. I slow. Bad men caught I. Brought I here. Locked I up. No food. No water."

Lem concluded that when the girl felt stressed, her English degraded. She was thirsty and half-starved. Her family had been taken away; she knew not where they were. She had been thrust into the equivalent of a dungeon and left to rot. And now, he, Lem Farnandis, son of her enemies, had been confined with her. How could she trust him? How could he trust her? Here it was again. Power. Control. The men above had both while he and the Indian girl had none.

Something inside Lem snapped. It wasn't anything physical, only the knowledge that he would return this girl to her family. Neither would he allow them to starve because a gang of blackguards had locked them up and thrown away the key. He turned to the stairs and stomped his way up to the bolted door. Amadahy remained below by the table, concern on her brow.

Lem could hear the muffled voices of Moore and his men on the other side of the door. Not wishing to overthink what he was about to do, he let fly with both fists against the heavy plank. "HEAR YE, HEAR YE, LOUTS!"

There was a general eruption of voices overlaid by the scraping of chairs.

"By the Bloody Devil! What fer goes on?" It was the growl of Tyger Moore himself. "Scarlet, ye lay about. Didn't I tell ye to square the lad away so's we could plot and plan? Bring 'em out. I'll take his tongue an' mark 'em yer kin with me own skinnin' knife."

The iron bolt was thrown, and the door wrenched open. Scarlet grabbed Lem's shoulder and propelled him into the room. All the men had apparently sprung from their chairs at the sudden noise, which made Lem's chest swell with pride.

"By the Hand of God, what be ye makin' such a ruckus fer?" Tyger's visage was one of wrath, daggers for eyes.

Praying that his voice would not crack, Lem said, "I'll not let you thirst and starve us to death!"

"What's this? Starve? Why I expressly saw ye fed proper and put to bed! I'll warrant ye figured to get out of yer predicament somehow's by playing the babe?"

Lem again said, "I'll not let you thirst and starve us to death! We demand fair treatment if we're to be prisoners! You cannot throw us in a dungeon without necessaries. We don't even have a chamber pot in which to piss!"

"We? What's this *we?* Are you speakin' of yerself as if ye be a mighty warrior with two heads instead 'o one? I'll not be nursemaid to no pretendin' whelp this night!" The one called

Moon Face leaned into Tyger's ear, whispering. Tyger piped up, "Oh ho! So, there be an Injun down thar with ye. A squaw near to yer own age, at that! A mite fine circumstance, ain't it, gents?"

There was a round of laughter at Lem's expense. Anger loosened his tongue, "It may be humorous to you lot, seeing as how all you're doing is robbing the hard-working folk hereabouts!" Silence immediately ensued. Lem knew he had stepped in the muck pile again.

"Lemuel," called Mr. Coleman from the fire, "come take this tray down to the lass. I've loaded it with a crock of stew, a loaf, a couple—"

"Shut yer trap, ale draper!" Moore stomped over to Lem as if to throttle him. Lem barely came up to the man's solar plexus. "Boy, ye've tried me patience to the quick. Iffin ye wants ta stay alive a wee bit longer, I'd take me meal and whatever else Coleman over thar's willin' to spare for that Injun and get yerself outta me sight. Dare ye interrupt me doin's again, I'll see ye whipped within an inch o' yer life. Do I make meself clear?"

"Aye, sir."

"Then git!"

Lem immediately turned heel and headed for the counter. Mr. Coleman placed the tray in his hands. Scarlet stepped behind him.

Mr. Coleman said softly, "I'll be down in a wee bit with water, blankets, and a pot. Mind the Injun. You can't trust her. Make sure to sleep with one eye open and leave the candle burning."

"Enough, Coleman! Lessen' ye want to join 'em," yelled Moore. "Send the boy down. We've got work to do. Scarlet, see to it an' git back here."

Scarlet steered Lem to the cellar door. Lem descended into darkness, thankful to Mr. Coleman for remembering to add a few spare tapers. Amadahy loomed up from the shadows to take the tray as he reached the tricky last step. She set it on the tabletop, eyes raking the food.

"Here," said Lem, "take a bowl. I'll ladle some stew for you."

Amadahy grabbed the bowl, hands shaking. Lem realized that she was starving, which angered him all the more. He couldn't understand how the men above could be so cruel, even if the girl was an Indian. Amadahy tested the temperature with a finger when he stopped ladling, found it bearable, and turned the bowl to her lips. In a few gulps, it was emptied. With a sheepish look, she held it out for more. Two more bowls finally filled her belly.

A sense of shame stole through Lem as he considered the treatment Amadahy had received at the hands of the dregs above. He couldn't quite understand the feeling, but it seemed that some people believed they were better than others simply because they had power. Studying the Indian girl, he noticed the similarity between her and his littlest sister, Caroline. Both had caring eyes; both were vulnerable. Why would anyone suffer harm to such an innocent? He certainly could not.

"Amadahy, would you like some bread?" Lem tore a piece from the loaf and offered it. She took it, appreciation written in her features. He took another chunk for himself as he composed his thoughts. They chewed in silence, each watching the other. After a bit, Lem felt that some agreement had been reached between them. It seemed that she wanted to escape as much as he.

Amadahy finished the crusty bread and stared at Lem's empty cider mug. He, too, was thirsty after the well-seasoned venison stew. For whatever reason, it was then the pilfered letter came back to mind. He fished it out of his shirt, and with trembling fingers, broke the wax seal and held it to the light of the candle.

The letter contained only one scrawled line: *Redbirds fly at dawn two days hence.*

"Redbirds fly at dawn two days hence," Lem whispered. "That's the whole message?" He glanced at Amadahy, unsure that she should hear this. But what is *this?*

Amadahy asked, "You took from them?" Lem nodded. She rolled her eyes and lifted the candlestick as if to ignite the parchment. The heat from the flame washed across the underside, and immediately faint brownish letters began to materialize.

"Wait! Hold the flame steady." Trying not to scorch the fragile leaf, Lem carefully exposed the rest of it to the heat from the taper. More writing appeared. When it seemed all the hidden letters had been revealed, he breathed aloud the shadowy words. "Redbirds fly at dawn two days hence. Advance arrives on the morrow. Remain vigilant at Easterwood's and Grindall's. By no means engage. Hold to secrecy in all matters. *T.*"

Amadahy unexpectedly touched the flame to the edge of the parchment. Lem hastily dropped it to the dirt floor. The sealing wax ignited. In seconds, the parchment was reduced to ash.

Lem was appalled. "Why'd you do that? It might have been important."

"They would slit our throats if they thought we saw the contents of that letter. Best remember the words and bury the remains." With that, she scuffed the ash with her moccasins until it was mixed into the dirt floor. "See? No see now." It was not a moment too soon.

As Lem tried to grasp the message's significance, the door above sprung open. Mr. Coleman, Moon Face, and Scarlet trooped down the stairs carting various necessities. While Mr. Coleman placed a heavy flagon of water and a tin dipper on the table, Scarlet shoved an unadorned porcelain chamber pot into Lem's arms. Moon Face dropped a chipped washbasin holding a couple of wool blankets next to the dipper. He gave Amadahy a boorish wink and rolled his eyes over to Lem. Chuckling, he turned and stomped his way back up the stairs. Lem's eyes sought Amadahy's of their own accord. He was stymied by the fury he found there, seemingly directed at himself. Scarlet let out a gruff bark of laughter, apparently at Lem's expense, grappled Mr. Coleman's arm in his craggy fingers, and forced the barkeep up the stairs.

Mr. Coleman's voice floated down, "Remember what I said about the Injun—*OOOFFF*." The door slammed. The bolt clanked into place.

Amadahy

8

Amadahy

Lem stared at Amadahy, uneasy in the face of her anger. Her eyes spoke daggers, and her bearing was ramrod straight. Though she wore a frown, her attractiveness was not marred by it. Lem's eyes roved down her braids, settling on the intricate necklace framed by her crossed arms. The adornment was made of minute seashells attached to a spiderweb of thread. Some were spiral and round like land snails, while others were pointy and twisted like corkscrews. When at last his gaze traveled to meet hers again, she stamped her feet indignantly.

"You no look hard like one of them!" Lem shied from her glare. "You no touch Amadahy! Lose eye! Lose hand!" She now brandished a small knife of fine white bone, her stance one of defense.

Lem raised his hands wide. "Amadahy, I'm not going to touch you." He nodded toward the ceiling. "I'm not bad like them. My father is a husbandman, a storekeeper, a miller—not a soldier—and certainly not a blackguard!"

The anger seemed to drain out of the Indian girl. She swayed slightly and lowered the knife. Lem could tell she was exhausted. He slowly reached for the candlestick. Raising the light higher to see her better, he chanced a question. "Are you of the Cherokee band?"

"Nay!" Amadahy nodded vigorously, pointing to herself. "I Cawtawbaw! Not Cherokee! Live three days walk at Rock Hill on the river."

Lem knew that Rock Hill was about forty miles north and east. "I've been told the Cawtawbaws were once a mighty nation, rivals of the Cherokees—an honorable people." Amadahy uncrossed her arms. He continued, "My family—we are honorable people. Our word is our bond, like the Cawtawbaws."

"We make promise, we keep!"

"To get away from these bad men, we will have to trust one another. Understand?"

"Aye!"

"Good. Amadahy, as God is my witness, I will never harm you. I give my word. Do you swear the same?"

"Amadahy makes promise to God also, but first must know how you are called." Her knife had mysteriously disappeared.

Heat rose in Lem's cheeks. He had not introduced himself. It was a wonder she had even spoken to him, a stranger. "I'm Lemuel Farnandis."

"I, Amadahy of the Cawtawbaw, People of the River, promise no harm to Lemuel Farnandis."

"Call me Lem." He held out his hand. Amadahy, a look of puzzlement on her features, gingerly reached out and shook it, once only.

"A handshake is how we seal an agreement," Lem said.

"It is well. Now, we sleep if we are to be strong for escaping on the morrow." Amadahy retrieved several blankets from the basin on the table.

"Tis true. We sleep now." Lem caught himself falling into the choppy rhythm of the Indian girl's speech.

Amadahy stalked off down the central aisle into the dark. "Bring light. Bring pot."

Lem followed the girl's receding form, chamber pot in the crook of one arm and candlestick in the other hand. Amadahy reached the final row of barrels just beyond the cargo doors and turned abruptly toward Lem. She yanked the pot away from him then slipped down the row toward the back corner of the stone foundation. Noticing that he was still watching, she dropped her blankets onto the nearest barrelhead and pointed toward him with a scowl. Her meaning was plain. Lem turned his back as she squatted.

Amadahy brushed past him a few moments later, bumping his arm. He almost dropped the candlestick, hastily cupping his palm to protect the guttering flame.

"Come. We go to sleep now." Lem noticed the faint smell of burnt pine needles riding the damp air. The girl's scent was not entirely disagreeable.

Amadahy turned down an aisle between barrels near the table. She placed one of her blankets on the dirt floor then laid down. The second blanket she unfolded to use as a covering. "Go to sleep, Lem Farnandis!"

Lem took the candlestick and found the opposite corner of the cellar for his own relief. He then retrieved a couple of blankets from the basin and left the candle on the table. Finally, he wrapped the blankets around himself and laid down across the entry to Amadahy's aisle. Anyone thinking to get at the Indian girl would have to climb over him or the barrels. Indeed, he would hear them either way, especially if they forgot about the trick step.

With the men stomping around and speaking loudly above, the possibility of sleep became a wish. At least the rough woolen blankets helped dispel the chill that had begun to creep through Lem's damp clothing. He hadn't been allowed to stay at the hearth long enough for his clothes to dry. He sniffled.

"Lemuel?"

"Aye?"

"Sleep will not come for me. I talk."

"What would you like to talk about?"

"You ask. I tell."

Lem thought for a moment. "How did you come to be in this cellar?"

"As you say, many Cawtawbaws die of white man pox…smallpox. Bad sickness. Since we are few now, we must make peace with brothers. Amadahy goes with family to visit mountain relatives in Tugaloo Town. They are Cherokees. We go to make trades. We cross over river at Grindall Shoals. I get caught by those above. Family run away."

Lem said, "My father once told me he used to trade cornmeal for furs with Indians paddling upstream past his mill. Where do they go?"

"We follow Occaneechee Trail along the Pacholet to Tugaloo Town. It is a fifteen-day walk. Some take canoes, but those must be carried over rocks a few miles further at the Iron Works. From there, portage becomes so frequently needed most abandon canoes and walk. Canoes can shave four or five days off the journey. My family, we use our travois to bring salt from the sea, smoked fish, furs, and jewelry to swap. It makes for a slower journey, but we can haul more to trade. Tugaloos make good leather and cloth. We bring much back to Cawtawbaw Town, though the journey is hard."

Her words contained a hint of pride. Lem pondered this as he spoke, "Papa once told me that, long ago, the area around Grindall's had been favored Indian hunting grounds. A few years ago, after a flood, I chanced upon an exposed Indian mound on the riverbank. I found flint arrowheads, broken crockery, and a beaded necklace. The necklace I gave to my mother. It was a leather string of colorful seashells. That was as close to the ocean as I have ever been. Have you seen the ocean?"

"No. Not go that far yet. My family makes trades with Chesapeake tribes. In winter, they bring fresh oysters wrapped in wet seaweed, salt for cooking and curing meat, and seashells. We make good trades. Oysters good to eat. Shells make decorations for lodges, even tools for scraping and scooping and holding things."

Loud voices interrupted their conversation. Moore's gravelly tone sank through the planks.

"Where the devil's me bloody communique? I'll warrant the dummy bamboozled me out upon the trail—filched it from me own pocket, he did. Sarch the blasted boy, Scarlet! Sarch 'em now! An' don't be gentle with the little catch-fart."

There were heavy footsteps, and the door smashed open. Scarlet descended the stairs carrying a brass lantern, the final step creaking as Lem predicted. Without a word, Scarlet grabbed Lem up, blankets and all, and rattled him, so his teeth clacked. Fetid breath laced with the smell of stale beer made Lem gasp. An evil laugh escaped Scarlet's deformed lips as he tossed Lem to the dirt and gave him a swift kick in the ribs.

Pain exploded in Lem's chest. He gasped and hugged himself as rough hands groped through his pockets and other places best not described. Another blow caused sparks to fly across his vision, and then the creak of the trick stair gave way to the slamming of the door.

Lem felt the warmth of blood on his cheek. His vision slowly cleared to see Amadahy hovering above him. She produced a soft leather chamois and used it to dab his forehead.

Lem offered a subdued, "My humble gratitude, Amadahy." The pain from the kick was subsiding. Gingerly, he propped on his elbows.

"What say I? Tis a Dutch comfort we burn letter."

"You were right. There's no telling what Scarlet would have done if it had been found. I owe you a debt. On my honor, I will repay you."

"No debt. You braved the bad men and brought food, drink, and blankets. We are…level." She waved a hand as if smoothing away wrinkles from a shirt.

Lem snickered, "You mean *even*? I suppose that's the truth of it. But it doesn't change our situation. We need to find a way to escape and warn our families."

"I fear my family captured or worse. I know not what to do." Amadahy removed the chamois from Lem's forehead.

Another eruption of voices from above brought fear into both captive's eyes. The heavy floor planks yielded a muffled rendition of the loudly spoken words.

"We have 'em. We have 'em, Captain Tyger. Caught 'em at the shoals skulking across in the dark! We lost two of our own in the takin'—Hoot Owl and Clap Claw. The little 'un poked Hoot Owl through duh mizzen, an' ole Clap took a bludgeoning from this sheer big 'un."

Tyger's voice screamed, "Ye was sleepin' at ye post, I'll warrant! Two o' me best an' ye let these here turncoats do 'em in. Yer not fit ter hold a candle, the lot 'o ye!" The rest was garbled as too many were speaking at once. Eventually, one voice rose above the others.

"Unhand me, you cur!" The pounding of flesh on flesh followed.

"Moon Face, take a detail an' head out for the rendezvous. Give over this message—*Two bluebirds twill sing.* Don't let no one stand in yer way, neither. Now go."

"*Two bluebirds twill sing.* Aye."

"Scarlet, take yerself an' Mr. Fussy an' one other of yer own choosin' an' toss these dogs in the cellar with them young'uns. An' by yer life, don't let any of 'em escape! I'm done fer a wink as I's been traipsing in me boots fer more'n three days. The rest o' ye lot be fair warned, I'll brook no more blunders, on ye very lives!"

Again, the stair door was thrown open. Lem could see shadows playing in the shaft of light from the taproom. A scuffle erupted.

"Unhand me, I say! Is this the manner whereby the King's soldiers treat prisoners? This barbarism is not to be tolerated!" The voice was rich, educated. Unfortunately, the owner tumbled down to land at the foot of the stairs in a groaning heap.

An animalistic roar overrode the shrieks of those struggling above. "Ye might a cotched us, but ye ain't gonna toss *me* down in 't hole without some reckonin' first!" Blows resounded down the staircase, some of which seemed hollow like clubs connecting with flesh. "AAAACCH!"

To Lem's astonishment, a bulky form tumbled down to crash into his compatriot. Moans and grunts erupted from the tangle of arms and legs.

Both Lem and Amadahy leaped forward to help their new companions.

9

Plotting

It took some doing to untangle the semiconscious men. Amadahy held the candlestick aloft while Lem helped the shorter and more youthful of the two extricate himself and prop against the foundation wall.

"Who are you?" Lem ventured.

"Ma…Major Joseph Caldwell McJunkin…at your service," said the man, "and my rather…erm…brawny companion here is Sergeant James Park. I'm afeared my ankle is sprained because of the tumble on the stairs. Please forgive my not rising to mark a proper introduction." The major winced as Lem attempted to remove his knee-length boot over the lame ankle. "My—umph—young sir, perhaps it would be best to leave the boot. After all, I may have to hoof it, and the swelling could make it unbearable to put the cursed article back on. Better to hobble away if one can than remain a hostage of these Tory ruffians, what?"

"Aye, sir," agreed Lem.

Lem switched his attention to the aged James Park, drawing

Amadahy's wrist to guide the light. He noticed that Park's countenance was battered, timeworn. His bald crown held a gash from which blood flowed copiously into a ring of dirty yellowish hair. Lem tore a strip from his shirttail and tried to dab the wound. Park began to mumble and bat at Lem's hands, forcing him to desist.

Every lineament of the man's body bespoke of immense strength. It reminded Lem of the story of Hercules that Momma sometimes read aloud at bedtime. Homesickness tried to spread into his chest at the thought, but he savagely thrust it away.

"May I inquire as to whom I have the pleasure?" Major McJunkin sipped water from the dipper Amadahy held for him.

"You may, sir," Lem began. "I am Lemuel Farnandis, and this is Amadahy of the Cawtawbaws."

"Ah, an Indian squaw. I could not tell in this meager light."

"I no squaw!" Amadahy shoved the dipper to McJunkin's hands, spilling water down his chest, and crossed her arms indignantly. "I not married yet!"

"My sincerest apologies, dear young lady. I'm not used to being around Indians. Hereabouts they are rare indeed." McJunkin retrieved his tricorn hat from the dirt where it had landed next to him and gave it a flourish as he pretended to bow from his seated position. He held out the now empty dipper, and Amadahy returned it to the table.

Park carped loudly, "Me noggin…it seems cracked. Oh, me poor, poor noggin." He tried to raise a bucket-sized paw to the offending spot but failed. Lem stepped in once more to clean the wound, but the sergeant gently pushed him away. His left hand groped for the table's edge as he pressed his broad shoulders against the foundation wall. He got his heavily muscled legs under his barrel-like torso and thrust upward. For an instant, it appeared the table would collapse under Park's weight, the heavy wood creaking and shaking ominously. Lem, Amadahy, and Major McJunkin shied back, fretful that Park was about to come crashing down again.

"I say, Sergeant, take it more slowly! That's quite a plum on your pate. As I was about to say, my companion and I desperately need to escape the clutches of these vile captors. I fear that if we haven't removed ourselves from this awful cellar and scarpered into the countryside by the dawn, we shall both be tortured for our hard-won information. I'll warrant an untimely demise would follow in short order. Wouldn't you vouch for my accuracy in this matter, Sergeant?"

"Mumph…aye…sir. Water?"

Amadahy set down the candlestick, refilled the dipper from the flagon, and handed it to Park. She then busied herself with the makeshift bandage Lem had ripped from his shirt, dipping it in the water jug and wringing it out.

"My, er, compliments to yer hospitality." Park took a swig then emptied the rest over the offending injury, water trickling down his cheeks and neck in bloody rivulets.

Lem observed that Park was recovering rather quickly, an impressive feat for one in such a maltreated state. In height, the old man stood over six feet, an imposing figure draped in a smelly buckskin jacket and filthy backwoods attire.

"Did me ears play tricks, or did I hear the name Farnandis bandied about?" Park took the strip of wet cloth from Amadahy and began to dab at the wound himself. She ladled water into the basin, which he availed himself of periodically in his efforts to cleanse the gash.

"Yes, sir. My father –"

"I know yer father, boy. Me an' him have made acquaintance

during me years o' travelin'. Can't miss the last stop fer provisions till Musgrove Mill when crossin' down ta Grindall's. Leastwise iffin you ain't planning to stop overnight at dis here Tory waterin' hole."

Excitement grew in Lem's chest. "Sir, did you perchance stop in at the store and speak with my father before crossing the river?"

Amadahy broke in, "My family were chased by the bad men, scattered. I got lost from them. Please. You see them?"

"Nay to both of ye, I dislike reporting. Me and the major, we were going to see Farnandis himself on some business of minor import, but someone's done cleared out all the folks hereabouts. I'll warrant the thievin' Tories what captured us up thar got a holt of 'em all. Me and the major, we've seen nary a soul till they trapped us crossing the shoals. It's a ponder and nuisance all bundled together. Now, what say we get to ciphering a way outta this sheer mess?"

"James, my good fellow, methinks we'll have to divulge a bit of our mission if we wish these young ones to aid us in our plight. Do you agree with that assessment?"

"I'll bend to yer judgments on the necessity, Major, sir. Sally forth, 'cause the night grows short, and we must be away if Providence suggests a method."

"Very well. I'll begin by recounting that a sizable irregular militia contingent is mustered over yon river, roughly a mile toward Asbury. They know not that Bloody Ban Tarleton and his merry men are planning a surprise bout as early as the morrow. Tarleton's forces have been slashing and burning a swath through Carolina from the Santee to Blackstock's. Why, at this very moment, they perch near the confluence of the Pacholet and Broad Rivers thirty miles to the southeast as the crow flies. To be sure, the sergeant and I paid dearly for that bit of information. It's not what I would consider common knowledge. The King's army is hot to catch unawares the good Patriots being led by General Daniel Morgan. Methinks that be enough details for now. We don't want to place the youngsters in no poorer circumstance than they've already been played."

"Now, Major," said Park, "I suggest we know a few facts in our favor. We don't want the lad and lass to think we're done fer. Firstly, the fiendish Captain Pad Moore will see to it that we are accosted at first light for our mission details."

"Meaning, Park?"

"Meanin' that someone has to open that door up thar, of course." Park pointed toward the staircase.

"True, Sergeant, true. Lemuel here seems a sturdy young fellow. Rather than seeing him and the lass placed into British servitude, I suggest he cause a ruckus as the door swings open. Likewise, Amadahy, in fact. Are you fast on your feet, young lady?"

"Amadahy quick like deer."

"Excellent! I say, we can't fail, good sergeant. Notice that the door opens outward away from us. If we doused the candle to throw ourselves into complete darkness, and if both Lemuel and Amadahy crouched at the foot of the top step, I suspect that as the door swings wide, the two of them could launch into the kneecaps of the unlucky visitor without first being seen. I would then barrel through the door and tackle the disoriented barbarian. Meanwhile, you, Sergeant, would arrive to assist in my efforts to flee on my bad foot. If Providence stays with us, the blackguards will not immediately become aware of our breakout. We may be allowed a repetition of the same trick at the outer edifice."

"You're a-doin' a whole raft of supposin', Major, sir. Well, supposin' there's more than one of them rascals a-standin' thar when the door swings wide? An', supposin' they be armed to the teeth? These poor young souls might be bite'n off more 'n they can swallow."

Lem took the last as a slur against his nature. "Major McJunkin, sir, Amadahy and I can do what you ask!" The Cawtawbaw girl nodded in agreement. "What I don't cipher is what will come next? Are we to run through any men remaining in the yard? Would we not be easy pickings for a musket ball if we did? What do we do after escaping into the woods beyond?"

"Aye, lad. Good questions all," said Park. "Major, sir, the element of surprise only stretches so far. What iffin we the two of us battered down the front door usin' one of them trestle tables up thar fer a ram? Might even take down a guard or two on the outside."

"Impeccable thinking, my good man. Regardless, we must consider the disposition of our young accomplices after the assault. No matter the results of our endeavor, there remains a sizable gamble once we breach the outer door. I do not wish harm visited on ones so young should our plans turn sour."

"I'll warrant Lemuel here has a thing or two up his sleeve should the opportune moment arise," observed Park. "Have I hit the nail on the head, me buddin' cock-a-doodle?"

Lem realized the sergeant was addressing him. "Yes, sir. I have sussed out a route for Amadahy and myself to avoid the clutches of those above so we can make it to the forest unmolested."

"Do tell," said the major.

"My father's mill is upstream from the ford by a few hundred yards. If Amadahy and I can make our separate ways down through the game trails to the river, we can swim across to gain the mill."

Park said, "Fer what purpose would ye wish to visit the mill? Methinks it would be the very place the Tory plunderers would sarch iffin they desired to reacquire ye."

Lem hesitated. For years Papa had drilled into him that family secrets were not for outsiders. But Papa was not here, and the situation was dreadful. He drew in a deep breath and let it out slowly. Papa would skin him for letting out this confidence.

The burly sergeant dropped his hands on Lem's shoulders, nearly crushing him to his knees. "Buck up, boy, and heed me words! Time's growing short. There must be trusting between us, or we're all done fer with the sunrise."

Lem met the intensity of Park's stare. With sudden clarity, he knew that baring all was the right thing to do. "My father believed that armed resistance against King George would be bad for business and destroy the Grindall's community. He favored preparation over regret, so he built a secret room in the basement of our mill. Only my family—and now you—know it exists. Papa keeps provisions of all sorts in that room in case of dire need. Supposing Amadahy and I can win through to that chamber without being recaptured, we should be able to emerge equipped for our mission—"

"Ah. And what mission do you propose for ones of such youthfulness?" asked the major skeptically.

Lem's face heated. "We can make our way to General Morgan and warn him of the coming attack!"

"Shuuush, lad," hissed Park. He gave Lem a shake, then removed his grip. It felt to Lem as if a boulder had been lifted away.

"That's our stock in trade," said McJunkin, ignoring the interruption. "We best be the ones to step in harm's way. Tis our sworn duty as soldiers. Shall we burden children with the weight of it? Nay. Best leave the dangers to the veterans, lad."

"Now, Major, sir, might I jus' say that young Master Lemuel

may have a point?"

"Go on."

"Supposin' we was to double our chances at reaching the General with our message by tasking them to carry it as well?"

"That would endanger these youths beyond my ability to accept, Sergeant Park." The major wore a frown.

"Not necessarily, sir, beggin' yer pardon. What iffen we sewed a copy of the vitals into each of thems' clothes, wrapped in oilcloth, of course, fer protecting from the elements?"

"By Jove, you may have it! And are we privy to such materials as to make these facsimiles in truth?"

"Me pouch inside me coat is loaded with a quill, scraps of rag paper, a tetch of oilcloth, a vial of India ink—even a needle an' length o' thread fer repairin' me clothes. They's above missed relieving me of these fineries, much to their woe."

The major said, "Treasure beyond price, good fellow. Now, let's get to it. Time's short."

Amadahy blurted, "Not go to mill! Not carry message. Must find family. Must know family safe."

"Would ye rather be coolin' yer heels in the back of a victuals wagon a-feedin' them's that in all likelihood stole yer kin?" asked the sergeant. "I'd rather be doggin' the enemy's hind tail sarchin' fer a chance to save 'em."

Amadahy closed her eyes and drew a few breaths. "I wish to apologize for my outburst, sirs." She opened her eyes and looked at each of the two men in turn with an unfearful gaze bespeaking a solid will. "My family is in terrible danger. It is difficult for me to give up searching for them when perhaps they need me the most." She crossed her arms and looked at her feet. "I fear for their treatment at the hands of those above, those two-legged beasts!"

Lem saw the same slack-jawed astonishment on the men's faces that had come over him when the Indian girl had surprised him with her English fluency. A smile crept across his cheeks.

"Well!" Major McJunkin wore a bemused expression. "Sergeant, there's more to this Cawtawbaw maiden than meets the eye. Wouldn't you concur?"

"Yes indeed! Seems ter me that the sq—I mean—Amadahy has cottoned onto the situation, 'cepting one thing. We're all paddlin' the same canoe. Danger!"

"Rightly so!" The major twisted his auburn beard until he grimaced. "What you say is beyond dispute, young woman. However, if the British catch Morgan unexpectedly, neither our welfare, nor that of Grindall's residents, nor your family will matter a whit. We will either be dead, imprisoned, or made workhorses for the duration of this bloody war with no prospect of saving anyone. With Morgan warned, there's a chance of pushing the British back across the Broad River. Then it might be possible to find your family. Have we come to an understanding, my dear Amadahy?"

"Aye, sir, we have. Although I wish it could be otherwise." Amadahy turned away. Lem thought perhaps she was hiding tears. His own was held in check, but the sentiment was there despite his attempt to bury it.

"A pact then, amongst us all." McJunkin held out his hand. Sergeant Park placed his paw on top. Lem followed suit, and then Amadahy. With hands stacked together, the major said, "By the Lord God above, who oversees the miseries and triumphs of the world, we shall each strive to reach General Daniel Morgan. Do ye so swear?" Four soft 'ayes' rose in agreement. Their hands dropped. "So be it. Now, Sergeant Park, with the skill and quickness I know ye capable, proceed."

"Major, sir?" interrupted Lem, "I pilfered a secret message

from Tyger Moore's pocket, and Amadahy destroyed it with the candle."

"Park, it seems we have met some daring compatriots. Prithee, tell us what this clandestine note bespoke." Both the soldiers fastened their eyes on Lem.

Before Lem could speak, Amadahy recited, "Redbirds fly at dawn two days hence. Advance arrives on the morrow. Remain vigilant at Easterwood's and Grindall's. By no means engage. Hold to secrecy in all matters. *T.*"

"Oh, ho! Park, we've been vindicated! Till now, we've only suspected the Bloody Scout had discovered Morgan's encampment. Now we know he has! Let us all keep this detail in our heads and set down the rest as proposed."

Lem watched in silence as the sergeant drew forth his tools and began the labor of copying the secret message onto four scraps of cloth. He handed off his coat, along with the men, to Amadahy. She used her bone blade to carefully slice the linings inside the armpits of all three garments. As Sergeant Park finished each copy, he folded it into a tiny square, wrapped it in oilcloth, and handed it to Amadahy. She then inserted the packet into the slit she had made and sewed it shut using the sergeant's needle and thread. Lem found it curious how the Indian girl could store a knife somewhere in her clothing without anyone noticing where she hid it. He wondered what else she could be hiding. Once Amadahy completed her sewing, no one could tell where she had placed the packets. He knew not where she hid her own copy.

"A masterful job, my dear! So, it seems we only must await the break of day to sally forth." The major's eyes were ablaze.

After quietly reiterating the plans for the morn amongst themselves, the four captives bedded down as best they could to catch a bit of sleep. Amadahy and Lem would make for the

Farnandis Mill if they chanced to obtain their freedom. After provisioning and rest, they would press onward toward General Morgan's last known whereabouts. The two soldiers would make separate tracks for the Patriot encampment. Splitting up would make it difficult for Tyger's men to recapture them all.

"Confusion to the enemy," toasted Major McJunkin with an empty fist. "Our course is laid, our sails billowed. May God have mercy on our souls."

10

The Escape

"Now, remember what I told ye, lad. All you haf ta do is launch yerself into the rascal's knees when the door opens," said Sergeant Park in a whisper—if one could call that great wheeze a whisper.

Lem gave a dutiful, "I will, sir."

The sergeant turned to Amadahy. "I wouldn't usually think of askin' a lass to do a man's job, excepting ye be an Injun girl, an' a tough pigeon. Do ye remember yer part in all this?"

"Amadahy crouches on steps below landing. Lemuel knocks man down. Amadahy screams, runs to front door. She falls at threshold as door swings open to trip guards rushing in."

Major McJunkin said, "I suppose we're as ready as we can be. As for my part in this venture, I'll storm the guards entering the front door while Park finishes Lem's man. If all goes accordingly, the four of us shall spring forth into the woods on differing paths. Since the sergeant and I are the most wanted amongst us, it is exceedingly doubtful that our captors will attempt to recover you two. Therefore, a few goodbyes are in order. Lemuel. Amadahy. May God be with you on your quest. Remember our warning. Stay far away from the advancing British Legion lest ye be captured. Lem would face conscription, but Amadahy would find herself in much darker straits. Your families have probably been captured and forced into British servitude already. With God's succor, they will endure until rescued."

"We're not afraid, sir!" cried Lem.

"Aye!" Ferocity radiated from Amadahy.

"Such bravery in ones so young," said McJunkin. "Should we meet again, you'll find me at your service."

Park said, "Iffin fortune smiles, we shall meet this side o' the Pearly Gates so's I may repay me debt to ye both."

There were handshakes all around. It warmed Lem's heart to know that the men held him in such high regard, especially considering that he might play a critical role in the coming action.

The little band broke up to fulfill their duties. Lem, overstepping the squeaky stair tread, quietly ascended to crouch on the landing before the door. Amadahy did the same; only, she remained a few steps below him. The major came next. Sergeant Park's great bulk caused the stairs to creak despite his care. Silence descended as the foursome awaited their captors.

Lem's legs had begun to cramp when footsteps sounded beyond the door. He readied himself. The bolt slid back, and the door swung into the taproom. Light filtered through the widening gap. Only half a breath longer—

Lem slammed his shoulders into the shins of one surprised Scarlet, the thrust so great as to knock the rogue's legs from under him. As Scarlet fell toward the stairwell, Amadahy sprinted for the entryway, shrieking. Park's two great arms reached out of the darkness to grab Scarlet by the head and jerk him through the door. Scarlet screamed—the only sound Lem had ever heard him make—that cut off abruptly with a sickening crunch. The bulky sergeant materialized wearing a grim smile, the major on his heels.

Park rumbled, "Gimme yer hand, Lem."

Lem reached for the outstretched paw and found himself standing almost before he could blink.

"Run, lad!" Park propelled him toward Amadahy as the front door sprang open. Two ruffians attempted to block the entrance. Neither could unlimber their weapons for their closeness.

Amadahy scrambled between their legs, unbalancing them further.

The major, weaponless, took advantage of the situation by simply plowing into them headlong. Both scoundrels landed in a heap on the porch. Unfortunately, the major, off-balance himself, stumbled over them. Lem saw McJunkin's bad ankle twist awkwardly, white pain shooting into his face.

Lem hesitated. There were yells from the story above. The ruckus had awoken the house.

"Don't look back, Lem!" McJunkin yelled. "Run! Run like the Devil's on your tail!"

Lem jumped over the tangled bodies. He found himself standing in the yard before the tavern, no one else in sight. Amadahy must have already made it into the woods. He spun at the edge of the trees to see the bearlike stature of James Park, Scarlet's dirk in hand, dispatch the sentries with quick slashes. He lunged from the porch to the major's side.

"Leave me, Sergeant. I think it's broken!" The major tried to thrust Park's hands away. Park threw the major over his shoulder in one mighty heave and launched into the woods.

Lem took that as his queue to slip through the underbrush. Briars and vines tugged at his coat and pants, but a faint trail had emerged that allowed his boots to remain unencumbered. Although his face and hands received scratches by his headlong rush, he pushed onward. Behind him, the sounds of the tavern awakening became audible, but especially one voice.

"Ye've lost me prisoners!" There was a pistol shot and the thud of something heavy hitting the floor. "Find 'em! Find 'em on yer lives or so help me Red Snoot won't be the only dog I plug this day!"

Lem recognized the ranting of Captain Patrick "Tyger" Moore, now known to him as a spy for Bloody Ban Tarleton, the British Legion commander. He redoubled his efforts, hoping beyond hope that he could lose himself thoroughly enough in the damp wilderness to prevent recapture.

As he struggled downhill, Lem mulled over last night's parley. The words of Sergeant Park rose to the forefront of his thoughts. "In case me an' the major be caught tryin' to escape, it'll fall to ye, Lemuel Farnandis. On your very soul, I charge ye with reaching General Dan. Iffin you believe in freedom and liberty, he must know the strength 'o the force a-creeping up his backside! Tis a man's task we ask of ye!" Lem decided this was indeed a man's job, as he swept wet limbs from his path with both hands. A warm glow lit in his chest, lending strength to continue his flight.

Judging by the brightness filtering through the pine boughs, the rain was letting up. Although the air was crisp, Lem freely sweated as he pounded downhill. Suddenly, the underbrush parted, and he burst out onto the river road below Major Littlejohn's millworks. Pausing to catch his breath, he frantically scanned the rutted, red mud track for pursuers. No one was in sight, thank the Lord. Stepping cautiously into the lane, he realized too late that his boots would leave prints.

There was no hope for it but to go on. Lem crossed quickly and ducked into the canebrake on the opposite side, praying any pursuers would think twice before following. The bamboo was thicker than his thighs and so tightly packed a grown man couldn't squeeze through without suffering the bite of sharp fronds and a beating from the flexible stalks. He wasn't sure even his slight form could force a way through to the river without taking substantial damage.

Crossing his arms to protect his head and face, he pressed sideways through the stiff, close poles. His coat, pants, and boots suffered much for wear. Every so often, he heard the rip of fabric. Momma would not be pleased.

Lem felt the sting of razor cuts across his cheeks and hands despite his best efforts to protect his bare skin. Once, his legs got splayed apart, boots wedged forward and back so he could barely move. Lem jiggled the tall poles to win free, causing them to shake and rattle alarmingly. Anyone within a mile would surely know where he was. Gasping, he extricated himself from the natural trap and paused to rest again. It was a blessing to hear the rush of water ahead, finally. Perhaps another thirty paces would see him through.

After a few more minutes of struggle, the last of the bamboo parted at the riverbank. Lem looked at the swollen torrent in dismay. The previous day's rainfall had caused the river to swell halfway up its banks. Even during dry spells, this stretch, being well above the swamp and the shoals, was deep enough to allow the big waterwheels at both mills to operate without scraping the bottom.

As he studied the situation, Lem recalled how he and his brothers would go swimming at day's end just below Papa's mill to wash the grist and sweat from their bodies during the summer swelter. Sukey's lye bar soap was strong enough to remove one's skin, but Mamma would not allow them into the house if they didn't bathe.

Lem caught himself. He had no time to reflect on the past. T'wasn't summertime, and home seemed no more than a faraway dream. He stared down into the turgid waters of the Pacholet, trying not to dwell on what he was about to do.

Stuffing his hat into his shirt, Lem drew a deep breath and plunged into the swift flow, feet first. Immediately his apparel became sodden, dragging him under the surface. He could not touch the bottom. The shock of submersion in such cold water caused his muscles to seize, a condition he had never experienced. As he struggled against his own body, the need for air seared through his lungs. Unwillingly, he gulped. The iron tang of the river water filled his mouth on its way to his stomach. A red haze clouded his vision.

Primal awareness of the closeness of death overrode his thoughts, at last releasing his muscles. Lem pumped furiously with arms and legs, panicky with the need to breathe. An eternity seemed to pass until his head broke the surface.

Spluttering.

Coughing.

Gasping.

When his vision cleared, relief washed through him, and rational thought slowly returned. He stroked and kicked toward the opposite shore. Several more times, he went under as he angled across the current. The struggle quickly drained his strength, but he didn't let up. His great hope was to attain the far bank before being carried too far downstream. Once around the coming bend, anyone waiting at the ford would be able to spot him. He quelled a sense of desperation as he went under yet again.

Breaking the surface once more, thoughts of Papa came

unbidden. "Lemuel, draw yourself up by your own bootstraps! Tis unlikely that help will be forthcoming during a time of need." Papa had turned away, leaving Lem to claw out of the cesspool behind the outhouse on his own. Old Bo had balked when Lem tried to lay the plow harness on him. The cantankerous mule had swung his head into Lem with such force as to land Lem in the muck pile twenty feet away. Papa was always one for hard lessons.

Strength waning, he reached for the limb of a fallen oak that was thrusting out into the river. Hand over hand, he worked along the trunk until he could scrabble from the water. He collapsed against the red mud bank, spluttering. A wave of nausea brought forth a gush of tannish stomach contents, the majority of which flowed down his chest. He was too tired to care.

For a time, thoughts faded. Eventually, uncontrollable shivering roused Lem from his stupor. Slapping his arms to spark a bit of warmth, he began to consider what may have happened to Amadahy. He knew she had made it clear of the tavern but had seen no trace of her since. Of course, Indians were far better at traveling without leaving signs of their passage. He would have to trust Providence that Amadahy would find her way across the river and make it to the mill. It was his fervent wish that she had not drowned, a plight he so narrowly escaped.

Hunger clenched his belly, allowing him to shake off the lethargy creeping into his limbs as he walked along the water's edge, making his way upstream. Since the bank was high, it was unlikely anyone looking down from above could espy him. Ahead, the creaking of at least one waterwheel met his ears, which meant someone was working. Otherwise, the wheel would be stationary. He moved forward slowly, hugging the riverbank.

Another few minutes brought Lem within a stone's throw of both mills. Indeed, he was correct in thinking one of the mills was operating. Littlejohn's undershot wheel spun lazily. The rumble of levers and gears covered the babble of the river. Billows of chaff coughed from the attic smutter flue. At least the workers at Littlejohn's would be so occupied with milling as to neglect any of Lem's doings. It occurred to him that perhaps Littlejohn's lay unmolested by Tyger's plunderers because Major Littlejohn himself was a known Loyalist.

Papa's mill was quiet, nestled against the riverbank in the shadows ahead. The strange silence brought on a mix of emotions. Devastation. Loss. He wiped his eyes with his jacket sleeve.

Before going further, Lem searched the far bank for prying eyes. Seeing no one, he quickly shimmied behind the great waterwheel, belly sliding against the mossy foundation stones until he reached the drive shaft. If anyone were to engage the wheel at this moment, he would be torn apart by the paddle struts.

Bracing himself against the wheel's rim, he pressed his hands to one of the smooth foundation stones. It was a large river rock somewhat broader than a man's torso. Papa had cut the stone to fall inward, given the proper pressure, thus providing entry into the foundation crawlspace beyond. The stone could then be fitted back in position so the exterior would appear again as a solid wall. At least, that's the way it was supposed to work. The stone should have shifted but felt as if something was blocking it.

Lem pressed harder, every sinew threatening to rupture. With a rasping sound, the keystone fell inward and dropped out of sight with a thud. Dank air met his nostrils. He crawled through the dark opening.

Captain Patrick Moore
1781

11

Provisions

Lem was grabbed by the neck and yanked forward! He lay prone, halfway through the foundation, belly chaffing in the hole, legs dangling outside. Something sharp pressed against the base of his skull. He was at the mercy of his captor, pinned.

"Aya tsiluga unega asgaya! No move! I kill! Who be thee?"

"Amadahy?" The pressure on his neck withdrew.

"Aye, Lem."

"Thank God!" Scrabbling forward on his elbows, Lem drew his legs inside. His eyes were already adjusting to the dimness. Amadahy's dark shape crouched before him.

"No find torch. No find candle either."

"I'll take care of it. But first, we need to replace the keystone." With Amadahy's help, Lem lifted the heavy stone and forced it back into place. "There. Now we should be safe. Wait here while I open the trapdoor. Then we'll crawl out of this mud. I don't know about you, but the chill has its grip upon me."

"I am cold. Clothes soaked."

"Perhaps there are some blankets in the storeroom. Wait here." Lem traversed the crawlspace on all fours, pebbles digging painfully into his hands and knees. Reaching the northeast corner, he gathered himself into a crouch and pressed his back against the wood above. He gave a solid upward thrust, and a heavy oaken trapdoor swung over with a loud thump. Dim light filtered through the opening. Using the doorframe, he levered himself out of the dank crawlspace.

"Amadahy, give me your hands." Straddling the opening, he reached down and began to draw her out. She proved surprisingly heavy, or he weak from the recent ordeal of the escape. Overbalanced, he nearly fell on her. Her bottom came down hard against the edge of the doorframe.

"Oomph!" Amadahy swung her legs around and stood, rubbing her backside. Sarcastically, she said, "Lem helps Amadahy most goodly. Strong. Like Indian brave." She held out her arm as if making a muscle, dark eyes filled with derision.

Lem flushed. Was she making fun of him for nearly dropping her? "I've noticed the quality of your English changes with the wind. Why is that?" He could hear the scorn in his tone and felt she deserved it. A slight flush appeared in her dusky cheeks.

Amadahy folded her arms. "Ahem! Me…I…am not used to speaking your English. It has been a few years since I attended the Indian School at Cawtawbaw Town. Before they moved away, the Reverend Sims and his wife discouraged us from using our 'heathen native tongue.' Sometimes the Reverend would swat my knuckles with his ruler if I spoke Cawtawbaw in class. I am glad they moved away. English is so confusing. Cawtawbaw is much easier."

Lem's mouth closed with an audible snap. He hadn't even felt his jaw drop. "I, uh, I didn't mean to hurt your feelings, Amadahy.

I only thought it strange to hear you speaking both ways. The Reverend and his wife must have been worthy teachers despite the punishment they meted out." Amadahy's cheeks reddened further. He added hastily, "I meant that as a compliment. Your English is as good as mine. Better. Without even a trace of a Southern accent. Nothing but pure King's English—"

"All this talk is so very goodly, but now we must move on. Much to do. Family to find."

"You're right. I need rest, though. Are you hungry?"

"Of course. I haven't eaten today. Have you?" Amadahy pierced Lem with a look of consternation. "I am freezing, still." With that simple statement, she began to shrug out of her shawl and doeskins, shellfish necklace jangling.

Lem panicked. "What are you doing?" Try as he might, he could not pry his eyes away from the now naked Indian girl. In the dim light, her skin was bronze, her shape—

Amadahy reeked defiance. "Lem Farnandis! You act as if you've never seen a naked person before! You told me of all your sisters and brothers. Why do you act so about my flesh? Does my form not appeal to you? Am I to understand that because I am an Indian, I am not good enough for you? Is that why you dropped me?"

"I…I…I…." Lem realized he was floundering like a fish thrown onto the riverbank.

"Humph!" Amadahy crossed to the wall beside the trapdoor. On pegs were old clothes, discards from Lem's growing family. She selected a heavy but motley short gown, stockings, woolen cloak, and a floppy hat made of felt. She was trussed in colonial garb in moments, all except for her feet. She drew on the stockings, the shape of her calves setting Lem's thoughts reeling. She looked up. "Are you going to stand there and catch your death, or are you man enough to do what needs doing?"

Lem was torn between a heated retort and shame. He could barely think. There it was again. Bare. He would show her. On another peg was a set of clothes he recognized as once belonging to his brother, Walter. They should fit now since he had grown several hands since last those clothes were worn. Boldly he strode up to the peg and began to strip out of his wet attire. Although every moment was an agony of bashfulness, it did feel good to get out of the soggy garments. He was warmer without them.

A snicker came from behind his back. Snatching the dry clothes from the peg, Lem hastily donned them. Once he put on the canvas pants, some of his discomforts subsided. He chanced a look over his shoulder to see if Amadahy was still watching. She was not. Instead, she was studying the contents on the shelves of the opposite wall. For some reason, an emptiness clenched his guts that had nothing to do with hunger. Was it disappointment?

Finding another set of stockings, he pulled them on. There was no use slipping his feet back into the wet boots. They needed a chance to dry. He looked around the dim interior of the chamber. A shaft of light was leaking through a small crack in the mortar between several oddly shaped stones. He realized the missing mortar would be close against the steep riverbank, probably invisible from the outside. He crossed over to the hole and stood on tiptoes to peer out.

The crack was perfectly aligned for shooting anyone approaching the mill by the same route Lem had just used. His estimation of his father's savvy rose a notch. Noting the clearing of the weather and midday approach, he turned back to the task of outfitting for the next stage of their journey. There was still plenty of time to eat and rest before they had to leave.

The walls of the chamber were covered in wide plank shelves.

Several were filled with hand tools, muskets, powder, lead balls, wadding, and a few knives. Others held casks and crocks of varying sizes, which proved to contain such foodstuffs as dried apples, raisins, plums, and blueberries. Cornmeal, flour, lard, cooking utensils, and other emergency rations were also stockpiled. Lem's mouth watered at the aroma of half-a-dozen smoked hams dangling from the ceiling. Each was well-preserved in layers of salt and pepper.

Amadahy was busy at a small table. He could not see what she was doing. Studying her rigid back, he noticed that she had bundled her braids and stuffed them under her hat. In semidarkness, no one would take her for an Indian. He was about to mention this excellent development when she turned toward him with a handful of sliced salt pork.

"Take. Eat." She forced the strips of dried meat into his hands. "I have found a cask of honey mead and a tap. If you would help find a mallet or hammer, I will tap the cask and pour us a drink."

"Where did you learn to do that?"

"Do you think Indians are foolish? Or perhaps you believe us to be ignorant. You whites seem to think you are better than other peoples."

"Tisn't true!"

"What about the Africans? Your kind brings the Africans to work as slaves in the fields, and the Spanish you drive out of your towns and villages."

Lem flushed. "Just so you know, I am part Spanish on my father's side, and my mother is Scot Irish. As for the slaves, my family did not bring them here."

"Your family may not have brought them in wooden ships stuffed like fish in a barrel, but you told me about Sukey and the other blacks that work on your farm. What makes you different from the slavers?"

"We may have purchased slaves for use as farmhands, but we did not capture and transport them. They are treated well. Papa clothes them, feeds them, and provides cabins with good roofs. It seems a good trade to me."

"Perhaps you would like to keep me then. I can work hard. Maybe you would like a squaw to care for you." Amadahy, furious, produced her white bone knife from somewhere in the folds of the short gown and used it to pop the cork on the cask. She then drew forth a wooden tap hammer from below the nearest shelf and deftly banged the tap into the bunghole.

From somewhere, she had found two wooden cups. She filled them and passed one to Lem. While taking his first sip, she emptied her own cup in one long swig and was already filling it again. Not to be outdone, he tossed back the sweet, fermented drink. Hence, this served two purposes. Lem's body began to feel most relaxed, and his temperament mellowed. He twisted the tap for more.

"You should eat first," Amadahy warned. "On an empty stomach, this type of beverage is not so good. There are nuts and dried fruits in those crocks and more meat slices here on the table." She pointed at each, acting as if Lem could do nothing for himself.

Admittedly, he did feel a bit lightheaded. It had been some days since any wine or ale had passed his lips. Dutifully, he stuffed himself with the dried fare, washing it all down with swallows of mead. By the time he was satisfied, nothing could keep him from a few hours of sleep.

12

Foray

When Lem sluggishly awoke, there was candlelight in the storeroom. It came from a triangular-shaped brass lantern hanging from one of the wall posts. His head throbbed and felt heavy as a cannonball.

"You're awake. Most goodly!" Amadahy was busy stuffing a wool blanket into a canvas knapsack.

Lem felt inadequate. This Indian girl had been shooting his marbles out of the Ring with her Taw at every turn. From the looks of it, she had been up and industrious for quite some time. She had loaded one haversack and was working on filling another. It was unnerving that a girl could outdo him. He clamored to his feet but kept his hands propped against his knees until the swirling in his head subsided.

"I told you to eat something before swigging down all that mead."

Lem forced himself to stand tall. "How long have you been awake?"

"Several hours. There was much to do before we leave."

"Why did you let me sleep?"

"You no good if too tired. You no keep up with Amadahy when the time comes."

Lem noted that she had switched to broken English. "I'll be fine. Not even an Indian girl can best me when it comes to scouting in the woods. I've been doing that since I was a boy."

"You still boy!"

Lem's temper flared. "And you don't know when to hold your tongue! It's one thing to be better at something; it's another to grind my face in it! Perchance you would like to search for your family by yourself?" Amadahy looked as if he had struck her a physical blow, to his immediate regret. Once again, he had lost control. "I'm sorry, Amadahy. I didn't mean it."

Lem concluded that she only switched to broken English when stressed. Seeing that she was already wearing her damp moccasins, Lem wormed his feet back into his own uncomfortably moist boots. He hoped that the short gown would hide her feet well enough from prying eyes.

Amadahy did not immediately rally from his earlier barb. Instead, she began fidgeting with the straps on the pack. "I'm sorry, Lem. I didn't mean what I said. I, too, am tired. Very worried. Do you remember what Major McJunkin told us? He said that the Tories have been rounding up all the rebel souls they can find to put them to work preparing for the coming of British troops. If my family has been captured, their treatment will be even worse than that of dogs. Worse even than that of Whigs. They will be lucky to keep their lives. You know this to be true."

Lem thought back to the Indian stories old High-Key Moseley told at the pig-picking last fall. Indians were not just run out of Grindall's. They were chased into their mountain refuges and slaughtered. The former Indian fighters at the gathering had said they were ensuring the "red vermin" would not return. Until now, Lem had not fully appreciated how merciless these veterans had been. Only the thought that the Indians had been just as ruthless toward the settlers held back his shame. Amadahy was justified to feel concerned about how her people would be treated if captured. She turned toward him, and, for an instant, their eyes locked in silent understanding.

"We must go," she said. "Much time has passed. Tis after sunset." Hefting one of the packs, she stuffed her arms through its wide straps. The bulk of it rode low against the small of her back. After she draped a haversack of food over her shoulder, she then lifted the remaining pack and held it forth so Lem could slip into it.

Lem found the canvas sack most uncomfortable. His attention was on situating the straps when Amadahy began to hang other items from his neck. First came a wooden canteen, then a ten-pound cartridge box of ammunition, and finally, a powder horn. "Since we need to move fast, this seems an awful weight," he observed.

"You must carry one more thing." She retrieved a Brown Bess rifle from the table and helped Lem shoulder it. "I loaded the weapon during your respite. The flash pan is filled with a measure of gunpowder. I covered it properly with the leather sock to keep out moisture. Try not to pull it loose."

Altogether, Lem's kit now weighed over fifty pounds, and his legs knew it. Indeed, he found these necessaries most cumbersome and said so. "Do we have to carry all these things? General Morgan is not so far away as to warrant all this."

"Papoose!"

"What say you?"

"Papoose—baby!"

For reasons unfathomable, laughter spewed from him like steam from a teapot. Amadahy, shocked at first, joined in just as heartily. It appeared that the pressure and strain of the last few days needed venting. Each clung to the other for support until the jollity had spent itself. When it was over, Lem discovered the girl held in his embrace. She realized it at the same time. They hastily pushed away from each other.

To divert attention from what had just happened, Lem cleared his throat and asked, "Have you packed food for both of us?"

"Ahem. Most certainly. And a pistol." She was looking down, her face hidden by her floppy hat. "I found a pistol in a box hidden behind all the crocks of dried foods. The pistol is in your pack. I did not load it."

That explained why the sack felt so heavy. Lem pulled his hat out of his shirt and restored it to his head. Like hers, it was limp from being soaked in the river. "Amadahy, how did you get here ahead of me? I ran straight for the river when we escaped from the tavern. I didn't slow down, nor did I see you in the woods."

"I ran to the small ford upriver from here. I think you call it Easterwood's Crossing. The water was only waist-deep there, but the current pushed me down once. It was easy to follow the riverbank to your mill."

Lem smacked his forehead, "Didn't think about Easterwood's! It would have been much easier. Nearly drowned crossing where I did." His regard for Amadahy increased a notch. After all, he had lived at Grindall's his entire life. Why didn't he think of that?

Amadahy turned toward the door. Flipping the latch, she crept out of the storeroom, listening for any sign of others about.

Sheepishly, Lem blew out the lantern and followed, gently closing the door. They ascended the plank stairs beside the vertical main shaft with light steps. Even in the darkness, Lem knew Amadahy was cringing as they went higher. The old wood creaked under their weight. The smell of mildewed flour was heavy on the air, probably caused by all the rain of late. No matter how well the mill was swept at day's end, there was an ever-present coat of creamy dust on all surfaces. They were most likely leaving smudged footprints for pursuers to find.

The burrs shone eerily white in a shaft of moonlight pushing through a fissure between the high shutters on the riverside wall. When they reached the landing beside the grindstones, Lem took Amadahy's hand and led her safely across the main floor between sacks of grain. She allowed this without remark, only extracting her hand once they reached the substantial double-door entrance.

Lem threw the latch and swung the doors outward. Amadahy glided between them, and he followed. He closed the doors and used the outer handle to shove the latch home. It thudded in place with a report like gunfire, rolling away through the surrounding pine forest. They both jumped.

Lem whispered, "We'd better go." They started up the wagon trail under the waning moon, the pathway's shale aglitter. Every step crunched, unnerving in the wintery stillness. Amadahy refused to follow, so side-by-side, they wound uphill, alert for any movement or sound. Lem noticed that Little Bear crouched low in the inky sky, the North Star in his tail pointing the direction they were moving. They would exit the trail at the top of the hill and continue northerly searching for General Morgan's encampment.

Suddenly, Amadahy's hand shot out to stop Lem. "Shhhhh…," she breathed, pointing to her ear.

Lem looked at her questioningly; she must have heard something he had not. His own awareness was so tightly wound now that thoughts of plunging into the woods to escape the unseen threat ran through his head. What had she heard?

As if in answer, muffled voices drifted down the hill, accompanied by footfalls growing ever louder. Whosoever they were, they moved quickly. Lem fathomed two possibilities, neither of which was favorable. These men belonged to either Morgan or Patrick Moore. If he and Amadahy were discovered, there could be dire consequences. Patriot soldiers might shoot, for they would be protecting Morgan's nearby camp. Likewise, their former captors might do the same or drag them back to the tavern as a prize for their cutthroat leader.

Lem cupped Amadahy's elbow and propelled them both up the embankment and into the pines, whereupon they crouched amidst the trunks. Lem speculated that whoever approached would find them handily but knew not what else to do. With all the noise he and Amadahy had just made, he prayed they would assume several deer had taken flight. Sadly, good fortune was not with them this night.

"Who goes there?" demanded a gruff voice. "Speak the password!"

Lem could scarcely breathe. He could make out two shadowy figures about thirty paces uphill standing in the roadbed. The forms were casting about, searching. They must be Morgan's sentries.

"We know you're there," the voice called out. "I say once more, speak the password! If you don't, we have orders to shoot!"

Lem knew the soldiers could not see them, but that wouldn't stop a lucky bullet. He nudged Amadahy so she would look at him. She nodded her consent to act for them both.

"FRIENDS," Lem shouted.

"You're about to die! Make your last words count!"

13

Side of Right

"We know not the password," Lem called back. "These past several days, we've been captives of a pack of Tory spies. They were being led by one calling himself Captain "Tyger" Moore. We only just escaped with our very lives. Beg you—we have important words for General Morgan."

The shadows put their heads together as if talking. Lem heard only mumbling.

One of the shadows called, "Where were ye incarcerated then?"

"The cellar of Christie's Tavern."

"And how many of ye be hidin' in them trees?" Both sentries began to creep forward.

"Just I, Lemuel Farnandis, and my…er…my sister…Sallie." He shot a glance at Amadahy. "Please, sir, we must see the general. Our message is from Major McJunkin and his aide, Sergeant James Park—Colonel William Washington's men. They were captured crossing the ford and thrown in with us. We, the four of us, broke away early yestermorn and scarpered with the selfsame goal of reaching the general with our messages."

"Beggin' yer pardon, sir," the figure on the right spoke raspily, "I can suss out the truth of this. So happens I knows the major. Me and him, along with a handful of us militia, was temporarily assigned to guide Colonel Washington to Hammond's Store a fortnight ago. We cleaned out them Tories holed up there, them's that'd been raiding up and down Fairforest Creek, terrorizing good folks in their own homes. Me and Major McJunkin split ways after Hammond's, him headed to visit Colonel Pickens and me returning here." Both shadows stopped moving.

"Be quick about it, Private."

"You in them trees, iffen you know the major, what's his middle name?" Aside to his superior, "The major's some more proud of his middle name. Tell's it every time he introduces his self."

Lem dredged his memory. Had the major told his middle name? Aye, the first words from his mouth back in the cellar. "Caldwell—Major Joseph Caldwell McJunkin."

"Tis right and true, sir." The shadows appeared to lower their weapons. It was hard for Lem to make out.

Finally, the superior said, "I still don't trust those I can't see. They could be the enemy gleaning rumors of General Morgan from the good Whigs hereabouts. There's been a lot of that. Some have been fed to the buzzards for holding their tongue, as you well know, Private."

"Aye, sir. That's for sure. But sir, I know 'em."

"Do you mean to say that you know those hiding up in the trees? Why didn't you say so? Time's short."

"I had to be sure, sir. Tis dark and all." For a few breaths, no one moved or spoke.

"I've seen enough innocent blood spilled," said the officer. "Come forth now with your hands high if you want to live!"

"Hold your fire! We're coming," Lem called. Both he and Amadahy raised hands and picked their way back down the embankment to stand before their new captors.

"That's far enough. Search them!" The private shouldered his musket and stepped forward.

In the light of the moon, Lem made out the familiar bacon-face of one he knew. "Mr. Foster! How come you put us through all that foofaraw? What a fright you gave us!"

"Well, Lem, it's me orders, don't you know? Can't be too sure of nothing in these times. How was I supposed to see it was you up thar in them dark trees? How do, Miss Sallie?"

Amadahy hesitated only an instant, then, "Doing fine, Mr. Foster, just fine." She added a coquettish swish of her gown. Lem thought it was a nice touch.

"My, how you've growed since I seen ye." Foster squinted for a better look at Amadahy.

"That's enough, Private! Let us be off whilst we still know the general's whereabouts. His tent will be moved again directly. Must be rough living like that, always worrying about capture."

"Corporal Ashberry, sir? These folks here are me neighbors, Lem and Sallie Farnandis. They's daddy runs the feed store and the mill we's been to so frequently for our hominy, and such."

"Have you spoken with my father or brother lately?" Lem asked.

"Nay," said the private. "Not in the last day or so."

"Corporal Ashberry, sir? My sister and I left our supplies and my own musket up in the pines. May we retrieve them?"

"I'll vouch for them, sir," said Private Foster.

"None of this shall matter if the general's tent is moved whilst we stand around eyeing each other. Retrieve your gear. And, Private Foster, I don't care a whit if they are your friends. See that the flash pan on his musket is empty, have him remove the flint, and keep a wary eye upon them until their message proves forthright."

"Aye, sir!"

Leaving the corporal to wait in the roadbed, Lem and Amadahy, accompanied by Private Foster, retrieved their packs and the musket.

When Lem lifted his musket from the ground, Foster reached for it.

"Sorry, Lem. Got to do as the corporal says." With that, he removed the protective leather covering from the pan and swiped his finger across to ensure there was no powder. Then, he unscrewed the flint clamp and removed the chip of stone. He called out to the corporal, "All's clear, sir!" He passed the musket and the flint chip back to Lem. Lem pocketed the flint.

"Fine. Come forth, and let's be away. The night wears."

"By the by, good to see ye, Lem. I heard ye was missed something fierce a few days back, but things have stood a bit chancy since then. Been meaning to thank you for saving my daughter, niece, and all them other maidens from the tyger."

"You've heard of that, sir?" Lem's face heated as he recalled the soft curve of Phoebe's exposed calf. He had almost forgotten that Phoebe was Nancy Foster's first cousin.

"Shore did. Them lasses couldn't stop tellin' it. You pulled off a man's job that day. Earned yourself the right to call me John." Foster clapped Lem on the back.

Lem felt a sense of pride swell in his chest. Papa had always told him there's power in a name. Now he thought he understood. "I'm in your debt, sir—John."

"Nay! I'm bound to you, Lemuel. I know one lass amongst my relations as had her head turned by a certain young wagoner."

The three made their way down the embankment again to meet with the corporal.

"Let's be off, then. Private, take up the rear guard."

"Aye, sir!"

The corporal strode away at a brisk pace, expecting the others to follow him up the hill. Lem and Amadahy complied, the rear taken up by Phoebe's father. Everyone was breathing hard, trying to keep up with the corporal. Lem noticed that Corporal Ashberry was only lightly burdened with his musket and cartridge satchel. No sounds could be heard above the thudding of boots and shuffling of gear.

It was late evening, already freezing. The moon winked from behind scudding clouds. Despite the cold, Lem sweated from the exertion. Silent pines crouched ominously along the rutted track, tugging at his fears. What of the Tory bandits? Were they lurking up ahead, waiting to spring out and destroy them all? Would the general be gracious or contrary? Could Amadahy pass muster as his sister to keep her safe from prejudice? Shuddering against such thoughts, he drew strength from his companions. Although he knew naught of Corporal Ashberry, the stalwart form ahead did much to bolster Lem's courage against such evil thoughts. He startled when Amadahy spoke.

"Brother? Should we have a care, or does all go well?"

John spoke first. "Everything's gonna be just dandy when we get to camp, Sallie. I'll fetch ye some soldier fare and watered ale. That'll bolster your mien."

"Our message for the general is dire," Lem said. "We must see him immediately upon arrival."

"That's not up to me or the corporal, but I'm sure you'll be passed right along. Best you follow the corporal's lead. Things are taut around camp, what with reports about spies and raiders."

"Enough talk," said Ashberry over his shoulder. "The lot of you are barely three lustrums old. Lack of experience loosens your tongues when you should suffer to hold them. Private Foster, camp business is not for the likes of these. Yesterday's friends can become foes on the morrow. These are evil times. Be vigilant. Speak no more until we reach our destination. That's an order!"

A quarter-hour passed in relative silence, although the treetops began to stir. Icy fingers of a fresh breeze were picking through Lem's sweaty woolens. Firm thoughts of dispelling the cold at a campfire began to vex him. It was his fervent hope that both he and Amadahy would be well-treated after these last harrowing days at the hands of Patrick Moore. It seemed as if a mantle of ice had ridden his shoulders ever since his capture. Evil times indeed.

A hand grasped his upper arm. Amadahy's eyes were black pools reflecting moonlight. Trepidation dwelt in them. She pointed her chin ahead. His eyes followed her prompting, but he could not pierce the shadows up the road. Then, sounds of a large contingent began to grow out of the darkness. At first, it came on as muffled clatters and voices. With every step, the noises grew until Lem could hear laughter, yells, horses whinnying, metallic clinks, and wooden rattles as of heavy equipment on the move. Each step brought the unnatural commotions closer. He was heartened to see the yellowish glow of many campfires above the treetops.

Finally, the small party reached the crossroad at the ridgetop. Lem longed to turn toward the store but knew that he had to follow through with his pledge to Major McJunkin and get the vital message through to General Morgan. Having crested the ridge, they followed the road northerly where it cut through a shallow ravine. Emerging from that, the road made a swath through fields of dead grasses and the spindly stalks of last season's corn harvest.

From ahead came a challenge out of the darkness, "Who goes there? Speak and be recognized!" Lem heard the snick of a sword being freed from its scabbard. He almost plowed into Corporal Ashberry when the latter came to an abrupt halt.

"Tis we, Corporal Ashberry and Private Foster, returning to camp with two messengers."

"And the sign?"

"Twill be a warm day on the morrow. Countersign?"

"Summer comes early this year. Step forward, Corporal, and well met." A tall, brown-bearded Continental Army captain, gold epaulet aglow on his right shoulder, had un-shuttered his lantern. The soldier wore an oblong leather patch over one eye, leaving the other brilliant blue orb to rake them all. Both Ashberry and Foster snapped to attention and saluted.

Ashberry spoke, "Sir, we caught these two approaching from the direction of the millworks down by the river. According to the private, they are his neighbors from along Sandy Run, the first creek below Grindall's Ford. That would be the farm belonging to that fence-rider, Henry Farnandis, owner of the mercantile perched on the north side of the ford." Lem bristled at his father being called a fence-rider but held his tongue. The corporal continued, "Lem here claims they were captured by that blasted Pad Moore this Saturday past. He also says they've got an urgent message for the general from Major Joseph McJunkin. Tis their tale that the major and his aide were captured and incarcerated with them in the cellar of Christie's for the last few days. Apparently, they contrived to escape early this morning. The account holds a ring of truth. Foster here confirms certain details as he personally served under the major at Hammond's a fortnight ago."

"Thank you for the thorough report, Corporal. You brought home the bacon this day. Now, what to do with them?" Lem felt the scrutiny of the captain's single eye keenly. He noticed a livid gash puckering from beneath the patch and rising toward the man's scalp. Thankfully, the officer's tricorn hid the rest. Lem shivered over what might be hidden by the leather.

The captain's face split into a voracious grin. "What ails you, boy? Never seen a battle wound?"

"Begging your pardon for staring, sir. There was a man—Scarlet he was called—that did Captain Moore's bidding. His scar was much like yours, only he hadn't lost an eye."

The captain barked laughter. "Not fit to hold a candle then, the lucky cur." To Lem's horror, the captain suddenly flipped Amadahy's hood back. Her braids spilled over her shoulders as the lantern was thrust near her face. She clutched at Lem's arm. "So. You wish to see the Old Wagoner, do you, my dear?" Everyone's eyes were on Amadahy. Lem struggled to keep his composure.

"Aye, sir. My brother and I carry an important message for him." To her credit, Amadahy did not flinch from the abrupt attention, nor did a hint of Indian inflection seep into her voice. Lem prayed fervently that no one noticed her Indian braids and resolved to have her remove them at their earliest convenience.

"According to reports, your father is a Spaniard. Such flawless, tanned skin bespeaks a high heritage. Ah, fair maiden, there is no need for discomfiture. I am but your humble servant." The captain turned his attention to his subordinates. "Tis proof enough in the truth of the matter to warrant passing them through, Corporal. Man this post with the private whilst I see them to the general's tent. He fervently seeks news of the enemy. They've arrived in the nick of time to fill the need!"

"Aye, sir!" Both the corporal and the private spoke at the same time.

"Fare thee well, the two of ye," added John. "Prithee, we all see the end of this action in short order."

"And to you also," said Lem. He took Amadahy's hand in what he hoped appeared brotherly fashion.

"Come, Lem. Come, Sallie. Let us proceed to complete your mission." The captain led the way up the wagon path with his lantern, leaving his underlings to guard in darkness.

As they traipsed along at the captain's heel, he maintained a lively repartee. He spoke flatteries to Amadahy while stroking Lem with compliments of bravery and savvy in the face of the enemy. The captain knew many facts about the Grindall's community. Lem held his tongue for details concerning his family. Surely there would be time enough for such questions after their audience with the general.

Flickers of light could now be seen throughout the woods, setting Lem's mind a boggle. There were hundreds of fires, which meant many hundreds of men. Smells of wood smoke and cooking rode the night air, setting Lem's mouth to watering. Laughter punctuated a growing hubbub. There was a general clamor of men, machines, and animals on the move.

"A small army," stated the captain. "Patriots all. You're in good company." With that, he thrust off the dirt track onto a well-worn footpath. Unfortunately, the path skirted a vault. "Whew! That's a ripe spot. Sorry, Miss. I wouldn't take a maiden through here except for alacrity's sake. The general's tent is nigh the other side of this pasture. We'll make a beeline for it once clear of these woods." The captain chuckled to himself, then continued his run of words. "My regiment, the Virginia Riflemen, arrived a few days before Christmas. Morgan himself had his very beginnings in our regiment of crack shots. Anyway, we had settled down on this farm belonging to one of your local bigwigs, see, a Tory by the name of Alexander Chesney. There were two hundred of us, and we were starving after our long march."

"I am acquainted with the man, sir. He and his family used to attend church with us and buy his staples from my father," said Lem, hoping to steer the conversation toward news of his family.

"Capitol! Then you knew him to be quite a sour Tory, and his wife also—Margaret, a Hodge from hereabouts—so I was told. Her husband being away, the old biddy was not pleased with us making camp on his grant. A feisty one, t'was she. When the matron saw us leading off a few cows with which to feed ourselves, she stormed right down from the big house in all her finery, leading a handful of pitchfork-toting slaves. Demanded we remove ourselves from her husband's property in the name of King George, by Jove! I told her my detail was sent to acquire beeves to feed our men, and she would have to take the matter up with my superior back at the camp."

Amadahy had gotten caught up in the narrative. "What happened then?"

"Whilst my detail had been away scavenging, General Dan and his batch of regular Continentals had marched in. They had crossed the country so fast to get here, we dubbed them the Flying Army—if you take my meaning. We related our treatment at the hands of Chesney's wife. The general was incensed. He made orders to pull up Chesney's fenceposts for firewood and raze all his property for edibles and other useful fares. We followed orders and left nary a blanket nor a change of garments. I say, wouldn't you agree that was an equitable arrangement considering how the thieving Tories have turned your settlement into a stricken hamlet? I haven't seen anyone hereabouts with two shillings to rub together since we arrived, with the exception perhaps of your father. For example, I met a lass on the road near the horse track two days past, calling herself Angelica. And a right angel she was to look upon, except her clothes. Her garments were in a deprived state. The poor lass told a tale of woe concerning her family that near curled me toes. She lives with her Aunt Anna, a Potter, she said. Well, the Potters were paid a visit by that Tory villain, 'Bloody Bill' Cunningham, a few days ago. Cleaned them out of everything, leaving not a morsel, just as we did Chesney and his ilk. It's mighty virtuous your father has not sided with those Royalist pains in the arses. He may have been riding the fence, so they say, but methinks the choice has been made for him. He must fall in with us Americans or end up like Chesney. Saw that old popinjay loading up his wife and child on a rickety wagon this very morning, no doubt fleeing back to the king which made him." The captain chuckled again.

Lem, sick to the heart, said weakly, "Aye, sir." His thoughts were a flurry of concern now for his family's sake. And what of his friend, Angelica? The suddenness of the Continental's arrival, the capture by Colonel T's spies, and all the rest that happened in only a short march of days—

"Have you seen any Indians?"

The question came from Amadahy. Lem was stunned. What was she thinking? Would the captain get suspicious?

"My dear, whatever would prompt such an inquiry?" The captain paused at the edge of the woods, surveying the encampment sprawled before them. He seemed to be taking his bearings. "There's been no Indian sign this side of the mountains in some years, except up north around Rock Hill. Those Indians are mostly tame, the Cawtawbaws."

Lem shot a warning look at Amadahy and thought to distract

the captain, "Sir? We were not told your name."

"Ah. An oversight on my part. I beg pardon. Virginia Company, Morgan's Sharpshooters, Captain Andrew Wallace, at your service. Close ranks with me now as we wind through the hustle and bustle. Mind you don't get trod upon by man nor beast." With that warning, he was off again, threading his way through the plethora of campfires.

Whilst the captain was distracted, Lem whispered in Amadahy's ear, "You're supposed to be passing yourself off as my sister. No one hereabouts speaks of Indians except in stories from a decade past when settlers were fighting to keep them out of Grindall's."

Amadahy cut Lem with a vulturine eye, "I must find my family. It seemed to me he was the perfect one to ask. He likes to spread tales and rumors." She dropped Lem's hand and closed the distance from the captain. Lem strove to catch them up.

Between the fires they went. As Amadahy wound through, the skirts of her short gown, draping from under her jacket, swayed provocatively. Heads turned, and silence descended. It made Lem bilious that such attention was landing on the very person he was trying to protect. There was naught for it but to pray the night continued to cloak her true heritage.

Some thirty A-frame tents, lit from within, arrayed the curvature of the pastureland—probably officer's quarters. Common soldiers were bivouacked around campfires, shabbily dressed in homespun or worn uniforms. Many had no shoes, their feet wrapped in rags. Groups talked in subdued tones while comrades slept in blankets nearby. Lem skirted several players that were shooting dice. They were keeping tallies with pebbles. A songster's melancholy baritone rode the breeze through the clumps of men. Smoke lay heavily overall, held down by the chill leading toward midnight. Chesney's pasture underfoot had been trampled by man and beast to naught more than a muddy plain during the heavy rains of late. Although the moon and stars were now out in full glory, Lem saw at most a hundred men in the vicinity.

On the rise ahead perched another tent, more prominent than others seen thus far. This pavilion was A-framed, had side panels to raise its height, and was made of flax linen like the rest. The perimeter was well-staked and taut ropes stretched from all sides for support. An additional rectangle of canvas extended from the roof to create a portico for the entrance. Lem estimated the tent sheltered an area of about five paces across by nine paces in length. It was bigger than his room back home.

"We're here!" Captain Wallace crowed. "Stand fast whilst I gain us admission."

Wallace proceeded across twenty empty paces toward a set of brawny guards who warmed their hands at a smoldering fire set near the tent's entrance. Lem assumed this cleared space was for the protection and privacy of the tent's occupants. The guards, affecting stances of angry bulls, straightened as the captain approached. Hands rested on the pommels of their sabers. Their uniforms were not as degraded as the others Lem had seen thus far.

"Hold!" commanded the guard on the left.

The captain stopped. Lem could not distinguish what words were exchanged, but the righthand guard turned, raised the flap, and stuck his head inside the tent. There were more unintelligible words spoken, then the guard straightened and pointed to Lem and Amadahy. Captain Wallace waved them over-enthusiastically. Lem locked hands with Amadahy again, and they stepped forward together. Like he, she too was trembling.

"General Dan will see you now," said Wallace as they came to him. "Did I not tell you of his interest in rumors of the enemy? He is most anxious to make your acquaintance. I'll be just outside here till he's done with you. After you've unburdened yourselves of your message, I've been instructed to lead you off to a nearby mess. I know you will appreciate the opportunity to sup and drink. The two of you must be famished after your trials and tribulations."

"Don't talk them to death, Captain. Send them in!" The command came from within the edifice.

"Aye, sir!" Wallace and the two guards stepped aside.

Amadahy entered, Lem following at her heels. The shelter's interior was well-lit. Half a dozen candle lanterns hung from a rope tied between two tentpoles. These meager flames had warmed the space slightly above freezing, which to Lem felt quite warm after days spent cold and wet. Before Lem was a table draped with maps, held fast by several pewter noggins. Atop them were feather quills, ink bottles, and blotters. There were two cots, one on each side of the entrance. The cot to the right was empty save a rumpled tick; the left cot held someone bundled head to toe in a heavy woolen blanket. Gentle snores filtered through the thick material.

"Ah. I see you've noticed my good comrade, Baron de Glaubech. Let's leave him be so he may recover his mien after an arduous day of travel."

Both Lem and Amadahy stepped backward as the general rounded his map table to greet them. Clad in a frontiersman's buckskin jacket, lindsey-woolsey hunting shirt, and wool breeches, the man cut an imposing figure. He was over eighteen hands tall, broad of shoulder, with arms thick like tree trunks. Lem's own hand was briefly engulfed in meaty appendages that had seen years of hard labor. Those selfsame hands gently drew Amadahy's wrist to lips for a brushing kiss.

"Welcome to my camp, young master, and miss. What news hast thou to impart, eh?" Blue eyes flashed expectantly from a congenial face.

14

The Encampment

By Lem's estimation, Brigadier General Daniel Morgan was neither young nor old but somewhere betwixt. He had not yet lost the vigor of youth, although his receding hairline was yellowish-white. It took all Lem's Scot Irish vigor to withstand the general's hot countenance.

"Speak your piece, lad. I'll not bite. Battered a few deserving skulls in my time." He punched fist to palm and gave a tightlipped smile.

"S-sir, I am Lemuel Farnandis, and this is my sister, Sallie. We carry vital words from Major Joseph McJunkin, as penned by his aide, Sergeant James Park." Lem chided himself for stuttering but held firm despite the general's scrutiny.

"Pray tell, are McJunkin and Park in good health?"

"When last we saw them, aye, sir. Excepting, the major had sprained his ankle."

"Alive if not wholly well. I'm sure their captors found them tough to chew. I've been told that the two of you, and my worthy scouts, were recently detained by that scoundrel Pad Moore. We're having a devil of a time rooting him out. He goes from one Royalist position to another, up and down Fair Forest Creek. Haven't seen those fair forests myself, though I wouldn't mind dipping a hook under the shade of a nice tree thereabouts. Ah, well, 'Time and tide tarrieth no man,' so says St. Marher. Get to the message."

"Begging your pardon, sir, it'll take but a moment to retrieve the packet. Sergeant Park copied out the message onto four pieces of linen, one for each of us. Sallie sewed the copies into our coat linings in our firm hope that at least one of us would win through to you, sir."

"Ingenious! Four chances to beat the odds! Would that all my officers displayed such wile."

"Sister, let us remove our kits." He and Amadahy began to shrug off their gear. The general lent a hand to the task, working with first Amadahy then Lem. In short order, they were unlimbered of cartridge boxes, canteens, packs, and the Brown Bess. All these items were laid on the empty cot.

"Ah. Where are my manners? Hold fast." Morgan retrieved three spindly stools from beneath his map desk and proceeded to spread them about. "My apologies to you both for my lapse of hospitality. Being constantly on the move has shorn much from my manners. Rest yourselves, I beg you." He held out a hand to steady Amadahy as she lowered herself onto a stool.

"You are most gracious, sir," she offered.

"'Tis nothing, my dear."

"Here, Sallie. Let us use my jacket." Lem removed his coat and gave the garment to Amadahy, then sat. The general joined them, perched like a hawk surveying his quarry. Deftly, Amadahy turned out the lining to expose the hidden seam she had placed in the right armpit. Once again, she produced the little bone knife from its unseen lair. Morgan reached for it, startling her. She recovered her aplomb and laid it in his palm.

"What's this? I've not seen such a tool since the one my cousin Dan Boone gave to Nancy, my eldest daughter. How come you by this Indian plunder, lass?" He turned the blade to admire the markings etched in the bone handle.

"T'was a gift from my father, sir." She seemed pensive.

"Oho! Just the trinket for a pretty maiden. Keeps the boys in their place, I should imagine." Curiosity satisfied, he held it out by the blade for Amadahy to retrieve. He leaned toward Lem and winked. "Take care with it, fair lady."

Amadahy's cheeks flushed as she replied, "I will, sir." She then diligently used the knife for ripping open the seam.

"Most ingenious. So many verbal messages have gone astray of late—the carriers falling prey to enemy ambush, no doubt."

"Tis nothing, sir," Amadahy said, eyes downcast. She exposed the hidden pocket and wiggled her fingers inside. Withdrawing the tannish square of oilcloth placed there by James Park, she put the packet on the table. The general seized it with sausage-like fingers and began to remove the oilcloth wrapper, talking all the while.

"Tut, tut. Such formality, and I being a plain man. Call upon me as simply Dan, I press you both. Rest assured, for one so worn with conventions, it would give me rare pleasure indeed to hear a simple greeting." The general's eyes gleamed encouragement over the audacious request.

Consigning the oilcloth wrapper to the dirt, Morgan rose from his stool and laid the linen open upon the table. Both Lem and Amadahy gathered themselves to either side. There before them was the fulfillment of their oath:

1100 redbirds plus two 3-pounders fly at dawn. J.P.

"Sir," said Lem, "This message, without the numbers, was part of a sealed dispatch which I purloined from Captain Moore's pocket two nights past. Sally and I burned and scattered the ashes before Moore discovered it missing."

"Did Moore chance to read it, Lem?" asked Morgan.

"Nay, sir. I broke the wax seal myself. Tyger Moore's none the wiser."

"Huzzah, Lem! Tis excellent news! Now, tell me, durst either of you recall the precise message?"

Amadahy responded by rote, "Redbirds fly at dawn two days hence. Advance arrives on the morrow. Remain vigilant at Easterwood's and Grindall's. By no means engage. Hold to secrecy in all matters. *T.*"

The general's eyes widened. "Praise God, you've delivered me a treasure trove! Such a sealed dispatch as this most likely had a two-fold intent. Firstly, to guide Moore's hand, and secondly, to inform Lord Cornwallis of his vassal's actions!"

Just then, a shout came from outside. "Make way, make way!"

Lem recognized the voice and exclaimed, "Sergeant Park! Sir…Dan…I mean, General, that's Sergeant James Park out yonder, the very man who copied this message!"

One of the guards yelled, "Hold, I say! No entry!" There were sounds of a scuffle, accompanied by several ominous thuds. Then, the tent opening was plugged by the bulk of Sergeant Park.

The sergeant wore a devilish grin. "Pardon the intrusion, General," he began, "but methinks the importance of our words will lift your—"

"General Dan," cried McJunkin. He moved past Park's elbow, revealing his dependence on a rough wooden crutch. "So sorry to disturb…Lemuel? Amadahy! Bless me, you're both safe!"

At that point, several things happened at once.

Lem was certain the major had just driven a stake through their deception. His thoughts raced. What would be the consequences?

"Halt, I say! Or I'll plug you through the mizzen!" A bayonet prodded the sergeant's back. Park's face went livid, but his arms shot up.

From the occupied cot came a pitched voice, "Merde! Cannot a mon get a wink in this dreary frontier?" A disheveled French soldier threw off his blanket with the flourish of a billowing sail.

"HOLD!" The very air seemed to harden as the brash command from General Morgan collapsed all action at once. "Guardsman, return to your post, for all is well! Baron, my sincere apologies for the disturbance of your long-awaited repose. Return to sleep if you may. Lem. Amadahy. Stand fast, but fret not."

As if time rewound, the saber withdrew, the so-called Baron lay down and pulled the blanket over his head in a huff, Sergeant Park lowered his hands and dropped his chin to his barrel of a chest, and Major McJunkin cleared his throat.

Such was the force of will radiating from the commander of the Continental Army, Lem felt as if he were standing next to a bonfire. He now realized that he and Amadahy were at the mercy of a new captor. The look on Amadahy's face told him she suffered similar trepidation. They could naught but beg for deliverance if chance would have it.

Morgan, seeming lost amongst his thoughts, absently stroked his unshaven chin. He began to pace but caught himself up. Abruptly, he turned to face McJunkin and Park. "Gentlemen. Put a damper on pleasantries and make your report!"

"Sir," began McJunkin, with noticeable relief, "the completion of the task you laid upon Colonel William Washington culminated successfully at Hammond's old store a fortnight ago. We offered those Tories proper redress for atrocities along the Fair Forest Creek, as I'm certain you are aware of by now. After chasing the Loyalists neigh twenty miles, they lit upon Hammond's to make their stand. Their regiment was decimated by our hand, with few escaping. Making hard inquires of the captured, we discovered that the pack of bloody, I mean to say, several infamous leaders managed to escape. Amongst those with luck was one reportedly named 'Moore,' perhaps the ruffian about whom we've heard prior words. Another was a Georgian called 'Waters.' Amongst those without luck was one Major Benjamin Wofford. Apparently, he is the traitorous brother of our own Colonel William Wofford, master and commander of the Iron Works and Fort bearing his very name at Lawson's Fork!" Here McJunkin paused to catch his breath, or perhaps for dramatic effect, and seeing no like sentiment continued his report.

"Park and I, being attached to Colonel Washington, chanced to gather some intelligence from our intrepid scouts combing the area around Hammond's. Apparently, the success of our actions did but aggravate Lord Earl Cornwallis, whom you know has appropriated comfortable lodgings in Winnsboro. One of our scouts, calling himself 'Jack' and riding a fine black mare, caught us up on the road to Fair Forest Creek. He blocked the way, proclaiming, and I quote, 'Dan hath kicked the hornet's nest!' Upon further inquiry, we learned from this 'Jack' that our scouts had Providentially taken an enemy spy who was leaving the vicinity of Musgrove's Mill. 'Jack' inferred that with persuasion, the spy divulged unwelcome news. He had delivered a sealed message from Lord Cornwallis to his ramrod, that butcher, Colonel Banastre Tarleton. Furthermore, the spy was privy to the message's contents. He was to return post-haste to the Lord Earl with an affirmative reply. Bloody Ban was informed of your whereabouts here at Grindall's and was instructed to 'push Morgan to the utmost.' Lastly, Park and I have it from Colonel Pickens—'Banny Tarleton is coming to give you a blast!'"

"Forsooth? There can be no mistake?" cried the general.

"Nay, sir. The sergeant and I bore witness to this awful truth and fought alongside these brave youngsters to bring it to you by hook or by crook." Sergeant Park shook his head, backing the major's bold statement.

At this point, there was another stir outside the tent. A feminine voice rose above the others, "But sirs, I must see the general. I have ridden in darkness and swum the river at risk of life and limb to carry grave tidings. Let me pass, I beg you, or all is lost!"

The guardsman, trouble creasing his face, pushed through the tent flap. "Begging your pardon, sir. There's a fair young maiden urgently requesting your attention. She claims—"

"Send her in, Captain!"

"Aye, sir!" The harried soldier left the tent. He returned moments later, escorting a bedraggled woman. Her dark hair was matted with debris, and both her dark cloak and gown were be-soddened. To Lem, she appeared swathed in castoffs.

It was plain the general no longer felt amicable, for he immediately demanded of the woman, "Identify yourself and state your business!"

The woman took in the imposing figure of the general and quailed.

"Speak, I say, for time is of the essence!"

"G-general," she stammered, "My name is Anne—Anne Kennedy. By the grace of God, I have found you. The enemy is at your doorstep!"

"How know you this?"

"My family resides in nearby Union District. Toward sunset this day, green-clad dragoons passed through our lands, absconding with every cow, pig, and chicken. We could but witness the force from our doorstep. Cavalry, sir, and upon our count, exceeding two hundred men. One macaroni wearing a fur-plumed helmet cantered up to us as we watched from our porch. He cheekily proclaimed, 'We confiscate these goods in the name of the King and Tarleton's Raiders!' It took till nightfall for them to be gone. I bade my sisters farewell and mounted my horse for a mad dash, knowing that I had a slim chance of finding you in the dark. The British are here!" She collapsed as she spoke this last. Park caught her and helped her sit on the unoccupied cot.

"Baron de Glaubeck, get thee up!" exclaimed the general. The disheveled French soldier unveiled himself yet again from the heavy blanket. Upon seeing Amadahy and Anne, his dark eyes widened. Hastily, he refreshed the upturned twist of his thin mustache, smoothed his goatee, and slicked back his hair. He then drew forth his black cockade, which had been his pillow, and used both hands to press it upon his crown. A speculative smile grew on his face as he openly appraised the two maidens.

"'Tis no time for dalliance, Baron! We have the means now to make good our bold plan. Get thee up, I say again! Go back and tell Billy that Banny is coming, and he must meet me tomorrow evening at Gentleman Thompson's on the east side of Thicketty Creek!"

"Sacre bleu!" exclaimed the Baron, struggling into his high-top boots. His protruding belly seemed to hinder his work, so Sergeant Park bent to assist him. "Oomph! What are you doing, lout? Unhand me, I say!" Lem was sure he had heard the little man's teeth clacking under Park's exuberance. Task accomplished, Park clamped the Baron's shoulders and lifted him bodily to his feet.

The Frenchman wore a mixture of indignation and embarrassment.

To the surprise of everyone inside the tent, a deep belly laugh rolled from General Dan. Lem noticed a single tear trailing down his cheek, such was his mirth. Finally, he said, "Mission accomplie, Baron! Now, make haste to Thicketty!"

Baron de Glaubeck gathered himself up to his full stature, short though it was, pridefully lifted his chin, and strode from the tent with a haughty "Humph!"

"And so goes the French volunteer," said Major McJunkin, smirking. "I must say, sir, that Frenchman wielded a mighty sword at Hammond's storehouse."

Anne Kennedy wore an appalled expression. "But, but sirs, how can you be so gay with the enemy upon your heels?"

"My dear young woman," said Morgan, "if I despaired over every piece of ill news received each day, I should melt into a puddle of misery. Is that the caliber of leader you expected to meet after such a harrowing and dangerous journey?"

"Nay, sir." Slightly abashed, Kennedy's eyes filled with growing respect. "Sir, one more thing I have for you." With that, she drew up the edge of her gown to reach into the top of her stocking. Everyone averted their gaze except Amadahy. "Here you are, sir. A dispatch from the ladies, my neighbors. It is a simple request for your attention as soon as may be. We have been sorely tasked of late by the Tory raiders and the British as of this day. It is much to endure, sir."

General Dan stroked his bristly chin, deep in thought. All eyes were upon him, and all felt the need for haste, yet he was not a man to be rushed. Lem could almost see the wheels of his thoughts churning through possibilities, forsaking the untenable and grasping the doable. The only sign showing the depth of such consideration was written in the ridges on the general's forehead. He looked squarely at Anne Kennedy when next he spoke.

"My dear Lady Anne, your services this night are worthy of the annals of history. A greater heroine I could not have imagined. Twill be my honor to have you escorted safely back to your home." The general then bellowed, "SENTRY! CALL FORTH LIEUTENANT BELL!"

From outside the tent came a snappy, "Aye, sir!" The sound of running feet and shuffling gear gradually faded as the soldier raced to follow the order.

Moments later, the crunch and jangle of several returning soldiers met their ears. The tent flap parted to admit a disheveled young officer who gave a sharp salute as he was shoved into their midst. "Lieutenant Bell reporting as ordered, sir!"

"At ease, Lieutenant. We're all friends." Lem noticed the general did return the salute, however, before continuing. "As you can plainly see, I have visitors, one of whom is this young maiden, Anne Kennedy." A pan-sized hand opened toward her. "Accompany Miss Kennedy to the mess tent for victuals, drink, and warmth. Care for her horse as well. She and her mount have been through trials to reach me. Tarry not, my dear, but certainly eat your fill and take what comfort you may under the lieutenant's care. To you, Lieutenant Bell, I entrust the safe return of this brave woman to the bosom of her true and faithful family. Whilst there, have your contingent make a sweep of the surrounding countryside and clear out any Tory ruffians thereabouts. Thereby the maidens and her neighbors may rest in peace. Once done, find us again at Thicketty!"

"Aye, sir! My men and I will be most honored to escort Mistress Kennedy safely home and take pure pleasure in routing any Tories we meet." The handsome lieutenant snapped off another salute.

He then offered his arm to the maiden.

Kennedy flushed as the lieutenant's attention lit upon her. She stood and linked arms with him at the elbow. "My heart goes with you and your men, General Morgan. May God shine upon your endeavors and give victory to the cause of Freedom!" With that, a proud officer escorted his new charge from the tent.

Turning his eye upon Lem and Amadahy, General Dan said, "My dear young master and mistress, please enlighten me before we go further. I must know the truth so jealously held within your breasts." The yoke of command harnessed those remaining in the tent. There would be no withholding information from General Dan.

Lem looked to the major. McJunkin gave a supportive nod toward the general. At that, something seemed to unclasp within Lem's chest. Taking a deep breath, he plunged ahead, "Sir, may I introduce Amadahy of the Cawtawbaw Nation?"

"Ahah. The People of the River. Steadfast allies. They have served us well as guides and trackers. Deer Tails, we call them. They tie deer tails in their hair, so we know they're friendlies and not Cherokees. Great numbers of Cherokees fight alongside the British."

Amadahy smiled, "Ye iswa'here." Everyone stared blankly at her except the general. He bowed gravely from the hip. Lem wondered what her words meant and filed the question away for a more appropriate time.

Amadahy's smile faded when the general asked, "What brought you here? Redskins…ahem…I mean to say, your People have long resided in Rock Hill."

She appeared suddenly unnerved. "My family…we travel to visit relatives across in mountains … we were attacked. I escape. Meet Lem. Meet major. Meet sergeant … I … am … uneasy." She drew several deep breaths to calm herself, then words spilled from her lips. "Please, sir, I beg you, help me find my family. They were captured by bad Tories days ago. These men saved my life." Her eyes glistened as she took in McJunkin, Park, and lastly, Lem. "I am indebted to them, but I must see my people saved also."

The general drew himself up and squared his broad shoulders. "Heed now these words I must regretfully lay upon you, Amadahy of the Cawtawbaws, and you, Lemuel of the Family Farnandis. Mounting a search for your missing relatives is currently out of the question." Both Lem and Amadahy tried to protest this announcement, but the general raised his hand for silence. "Your vexation with me is understood but misplaced. The danger is too great on several scores to release you freely or send forth search parties into these angry woods. Your likely recapture by the Loyalists would ensure a most painful circumstance as they would wring information from you."

Lem interrupted, "Sir, we don't know anything of import—"

"Be still! I shall have my say! It so happens I have knowledge of the current plight of the Family Farnandis and of several other prominent folks hereabouts. They have been rounded up by Loyalist troops, their wares commandeered, and themselves conscripted to serve the whims of the British. Upon penalty of death for insubordination, they serve in menial capacities as cooks, launderers, muckrakers, blacksmiths, and such. Of the Indians, I have no firm knowledge, though I suspect much the same for them." Lem's heart froze in his chest at these words. He sought Amadahy's eyes as the general continued, "Many families have felt the sting of conflict with the Crown since this dirty war began. My heart bleeds for them all, but Liberty is not free. Whilst I cannot assuage your desires immediately, I offer this token. Upon my word of honor, once the grip of the enemy is lifted from these lands, I shall have my scouts look to the whereabouts of both families. I prithee God sees you reunited. Till then, you shall remain in my charge."

Lem was stunned. It was as he suspected. Amadahy and he had leaped from the frying pan into the fire. They, indeed, had new captors. He looked to McJunkin and Park for compassion. Finding none, he sought the general's face for some manner of leniency.

"Now, now. There's no need to fret. You'll not be consigned to the briny deep this day. Nay, here's the thick of it. Our danger is so great, our demand for stealth so indispensable, I must ask of you an even greater sacrifice in the cause of Freedom."

Lem held his breath. Somehow, he knew the next words from the general's mouth would seal their fate. Power. Control. Again, he had none, and this time the general had all. In the name of the Lord God Almighty, Lem prayed the general used his authority well.

15

Oaths and Duties

"Major McJunkin and Sergeant Park, I now charge you as witnesses whilst these two make their solemn oath," said General Morgan.

Both men spoke as one, "Aye, sir!"

"Lem. Amadahy. I will now ask you to affirm the Oath of Allegiance and Fidelity. Raise your right hands and repeat my words truly and faithfully. I, (state your name)," Lem and Amadahy did so, "do swear that I will bear true Faith and Allegiance to the State of South Carolina, and will faithfully support, maintain and defend the same against George the Third, King of Great Britain, his successors, abettors and all other enemies and opposers whatsoever, and will without delay, discover to the Executive Authority or some one Justice of the Peace in this State, all plots and conspiracies that shall come to my knowledge against the said State, or any other of the United States of America."

"You may both lower your hands. Now. In my capacity as the

Executive Authority here present, I offer you, Lemuel Farnandis, the honorable position of alternate drummer for the Second Spartan Regiment of Militia under Colonel Thomas Brandon. Tommy just lost one of his to the flux. This is the selfsame regiment in which Major McJunkin and James Park now serve with distinction." Turning to Amadahy, Morgan said, "And to you, Lady Sallie, I offer a most vital occupation. I ask that you join with the women of the Second Spartans. Though the bulk of my camp followers was disbanded weeks past, as we had needs of speed, those few willing lasses that could ride horses remained behind. These perform the drudgery of domestic chores such as cooking, laundering, sewing, and assisting in the infirmary. Their services make it so the common soldiers may have some small comforts, although the women themselves share in the hardships of the men. Stick with them, and you may yet live through the war." Morgan then withdrew two guineas from a leather pouch in his jacket pocket. "To seal the bargain, I place in each of your hands a small payment for your past and upcoming services rendered to the Continental Army."

Lem was astonished. It was more money than he had ever held—and in gold coin—not worthless Continental paper. "Th-thank you, sir." He drew forth his own goatskin money pouch from an inside pocket and dropped the gold coin next to two coppers. Tying it off again, he stuffed the bag back in its pocket, buttoning it up for safekeeping.

"That should see you both through the end of the war with food in your belly and shoes on your feet, though there's little enough of anything to be had these days. Guard it well; spend it wisely. I caution you."

Amadahy remained silent but secreted her coin away, although Lem knew not where she hid it. Suddenly, she looked up at

Morgan. "Much wampum. How can you spare it…for an…Indian?" Her eyes were moist.

"My dear, I have fought my share of Indians. Came close to getting brained by a Shawnee tomahawk. One day, perhaps, there will be time enough for a full discussion on the subject. Suffice it to say, I have fought against and alongside Indians all my life. Not all Indians are heathens, nor are they all saints. I cannot fault a warrior for defending his home and family from those who would take both. However, I can fault the same warrior siding with my enemy, intent on driving me from home and killing my loved ones. For good or ill, your people and mine have been thrust together. We must proceed as best we can against our common enemy in King George III. To this single cause, I have committed all that I am and all that I have. Unless we join as one nation under God and shirk the yoke of tyranny, no man, Indian or otherwise, will live free of oppression in this New World. I have no right to meddle with another man's property, his ox or his ass, his manservant or his maidservant, or anything that is his. Neither does he have the right to meddle with anything that is mine. If he does, I have a right to defend it by force. This is my land, and so shall I do."

For a moment, the great man held his tongue in reflection, then his brow cragged as it wrestled with hard thoughts. All in the tent awaited Morgan's next words with bated breath. Lem knew those words would seal his fate and that of Amadahy.

"Men, and Lady, from this point forward, I desire the rumor spread that the son and daughter of a local farmer brought forth vital information of the forces that will oppose us. Thus, a merrier welcome they should receive of their fellows. Make it known that Sallie shall be joining the camp followers. Those women will appreciate her help and see her through this action. There will be few questions asked because the need is so great. Under no circumstances should it become known that we have a Cawtawbaw amongst us. My fair maiden, tis not glamorous work, but a most vital and appreciated service. Should our condition sour, you'll doubtless be pressed to serve the British at the same loathsome tasks. Best maintain your ruse as Lem's sister in any case."

"I shall do my best, sir," said Amadahy. She seemed ill at ease yet resigned to her plight.

"The same goes for you, Lemuel. Better alive and tapping a drum than dead of a ghastly wound, although carrying drumsticks does not preclude the former. Lay low when necessary. Upon the battlefield, a drummer must keep his head. I've seen too many boys drop their drums in the heat of battle and take up the sword in vengeance. Once done, there's no turning back, young sir. For my own part, I would see you both returned to your homes and families safe and sound."

Lem said, "Aye, sir. But sir? I know naught of drumming. Who shall teach me?"

"Twill be I, lad," James Park stepped forward to stand between Lem and Amadahy. "I'll have you tappin', draggin', and flamin' the beat in no time. My first duty was drumming when we was fighting the Indian Wars. Begging your pardon, Amadah…ehem…I mean, Sallie."

"Excellent, James," interjected Major McJunkin. "I shall apply myself to getting the both of you settled into the outfit.

Morgan said, "Very well. We've settled this matter for the best, methinks. Our business is concluded, and the time has come to part. The Foe nips our heels, and we must feed him a bone lest he becomes ferocious all too soon. Go now, all, with my deepest gratitude and respect. Harken my command of silence as to our best-laid plans."

"Thank you, General Dan," said McJunkin. "Come, Lem. Come, Sallie. Stick by my side now, and I shall lead you to your new situation." McJunkin laid gentle hands upon their shoulders and turned them away from the map table. Already the general was engrossed in the study of the parchments. Both McJunkin and Park assisted Lem and Amadahy back into their kits, the Brown Bess's sling riding uncomfortably across Lem's shoulders. He attempted to shift the strap to a more suitable position as Park held open the tent flap. They filed out.

Just as the flap dropped closed, General Morgan roared, "ED GILES!"

The sentries to either side of the entrance jolted as if struck by lightning. Lem's heart flew to his throat. From a nearby campfire, a thin figure struggled to rise. He tripped over a bundle at his feet. "Beg pardon, John," he said. Recovering, the soldier hastily smoothed his hands through his hair and down the remnants of his uniform before launching toward Morgan's tent.

McJunkin spoke softly in Lem's ear as they walked away, "That would be Major Edward Giles. He's a good chap to know despite his awkwardness. We're all a bit inelegant when awakened from a sound sleep, what? I'm sure General Dan has good reason to stir his aid-de-camp. Matters are about to heat, I'd venture."

The four moved off. Lem and Amadahy followed at McJunkin's heels, with Park trailing. They wound through the bivouacked militia strewn about the open pastureland, making for a row of tents bunched up against the edge of the forest toward the north. The smell of woodsmoke remained prevalent. As they progressed, Lem noticed how sparse were the men strewn about the fires. It seemed there should have been six or seven soldiers to each fire, yet most of the flames were kept fueled by only one or two.

Before Lem could speak, Amadahy asked, "Major, sir, why are there so few men?"

"Good question, dear *Sallie*." McJunkin sounded jovial. "General Dan, being a wily sort of fellow, wishes to convey a certain message to that popinjay, Bloody Ban. The woods hereabouts have eyes, you know."

"Beg pardon?" Lem interrupted.

"Iffin you was a-wantin' ter mislead—" began Park.

"Now, now, my good man. They should learn to use their noddles, don't you agree?"

"As you say, Major."

"Where was I? Ah. Suppose a large group of bullies chased after you, Lem, you, Sallie, and perhaps a few more of your friends. Their design is to beat the lot of you for daring to stand against them over some moral high note of contention. Imagine these happen to be stout pugilists, heavily muscled, whilst yourselves are barely willow branches. What would you do?"

Amadahy was again quick to answer. "Hide our numbers. Create confusion. Move quickly and silently."

"Smart lass!" exclaimed Park. "Them's Injun tactics!"

"Sergeant! Hold your tongue, man!"

"Oh. Sorry, sir. Me mouth ran off before me tongue knew the better of it."

"Don't let it happen again!"

"Narry shall I, sir."

"Sallie, that was an excellent observance."

Lem considered what had been said. Other circumstances came to mind where the same situation had occurred right at home. Mamma had asked Lem and his brothers to round up the chickens because they had somehow escaped the henhouse during the previous night. The hens were scattered all over the barnyard. He and his brothers sought them out, but t'was Lem's ill-luck to come upon a dozen hens bunched up in one of the horse stalls. Hot Spur dove down from a high beam and cut Lem's back to ribbons with his sharp talons. Even now, as Lem made his way through the dark encampment, recalling the rooster's punishment made his shoulders bunch.

"Me lad, I take it you have no thoughts to share on the subject?" Major McJunkin had dropped back to walk alongside his charges.

"Sir, in addition to Sallie's tactics, I would add that a small group would be afeared of becoming surrounded by the bullies. They would be looking for a place to make a stand. If their backs were to the wall, they could not as easily become encircled and crushed by greater strength and numbers."

"Excellent! Park, it seems we are up against some rather spritely young minds. I'd wager these two have noted General Dan's penchant for all things Indian. Ah, but here we've arrived at last. Best belay further discussion for a time."

"LAWS A MERCY!" A dark shade rose out of the night to block the way.

Lem knew that voice. "Sukey! Oh, Sukey!" Of a sudden, he was whelmed in the pungent scent and ample form of the black family servant. Only the whites of Sukey's eyes could be made out in the moonlight. Had it been daytime, the moisture streaming from his own would have blinded him anyway.

"Unhand the boy, negress! You're going to smother him!"

Lem was released, fresh air filling his eager lungs.

"Have you naught to say to young *Sallie*, here?" Mcjunkin admonished.

Lem leaned forward as if to hug Sukey again. Instead, he thrust lips to her ear. "Play along, Sukey," he whispered.

The black matron dutifully engulfed Amadahy. "Why, child. Iffin I didn't know better, I'd say you done growed a foot in a week!" Amadahy's arms flailed about until she was released. She stepped back to Lem's side, mouth hanging open.

"Sukey?"

"Joseph?"

"Now, now. You know the protocol. No calling by given names. Rank and surnames, madam, unless addressing another of the same rank."

"Whatchu want of me, *Major?* You knows I got no rank!" Lem recognized the tone of irritation in Sukey's voice. McJunkin was about to get an earful unless he smoothed her feathers.

"I thought perhaps you forgot yourself, what with having just discovered several of the Farnandis children alive and well. Park and I have pressing business, so I beg you, see to their needs whilst we attend our duties. Word has come down that we will break camp in a few hours. These ones are no doubt quite depleted after their trials. I'll leave it to them to tell their harrowing tale once they've supped and rested. Keep Sallie near your bosom when we ride. I shall send for Lemuel once we move out. Park shall scrounge him a horse and teach him the drum."

Sukey, having regained her humor, said, "Lemmy? A drummer? He'll make a good 'un, the number of times I've had to rap his skull to make a point. Tis a wonder he has any hair left to hide under his cap. He'll make a good-un, Major, sir, or I'll take to drumming meself."

McJunkin chuckled. "Good matron, you have my gratitude. James, shall we see to what may be cooking at Colonel Brandon's fire?"

"Tis as good a notion as ye've had of late, Major. Me stomach has long been a knotted rope. Think ye we find forty winks as well?"

"That, Sergeant, may be a vain hope. Nevertheless, we shall sally forth and see to what we may." An orange glow highlighted their shadowy forms as they strode away toward an A-framed tent with a large fire.

Sukey rounded on Lem. "Wha'chu been a-doin'? I's thought you's dead and gone! I done fount Old Bo just a-standing in the road day befo' yesterday—yo birthin' day! An' you weren't nowheres to be found. Oh, honey child, I's so glad to see you ain't a ghost!"

Lem held up his hands to slow her down. "Sukey, the major's right. Sallie and I haven't eaten or rested since early this morning. Do you think we can find some scraps and a place to bed for a while? I promise we'll tell you everything after we've recovered our wits and strength."

"My, oh my. What a prattler I is. Sho' honey, I knows jus' what to do. Y'all come on with me, now." She grabbed both Lem and Amadahy around their waists and steered them off toward the edge of the woods.

16

The Respite

Sukey brought Lem and Amadahy to a picket that had been tied off between several large oaks rooted at the field's edge. Suddenly, amongst the beasts, a mule brayed. The sound was a cross between a whinny and a wheeze. Lem rushed forward to throw his arms about the neck of Old Bo, once again feeling the trickle of moisture on his cheek. The mule nuzzled at Lem's side fondly, jouncing him. The unexpected commotion set the line of horses to nickering and shuffling.

"Ho, there! What goes?" Apparently, the picket was being watched over by a sentry.

"Why, tis jus' me an' a some of my family that's done raised from the grave."

"Is that you, Sukey?" There followed the clinking and tramp of a soldier carrying full gear.

"Sho' is, Lit'l Nick!"

"Awww. Sukey. You know better."

"I's supposed to call you *Sergeant* Jasper after all's we been through? You's gettin' to be as bad as Joseph! Bet you can't even fit in yo britches! You ain't gittin' no more o' my cathead biscuits iffn you keep on treatin' me poorly!"

"Hush, now. That's no way to be." The shadowy form of Nicholas Jasper rounded Bo's head. Jasper shifted a long rifle from one hand to the other to keep from clunking the mule. Lem stepped back, allowing the soldier to draw near.

"Who's this you've got with you, Sukey?"

"Don't be tellin' me you done fergot yer own neighbors so fast! This sheers Lem and Sallie Farnandis, o' course!"

"You know I can't see nothing in the dark!" Jasper seemed to be squinting.

"You can't see nothin' in the daytime, neither. Near squashed you just the other week under a sack o' flour that you was supposed to be catchin'! Busted the sack all over yerself. An' you havin' all them mouths to feed! Liza, Phoebe, Rachel, Polly—"

"Hey, Lem. Hey, Sallie. My heavens. Both y'all done grown a bit since I seen you last. Been wanting to thank you, Lem, for saving Phoebe and all them other girls from that tyger. Methinks it took some expert driving."

"T'was my pleasure, Mr. Jasper." Lem was about to say more, but Sukey swelled up like a mother hen.

"Sergeant Jasper, I's supposed to get these two young'uns fedded and bedded. Now, get on back to yo work so I's can get on to mine."

"I'm supposing you're right, Sukey. Lem, Sallie, sure am glad y'all are safe. Can't say as much for the rest of the Farnandis clan." Those words chilled Lem's heart.

"Sergeant! Get on, now. Lemmy, don't you fret. I'll tell you all 'bout it later."

"Aye, madam!" Nicholas Jasper's lanky shadow rounded Bo's

head again. Lem could see the swish of a long gray beard in the meager starlight as the man trod down the picket line. He paused now and again to scratch at an ear or rub at a muzzle. The horses quieted under his ministrations.

Sukey was already rummaging in the pack carried by Old Bo. The savory smell of smoked beef wafted across Lem's nose, causing his mouth to water and belly to rumble. He hadn't realized he was so hungry, but there had been no chance to stop for victuals all day. Sallie, as he was forcing himself to think of Amadahy, was shifting restlessly from one foot to the other. She was famished too.

"Here, young'uns." Sukey thrust a handful of the dried meat and a corn muffin into each of their hands.

Sallie stuffed her mouth immediately with the bread. Lem refrained from gorging, afraid the dry fare would make him choke. Indeed, Sallie began to gag.

Sukey unslung a wooden canteen, uncorked it, and thrust it to Sallie's lips. "Here, child. Sip this quick."

Sallie gulped several times to clear her throat. "I am…in your debt." She continued to clear her throat as Sukey tilted the canteen against Lem's lips. He gulped too fast, spluttering.

"Easy, Sukey. Are you trying to drown me?"

"Take it yo'self, then." Sukey turned away to rummage through the loaded sawbuck riding the mule's back.

Lem juggled the foodstuffs to take the canteen. A few swigs later, his tongue discerned the flavor of spruce beer, although it was heavily watered. He handed the canteen back to Sukey with a word of thanks. She slung it back over the pommel and continued digging through the sacks.

"Here they is. Thought I wouldn't find 'em in the dark." Sukey withdrew several heavy blankets and draped them over her arm.

"You'uns 'bout done eatin'?"

Sallie spoke. "I am at your service, Mistress Sukey. The fare was good. Excuse me for a short while, I beg you. I must attend to some personal needs." With that, Sallie stalked into the dark woods.

"Who she be, Lemmy?" Sukey uttered these words as soon as Amadahy was out of earshot.

"A friend, Sukey. Best hold your tongue of anything you may suspect. It is crucial that *Sallie* be passed off as my sister. Will you trust me on this?"

"Course I will! I ain't no snitch. She's Sallie Farnandis till I's told otherwise, an' I'll pound anyone sez other how. You will tell me when you can, won't you?"

"Certainly, Sukey. Do you have any word of the rest of the family?"

"Laws, I wish I did. General Dan's sentries picked me up almost the minute I found Bo. I ain't had no time to meself since. They's got me cleanin', and cookin', and sewin' up socks, and such not. These po' soldiers—specially them militia boys—they's got no food an' wearin' naught but tatters. Too cold for that, I tell ye. When they cotched me, I led 'em back down to da mill, and since then, they's been goin' an' gittin' sacks to feed everyone. Lemmy, they wuz starvin'. I'm show yo' papa wouldn't begrudge 'em."

"That is the truth of it, Sukey. Here comes Sallie. I think to avail myself of the trees as well, then let's all get some sleep. I'm near dead on my feet."

"Sho', Lemmy. Po' child."

Lemuel left Sallie in Sukey's good care while he relieved himself. The old negress was chatting her up merrily, at the same time forcing the girl to settle amongst the roots of the hoary oak. Lem smiled to himself. It was a stroke of Providence that Sukey was with them now. He found privacy amongst the branches of a scrub pine, then returned to the others. He noticed that "Sallie" was already wrapped in a warm blanket, asleep beside Sukey.

"Here, Lemmy. Settle right cheer next to me." Sukey patted a trough between the oak's massive roots. Lem laid his gear off in a pile next to the trunk, then followed Sukey's advice. Sukey spread another heavy woolen over him as soon as he had settled himself. The blanket was thick and coarse, but Lem was grateful for the warmth, as the night had grown colder yet. The moment his eyes closed a dreamless sleep took him.

"Get on up, there! We're moving out!" Someone was shaking him. It seemed to Lem that he had just closed his eyes; such was the sluggishness in his limbs. The shaking continued. "Lem! Wake up, boy!"

Something was tickling Lem's cheek, and the voice sounded familiar. Lem cracked an eyelid. "Mr. Foster?" As Lem tried to rise, his face met John Foster's beard.

"Tis I, with certainty." Foster straightened so Lem could stand. "Major McJunkin said for me to come get ye and bring ye to Sergeant Park. They've been pushing us militia to call each the other by ranks. I've known Joseph and James for ages. It gravels me to call 'em by rank, especially with me being a private. Look here what I'm showing ye now."

Lem tried to focus his eyes but failed. As the moon had set, it was dark. All he could make out was something white riding in John's hat, something like a feather. No. A piece of paper?

"See? It's a strip of white linen. Since we irregulars look the same as them Loyalist volunteers on the other side, what with our homespun clothes and such, this here white ribbon tells them we're Patriots, don't you know? Otherwise, we'd be shooting at each the other. Here's a piece for your hat. James said to sew it on well!"

Foster's exuberance had disturbed both Sukey and Sallie. They had begun to stir.

"Tis time to rise and shine, ladies. We're on the move. Word is we're off for battle."

The three of them stood and stretched while Foster looked on impatiently.

"Sukey," said Lem, "I've been ordered to attend Sergeant Park. Private Foster here is supposed to take me to him. I don't know when I'll be catching up with y'all again, so farewell." He reached around her wide frame and kissed her cheek. She hugged him tightly.

"Don't you fret none. I'll see to Sallie. An', you knows I kin take care of myself!"

"Sure, I do." Lem thought about the deserved whippings she used to mete out to all the Farnandis boys. His own backside had seen the stripes of her switch many times. Bending to retrieve his gear, Lem kept talking. "Sallie, I'll return as soon as I can. Stay with Sukey so I can find you." He gave her a brotherly hug. To his surprise, she kissed his cheek and returned the embrace wholeheartedly.

"Stay safe, Lemuel. I'll be waiting."

"Let's go, Lem. Sergeant Park's not a patient fellow when things need doing. Ladies, I bid you farewell. Don't dally lest you wish to be left to the enemy!"

"Lemmy, be a good drummer. Your papa would have been so

proud!"

Lem had already been at John's heel for several minutes before realizing what Sukey had said. The words "would have been" burned in his guts like molten lead. What happened to Papa? Catching up to Private Foster, he asked, "Have you any word of my family?"

"Shoot no," Foster said. "Have you been hiding under a rock? Everything's been in a terrible fuss these last few days, ever since that ne'er-do-well Jack Beckham came through Grindall's this Sunday past. He was riding his big black mare at full bore, clay pipe stuck in his mouth as if it was Gabriel's Horn. Cotched a group of us huddled up around the hearth at your papa's store, trying to stay warm. Recollected to me of Paul Revere, he did, hollering about the British a-coming! Of course, we knew they'd be coming by land, heh, heh. Before we could say *boo,* Jack was back on Maw and lit out again, straight for General Dan. We were all astir, let me tell you. Every able-bodied man went straight home to get his musket and bid his family farewell. Last I saw of Henry, he was trying to sidle old Private High Key out the door so's he could head for home his own self. Hey, Phoebe's taken a shine to you, don't you know? Been pining ever since she heard tell of your disappearance. Where was you, anyhoo?"

Lem thought fast. "I was hiding out down at the mill."

"Oh ho. And didn't tell nobody, not even Sukey, where you wuz?"

Lem desperately wanted to sidetrack this conversation before Foster could start asking questions about Sallie. "No. Sukey and Walt had gone home, so I couldn't tell them. Mr. Foster, why do you call Mr. Beckham a ne'er-do-well?"

"He may be a most active Whig and fearless scout, or so they say, but I know the Mistress Beckham does all the work of feeding that baker's dozen of young'uns whilst he pulls a cork! Course, he's a mighty fine horse trainer and blacksmith when not distempered."

Lem spoke boldly. "It seems to me if Mr. Beckham puts his life on the line to warn folks hereabouts of the British, he's paid for his sins."

"One might say that." Foster paused, then angled to a new topic. "Did you hear what happened to them Potter's yesterday? No? Well, let me tell you, they had a fine time of it. Adam Potter's been away who knows where these past several weeks. Potter's another one that likes to pull a cork. Anyways, seems how a passel of them Tories paid his Mistress Anna a visit. Them evil filches done burnt the straw roof off the Potter's hut, stole every scrap of food and linen—cooked up every one of Anna's chickens right before her very eyes! When they found out that smallpox was in the house, they burned the goods and left Anna to struggle along. It could be why they didn't take her wedding band, or maybe it was so stuck in her flesh they couldn't get it off without cutting her finger loose. I noticed how that ring was seated one day at the Meeting House when she lit the candle lanterns. Buried right in her flesh, that ring was, like a hundred-year-old nail growed over by tree bark. Well, the mistress gathered up her brood and laid 'em all in the manger atop some straw, then crawled in herself, covering the lot of 'em over with corn shucks to keep warm.

"You know how cold it's been lately. If it weren't for the Potter's adopted child, little Angelica Mitchell, they'd be starved or froze out by the end of the week! Angelica's been going around begging the neighbors for food and blankets. Tis a shame Joab and Mary Mitchell done moved back to Boonesborough. The Potters sure could use some family right now. I don't count sister Elizabeth Beckham. Being hitched to that Jack means the poor woman has had a hard life. Seems to me all three of them sisters got a right raw deal when they moved to Grindall's with their husbands. Things would've gone better for 'em, their daddy being high sheriff of Granville County, Virginia an' all, don't you know?!"

By the time they arrived to meet James Park, Lem was in such a deep depression he wished he could put a damper on John Foster's mouth. The militiaman had been running Lem through the mill with tales of woe. As a miller's son, Lem understood the allusion of being crushed beneath a millstone all too well. The only thing he gathered that might concern his own family was that the Beckhams, Fosters, Potters, and Jaspers were all near neighbors at Sandy Run. If the Tories visited Angelica's home, they likely stopped at his own on the river road. Lem felt mightily relieved that James Park appeared at that moment to put a stop to John Foster's incessant chatter.

"John, I'm beholding to you for fetching Lem here whilst I was indisposed. I've got him now, so we'll head on up the road to Thicketty. Be seeing you. Come along, Lem."

"Nice talking at you, Lem," said Foster. "Catch you around the campfire, James. If naught there, then at the happy hunting grounds!"

Lem walked alongside Park in silence for a while before mentioning, "I'm beholding to you, sir."

"Lad, I know that man. He runs off at the mouth like a meandering creek. I take it he was treating you to rumors of the latest happenings?"

"Aye, sir."

"I wouldn't put much stock in it if I was you. Camp gossip, no matter how close to home, is still gossip. That's the way the officers want it. Till it's all said and done, it's nothing more than talk. Trust me on this. Talk."

"Aye, sir."

"I ain't a commissioned officer. You don't have to call me 'sir.' Sergeant will do."

"Aye…Sergeant."

"That's better. Now. I've got to teach you the drum signals. Unfortunately, we must do this as we ride, and do it quietly."

"How now?"

"Oh, we'll get your drum and sticks. Once you're mounted, you can practice by tapping on your leg."

"Aye." Lem did not see. What he did notice was that the Great Bear constellation had spun itself down toward the treetops. That meant it was early morning, perhaps half past midnight. Yawning, he asked, "Do you think it possible we will get more sleep this night?"

"Fair to middling, I'd wager. Tis only eleven miles hence. That should bring us to Thicketty a few hours before dawn. Time enough then to sup and rest."

Lem had been walking along without taking in his surroundings. His breath came in white plumes. Frost had settled in the grasses and now crunched beneath his feet. The sky was devoid of clouds, exposing myriad stars. Luna hung low on the horizon. Along the dark tree line ahead loomed an oak of mighty proportions. This was a majestic tree of such girth that four grown men could not have stretched arms around it with fingers touching. The lowest limb hung like the mainmast boom of a first-rate warship. Unless Lem's eyes deceived him in the dark, there was a loop of rope dangling from it.

Goosebumps prickled his forearms. This had to be the Hanging Tree he'd heard tell of at the store! Papa had forbidden trespass upon the Chesney property. He warned that one was as like to receive a ball in the gullet from that devilish

Tory Alexander Chesney as any cordial greeting. Hence, this was the first time Lem had laid eyes upon the infamous timber.

"By the lay of your countenance, I suppose you're on about the hanging of that Tory spy a few days past," observed Park. "This here's the place they done it, alright. Heard tell some of Colonel Washington's dragoons was down from the Iron Works the same night we was all locked in the cellar. The torrents we was having done flooded the river, ye know. Cotched the lowdown scoundrel sculking about the officer's tent during one of them downpours, so they say. Had him strung up in a thrice."

Suddenly, the thunder of horses met their ears. Lem and Park both turned as the call came across the field, "Make way! Make way!" The foremost of the riders carried blazing pitch pine brands to light their progress. They would likely not see Lem and Park standing in the road. Park must have had the same thought. He planted a big hand between Lem's shoulder blades and propelled Lem toward the base of the oak.

The unit of riders passed beneath the oak's great limb on their way toward Asbury Road. That would bring them near Mr. Gouldelock's cabin a mile north at the crossroads. From there, they could go one of three ways, towards the mountains, Rock Hill, or Winnsborough. Distracted by his suppositions, Lem jumped when a silky black horse neighed at his side.

"Caught you unawares, did they?" Park chuckled. He was patting a big chestnut on the neck. "Here now, let me introduce you to your mount. This here's Bonnie. They tell me she's a spritely maiden and a smooth rider. Takes well to the knee instead of the bit. Be gentle on her reins. We've got a long journey ahead of us, so we'll not be wanting to wear her down too soon."

"Aye, sir. I mean, Sergeant. Are we following those riders?"

"For a ways, for a ways. Did ye happen to notice who was amongst 'em? T'was General Dan. They was keeping him safe and moving him fast. He'll arrive ahead of us, for sure."

"Where are we bound?"

"Suppose there's no harm in letting out a morsel now. Thanks to the messages delivered by the four of us good Patriots—five iffin ye count that handsome lass Anne Kennedy—the army's on the move. Here, let us pack as we speak. Needs get we on the road."

For the next few minutes, Lem tied his kit behind Bonnie's saddle, applying gentle hands to her neck and rump to help her become familiar with his touch. He made soft clucks of the tongue as he worked. It was a challenge to fit the haversack and cartridge box behind the saddle because the drum was already slung offside. He draped the canteen over the pommel. The Brown Bess had to remain across his shoulder.

After seating his hat more tightly on his head, Lem grasped the reins in his left hand, threw his boot into the stirrup, and mounted Bonnie. Testing her response, he applied a soft knee to her nearside and draped the reins gently toward the same. Bonnie responded by stepping off to the left in a tight turn. He reversed the maneuver, and Bonnie turned back to the right. Satisfied that the mare was faithful as James had described, he drew back slightly on the reins with a "Whoa, girl." The horse stopped moving, but the feel of pent strength flowed up Lem's legs. She would serve him well.

"Take care of her, Lem. Horseflesh is hard to come by during these times. Let's be off, shall we?" With that, James Park swung up into his own saddle. His stature so swamped the humble animal, Lem wondered if the dark gelding would hold up to the abuse on the journey.

Park seemed to be having the same misgivings. "We'll take it slow for a time. Let the beasts warm to their labors. Stay beside me, now, so's I can go over the necessaries with you." He stirred his horse. For the initial furlong, they traveled with only the sounds of leather, harness, hoof, and the steady beat of the drum thumping against Bonnie's flank. Then, they came upon the same road General Dan and his riders had taken. Lem could tell the track had been well churned by many travelers, but the mud was frozen, making it easier on the horses.

Eventually, they reached the forks. To the right, one could travel to Love's Ford on the mighty Cawtawbaw River. Ahead, one could visit the Sims-Marchbanks Meeting House for church, or further along, Amadahy's people in Rock Hill. The left branch was known as Green River Road, or Asbury Road, depending on which direction one was traveling. They took this branch heading northwest away from Asbury and Grindall's Ford. Lem felt a catch in his throat. He was leaving the familiar lands of his home for unknown territory without knowing the disposition of his family.

"Keep a sharp eye out. There's bound to be travelers on this road tonight. General Dan ordered up a hasty move to Thicketty Fort. Draw out them drumsticks from their holster and let us ply the trade a while."

Lem turned in his saddle and retrieved the two sticks from their sheath. "How do I hold them?"

"There's two ways—straight out or left inward and right outward. The latter I find to be of more comfort when the drum is slung low at your right thigh. Here now, let me show you." Park laid his reins across his mount's neck and took the sticks. The long dowels shone white in his hands but seemed mere toothpicks in proportion. He then drummed a beat against his thigh. “See there. Nothing to it.” He passed the sticks back to Lem and took his reins up again. “Now, since we’re plodding along, just lay them reins upon her neck, and let’s get to practicing the rudiments.”

Lem did so. The mare continued under his knees as he tried slapping the sticks against his own thigh. He found that holding the stick backward in his left was easier for the angle.

“The primary objective of the regimental drummer is the issuance of commands. Knowing the strokes to carry off the commands is vital to the unit, a matter of life or death in the heat of battle. Heed me, now.”

“Aye, Sergeant.”

“Right. We’ll start with the basics. First off, what’s called the Long Roll. It tells all the soldiers in range to come the ready and be braced for imminent danger. It goes like this....” As they slid beneath silent pines, across rolling hills and shallow valleys, Park demonstrated the stokes and explained the corresponding orders for the next hour.

Mostly, the commands were plain, as were the rolls, taps, and flams that accompanied them:

The last command Lem hoped never to use and said as much

Long Roll	sudden danger
Reveille	awaken the troops
Supper Call	come to supper
Tap-Too (Taps)	go to bed
March	formation movement
Church Call	come to worship
To Arms	get weapons
Preparation	make ready to fire
Fire	discharge weapon
Charge	move quickly toward enemy

"We're both in accord on that score," Park agreed. They rode on in silence for a period, letting Lem try his memory. Now and again, the sergeant would tap out a correction.

The chill deepened as the night wore. Lem finally gave up the drilling and thrust his fingers into his armpits. It was no use practicing further as they were stiff from the cold. It was a blessing to be traveling slowly. Otherwise, he would be forced to hold the reins. He noticed that James was doing the same. They were gambling that nothing spooked the horses as they passed through the wilderness.

"Tis time for some plain talk, Lem," said Park after a lengthy silence. "Know you the import of your position, so now to the certainties of it. Have you every kilt a man?"

The question took Lem off guard. He stammered, "No-no, sir."

"I knowed the answer already." He broke off suddenly. Lem could see movement ahead at a bend in the road, forms backlit by the waning moon.

"Not to worry, Lem. Them's most likely Morgan's Rifles under Major Triplett. They were trained by General Dan himself in Virginia. Notice them long barrels sticking up? Kentucky long rifles. These boys are the best sharpshooters there is. Should be more than two hundred of them. The lot of them took out an hour or two before us, on foot, of course."

Lem noticed that Park rested a hand on his pistol bucket. "What if it's the enemy?"

"In that unlikely event, turn tail and bolt back the way we come."

By then, they had reached the back of the column. Indeed, it was the Virginians. As Lem and Park proceeded to pass them, the line made way by stepping to the shoulder of the road. Now and again, a soldier would murmur a greeting, which Park would return in kind. Lem realized the troop's movements, while not stealthy, would nevertheless be difficult for an enemy to decipher this late at night.

After a quarter-hour, Lem and Park saw the column behind them. Park said, "Back to our earlier pow-wow. You ain't never kilt a man, nor have you ever seen one kilt before your very eyes, I'll warrant."

"'Tis true," said Lem. He was anxious as to where this conversation was leading.

"Then, mark me words, young Drummer Lem. I can't prepare you to sit idle whilst your comrades are cut down by enemy balls or shredded by redcoat swords, but that ye must do! There's no apt way of describing the blood and gore. Seeing firsthand the slaughter is the only way to grasp the horror." Park went silent for a few breaths, then, "General Dan hit uponst it. Many a drummer, flagbearer, and fife man have been overcome by the heat of battle. Seeing one's friends, one's brethren in arms, go down in the field brings on anger the likes of which you've never felt. This anger can barely be described as blind rage. Tis a thirst for blood slaked only by killin'. Plain words cannot define it.

"Take heed, now. Leave the fighting to the soldiers and keep the drumming to yourself. No matter how great the urge becomes to lay aside your drum and join the fighting…do not…." Park's voice trailed away. For a time, they rode in silence. When the sergeant spoke again at last, there was a catch in his voice. "Would that I could spare you the horrors soon to be witnessed."

Lem was sure he caught a muffled sob from this bear of a man. Hearing it struck dread in his heart. He was riding headlong into a predicament of which he knew naught!

17

Thicketty Fort

Another hour was spent in relative silence, broken only when passing other travelers along the route. Some were simple backwoods militiamen, clothed in rags held together with string. Others were regulars of the Continental Army. Once blue and off-white, their uniforms were now tatters of gray and tan. All wore expressions of weariness, their sagged shoulders telling tales of hardship. Park's earlier warnings had kept Lem's mind aswirl with vague imaginings of Death.

Bonnie splashed into a swollen creek, icy water spilling over Lem's boot tops. He gathered his thoughts and took reins in hand once again to ensure the amiable horse kept moving. Of a certainty, he did not wish to fall from the saddle if she stumbled on slick river rocks while attempting to take a swig.

"Nearly there, Lem." Park had taken the lead. "Just one more bend of the road, and we'll arrive at Thicketty Fort. I suspect the general may be holding council there with Bill Washington and other commanders. We'll get a bite, a nip, and a few winks. There'll be no comforts, but at least it'll be dry. I'll lay you don't miss the rain any more than meself."

Lem said, "I'm so tired I suspect that a few mouthfuls of food will have me be laid out, want or no."

"I kin the feeling, sure enough. Thicketty Fort's the selfsame place that nasty plunderer Patrick Moore and his Tory filth used to hole up. They'd sally forth to pillage the Whigs from hereabouts all the way down to Grindall's. We run him out of here—spared his life and the lives of his bloody thieves to boot—and then he captures us and throws us in a cellar. Humph! I'll wager that Major McJunkin didn't lay on about his niece's encounter with Moore."

"Nay, sir. Tis the first I heard tell," Lem said dutifully.

"Well. Himself and his plunderers showed up at the house of the major's brother, Sam, on an ill night some months back. Stripped the bedlinens, wearing apparel, anything that weren't nailed down. Kilt nobody. Took everything—except one quilt. The major's niece, Jane, bold she was. Stalked right up to that devil Bill Haynesworth. You met him. The one they called Scarlet. Grabbed a-holt of the blanket and began a tug-o-war. The contest was fearsome. Old Bill slipped and fell on his back to the mud. Before he could get up, little Jane slammed her foot in his chest and held him down till he was panting for breath. She wrestled the blanket from his grasp and retired from the field triumphant! Heard tell Bill was so harassed and shamed by his men, he slunk away to brood. Wish I could have seen it. All this happened before we could run them out of the fort. Speaking of the fort. Here she is, such as she is!"

The sturdy log structure of Thicketty Fort, not much bigger than a family cabin, stood in bold relief upon an open swath surrounded by woods, backlit by many campfires. Lem could make out an indeterminant number of men cooking at the fires. He guessed they were preparing breakfast, judging by the savory aroma of frying bacon. His belly rumbled. Tallying the number of hours since leaving Grindall's, he figured it to be about four in the morning. Only a few more hours of darkness remained to get food and sleep.

"Let us find our regiment and see to the horses. Best handle the needs of the beasts first if we expect them to see to ours, eh?"

"Papa says the same," said Lem.

"Ahem. Sure, Lem, sure."

Lem caught a duskiness in the sergeant's tone. Before he could inquire into it, the hustle and bustle of this new camp intruded. It seemed everyone had tasks to perform. With so many pressed into close contact, the odor of unclean humanity lay heavily on the air, sullying thoughts of bacon and grits. He would gratefully avail himself of the necessary trenches if he could discover where they were. Taking rest amongst all this commotion was of concern.

"HO THERE! Is that Sergeant Park I see over yonder? Come hither!" This came from a tall figure silhouetted before a fire just inside the edge of the forest. Behind him was a tent. Other fires were set throughout the woods, probably along a curving ridgeline.

"Tis I in the flesh! Unless me ears be failing me, I'm supposing I heared the voice of Captain Nate Jeffries?"

"The same, my good fellow. Draw up your horses and join me for a spell. I hath the rumors, and I hath the rashers."

"Ye have convinced me of the notion. Be right with ye, Captain, sir." The sergeant flew from his horse. "Dismount, young Lem. Stick beside me whilst I uncover what Captain Nate wants doing."

"I heard that, Sergeant. I want nary a thing except for a touch of gossip. Come over by the fire. Private Gillham here will see to your mounts. Our pickets stand nigh with fresh water and hay, offering sound treatment for the beasts. Ah, I see you've brought a new drummer. Good show, old boy!"

Lem handed off the reins to a fellow only slightly older than himself. A splotchy beard showed little promise of hiding Private Gillham's cadaverous cheeks. "At your service, Private," he said.

"Naw, sir. I'm at yer'n—name's John Gillham. Yew can call me Gilly. Ever'body does." The man's face split into a happy, albeit snaggletooth grin. The combination of features resembled the rictus of death.

Lem's jaw dropped.

"Most folks do that when I greet 'um." Private Gillham took the reins from Sergeant Park and led the horses off into the shadows.

Sergeant Park cleared his throat. "This here's Lem Farnandis, Captain. He's a brave lad. Him and his sister both. She's been attached to the camp followers and should be coming up shortly. They was preparing to move everyone out of Grindall's as we was leaving ourselves."

"I'm sure it's quite the tale, Sergeant. Do tell whilst we break our fast. There's a stack of plates and forks just inside the tent flap. You'll find tin cups and a water bucket. Bring your cups, and I'll slake your thirst with a touch of rum ration. He was holding a leather flask.

Lem spoke up. "Sir, begging your pardon. Prithee, where may I find the vault?"

"No vault. Didn't have time to plow one out. Head straight down the slope behind my tent. You'll come to a ridge with a steep drop. We've roped it into a kind of gurney. See you don't take a spill." The captain chortled. It recalled to Lem the way hens clucked over their brood.

Leaving the men to their talk, Lem hurried off into the white pine forest as directed. The carpet of long needles muffled his footsteps. Boughs trimmed with icy fingers swiped his cheeks.

His ears pricked up as a familiar clatter grew to meet them. There was a mill nearby! Some time back, he had heard tell of a mill at Thicketty—Burr's, Byce's, Buece's, Byer's—well, no matter. Ah, he remembered now. Papa mentioned it with an envious tone—Buice's. It was said to have three great burrs. One for grinding corn to flake, one for powdering wheat, and one for driving a vertical lumber saw. That's it! Papa's jealous of the saw. With another burr, Papa could make a fortune at cutting planks for construction! The army's wants must be pressing since the miller was ousted to run this night.

Lem came upon the ropes about fifty yards behind the tent. Primarily by feel, he discovered a makeshift cradle consisting of three taut, heavy cords tied between two close trunks. The rig was stout enough to support a man. Next to the tree on Lem's right hand sat a couple of water-filled buckets, stars reflecting near their rims. Several wooden rods stood in each bucket. Lem picked up a corn cob from the stockpile beside the buckets. He grimaced in disgust at the thought of having to spear one with a rod, douse it in a bucket, then use the dripping roughage to clean himself. Fervently wishing to avoid any unwanted adventure, he dropped his breeches and sat carefully on the lowest rope. The higher cords supported his back and prevented a fall into the ravine. To dangle one's privates over the edge of a cliff in the dead of a cold winter's night was an ordeal he hoped to avoid in the future.

Once done, he returned uphill. Drawing near the tent, he overheard the voice of James Park telling Captain Jeffries about someone's family having been burned out down at Grindall's. His ears prickled to hear more. The discussion stifled as he rounded the last tent stake. Park had a hand clamped over his mouth, and the captain wore a guilty expression.

Jeffries was the first to breach the awkwardness. "I say, Lemuel, you seem no worse for wear, what? Found your way down and back. Here, take my utensils and fill your belly." Lem took the proffered plate, cup, and fork. "Gilly's outdone himself. Scrounged up slabs of bacon. The grits received fair treatment with salt and pepper, a rarity for sure. Provided a royal feast, has Gilly!"

Park belched loudly. "Erm…that's better." He tipped a ladle-full of bacon-chocked grits onto his plate for another round, then handed over the spoon. "Stuff yourself, Lem. Don't never know how long you'll suffer betwixed meals on the trail."

"Positively dead-on, Park," agreed Captain Jefferies.

"Sirs, may I inquire—" began Lem, as he filled his plate.

The captain turned to speak, but Park cut in, "Ye may, but not just now. Here. Gimme your cup. Take a bit of this rummy water. It'll stiffen your countenance for what I must report." The sergeant took the cup from Lem's hand and held it out for the captain to fill with a full measure of spirit. When Park handed back the cup, Lem sniffed it. No water was in evidence.

"Here, let's pull up a stump," said Jefferies, "so the three of us may chat away in comfort by the warm fire."

Lem and James each chose an upturned log and sat. Lem placed his cup beside his boot and began to eat. After the first bite, he shoveled down the food.

"Told you he was starving, Park. Have you forgotten what it was like to be a growing lad? I couldn't keep my belly full as a young'un. My mother complained that she could never leave the pantry without the nine of us children raiding it!"

The conversation continued along those lines as Lem refilled his plate twice. Finally satiated, he laid the plate down and took up the cup.

Park sighed. "Lem, sip that slowly now and listen to what I have to tell ye." Both men were pulling long faces. Snatches of recent conversations began to fall together. Past tense concerning his father. Odd looks from Sukey. Every sinew in Lem's body stretched taut as he waited.

"I'll cut straight to the chase," Park began. "Word came after Major McJunkin and me left ye with Sukey that raiders had been at your papa's store. Even before ye was woken to be brought to me, another scouting party arrived with word that several homes had been burned out down around Sandy Run creek. By what ye told us when we was down in the cellar, the major and I are fairly certain one of them houses was yours. Chicken coop, big barn, sweet well with a capstone in the center of the backyard—"

"It was a spent millstone. Our family is the only one with that type of cap." Dread was overtaking Lem's thoughts.

"Take a swig from your cup," suggested the captain.

Lem did—and choked. The liquid burned down the back of his throat. When he had recovered, James started talking again.

"Lem, here's the worst of it. Two bodies were found in the driveway beside the smoldering ruins. One was a dark, stocky man with a thick black mustache upturned at the ends. The other was his spitting image, excepting much younger, slightly taller, and cleanshaven. They was stove through their chests by bayonet, their own muskets discharged. Someone had laid their weapons lengthwise uponst them, fitted their hands to the stocks, and closed their eyelids. At least whoever they was done that much for the dead. Narry another soul was seen after a thorough search of the remaining structures. The detail took the burial of the bodies unto themselves, placing them where they was found. Swords were broken, tied into crosses, and drove in the ground as markers for the graves. Lad, I'm so very sorry for your loss."

"I wish to offer my condolences, and my services, young Lem. Call on me at will." There were tears in Captain Jeffries' eyes.

Stunned by the ill news, Lem suddenly found himself overwhelmed. Park and Jeffries averted their eyes as an uncontrollable shaking overtook him. Both Papa and Brother John gone? Dead. His entire family missing. These thoughts cleft his heart. He looked up to James but could only see a blurry visage behind the firelight. Unbidden, a recollection of Amadahy standing beside a keg in the candlelight came to mind. Now, he understood how she must feel. Raising his unseeing eyes to Heaven, he implored, "Oh Lord of Hosts, God of our Fathers, I beg you, lead the remainder of our families to safety. Bless them and keep them until found and restored to us. Amen."

There came a murmured, "Amen," and "So be it," then boots champed, and the cold edge of the tin cup was pressed to Lem's lips. He had not the will to turn it away.

"Take the rest of this," murmured Park. "Swallow it down quick. That's a good lad. Now, the captain has prepared his cot for you. Let us put ye to rest. I'll come for ye when it's time to break camp."

Lem was lifted to his feet. A few steps later, he was laid out and covered in a heavy blanket. The rum that had seared his throat now radiated throughout his limbs. He was more comfortable than he had been in many days. Warm. Adrift. Despite the hard news, his eyes closed. For a time, he was mercifully oblivious to any goings-on at the fort.

18

Of Mice and Catamounts

Something had awoken Lem from his deep slumber. As senses mustered, he noticed the predawn light through the rolled-back flaps. There was much clamor outside. The regiment must be on the march! He swung his legs from the cot only to discover his boots had been taken. Ah. There they were, sitting at the cot's foot. He reached for the nearest of the bedraggled leathers and undertook to draw it on. The task nearly defeated him as his surroundings began to spin. Lem realized he must be suffering the aftereffects of the rum. Never had he drunk it straight, only a weak dilution to keep the water safe. Unwillingly, his guts spewed onto the dirt.

"My, that's a bother." Captain Jefferies was looking in with a wrinkled nose. "Never you mind. Word's come the Old Wagoner is consulting with his colonels this very instant over at Gentleman Will Thompson's. That being only a mile or so to the east, I expect orders to be relayed at any time. Heard tell that old Will is a capable horseman under Ben Roebuck's command. Good of him to offer up the use of his house for the plotting of the bigwigs, what?

"Scouts say the enemy has been lured across the Pacholet at both Grindall's and Easterwood's fords, drawn over by our evacuation of those areas. Orders have come down to break camp and make for higher ground. Thus, Sergeant Park has gone to retrieve your horses. There's no time to dawdle. Reveille has sounded, and the march is underway. You'll soon discover why General Dan's command has been dubbed the Flying Army! Now, pip, pip, pip!" Jefferies turned to shout, "Gilly, get in here and fix poor Lem to his kit, stuff him with what victuals may still be had, and hand him off to Sergeant Park. I'll take a gander at the lay of things up at the fort and shall soon return, but only briefly. Have my horse at the ready post-haste and see to your own. Keep your powder dry, Lemuel Farnandis. May God spare you to see the end of all this." The captain withdrew.

Private Gillham entered the tent. "Eeeeyuuuk! Wha' chew been a-doing in here?" Gillham used the side of his foot to scooch dirt over the vomit. Lem noticed the scrawny man had bound the remnants of his shoes to his feet with strips of cloth. Upon catching Lem's gaze, the private said, "Yew shore got some mighty fine boots thar, mighty fine."

The emaciated fellow leaned down to assist Lem into his jacket. Foul breath wafted over him, dredging up thoughts of Tyger Moore. Until now, Lem believed Moore's respirations to be the worst he had ever encountered. He gasped, "Many thanks for your assistance, Private. I can take it from here."

"Come on then. Let's git yew some hominy!" Gilly led the way out. Lem noticed how threadbare the seat of the man's pants had become, and the sorry state of his hunting coat—splotchy, split seams, shredded cuffs—hands wrapped in linen rags.

Lem stepped from the tent into a whirlwind. Looking off

through the pine boughs, he saw men running to and fro. Some were saddling horses. Others were donning gear. Still others, like Private Gilly, were attending higher-ranking soldiers. All the faces he could see held a grim temper. Before him, no more than a few hundred feet away, sat Thicketty Fort.

It struck him that the edifice was hardly more than a single-family dwelling. However, the timbers used in its construction were much thicker. Soldiers were bunched at the door. That must be where Captain Jeffries had gone.

"Here now! Take this an' start eatin'!" Gilly shoved a plate of grits into his hands, followed by a spoon. The private stalked off through the woods without further comment, leaving Lem to his own devices.

Wiping the spoon on his breeches to remove crusted debris left by its previous user, Lem willfully shoved a dollop of lukewarm hominy into his mouth. It was flavorless and coarse, yet it settled his stomach. Using the toe of his boot, he pushed several half-burned brands into the dying embers in hopes of knocking the chill from the air.

At a shout, he looked up to see a group of riders fast approaching. They thundered off the main road, swept across the trampled field before the fort, and pulled up to its door. From the stature of one rider, Lem suspected General Dan had just arrived from his rendezvous at Gentleman Thompson's. The hulking figure stood up in his saddle and started shouting orders at the gathering crowd.

Lem caught a few words as he scraped his plate clean. Chief amongst them were, "...crack my whip over Ban...leave everything...make for Saunder's...let us away, Baron...." With this last, the horsemen wheeled almost as one and strove back the way they had come. Those at the fort steps disbursed in a rush.

Commands rang out from every direction.

"Lemuel Farnandis! I'm proud to find you on your feet and raring to go instead of sulking!" It was James Park leading the horses. "Here now. Drop that plate and let us be away!"

"Where shall we go, Sergeant?"

"You're what we call an 'irregular' now and as true as me own brother. That's the way of it when a man shares the pains o' life as we have. That don't change the fact that you're in militia service now. Make sure to henceforth call a soldier by his rank. Some's can be real sticklers."

"Sergeant Park, pray tell, whom do I serve?"

"A mighty question with a mighty riposte. Ye now serve the pleasure of the finest unit in this here command—Colonial Brandon's Second Spartan Regiment!" Park tossed over Bonnie's reins and remounted his own horse. "Saddle up, Private Farnandis! We've some miles to go before day's end."

"Aye, Sergeant!" The exuberance of his large companion and the consternation written in his mount's hazel orbs brought an unexpected smile to Lem's cheeks.

Lem and the sergeant made their way back out to Green River Road. In daylight, this track appeared quite rutted and broken. With the coming of dawn, the frozen surface was fast thawing. Rivulets of water had begun to drain away, creating small brooks in low places. They joined in behind a clump of militiamen who were shifting around to avoid becoming mired. More than a few curses flew into the burgeoning day.

Park said, "T'would be a fine idea to review the drumming signals, Private, the pace being sluggish. Methinks I'll discover the whereabouts of our regiment so's we can join 'em. We was in such a sweat last night to get here that we didn't properly report our arrival. Wouldn't want Major McJunkin sending out a search party.

I shall return for you. Practice well!" With that, he pulled out of line and stopped so he could watch the troops pass.

"Aye, sir," Lem called after. He drew the drumsticks from the sheath and began reviewing the strokes. He was ignored by the struggling walkers. In short order, he had to take up the reins again, for the column huddled at a swollen creek.

Glad to be horsed, Lem sheathed his sticks and pulled Bonnie further to the side. It would be easier for those afoot to cross without the worry of being trodden upon by a horse. He figured to wait on the sergeant to catch him up.

Lem recalled a map his father had once hung on the wall at the feed store, a hand-drawn affair that showed the surrounding country within twenty miles of Grindall's. The Green River Road was a northwesterly line from Asbury to the Blue Ridge Mountains. Cutting through it was Little Thicketty Creek, about halfway between Grindall's and the foothills. The creek was a minor offshoot of the Broad, the same watercourse in which the Pacholet itself emptied. By Lem's estimate, this must be Little Thicketty. To bolster his confidence on this, he was able to see the hump of a ridge just over the trees. That must be Thicketty Mountain.

Shouts interrupted his musings. Swift as an arrow, a single command was passed from the distant rear of the column.

"RUN FOR YOUR LIVES!"

Soldiers launched themselves into the water and struggled across the knee-deep flow. Upon reaching the far bank, they fled up the road as if their forty-pound kits weighed naught but a feather.

Bonnie began to prance, forcing Lem to tighten the reins harshly. The onrush of panicked militiamen was oblivious to her stamping legs, surging around the nervous animal, risking broken feet or worse.

Frantically, Lem looked for some sign of Sergeant Park. To his dismay, he saw a contingent of green-clad dragoons with plumed helmets round the bend at the rear of the column. They drew swords and charged.

It appeared that a small contingent of Roebuck's cavalry had been following the column. They now turned to meet the newcomers head-on. The ring of steel on steel spurred the fleeing militia to greater efforts to cross the stream. Lem marveled at how quickly the road cleared of infantry. Shortly, he was alone this side of the creek with naught between him and the struggling cavalry. Those few Patriots would rush in for a slash and retreat thirty or forty paces. The green dragoons would drive forward and close the distance. He could now make out individuals in the fracas. Chief amongst them was none other than Sergeant James Park. It seemed he was beset by no less than three green dragoons.

Lem unslung the Brown Bess, removed the leather cover from the flash pan, checked that the flint was in place, and leveled the rifle. Attempting to aim, he despaired those men and beasts were in such close quarters. It was then his eyes fell on a single dragoon hindmost of the melee, not taking part. Instead, the man seemed to be shouting orders. Lem calculated it to be a long shot, though not further than a buck he took last fall. With care, he raised the barrel, accounted for a slight drop of the ball over such a distance, and gently squeezed the trigger the way his father taught him.

Bonnie reared at the explosion of sound, light, and smoke, but not before Lem had the satisfaction of seeing the plume shorn from the dragoon's helmet. He may not have hit the soldier, but the nearness of the ball stuck fear into the dragoon's haughty continence. The soldier turned and fled with his men while Lem struggled to remain seated, wrestling Bonnie into submission. That

Bonnie might not be trained to the gun, as all the horses belonging to Papa were taught from birth, had not occurred to Lem. By the time the poor animal calmed, the fight was over. Park lay supine in the muddy road, a sight that quailed Lem's breath. The Green Dragoons were retreating around the bend with a prisoner. They showed no sign of rallying, so Lem shook Bonnie to a gallop.

In moments he reached Park's side. The other men were attempting to help the sergeant gain his feet. Lem could see blood streaming from a shoulder-to-elbow slash on Park's left arm. Hands were trying to wrap the arm in rags, but the sergeant struggled.

"T'aint nothing but a scratch, I tell ye! Leave off, now! I'll see to it meself!" Park shook free of the would-be orderlies, his face a thundercloud. Lem recalled that look from back in the cellar when Amadahy had attempted to bind his head wound. The big man clearly had naught much luck of late, which put him in a foul mood. Rounding on Lem, he shouted, "And you! What are you still doin' here on this side o' the creek? All the rest of the militia had sense enough to run. What good was our little talk about losing your head in the heat of battle and taking up the sword?"

Abashed, Lem struggled to say, "I—I couldn't let them capture or kill you, James."

"That's Sergeant Park to the likes of ye! Tis unlikely you'll see the morrow at the pace you've set for yourself!"

Lem was surrounded by grim faces but mustered his courage. "To mine eyes, it appeared you were going to die. I beg you, forgive my desire to stave off such a dread circumstance. T'was within my power to prevent it, sir, and I would do the same yet again to save a friend's life!"

"Hear, hear!"

"Tis a right and true friend he be!"

"Bravely spoke!"

"Sergeant Park," said a clean-shaved man, rugged of appearance, clothed in worn buckskins, "I command you, release your dampness of spirit. This is one true gem. Think you, he remained behind whilst all others fled before the enemy. Orders to the contrary would nary have stayed them. His quick wit saved our very lives!"

"Aye, Colonial Roebuck, sir," rumbled Park. "Still, the boy is a drummer, not a soldier."

Roebuck's eyes blazed from beneath his wide-brimmed felt hat, "Be that as it may, he hath served well. Volunteers are we, with no formal soldiering. All that we lack in discipline, we make up for in heart! Let us now catch the rest of the column lest the enemy return in greater numbers for a slaughter." He remounted his warhorse, a stout bay gelding of sixteen hands, and led off at a trot.

The half dozen men surrounding Lem and Park broke up and made haste to gain the colonel. Lem soon found himself riding next to Park as they formed two fast-moving columns.

Park remained silent, stealing hard glances when he thought Lem was not looking. Thicketty Mount gradually slid past to the right and fell behind. Long since had they waded the mountain's namesake creek. The road became more arduous, curving around hillocks, washouts, and ravines. Rounding one such protrusion, they caught up the rear of the infantry. Upon sighting the horses, the column nearly broke again.

"Hold fast yon Spartans!" Roebuck yelled with confidence. The colonel galloped his horse up the militia line toward the head of the column, waving all the while.

Cries arose of "Tis Roebuck…the colonel's a-coming…Halloo and huzzah!" Somewhere ahead, a rendition of *Yankee Doodle* was struck by a shrill fife to the beat of a drum. The column reformed and moved forward at a doubled pace in reply to the martial music. Lem had never heard such a melody, and the lively tune did much to stir his blood.

The other five riders, not to be outdone, threw various farewells at Lem and Park as they chased after Roebuck. One fellow removed his dilapidated tricorn and gave an Indian whoop. The rest did the same and kept it up as they passed their walking fellows. A fierce roar erupted, accompanied by the shaking of fists, swords, and muskets. Where there had been a dejected regiment trudging through the mire and hardship, now strode heartened men with fierce determination.

"Lifts the drudgery of soldiering, that. Drumming and fifing. Cheering." Park uncorked his wooden canteen and offered it to Lem as their horses ambled along behind the column. Lem took a swig with a murmured thanks and handed it back. It seemed the sergeant had finished nursing his bile and fallen into an erstwhile mood. His next confirmed Lem's suspicions.

"I was just recollecting a boy I met a mere few days ago. Trapped like a mouse in a cage, he was. Treated sorely by that vile predator, Captain 'Tyger' Moore. That boy was in a sorry state when we met. Something has happened to him ever since, and tis a true wonder. I seed that boy grow to manhood before me very eyes. A man, I say!"

Lem turned to meet the full countenance of the sergeant only to see a face ruddy and bloated like a crying babe.

"For saving me life, I am beholding to ye." Park straightened in his saddle and swiped the moisture from his cheek with the back of his weathered hand.

Lem was stunned. The horses plodded along a while before he found his voice. "T'was my true pleasure, Sergeant."

"Hang the protocol! Call uponst me as James! James Matthew Park, at your service!"

19

Cow Pens

With the sight, sound, and smell of hundreds of laboring militiamen so close at hand, Lem sought a respite. Full of fatigue, he watched dejectedly as a gaggle of geese winged along beside Green River Road as if spying upon the progress of the regiment. The Broad River gushed down from the Blue Ridge Mountains, not five or six miles to the east. He also recollected that the Thicketty and the Pacholet lent their flow to swell the Broad about a dozen miles below Grindall's. General Dan, he reckoned, must have aims of crossing that imposing watercourse. Surely that would be a danger to those making an attempt, what with the water riding high after last week's flooding. What if the British came on them during such an undertaking? It would be a slaughter.

"…as I was saying, we should be coming to our destination in short order. Saunder's, they call it. Some cow pastures—are you hearing me, Lem?"

Lem snapped out of his doldrums. "My apologies, James.

Weariness overtakes me."

"I knows the truth of that. Sore of the saddle be me rump. Notice ye the lay of the land hereabouts? The trees are thinning, and the underbrush fading. Tis as pretty a land as can be."

Forcing himself to vigilance, Lem took in his surroundings. Indeed, James was right. They were rising at long last from the dense forests into a tableland dotted with stands of hickory and oak. Scrub pine and thickets were no longer in evidence. Grasses tall and lush grew in their stead.

As the horses trod on, the ground climbed gently until Lem saw the deep shadows of the Blue Ridge for the first time in his life. Reining in, he rested Bonny and took in the natural beauty of it all. Park joined him.

"James?"

"Hmmm?"

"Have you ever born witness to such magnificence?"

"Aye. Tis God's own abode, them mountains. Their beauty does naught but treble from here to Shenandoah. Fighting Cherokees and such, I seen more of God's fine work than I have a right. Such ugliness there is in the world. Tis the way of it. Makes one value these rare sights all the more."

"How long have you served?"

"Too long, Lem. Too long."

There came the rumble of hooves from behind. Lem and James spun their mounts. Lem had not realized the road had been rising out of the forests between several creeks, so gentle had been the incline. He could clearly see the approach of thirty or so cavalry riding fast. From the forests and low-lying bogs to either side of the road, more riders joined them. Lem wondered that they had passed through those very trees and obstacles without noticing the presence of so many horsemen.

"Them's our scouts a-coming outta the woods. They've been keeping pace watching our flanks for miles, ever since them bloody dragoons cotched us." Lem saw James shrug his shoulder and wince.

"Should we make way?"

"Aye. They's still a ways off, but let's give 'em room. I needs ter stretch me legs anyhoo." He dismounted and led his horse to the roadside. The beast promptly dropped his head to the rich grass and pulled a wad. "Here now, Hairy! That's enough of that! Don't want you getting the colic now!"

"Harry? Did mine ears hear you call upon your horse as Harry?"

"Just look at the beast, shaggy like a long-haired dog he be!"

"Ah. Hairy. I see." Lem turned away with a smirk.

By then, the approaching riders were nearly upon them. Except for a single dragoon, the lot did not slow upon seeing Lem and James. This one drew up in a skid of mud and dismounted.

"Sergeant Park! Lemuel Farnandis! And in good health from Grindall's and Thicketty!" Major Joseph McJunkin attempted to grab Lem and James into a hug but failed miserably. The sergeant's bulk was simply too significant an obstacle for one of average stature to pull it off. In the end, the major had to settle for clapping shoulders.

"Yikes, Major! That hurt!" Park tried to protect his sore arm from further abuse.

"Sorry old chap. Didn't see the scratch!"

"Scratch! I get a twinge with every move!"

"Not to downplay your hurt, poor Sergeant, but there's a few that's seen worse. Buck up, man! Buck up!" McJunkin turned his jovial visage on Lem. "Lemuel. The tale I've heard this day. Savior of Colonel Roebuck and his officers. Savior of the column. Savior of James Park. Dan's Virginia Sharpshooters themselves can only boast of such a shot. They use Kentucky long rifles known for accuracy at a distance! You squeezed off a ninety-yard shot with a forty-yard Brown Bess! Bravo, young Lemuel! Bravo!"

"Many thanks, sir." Lem's cheeks were hot.

"Quite my honor. Now, to the grave news. Those green dragoons that overtook you on the road were none other than an advance scouting party for Bloody Ban Tarleton—what's the matter, lad?"

Lem had slapped his forehead. "Tarleton. Colonel T. I should have realized…" he trailed off.

"That you were captured by the lapdogs of The Green Dragoon? The Butcher? The Bloody Scout, bloodiest of them all? The infamous leader of Tarleton's Raiders? Lord Earl Cornwallis' merciless creature who gave rise to the terrible phrase, 'Tarleton's Quarter,' with the meaning 'none to be spared?' T'was a wonder that we escaped his minion's clutches with our lives. Pad Moore holds naught a candle to his handler, thanks be to God!"

Lem felt a chill despite the warmth of the sun now resting upon the brow of the far mountains. He had never heard such passion in a speech. It drove his need to ask, "How did Tarleton earn such despicable titles?"

"I met a field surgeon last year," said McJunkin, "a Dr. Robert Brownfield. The man was witness to the Waxhaw massacre this May past. He said, and I quote, 'Tarleton with his cruel myrmidons was in the midst of them, when commenced a scene of indiscriminate carnage never surpassed by the ruthless atrocities of the most barbarous savages.' He went on to say that few of Colonel Buford's command was spared, even under a flag of truce. Tarleton ordered every Patriot, whether dead or wounded upon the field after the battle, run through with bayonets." This tirade seemed to have worn McJunkin down, for he placed hands upon his saddle and bowed his head.

"Major?"

"Aye, Lemuel?" He sighed.

"'Tis not the same army coming to do us in?"

"Aye."

"General Dan will turn the tables on him."

"Prithee, you are in the right, young Lemuel."

"May God have mercy on our souls," pled James Park.

"Should He not, none will. Now, the time has come to join our fellows for a long night. Shall we away, my friends?"

With that, Lem gave an affectionate pat to Bonny's neck and climbed to his saddle once again. Fatigue was becoming second nature to him, as it had been nearly thirty-six hours since last he tasted a whole night's sleep. His belly rumbled, a reminder that meals had come and gone just as James said they would upon the trail.

Turning onto Green River Road, Lem observed the redness of the setting sun, now behind the mountains. It promised to be clear and icy on the dawn. Lem cast over his shoulder toward the shadowy forests from whence they had emerged. A stab of longing gripped his breast. Never had he been gone so far from home and for so long. Would that he could see his family again, all safe and comforted. His birthday celebration, only these three days past, seemed another lifetime ago. Both James and the major must have sensed his melancholy, for they let him ride ahead, holding back to talk amongst themselves. He was glad of it.

Bonny plodded along, her equine head drooping in fatigue. The gentle sway of her gait sent Lem's thoughts adrift. Unbidden, concerns for Sukey and Amadahy loomed. Where were they? What were they at? Were they safe and sound? It was his firm hope to see them rejoined with loved ones, yet he felt powerless to arrange that ambition. Letting go of that failure, his thoughts turned to the raising of cold stone markers above the heads of his father and brother.

Pain, as of a fist squeezing his heart, brought tears to his eyes. So long held in check, grief abruptly forced itself upon him. There would be no postponement this time. No holding back. His body was wracked by its struggle to cleanse away the manstealing sorrow. Lem was thankful for the descending twilight, for he felt deficient of vigor. A man was not meant to weep as of a bantling. Quickly the torments had come. As speedily, his heart was unhanded, much to his relief.

"Whoa, girl." Bonny halted without the need for reins. She, too, was spent. Lem drank deeply of the chill air, allowing the remnants of his trial to drift away on the plumes of his outbreath.

He took notice that the road had continued to gently climb. Before him now, the lane wove through a large field roughly the shape of a rectangle. The darkness was growing. Campfires had been struck to either side, mimicking the fireflies of springtime, winking amongst the grasses and clumps of trees. Lem was awed by the numbers, far more than ever he had seen. Before every blaze, there were the flitting shadows of many men.

"'Tis a correct assumption, Lemuel," said McJunkin, drawing next to Bonny's nearside. Hairy nuzzled Lem's elbow on the offside. Such had been his distraction that the men had caught him up unawares.

"Assumption, sir?"

"Surely. Tis spot-on, I say, to believe that Tarleton, bonny youth that he is, shall get a comeuppance on the morrow. One constancy hath the British. Conceit. That shall be their undoing."

Park rumbled, "'Tis true, God be willing."

"Follow now, Lemuel, be not vexed, for we shall meet food

and repose this evening. Come break of day, our regiments shall be fresh as daisies upon this killing field when the Redcoats arrive, bedraggled of a forced march all the livelong night. Twill make all the difference we shall need for victory, I say." Lem coaxed Bonny to walk between the other horses as they descended to the camp.

"You'll have your work cut out come morning," warned Park. "If you've been a-practicing your strokes, that is."

"I shall comport myself well on the drum, methinks," Lem replied.

"See you my point, Sergeant? Such is the nature of fledgling men. Mind you, tis only supposition. Tarleton shall attack at first light if he holds to his usual methods. The fear of Death has yet to bite him—nor thee, Lemuel. Ah, to be so young again, eh Park?"

"Don't halloo till you're outta the wood yourself, Major, sir." Park chuckled merrily.

"No need to be uncouth, Sergeant! Think now, tomorrow be Woden's Day, and he shall lead us on the Wild Hunt to triumph over the giants of frost and ice!"

"Well done is better'n well said. Sir."

20

Preparations

Drawing nigh the encampment, Lem's curiosity was peaked. Every direction offered a new activity. Straight before him was the most curious of all—General Dan standing upon the back of a wagon—shouting. A bonfire was built to illuminate the area, and at least fifty men were gathered to witness the spectacle. The three weary riders, McJunkin, Park, and Lem, pulled in to hear the news, dismounting at long last.

Much of the general's speech concerned the deployment of units, sentries, pickets, and such. His words ran to expectations of the enemy's approach and to their weaponries. At times, soldiers would erupt in accords of "Hear, hear!" or "Indeed!" Other times brought the discords of "Fie!" or "Nay!" These last usually came in response to some well-placed slur upon their wearied and famished state after the all-day march. White hair flying wildly from beneath his hunting cap, the general boasted, "On this ground I will beat Banny Tarleton, or I will lay my bones!" The crowd went mad, chanting, "Tarleton's Quarter!" Hats sailed into the air.

"Come, Lemuel. Tis enough for now. Let us find our regiment. My belly cries for sustenance. The aromata from the cookfires cannot fill the need!" The major led his horse away from the throng. Lem followed with Bonnie. Park brought up the rear with Hairy. They skirted the crowd and continued up the road through a grove of leafless peach trees, or perhaps apples. It was hard to tell the difference in winter.

After passing from the barren grove, they came upon a well-lit cabin of some quality. Scattered beyond this house were shadowy barns and corrals, all seemingly devoid of livestock. They formed a hamlet of sorts, grouped together as they were.

Standing on the porch was a sharp-featured lean man shaking a musket. He was arguing with three uniformed Continentals established in the yard. Two of them held torches. Behind the man was a bellicose, grand old woman with arms akimbo. Another stout matron, younger but of similar features, blocked the doorway. At her skirts were two pale children, a boy, and a girl, their eyes fearful. The family was well-attired compared to the soldiers, whose uniforms were tatters. These were wealthy people.

Lem noticed that Patriot campfires surrounded the farm to create an island of normalcy amid chaos. There was much noise from the horde of men, which had set a couple of heifers to lowing. The cows were firmly corralled alongside the cabin. The stacked rail fence of their enclosure reminded him of those back home. Lem's spirit stirred for the little family, though he did not crave to witness what must happen. His own hollow insides bespoke that.

"Master Saunders, sir, we beg your generosity in this matter. Our men have needs of sustenance. A guinea, sir, the very last of our regimental hard coin for one more of your beeves."

Saunders erupted in an English nasal tone. "Ye rebel Overmountain Men came down through here back in October. Cleaned me out—stole near every chicken, pig, goat, and bovine! Me three remaining heifers are all that's been left for feeding me own brood the rest of this long winter! What good will they be, come Spring, when ye've already eaten me last bull? Without him, there's no rebuilding me herd!"

"Another reason to sell us one more cow, sir. Tis only a courtesy, our offer to pay. Tory or no, I cannot see a man's children starve by my own action. Be that as it may, these militias must eat! We aim to have your cow!"

"Nay says I! Narry a single stone will I sell ye! Now get off my property and take your rabble with ye!" Saunders shook his musket again.

"Sir, dost mine ears deceive me? Rabble, say you?"

"Lemuel, take my reins." Major McJunkin tossed them over as he sprung from his horse. He was already moving toward the cabin. "Here, now. What seems to be the trouble, Corporal?"

The corporal noted the rank upon McJunkin's shoulder and snapped to attention. "Sir, we are trying to purchase a cow, but *Master* Hiram Saunders is not having it! Landed gentry or no, his latest insult demands retribution! A right Royalist swine is he. If it weren't for the children—"

"These strongarms are trying to relieve me of my beeves," Saunders spat. "One gold piece isn't near enough! The welfare of my family is at stake here. Honor-bound ye be, says I, to leave us sustenance against starvation!"

"Fie, sir!" exclaimed the corporal. "Your affiliates do not leave wherewithal for the Whigs! They take all and laugh along the way! We plan to leave enough for your belly, and we offer to pay for the part we require."

James eased off Hairy and stretched his stiff joints. "Lem, take holt of me stalwart beastie." He passed the reins off and sauntered toward the house. His shadowy form reminded Lem of a bear walking on his hinds.

When James entered the torchlight, Saunders stepped back. "Aaaaaack! Don't think ye to intimidate me!"

"We mean not to do any such thing," said McJunkin. "Can the sergeant help it if he was born part bear, part man, I ask you?"

"I've got me gun!" Saunders jiggled it for emphasis.

The corporal said, "Look around, man. There are many firearms—"

McJunkin broke in, "—and many more shall come tomorrow. Doubtless, those yet to arrive will spare your precious cows or your very lives! Tis Bloody Tarleton we expect to meet! If you have your wits about you, take what you can from the house and head toward the mountains this very instant!"

"Banastre Tarleton's Legion? At me own cow pens on the morrow?" Saunders seemed to fold in upon himself.

"The very same, sir," said the corporal. "The battle is sure to be fierce. No one wishes to see your family caught in the crossfire."

"Tis true," growled Park. "And Bloody Ban won't care a whit fer the wee ones amongst you. Best get out now whilst you can."

"Take the gold, Papa!" The woman in the doorway stamped her foot. The tone of her voice reminded Lem of his own mother.

"But Honey Pot?" whined Saunders.

"I said take it! Take it now and let us be off! Think of the children!" She was clutching at the young ones.

"Sensible woman ye have," observed Park.

Resignedly, Saunders held out his hand for the coin. The corporal placed it there. Saunders lifted it to his teeth and bit the corner. Thus satisfied the coin was indeed gold, he said, "Take the cow and be hanged, the lot of ye!" He shooed his wife inside, and with the grandmother upon his heel, stalked into the cabin and slammed the door.

"Colonel Howard's Continental Light Infantry is at your service, sir!" called the corporal after him. He turned to McJunkin with a lively grin. "I shall report to my commander this worthy ending to a dreadful happenstance, sir."

"Tis nothing, Corporal. My man, Park here, deserves all the credit. Who could stand against him? Know you, where might I find Colonel Brandon's Second Spartan battalion?"

"Ahhh…the Second Spartan? The next camp is under the flag of Colonel Andrew Pickens himself. If you continue up the road, with certainly you shall obtain further directions from there."

"Indeed! Well, Corporal, may fortune favor you! Come, Park. Let us be off." McJunkin stalked toward Lem, Park at his heel.

The corporal and his torch men rounded the house to choose a beast for slaughter as the major and sergeant joined Lem astride their mounts once more.

"All's well that ends well, so they say," McJunkin observed. "Ye gods, my very bones ache of weariness, Sergeant. Let us a way to find our lodgings and take refreshment."

"Aye, sir," Lem and James chorused.

The road led straight to Pickens' militiamen as described. McJunkin brought them to the nearest bonfire. Upon seeing no officer's tent, he reared up in his saddle, cupped hands to mouth, and summoned a strength of lung from where Lem knew not.

"SECOND SPARTANS—SOUND OFF!"

Far to the right came many halloos. A high-pitched voice cut through the din, none other than that of Private High-Key Moseley, "Best of the Carolinas!" The sing-song announcement set off a round of chants that began as "Carolina, Carolina!" Those near Lem countered with "Pickens, Pickens!" Soon, others could be heard echoing across the field and filtering through the scattered trees—"Howard, Triplett, Washington, Seventy-First Cavalry," and many more individual companies sounded off.

McJunkin lowered to the saddle and turned. "Let us take our leave, gentlemen." He led off in the direction of the Spartans, weaving his horse among the throngs of cheering soldiers.

Lem was heartened by the enthusiasm. Even Bonnie must have felt the thrill, for she kept her step and head high. She was treated to strokes on the neck and flank and Lem to friendly waves and cheerful faces as they passed. They went from fire to fire until finally achieving their day's goal. Before them stood a hastily rigged entranceway of lashed poles sporting a rag banner that read, "Second Spartans, Col. T. Brandon, Cmdr." To both sides were sentries at attention, saluting the major as the trio passed through.

Shouts of "McJunkin! Major McJunkin's come!" filtered down through the camp. Someone yelled, "We've got a new drummer!" Cheers went up, warming Lem's breast. A runner sprang into the center aisle between bivouacked soldiers and raced ahead of their small procession.

Odors both pleasant, like woodsmoke and roasting beef, and unpleasant, like unwashed bodies and detritus, assailed Lem's nose. After the freshness of the open country, it was somewhat off-putting. Still, the neatness of the camp was impressive, especially when compared to the rout Lem had witnessed earlier in the day when Tarleton's advance party had discovered the column. The center path had been swept free of horse droppings, rubbish, even pebbles.

Lem found a hunk of warm beef rib thrust into his hand, the savory aroma making his head swoon. He thanked the one who delivered the meat unto him and delved in ravenously. Grease rolled down his chin and wrist. Both Sergeant Park and the major were also treated to ribs, which they ate just as ravenously. When they had picked clean the bones, Lem followed McJunkin's lead and tossed his toward the nearest fire, after which a militiaman kicked it in. Licking his fingers clean, he dried them on his breeches. He felt strengthened, and his head had cleared.

Now they were gradually descending toward a handful of tents. Hickories surrounded them. Before these domiciles was a large fire encircled with fieldstone. Adjacent to the warm flames were a dozen men in various positions of repose. Some few used sawed logs for seats, some sat cross-legged on the ground, and one individual rested perilously on a rickety chair in front of the farthest tent. This sturdy militiaman wore a full auburn beard upon an amicable mien. Gray eyes blazed from beneath overhanging crags. A robust nose and full lips completed the portrait of good Irish stock. He stood, grinning toothily.

"So good to see you alive and kicking, Major!" said the Irishman. "Sergeant Park—no less imposing, I see! And who have we here? Is this the new drummer ye've brought me? I've heard tell that he singlehandedly ran off some of the Bloody Scout's finest horsemen this same day! Get ye all down and join us." To no one in particular, he added, "Gather up their spent beasts and see them attended!"

At this juncture, all the men were on their feet. Several came forward to assist with the dismounting and unpacking. Gratefully, Lem consigned the Brown Bess to the hands of a sergeant. This man suspiciously had the same coloring as Brandon.

Catching Lem's questioning eye, he said in brogue, "Aye, lad. Tis me own brother, Colonel Thomas Brandon yonder." He thrust out a firm hand to Lem. "Sergeant Richard Brandon, at your service. Methinks to stow your essentials in me tent here for safekeeping. As quartermaster, I bear witness to the shortage of canvas, mine being greatly shared already. Storage below me cot—that's the best I can do at the mo'. I'll take ye to the musician's fire for bedding down. Got a short scrap of linen canvas to throw over ye and yer drum. You've me permission to poke through yer belongings when needs be. I suggest ye pay a visit to the supply wagon and draw an extra blanket. This night will be a cold one if ever my bones be truthful. Don't let them women tell ye contrary!"

"Where are these women of which you speak, sir?" Lem was ready to take his leave and find comfort in sleep.

"Why, ye'll find them two darkies under yon tree. Showed up in the wee hours this very morn drawing a wagonload of cornmeal, saints be praised!" The sergeant threw out an arm toward a small fire well beyond the back of his tent. "If it weren't for them two helping with me inventory, I could naught get me job done! A word of counsel. The vast negress hath a sharp tongue—more bark than bite, methinks. Tell her I sent you, and holt yer ground when she growls at ye!"

Lem's knees trembled. Could it be? "Sergeant, sir? These women—perchance are they Sukey and Sallie?"

The sergeant was flummoxed. "Pray tell, how came ye to know of them?"

Over his shoulder, Lem called back, "We're family!"

"Well, I'll be swaggered!"

Lem was nearly overcome by excitement and longing. Struggling through dried clumps of grasses in the dark, he almost went down several times. Drawing nigh the wagon, the females peered toward him.

Sukey cried out, "Oh my good Lawd above! It be Lemmy! Lemmy's done come back to us. Oh, Lawdy, Lawdy!" She lumbered to her feet and flung herself at him, crushing the wind from his chest.

Amadahy hopped up but remained still as Lem came into the firelight.

When at last Sukey released him, Amadahy stepped in. "My brother, it fills me with great joy to see you," she said formally. Lem reached out, and she fell into his embrace. When at last the Indian girl drew away, his shoulder was damp. Her tears pierced his heart.

Sukey was still muttering about their good fortune when of a sudden, she asked, "What happened after you hove off last night?"

"Tis of trifling importance, and yet a long and thrilling tale, O' Great African Queen. Grant me leave to tell it on the morrow, I beg you. I'm bone-tired." Lem gave her a bow from the hip. This unexpected return to their usual humor fetched a burst of laughter from Sukey. She was joined by Amadahy. Lem could not hold back. The three indulged in shared mirth for a few moments to ease their woes.

The mood was short-lived, however. From the direction of Colonel Brandon's tent came the tramping of many feet. The gibbous moon did little to ease Lem's apprehension over the specters now emerging from the shadows. He stood before Sukey and Amadahy warily, thoughts that somehow his Indian friend had been found out. His fears were allayed upon recognizing the bulk of Park emerging from the dark. The sergeant was followed by

Richard Brandon and a few others Lem had noticed earlier at the colonel's fireside.

"Thar ye be, Lem! Had me worried when ye disappeared without a lettin' on. Sergeant Brandon here told me where you'd likely—" James Park stopped dead, eyebrows swamping his temples. "Am…uh…I…Sallie?" He stepped forward to engulf Amadahy in a bear hug. When he finally let her go, Lem was sure he saw a glisten in the big man's eye. "Good to see ye safe, me girl," Park managed.

Lem took advantage of the lull in the conversation. It seemed that James had stunned his compatriots with his attentions to Amadahy. "Sirs, may I present my sister, Sallie, and my family's most beloved retainer, Sukey Farnandis?" He knew that Sukey, cherished as she was by his family entire, was still yet a slave in the judgment of the world. Acceptance of her as of his own blood was beyond hope. He was wrong.

James Park swept Sukey from her feet as if she weighed nil and planted a kiss full upon her lips. Easing her to the ground, he said, "Tis my great honor to meet ye at long last! Lem hast spoke of ye as one put upon the highest pedestal. God hath graced our meager forces with your willing hands! I, James Obadiah Park, am at your service."

Sukey, eyes rolling back in her head so only the whites could be seen in the firelight, said, "Laws a mercy!" She promptly swooned into Park's arms. With difficulty, he eased her immensity to the ground, where she sat fanning herself with her hands.

The gathering rolled with merriment. Lem looked to James in humble gratitude and was acknowledged with a wink.

Sergeant Brandon spoke. "Park, my good fellow, tis my brother's wish for entertainment. Let us away with these fine people. I've yet to introduce Lem to his fellows, and time flies."

With that, all those gathered, including Sukey and Amadahy, were escorted to Colonel Brandon's presence and made comfortable at his fireside. All excepting Lem. His was a different plight.

As the group passed before Sergeant Brandon's tent, the sergeant grabbed Lem's arm to hold him back. Rummaging to retrieve Lem's drum, he said, "Here tis, Lem, your instrument of office. Didst Park make mention that ye have a bit of rank to your name by holding this here thrummer? Nay? Well then, hear ye. Any of the ranks of private is at your command, young Lem. Call it professional courtesy, since ye be engaged at odd times whilst the rest of us be off duty, so to speak. Drummers fall between privates and corporals. Ye have the right to a morsel of assistance once upon a time—but don't think ye to abuse your newfound influence. Now, let's be off to serve at the Colonel's pleasure."

Lem was shaken. That answered a question that had been burning in his mind. Privates Moseley, Foster, and Gillham had all been compelled to see to his needs. It had not occurred to him the reason beyond simple gentility. He hung the shoulder strap over his neck, adjusted the drum to his right hip, and withdrew his drumsticks from their sheath.

"Song. I want song!" demanded Colonel Brandon as Lem drew near the fire. "Bring forth the fife and drums!"

Into the circle came two men carrying their instruments of trade. The first was a crumpled old man, clean-shaven, with thin yellowish hair and few teeth. He clutched a handmade wooden fife with his claw-like fingers. The other was a decade younger perhaps, taller, and darker of countenance as Lem himself. His hair was black and stringy, creeping from under a flat moss-colored Scotch bonnet. From his shoulder dangled a taut-rope field drum, not unlike Lem's, only his was emblazoned with colorful images of a martial design.

"Where be my greenest drummer?" demanded Colonel Brandon.

"Go on, now. Ye've been summoned!" Park reached over Sukey and Sallie to propel Lem into the firelight. A fright came upon him what with all the eager stares. T'was his first performance before an audience. Nor had he the full training. His new companions acknowledged him with cordial nods, then the tall drummer ticked off a cadence. Lem raised his own sticks and struck a simple beat. He was rewarded with a smile from his new partner. After a few bars, the old man raised his fife to his lips. He blew a piercing melody Lem immediately recognized—*Free America*—an old ballad by Joseph Warren. The men around the fire raised their voices in song:

That seat of Science, Athens,
And earth's proud mistress, Rome;
Where now are all their glories?
We scarce can find a tomb.
Then guard your rights, Americans,
Nor stoop to lawless sway;
Oppose, oppose, oppose, oppose,
For North America.

We led fair Freedom hither,
And lo, the desert smiled!
A paradise of pleasure
Was opened in the wild!
Your harvest, bold Americans,
No power shall snatch away!
Huzza, huzza, huzza, huzza,
For free America.

Torn from a world of tyrants,
Beneath this western sky,
We formed a new dominion,

A land of liberty:
The world shall own we're masters here;
Then hasten on the day:
Huzza, huzza, huzza, huzza,
For free America.

Proud Albion bowed to Caesar,
And numerous lords before;
To Picts, to Danes, to Normans,
And many masters more:
But we can boast, Americans,
We've never fallen a prey;
Huzza, huzza, huzza, huzza,
For free America.

God bless this maiden climate,
And through its vast domain
May hosts of heroes cluster,
Who scorn to wear a chain:
And blast the venal sycophant
That dares our rights betray;
Huzza, huzza, huzza, huzza,
For free America.

Lift up your hands, ye heroes,
And swear with proud disdain,
The wretch that would ensnare you,
Shall lay his snares in vain:
Should Europe empty all her force,
We'll meet her in array,
And fight and shout, and shout and fight
For North America.

Some future day shall crown us,
The masters of the main,
Our fleets shall speak in thunder
To England, France, and Spain;
And the nations over the ocean spread

Shall tremble and obey
The sons, the sons, the sons, the sons
Of brave America.

Both musicians clapped Lem upon the back when the tune was ended, smiling. The oldster called himself Jake Polk, and the one of middle years, Chand Aubrey. They laid it out plain how good it was for Lem to join their little band, offering heavy praise upon his novice drumming. Lem warmed to them graciously.

For some while to come, the soldiers implored more music. Wood was thrown on the fire. Many a cup filled. When Lem looked around, he realized that the crowd had grown. Militiamen throughout the camp had wandered in to lend their voices to the tunes. They took what cheer they could on the eve of battle. This notion stirred Lem to his core. The firelight swam in his sight until he swiped the moisture away with his sleeve.

"Tis a dance we have needs of!" exclaimed the colonel. Immediately the crowd took up the chant, "…a dance…a dance…a dance."

Lem looked to his fellows, unsure.

"Just keep the tempo, Lem! That's all you've to do," hollered Jake over the chanters. He bobbed his head to the beat he wanted, so Lem struck the drumhead in tempo. Chand Aubrey added flourishes and drags. When several cadence measures suited Jake, he launched into a popular ditty that brought cheers, whistles, and claps. All around, men linked arms and spun. Park hooked both Sukey and Sallie and lumbered in circles. Laughter and gaiety abounded. Lem's weariness vanished as he became enamored with the music.

As the dance ended, shouts came from the back of the throng. "The general's a-coming! Make way for General Dan!" Versions of the notice made it all the way to the fireside, at which point

Colonel Brandon commanded, "Drummers, give *The Roll!*"

Lem observed as Chand tapped out a continuous tremolo. These stokes he had not yet mastered, but seeing it done, mimicked as best he could. All eyes were now fastened upon the central aisle. The militiamen parted to either side, as did the Red Sea by God's power through the outstretched arms of Moses. Cheers announced the arrival of General Dan and his entourage. Lem saw they were walking and shortly understood why. The general shook hands and made jokes with the men as he strolled along. Many firebrands were held aloft to light his way.

Snatches of the general's banter reached Lem's ears as a hush gradually fell over the crowd. "…keep in good spirits, and the day will be ours…the Old Wagoner will crack his whip over Ban in the morning, as sure as I live…so, a pretty maiden awaits you back home…tis a boast, sir, a boast…all I ask of ye is just hold up your heads, boys…three fires and you are free!"

The general came to the fireside, greeting Colonel Brandon and his officers. After shaking a few hands, he turned back to the men. It was then his eye lit upon Lem. "Ah, well met, young Lemuel! Making a mark for yourself, I see. Maidens do adore a man who can play his instrument with a lively beat!" Lem's face heated as the crowd roared.

Morgan raised his arms for attention. "Hold your tongues and I'll tell you a tale," he began. "Many of you know I had my start as a wagoner." Shouts of "no…cannot be…nay" gasped his listeners. He raised his arms again, then continued. "Aye. In my youth, I was a skilled pugilist and rowdy. Now, now. Settle down. Tis true, I say—a rowdy! A quarter-century past, in the springtime, I was delivering a wagonload of goods to Fort Chiswell, Virginia, when misfortune befell me as of a load of brick. A British lieutenant took grave offense at something I said and abused me with the most violent of tongues. Well, I could nary brook the outrage, such was my spirit at the time. I forthwith clenched my fist and pummeled the officer senseless to the ground." [cheers] "Court-martialed, was I, and on the very spot!" [nay, nay] "Sentenced to five hundred lashes, I say! Being immediately stripped of my shirt and laid into by the strokes of a strong boy, I counted each sting as my flesh was laid to ribbons. When the terrible punishment was met, the sorry Britons missed the allotment by one! Four hundred ninety-nine lashes only had I received. They owe me one still!" With that last testimony, he stripped away his jacket and shirt, turning this way and that, allowing all to bear witness to the truth of his words. The scars upon Morgan's back struck Lem as a monstrous tragedy. The witnesses went dead silent.

Replacing his garments, Morgan once more addressed the crowd, "Tomorrow, I shall pay them back for every stroke! Let them try to bring the last! The glory of victory shall be ours!" He thrust both fists skyward. The militia erupted in cheers that could not be staid. Morgan placed a hand on Lem's shoulder and bent to speak in his ear, "My God be with you and grant I see you in good health at the end of this campaign. I'm off to hearten the other companies." Morgan called his entourage to him. They formed a vanguard and ushered him out of the excited camp.

Upon seeing General Dan on his way, Colonel Brandon called for Chand to play *Tap-Too*, a signal cadence Lem had not yet learned. It was a call for the soldiers to retire to their quarters and sleep. Lem suddenly longed for his bedroll. It had been the longest day of all thirteen unlucky years ascribed to his name. Would he live to see another?

21

Strokes

The assembly broke up at the strike of *Tap-toos,* and men went back to their fires, restoking them against the chill and finding what comfort they could in their blankets. For most, t'was certain in Lem's mind, the night would be long and fitful, knowing what was expected come sunrise. Beyond exhaustion, nerves frayed, Lem was unsure he could close his eyes.

"This evening has been most agreeable," stated Colonel Brandon to those few officers still encircling his fire. "A light spirit accompanies me as I retire tonight. I bid you all dreams of loved ones and sweethearts. Unless some change in prospects occurs, sound *Reveille* two hours before daybreak. Fail me not. Good night!" With that, he entered his tent and dropped the flap.

McJunkin joined Lem and his new companions. "Lemuel. Must that you bed down next to this fire. Tis your duty to stick with these vital signalers if the colonel wants for drumming. Park shall escort Sukey and Sallie back to their wagon and obtain several extra blankets for your bedding. I recommend you say farewell to them now, as the field will likely begin to heat at break of day." He then addressed Sukey alone. "Fine negress, come reveille I beg you take Sallie upon your wagon and go to the rear of our lines with the camp followers and surgeons. I would see you safe amongst the baggage carts, for they are well-guarded."

"Yaw'sa, I will."

"And now, for my own part, the day is done. May God grant succor and strength to you all." Major McJunkin left for his tent.

Lem said his goodbyes to Sukey and Sallie, a moist affair, then sought the trenches. T'was cold, but not bitterly so. As he saw to his relief, Sukey's voice drifted down through the sparse trees. She was saying, "Lawsy, that was the most' citement I's seed in many a moon!"

Amadahy's softer tones responded, "You reckon the passage of time by the moon? I thought only Indians marked time by the lay of it. Are you part Indian, Sukey?"

Sukey chuckled. "Could be, Sallie. My boy, Big Tom, and his boy, Little Tom—they shore believed it true. Iffin I tolt 'em to git home by dark, they'd better! Iffin the moon done showed up befo' they did, I'd give 'em both a good lickin'! Big Tom, he'd say, 'Mamma, you shore you ain't part Injun? How you knowed we be late when you ain't got no timepiece?'"

Amadahy asked, "What about those weeks when the moon shows its face during the day?"

James Park's laughter drowned out the rest. Lem tracked the sergeant's heavy footsteps back to the ring of officer's tents. His own thoughts drifted to Big Tom and Little Tom. He wondered if they ever emptied the catfish traps and made it over to help Mamma cook his birthday dinner.

When he returned to the colonel's fire, James was gone, and the musicians had taken to their bedrolls. Jake was snoring gently, but Chand was tossing and turning. Lem's blankets were stacked on a piece of canvas beside his drum. He moved the drum to sit at his head, spread a blanket across the canvas to soften the ground, then unfolded and used the other two for covers. From what he had seen, most soldiers had but one blanket. He was indeed blessed.

Just as his eyes closed, Chand whispered, "Lem? Cover your drum with part of a blanket to keep the dampness away. Moisture will temper the drumhead. It could split when you hit it. The Officer of the Day carries a clock watch. He'll be around to wake us when it's time for *Reveille*—and he'll be punctual, I'll warrant. Rest well."

"Aye, Chand. Don't let the bedbugs bite."

Lem lay awake for some time, unable to quell his thoughts. Eventually, he fell into a restless sleep. He dreamt of angry men squabbling about vague tax levies, bustling taverns, dank cellars, Indians running for their lives, and corn grinding to powder beneath great stones. These stones became a king and his court. The nobles were crushing bones beneath their feet. Graciously, the dreams resigned for a time. All too soon, a boot shoved his rump, and not gently.

"Time for ye lay-a-bouts to rise and shine! Don't be making me come back here to roust ye out again!" Footsteps faded.

Lem groggily threw off the blankets to find both of his companions already up and stretching by the fire. Someone had poked in a few fresh faggots, reviving the flames. Stifling a yawn, he stood.

"Make ready your drum, Lem. Tis time for the strokes," Jake said.

Lem retrieved his drum, shouldered it, and grabbed his sticks. Chand put on his own drum; Jake pulled his fife out of his haversack. They came to flank Lem, Chand on his left and Jake on his right—only they faced toward the encampment. An elbow to the ribs convinced Lem to turn around. It was still totally dark except for the stars above and the glow of dying campfires.

Jake said, "Ready. Set. Play!"

Chand gave his drum a series of whacks that Lem tried to imitate. Jake's fife rent the air with a high-pitched warble that made Lem think his head would burst. From nearby came shouts of "get up ye lazy dogs…so ye think to sleep in do ye… I'll put me foot up a dark place…" and variations on the theme. From farther away, other drummers roused their companies. The upsurge of noise reminded Lem of how Papa's mill would eventually fill the countryside with creaking and rumbling once the great wheel was engaged.

"That's done it, Lem! My belly feels awfully empty. Let us break our fast now." Jake rounded the fire, stuffed his fife back in his sack, pulled out a skillet, utensils, and a portion of his daily rations. He turned to Lem. "What goods have you to add to the pot?"

Lem rummaged in his kit for the hunk of pepper-cured ham that Amadahy had packed. His friends murmured in delight over its advent. They had run out of meat days ago, subsisting mainly on cornmeal cakes and mush ever since.

Chand handed Lem two pots to be filled from a clear rivulet at the base of the hillock. When Lem reached the tiny flow, hails of greeting came from others crouched along the bank. They were washing, shaving, scrubbing, and filling vessels. Lem walked upstream to find an unsullied flow to fill his pots, then climbed the hill back to camp. While Chand set cornmeal and coffee simmering on the coals, Lem heard words that chilled his heart.

Jake asked, "Do ye 'spect we're gonna make a run fer it?"

"Whatever for?" James Park bristled. "General Dan, he don't

run from no man!"

"Then why are we sitting here in a cow pasture instead of trying for the mountains?" asked Chand.

Jake rubbed the stubble on his chin. "Trusting to General Dan's wiles, I'd say he was unsure whether we could make it that far before the Britons caught us up and surrounded us."

Lem interjected, "Why not flee northward across the Broad at Cherokee Ford?" It was a question that had badgered his thoughts during yesterday's trek, as the ford was only six miles northward. Papa's map marked it clearly as the most used by traders between the Carolinas.

Park said, "More of the same, eh? Tired troops, high water, difficult crossing. Let us leave off supposin'. What I know is that we was ordered out to these here cow pens in a mighty rush—two o' the clock, mind—yesterday morn. Most of us had to leave our meals still cooking in the pots back at Thicketty—over five hundred militiamen. T'was a long day on an empty belly. I could nary sleep, so's I got a few bites and packed my pots. Most were in their blankets when the order came to skedaddle. Now, think ye, would General Dan want to starve his men on the eve of conflict? Nay, says I. T'was a rouse, a sham. The Old Wagoner was playing the piper to that arrogant rat, Bloody Tarleton!"

"I'll lay the general wanted it to make it seem we was on the hoof to draw them across the river," said Jake. "T'was a disgrace, though, having to leave all that food on the cook fires. Ain't no denying it."

Chand mused, "Makes a crumb of sense. We started moving these two days past, leaving only a token force patrolling the banks of the Pacholet between Grindall's and the Iron Works. Then, we reposed at Thicketty whilst the enemy thought us still at Grindall's."

"Heard tell the one thing The Butcher cannot abide—watching the enemy flee before him," said Park. "Drives him mad to think his quarry might be gettin' away. He's the hound after the rabbit's tail, says I!"

Lem struggled to grasp what he had heard thus far. "I twig the pretense of flight to goad the British commander into rashly making chase. Jake's observance of leaving the victuals cooking has me stymied. Why would General Dan feed the enemy whilst his own troops suffer the lack, pray tell?"

Park raised an inquisitive brow. "A query for a query, young Lem. Didst you find the swift march of yesterday tiring?"

"Aye."

"And we was only going a few miles—barely eleven. From Grindall's to these cow pens sum near twenty-two if you consider all of them twists, turns, gullies, hills, and valleys. We endured it over two long days. The Bloody Scout, now, he adores force-marching his troops at night—known for it! Why, if he thought we was on the run, he'd press his army for the full length of it without a break, mark my words! More to the point. What's the first thing you did when you got here yesterday, lad?"

Lem thought back. Much had happened. Then it came to him. "I wanted for nourishment and sleep," he replied.

"Good answer. Now compound it a bit. I heard tell Tarleton's troops have been beating ground since Sunday past. That's five whole days pushing from down at Musgrove's Mill, across the flooded Tyger and Fairforest creeks, to attain Grindall's Ford. Miles of hilly country scavenged for every nibble by their own Loyalist dogs. They'd be tired and starved, having traipsed close to forty miles in such a short time."

Lem harkened back to the night he met General Dan above Grindall's. He had been enticed by the smell of bacon frying on numerous cookfires. Still, he was confounded over the few men in evidence. Now he understood. It was a nasty ruse, and right sneaky one, to play on hungry soldiers having no respite in sight.

"Point well made, Sergeant Park." Chand looked thoughtful. "If I was on such a tramp and chanced upon food still warm and juicy, I'd take nary another step until I'd slaked my thirst, filled my belly, and pulled a few winks."

"I'd be doing the same," said Jake, "and hang any commander to say different!"

"I find that line of thought most intriguing," said Colonel Brandon, easing from his tent to join them at the warm fire. A wry smile lifted his red beard.

"No offense, sir!" Jake sprang to his feet, a maneuver that Lem found remarkable for one so old.

"None taken, my man." He held out a tin cup to Chand. "Strong coffee, I pray?"

Chand poured the black liquid. "Aye, sir! Just the way you like it!"

"At your service for the black gold, Chand. However did you scrounge it? Nay, best keep that to yourself. Gentlemen, your deliberations intrigue me. Being privy to much more of the general's executions, I'll divulge this much by way of confirmation. The plot is a combination of many factors coming to a head, the most important of which is we have staked out the ground on which we will fight. We're beholding to Captain Dennis Trammell of Roebuck's Regiment for that. He lives about a mile from here. Knows this pasture like the back of his hand, every draw and gully of it. He and General Dan spent yestereve scheming up a few traps and troop deployments. The enemy knows not the lay of the land nor the full measure of the forces awaiting him. Our far-flung scouts have kept enemy spies at a distance. Further, as you said, the British foot and horse shall arrive fatigued whilst we are well-rested and full of wrath. Therefore, we will take the day!"

Lem noticed the light of dawn approaching. The sky promised a cold, crisp day devoid of clouds. "Colonel Brandon, sir?"

"Lad?"

"May I ask, sir, how many men strong are we? I have counted over five hundred, but surely that is not the fullness of it. The message I delivered to General Dan described the British at some twelve hundred of infantry, cavalry, elite guard, fusilier, and artillery."

Brandon was taken aback. "It escaped me that you brought Sergeant Park's message to General Dan faster than the author himself." He chuckled. "Very well. We are near equal to Bloody Ban's legion. The fight will be won or lost before midday. We have much on our side besides pluck and nerve. Despite his lack of formal education in the military arts, General Dan is an undefeated strategist. This does not mean we shall win the day handily, for war is a bloody and uncertain endeavor. Be stalwart, my signalers! Keep these conjectures between you. Don't let them out. Understood?"

"Aye, sir," replied all three musicians. Lem's trepidation raised a notch. The sound words from the colonel did naught to bolster his confidence. He was refilling his cup when a distant rumbling split the cold air of dawn. It matured into a company of scouts riding pell-mell down the Green River Road, shouting as they approached.

"To arms! To arms! The enemy is uponst us! The British are coming! The horsemen passed swiftly out of sight, heading northwestward to warn other battalions.

Lem could see men springing to life across the broad field and throughout the open woodlands. Fires were kicked out. Swords buckled. Muskets were brought to hand. The din of so many abruptly on the move swelled across the tableland.

"So it begins," Colonel Brandon said resolutely. "Rise my brethren. Tis time to call forth the dogs of war. Sound *The Alarm!*" Tossing his cup to the ground, the colonel stalked away to join a gathering of his officers at the mouth of the semicircled tents.

After donning his drum, Lem lined up with Chand and Jake to face the camp again. Chand loosed a hardy roll, taken up by Lem. Jake trilled upon his fife. The thrum of the combined instruments made Lem's ears ring. Time stretched; his arms grew tired. Just as it seemed he could no longer sustain the roll, it was over. The clatter and yells of the assembling regiment were a quiet blessing in comparison.

"Lem? I've got something for you." Jake pulled a tomahawk from his pack and tied the leather thong of its sheath around Lem's waist. That done, he said, "Can nary be too careful. Took that off a Shawnee back in my Injun fightin' days. Use it only if you must defend yourself, but do not lay off your drum! Heed my words. Once the battle is pitched, our station is by the colonel and the majors awaiting signal orders. That don't mean we're safe! Above all else, we, the three of us, must stick together. Our purpose is to deliver commands where no raised voice can pierce! The company flag will join with us so our fighters can know where to rally if needs be. Things become confused on a battleground."

All the while he talked, Jake had been shepherding Chand and Lem up the central aisle of the camp, keeping pace with Colonel Brandon, Major McJunkin, and others of rank whom Lem did not know. Sergeant Park rushed up from the side.

"Lemuel!" Lem found himself swept into Park's embrace despite the large field drum in the way. "I must be off, Lem. Stick by these good fellows. They've seen action and know what to do.

I shall see you by God's grace after all 'tis said and done. Hold yer heads proud, the lot of ye!" With that, he turned away and was quickly surrounded by militiamen seeking instructions.

The trio reached the camp entranceway. A work detail was dismantling the flagpole. One stalwart fellow lifted the pole from its supports and handed it to the young man Lem recognized as Private John Gillman. Gilly's eyes were alight with excitement as he rushed up, waving the rust-colored regimental flag in greeting. To Lem, the flag looked like the remnants of upholstery ripped from a chair back.

"I seed you come in last night, Lem! You looked slap beat. Tried to say 'halloo,' but me mouth was full." The man's cadaverous mien rounded on Chand and Jake. Who ye boys be?" His grin was as snaggled-toothed as Lem recalled, but his eyes were somewhat wandering, each in a different direction. This Lem had refused to notice before because it was so unsettling.

Predictably, Chand and Jake wore frozen expressions as Gilly's presence bored into them.

"It's jus' like I tolt ye, Lem. I get that look from ever body." He stuck out a grubby hand with fingernails black with impacted dirt. "Yew boys can call me Gilly."

Jake cleared his throat, "Gilly, stick to our heels. Them boys on the field will be looking to the flag for orders. Let's keep moving." He set off toward a gathering of officers up the road. They bypassed ranks of militiamen priming rifles. Lem was awed by the speed with which the troops were mustering.

Jake called, "Them making the front line on the left and hiding all in the trees are Georgian sharpshooters, five hunderd of 'em." Pointing across the road, he added, "Them over yonder way are North Carolina militia brigades—crack shots themselves."

The sun lifted above the forests where Green River Road

emptied onto the field. Lem wondered at the wrath on faces now in silhouette, the disrepair of their raiment made plain in the stark light. Strips of white hung from most hats, barely discernable from the rest of their ragged attire. Lem checked his own hat to certify the white slip was still attached. As he restored it to his head, a cheer went up from the offset lines of sharpshooters.

Shielding his eyes against the sun's rays, he saw General Dan's entourage galloping toward him. When they reached the point on the road between the Georgians and North Carolinians, they drew up. From atop his warhorse, the general raised his arms for quiet. Immediately a hush overspread the field.

"Banny's coming!" General Dan shouted.

Brigadier General Daniel Morgan

SAUNDERS'
WASHINGTON'S CAVALRY
HOWARD'S CONTINENTALS
LEM
X
PICKINS' MILITIA
MORGAN
SHARPSHOOTERS
N. CAROLINA
BATTLE OF COWPENS
JANUARY, 17, 1981
MAP BY RICHARD C. MEEHAN, JR.

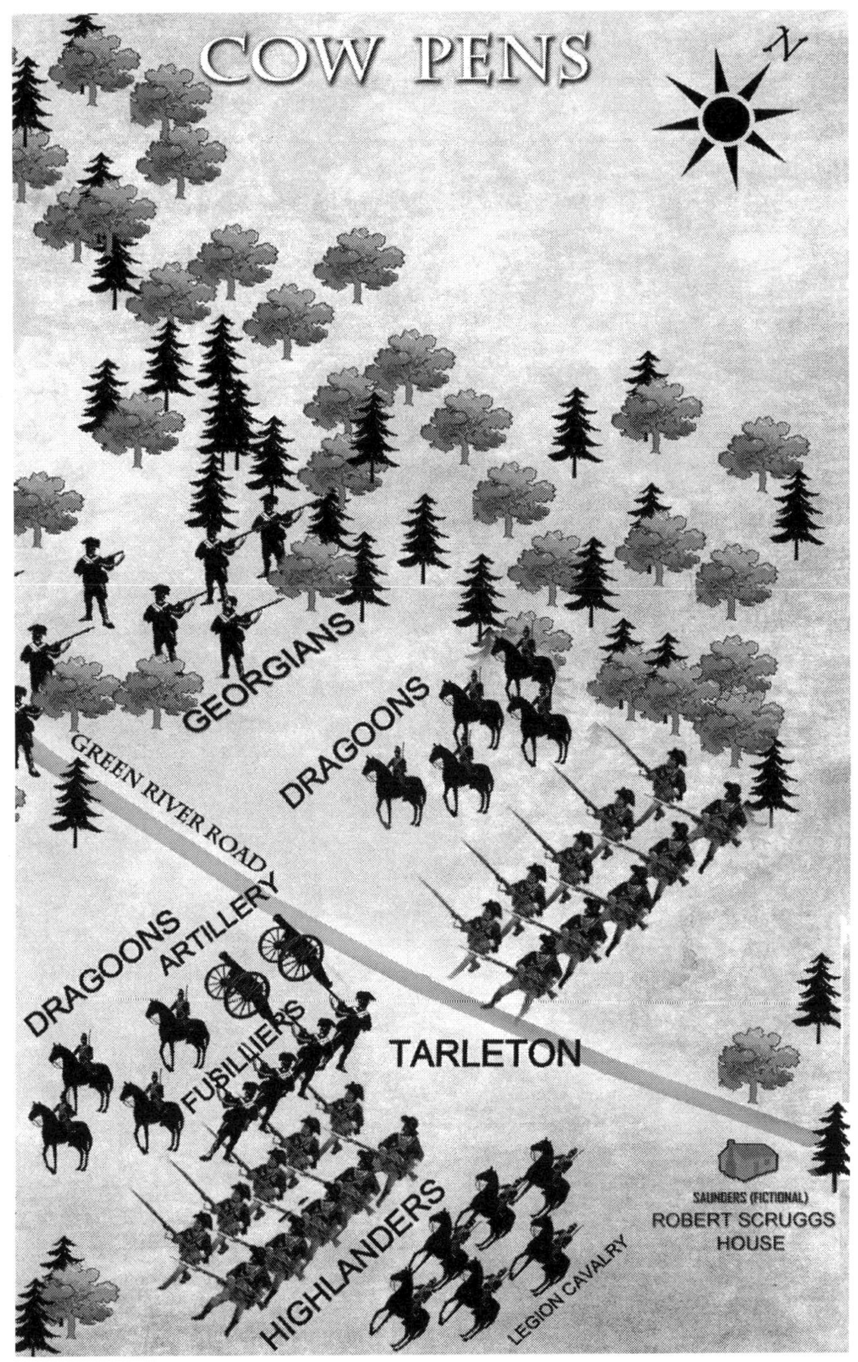
COW PENS
N
GEORGIANS
DRAGOONS
GREEN RIVER ROAD
ARTILLERY
DRAGOONS
FUSILLIERS
TARLETON
HIGHLANDERS
LEGION CAVALRY
SAUNDERS (FICTIONAL)
ROBERT SCRUGGS
HOUSE

Coloniel Banastre Tarleton

22

The Storm

Brigadier General Daniel Morgan, commander of the joint regular and irregular soldiery, Continental Army Southern division, bellowed, "I've heard a lot of tales about who are better shots, the men of Georgia or Carolina. Here is your chance to settle the matter and save the country in the bargain. Let me see which are most entitled to the credit of brave men, the boys of Carolina or those of Georgia!" He pounded his fist into his palm. Competing yells erupted from both sides of the field. Lem realized the general was pricking the rivalry between his sharpshooters, and they were rising to the challenge. General Dan called for silence again. "Remember now, reserve fire until you've seen the whites of their eyes! Deliver me two well-directed rounds and drop back behind your fellows so they may get a chance!"

Jake elbowed Lem, whispering, "That be us he's talking about—Colonel Andrew Pickens' South Carolina Militia, all total at roughly seven hundred men. Them shooters will be counting on us to give 'em cover as they fall back. We won't let 'em down!" He stood tall and wore an expression of great pride.

Morgan finished delivering his speech to the sharpshooters and turned his horse toward Colonial Pickens' line. Brandon and his officers followed in the general's wake.

"Come on, boys," Jake led off, angling toward the right of the Carolinians where Morgan and his guards had settled. By the time they caught him up, the general was amidst another full oratory.

"I ask but an ordinary display of manhood to obtain certain victory," said Dan. "Flight upon the field would certify mutual destruction, whilst safety, advantage, and honor will be gained by courageous resistance. I have no doubts about the result if you of my fine militia perform your simple duty! You volunteers have achieved so much with so little! Remember now the victories you have wrought. Remember, too, the atrocities perpetrated upon you. Do not break on any account. Fire low and deliberately. If forced to retire, rally on the eminence in the rear, where, supported by cavalry and militia, there can be no defeat!" Here ending his speech, General Dan and his guards passed through the lines at a gallop towards yet another skirmish line nigh a hundred yards further on.

"Jake, who are they?" Lem pointed to the blue-and-white-uniformed regiment stretched tidily across the grassland.

"Howard's Continentals—regular army. Over three hundred trained troops. Them's *our* fallback in case we have need to cut and run."

Chand said, "I certainly hope we do not!"

"Same for me," said Gilly, rolling his eyes wildly.

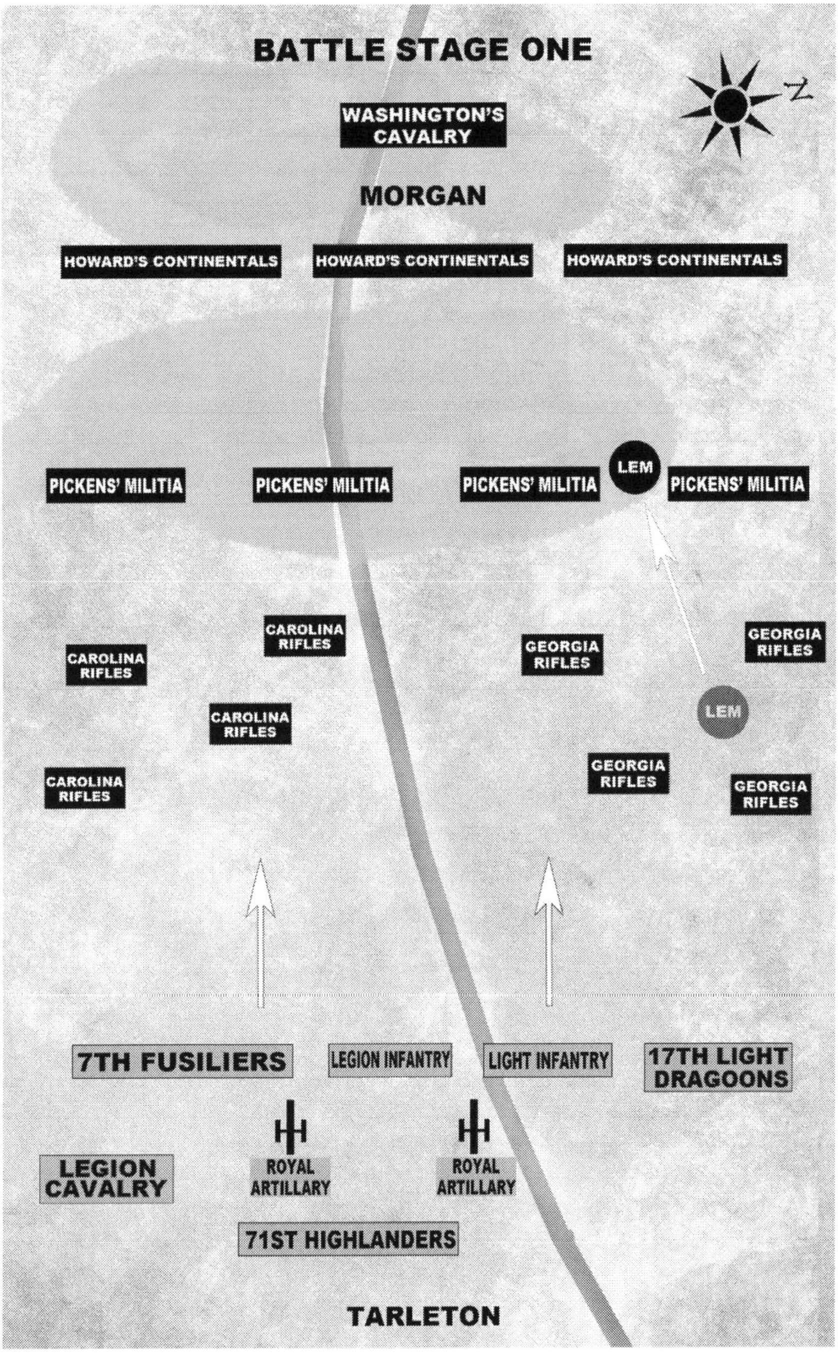

BATTLE STAGE ONE

WASHINGTON'S CAVALRY

MORGAN

HOWARD'S CONTINENTALS
HOWARD'S CONTINENTALS
HOWARD'S CONTINENTALS

LEM

PICKENS' MILITIA
PICKENS' MILITIA
PICKENS' MILITIA
PICKENS' MILITIA

CAROLINA RIFLES
CAROLINA RIFLES
CAROLINA RIFLES
CAROLINA RIFLES

GEORGIA RIFLES
GEORGIA RIFLES
LEM
GEORGIA RIFLES
GEORGIA RIFLES

7TH FUSILIERS
LEGION INFANTRY
LIGHT INFANTRY
17TH LIGHT DRAGOONS

LEGION CAVALRY
ROYAL ARTILLARY
ROYAL ARTILLARY

71ST HIGHLANDERS

TARLETON

"Never can tell," said Jake gloomily.

Colonel Brandon had chosen a hillock from which to direct his Second Spartans. He waved the signalers over. From this vantage, Lem could see in all directions. Next to them was Roebuck's Battalion. Colonel Roebuck was returning from the Continental battleline, riding a steadfast bay. He cantered along his company offering encouragement. Cheers were raised. Other battalions up and down the field added to the ovation.

The sun crested Thicketty Mountain. Awash in its yellow rays, a company of green-clad, feather-helmeted dragoons spilled from the forests where Green River Road met the tree-dotted fields of the cow pens. It was the very place Major McJunkin had met up with Lem and James Park yesterday, barely four hundred yards distant. Lem could even see Hiram Saunders' cabin off to the right beyond a copse of trees. A moment of terror rooted him to the spot as he realized his situation was at once dire and genuine.

He was smacked on the cheek. "Boy! Don't be frettin' what can't be stopped. Them British have come, and that's a fact. Best you live up to it!" Lem's trepidation subsided as Jake's gray eyes, filled with an inner fire, found his. "That's better, lad. Stick with me, now. I know what to do to keep us alive. That goes for the rest of ye too. Don't forget—we must stick each to the other!"

Chand and Gilly had gathered around, dread chalking their skin. Lem wondered if that's how he looked to them. Of the four, only Jake remained calm and focused. When the old man stepped back, Lem could see that many redcoats had formed lines behind the dragoons. The British crawled across the field like ants from a ruined nest.

"Colorful, ain't they?" Jake's voice sounded stressed. "Look to the one at the front of it all, prancing like a mallard drake. That there be the Bloody Scout in the flesh!"

Lem quickly picked out the man from his fellows, astride a tall black horse and wearing a helmet sporting voluptuous plumes beyond any worn by his men. So. This was the enemy. A man like any other, only better clad than most—and relatively young. Tarleton appeared to be yelling orders. Of a sudden, the infantry dropped their packs and blanket rolls. At the same time, the Green Dragoons split into two units, each of roughly fifty horsemen. A team trotted to either flank, positioning themselves to protect the foot soldiers from a cavalry charge. Despair was edging back into Lem's thoughts. Hair on his nape and along his arms stood on end as a roar swelled from the steadily advancing British Legion.

Behind him, General Morgan rode the line of militiamen once more, shouting, "They give us the British Halloo, boys. Let us give them the Indian Halloo!" The war-whoop, known so well by every frontiersman, swelled in defiance until it drowned out the British voices.

Lem heard the scattered *k-pow, k-pow,* of overly excited militiamen opening fire from behind trees. Some redcoats fired back, although they were out of musket range. So far, no one had fallen. The British came on without slowing.

"Sound *The Preparative!*" Colonel Brandon's bellow came from behind Lem's head. He had forgotten that the colonel and his advisors were so close. Chand and Jake were already heralding the command whilst he fumbled with his sticks. Distant drummers could be heard taking up the signal. When the drums stopped, calls of "Make ready!" echoed up and down the militia lines. Muskets were raised.

Led by Tarleton and a small party of cavalry, the British infantry had advanced to within four hundred yards of Lem's position. The militia ranks were moving forward on both sides, but not Colonel Brandon or his advisors. They remained steadfast upon the small knoll with a clear view down the field.

Brandon directed, "Shoot the epaulet men, the officers! Aim low! Pick them out! FIRE!"

Finally getting his sticks to hand, Lem joined Chand in a continuous battle drum roll. Although Jake's hands flew over his fife, the small instrument could not be heard above the tumult.

Carolina and Georgia Sharpshooters to either side of the field volleyed from behind tree trunks, a most unusual ploy. They must have been true marksmen, for each pop brought down a redcoat. Tarleton and his party had progressed ahead of their troops, probably hoping to better understand the American positions. Thus, the Bloody Scout suddenly found himself in a crossfire. This seemed to discomfit him, for he turned his horse and, followed by his party, plowed back through his lines out of harm's way. In classical British form, the redcoats continued up the field.

Moments later, Lem saw a detachment of dragoons break toward the Carolina militia. They fired at the horsemen and then retired slowly as Morgan had ordered. Around fifteen British assailants went down under the volley.

Now Lem discovered where Tarleton had gone. While his light infantry had been advancing on the left, the two three-pounder cannons had been wheeled forward. One now sat beside the infantry; the other was drawn up next to a hearty group of fusiliers. The green dragoons and legion calvary still covered both flanks.

For the first time, Lem heard the boom and felt the concussion of cannon fire. Even at greater than a hundred yards distant, the sheer power whuffed against his chest and rang in his ears.

"They're firing up the hill at Howard's Continentals along the ridge," bawled Jake. "Must be trying to break 'em up.

Them's our fallback point!" His eyes were filled with terror.

Lem swallowed his fear. "What do we do?"

"Stand fast, boy!" Lem's knees could barely sustain him as it was. He was going nowhere. With supreme effort, he quelled his shaking.

The air was rent with sporadic bursts from Pickens' regular militia. It recalled to Lem the sound of corn kernels popping inside a hot kettle. As instructed by General Dan, they fired and dropped back to allow the ones behind a chance. Lem noticed the sharpshooters followed the same pattern, with the effect that the skirmish lines gradually moved backward as the British advanced up the field—toward Lem!

"Looks like we've gotta move!" Jake stuffed his fife into his jacket. "Get ready!"

Lem found himself surrounded by Gilly, Chand, and Jake—front and center of the oncoming British Legion. The sharpshooters were backing towards them. Cannon fire continued to pound Howard's Continentals.

Then, as if General Morgan's will settled over the field, the sharpshooters stopped retreating and laid heavy fire into the British front. Countless men went down, and many of those wore epaulets.

Disorder had come to the redcoats, their advance faltering scarcely a hundred yards away. The British reformed quickly. Stepping over their fallen comrades, they again advanced, to their credit.

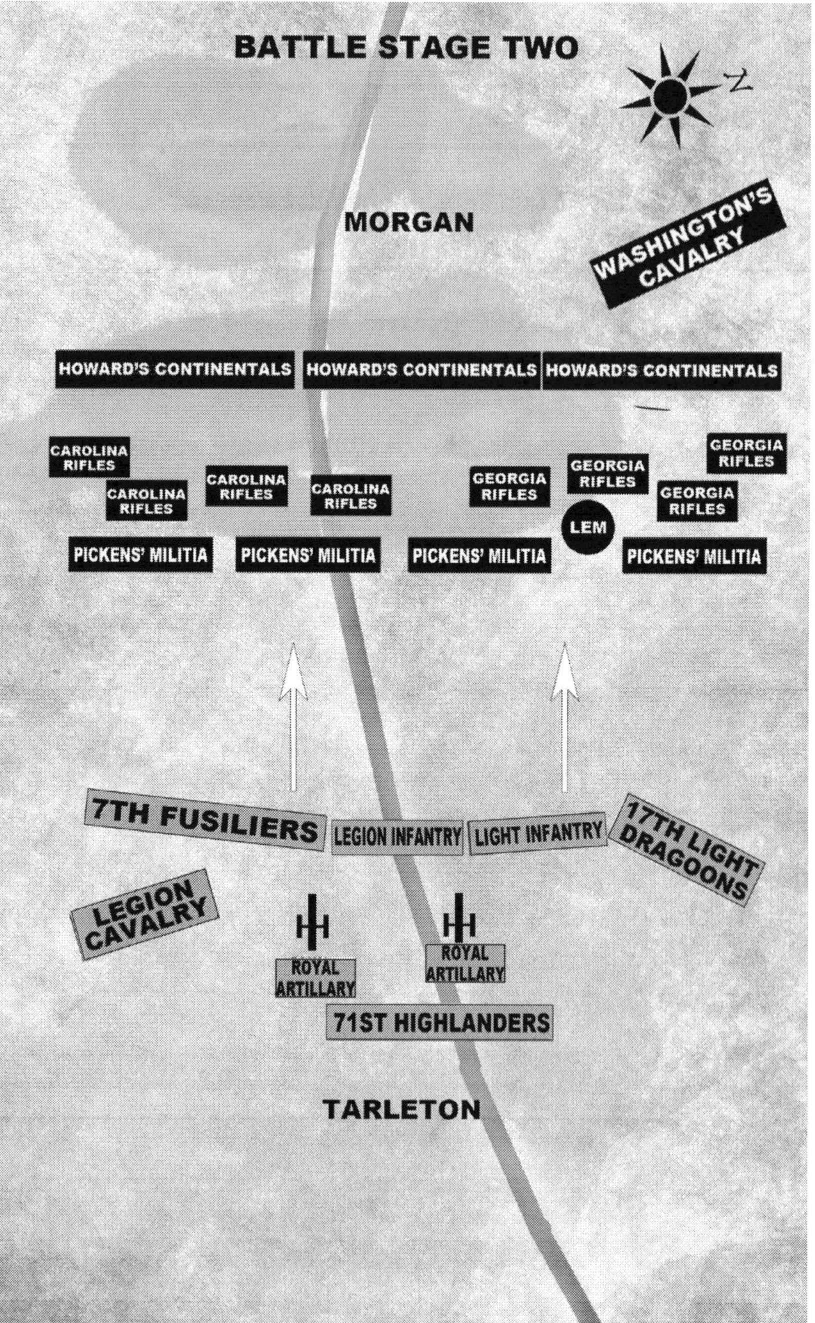
BATTLE STAGE TWO
N
MORGAN
WASHINGTON'S CAVALRY
HOWARD'S CONTINENTALS
HOWARD'S CONTINENTALS
HOWARD'S CONTINENTALS
CAROLINA RIFLES
CAROLINA RIFLES
CAROLINA RIFLES
CAROLINA RIFLES
GEORGIA RIFLES
GEORGIA RIFLES
GEORGIA RIFLES
GEORGIA RIFLES
LEM
PICKENS' MILITIA
PICKENS' MILITIA
PICKENS' MILITIA
PICKENS' MILITIA
7TH FUSILIERS
LEGION INFANTRY
LIGHT INFANTRY
17TH LIGHT DRAGOONS
LEGION CAVALRY
ROYAL ARTILLARY
ROYAL ARTILLARY
71ST HIGHLANDERS
TARLETON

This time, the sharpshooters could not hold. They broke for Pickens' mainline, swarming around Lem. The three musicians and the flagman found themselves caught in what seemed a rout. Suddenly, the sharpshooters stopped to reload, not fifty yards behind Picken's men.

"Don't just stand there, boy! RUN!" Jake grabbed Lem's arm and spun him around. The British must have believed victory was at hand, for they were now giving chase to the retreating militia, letting up a thunderous roar as they came.

"Hurry, boys!" To Lem's amazement, Jake had outstripped him. Of course, Jake wasn't encumbered by a heavy drum or carrying a flag. Nevertheless, Lem's legs pounded faster than ever—as did his heart.

Pickens' men opened ranks to let Colonel Brandon and his officers, musicians, and flags through. Spent sharpshooters, both Carolinians and Georgians, had now reloaded and joined the stalwart skirmish line. Lem and his fellow signalers crossed through just in time. Pickens' militia laid out a solid volley.

Trying to catch his breath, Lem saw the British lines falter against the hail of bullets. Many a redcoat suffered destruction of flesh and bone at such close quarters. The horrible screams of the dying on both sides and the images of mutilation seared into Lem's memory. Everywhere he looked, the fallen writhed in blood and gore. Yet, the militiamen held their ground amid the chaos.

"Take a hand to yer hatchet, boy!" Jake was shaking Lem's shoulder roughly. Events around him seemed to be moving slowly, even his own fingers as they unlimbered the tomahawk.

A cluster of British foot soldiers, who had broken away from the main front, was rushing forward with bayonets. They were joined by a unit of Green Dragoons, swords raking Pickens' militia to protect their infantry from additional fire.

Out of the smokey haze, a youth of perhaps sixteen rushed toward Lem, face a mask of intense hatred.

Lem froze.

"LEM! LOOK OUT!" Lem was thrust aside, drum entangling his legs. Twisting as he fell, he saw the young redcoat make a thrust. The bayonet point glistened wetly in the sunlight where it protruded from James Park's back. Park sank to his knees, then toppled sideways. The redcoat, tricorn askew, struggled to extract his bayonet from Park's body.

Lem's body was kindled to wrath. Such was its fervor, his vision reddened. Casting aside the drum, he scrambled to his feet and sank his tomahawk into the redcoat's forehead. For the barest instant, the man's eyes locked with Lem's before he crumpled lifelessly to the ground. Unreasoning, Lem reached down to wrench the redcoat's rifle from his death grip, snapping several fingers. When the bayonet still would not come free of James' body, he discovered that the sergeant had the barrel clamped firmly in his hands. James was staring up at him, gasping for breath.

Seeing no further threat nearby, Lem dropped to his knees in a pool of his friend's blood. He let go of the rifle, which brought agony to James' profoundly creased face.

"L-Lem. Me time's come." His once deep voice came only in gasps. "Would that I could've spared you the killin'…vengeance be mine, sayeth the Lord." Park's body was wracked by coughing. Blood bubbled from his mouth. When he finally continued, Lem had to bring his ear close. "'Tis fittin'…me old life be put down for yours. Grieve not, for mine has been…joy…full…." The sergeant's body gave a spasm, and one final breath rattled from his lips.

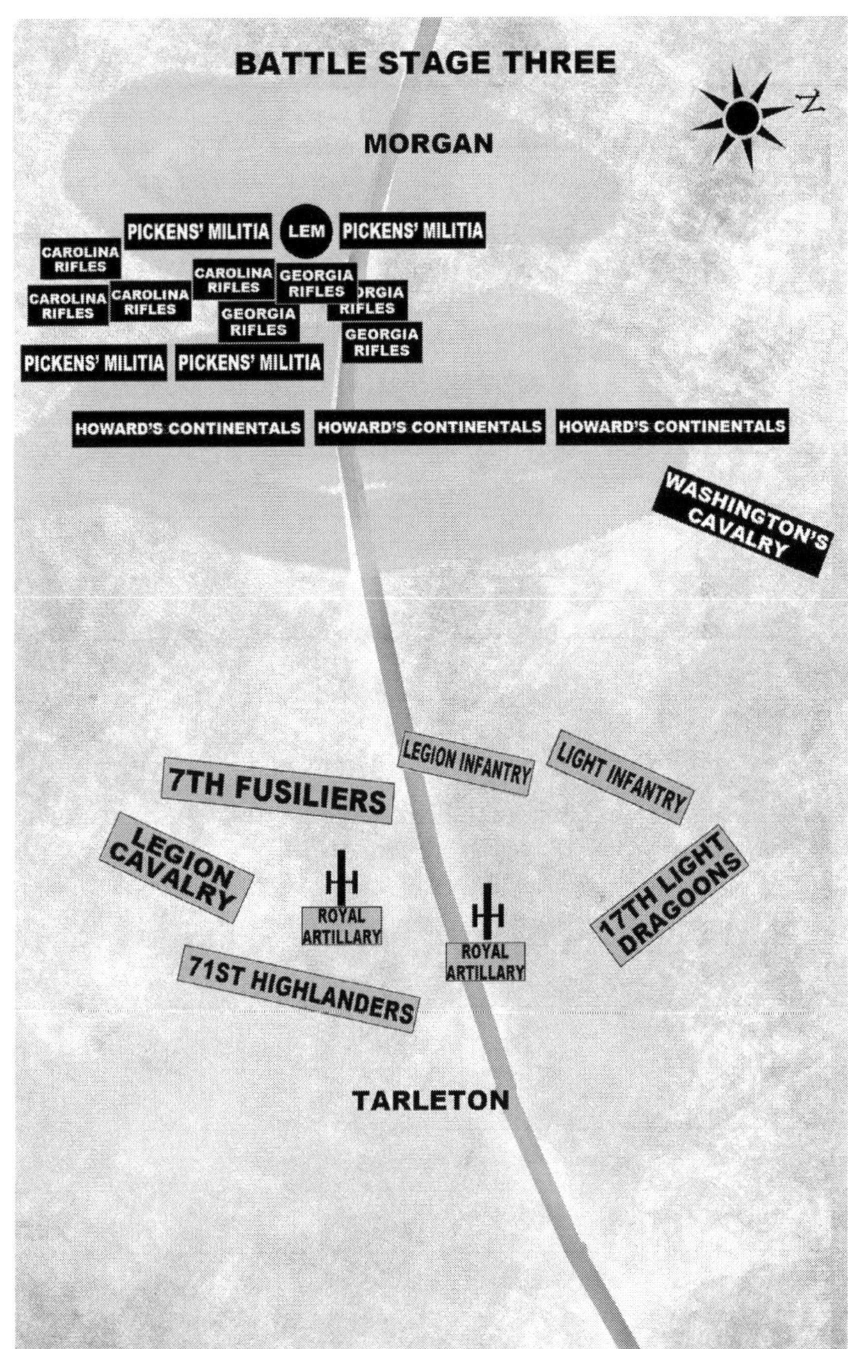
BATTLE STAGE THREE
MORGAN
PICKENS' MILITIA
LEM
PICKENS' MILITIA
CAROLINA RIFLES
CAROLINA RIFLES
GEORGIA RIFLES
CAROLINA RIFLES
CAROLINA RIFLES
GEORGIA RIFLES
GEORGIA RIFLES
PICKENS' MILITIA
PICKENS' MILITIA
HOWARD'S CONTINENTALS
HOWARD'S CONTINENTALS
HOWARD'S CONTINENTALS
WASHINGTON'S CAVALRY
LEGION INFANTRY
LIGHT INFANTRY
7TH FUSILIERS
LEGION CAVALRY
ROYAL ARTILLARY
ROYAL ARTILLARY
17TH LIGHT DRAGOONS
71ST HIGHLANDERS
TARLETON

As quickly as the rage had come uponst him, it left Lem shaky and sick. He turned his head away from Park's fixed stare and retched, stomach contents splattering the dead redcoat's jacket.

Reason must have fled for a short time. Lem only knew he had been laid next to his drum. There were many legs all around and voices to match.

None of them overrode that of General Dan. "See, you? Banny's men falter upon the field. They fail of strength and spirit. Go forth and press our advantage!"

Orders were issued, and drums rolled, the playing of which Lem was not a part. The legs around him dispersed. He sat up and drew several gulps from his canteen. This helped to clear his head, so he chanced to stand. Looking about, he discovered that he was at the crest of the field with Howard's Continental regulars. Someone had moved him nearly a hundred yards up the hill away from the British. He could see Pickens' militia, including his own company—there was Gilly with the flag—in apparent retreat toward the mountains.

As Lem tried to gather his wits, a hawk-faced officer riding a warhorse galloped toward the Continental line yelling, "To me, to me!" There were chants of "Pickens…Pickens," and the militiamen immediately turned, reformed lines, and headed back toward the British Legion.

This was a signal. Colonel Washington's cavalry raced around the slope to Lem's left, skirting Pickens' line to engage the flank of the irresolute British. With Patriot horsemen hot upon their tails, a flight of Green Dragoons, swords slashing, brushed across Pickens' men to prevent their firing at the confounded British foot soldiers. Washington's cavalry was in heated pursuit, further hindering a concerted volley from the American militia.

Drum signals roared. As a unified force, Pickens' men swept

toward Lem reloading muskets as they came. Folding through and around Howard's Continentals, they cleared the killing field. It was just as General Morgan had planned. The militia had given their three shots and dropped behind the Continentals for protection. Now the enemy faced a deadly volley.

Meanwhile, the British infantry had awakened from their indecisiveness, marching toward the waiting Continentals. At this moment, Colonel Pickens' men, now reloaded and full of wrath, swarmed over the hill to bolster the American front. The full force of the Continentals, including the horse soldiers and irregulars were now engaging Tarleton's legion. Men fighting and dying, flintlocks popping, drums and fifes playing, and blasts from the three-pounders made a great cacophony in the early morning.

Lem stood near General Morgan, his advisors, messengers—and a younger drummer boy. The lad was sitting upon his drum at Morgan's feet, grasping his knees in a hug. Their eyes met across the hilltop. The boy could be no more than nine years old, yet his mien was that of a withered old man, haunted. Lem understood the feeling. Dragging his view back to the raging battle, he firmly shut the door of pity that had opened for the lad. There was nothing he could do.

For a while, victory hung in the balance. The British were, after all, crack troops and would not be easily vanquished. They struggled to maintain their lines, but Washington's cavalry turned about and charged down the remaining dragoons who were guarding the British forward infantry. There was much slashing and stabbing of hand-to-hand combat. Limbs were shorn. Guts spilled. Screams of agony lifted above the mayhem. Tarleton's legion ground to a halt.

Just then, Morgan roared, "Face about boys! Give them one good fire, and the victory is ours!"

Colonel Howard issued the order to "Charge!"

Still grasping his tomahawk, Lem set his feet to moving along with the throng of nearly eight hundred mixed soldieries, straight at the British line. Washington's cavalry dispersed the dragoons then turned once more to come at the British rearguard. With no protection from their horsemen, the British infantry faltered…and surrendered.

Lem, furious over the loss of James Park, took up the sudden plea of many blood-lusting Americans, "TARLETON'S QUARTERS!" Show no mercy! The slaughter of the remaining British legionnaires hung in the balance.

It was then that Morgan, Washington, Howard, McJunkin, Roebuck, Brandon, and many other officers took the field and demanded "mercy." Lem couldn't hear all the words, but the work of slaughter was averted. Murmurs he did hear were those of "for the best…more honorable than the bloody enemy…enough killing for one day…" and the like. Lem had seen enough death and was glad when the swords of British officers were surrendered to their counterparts in the American forces.

The field was beginning to calm when a scuffle started at the back of the British lines. The two cannons were being carted away by their firing teams. These carts were guarded by the remainder of the Green Dragoons. Tarleton himself led the retreat, surrounded by a handful of mounted officers.

Colonel Washington noticed this quiet departure, for his

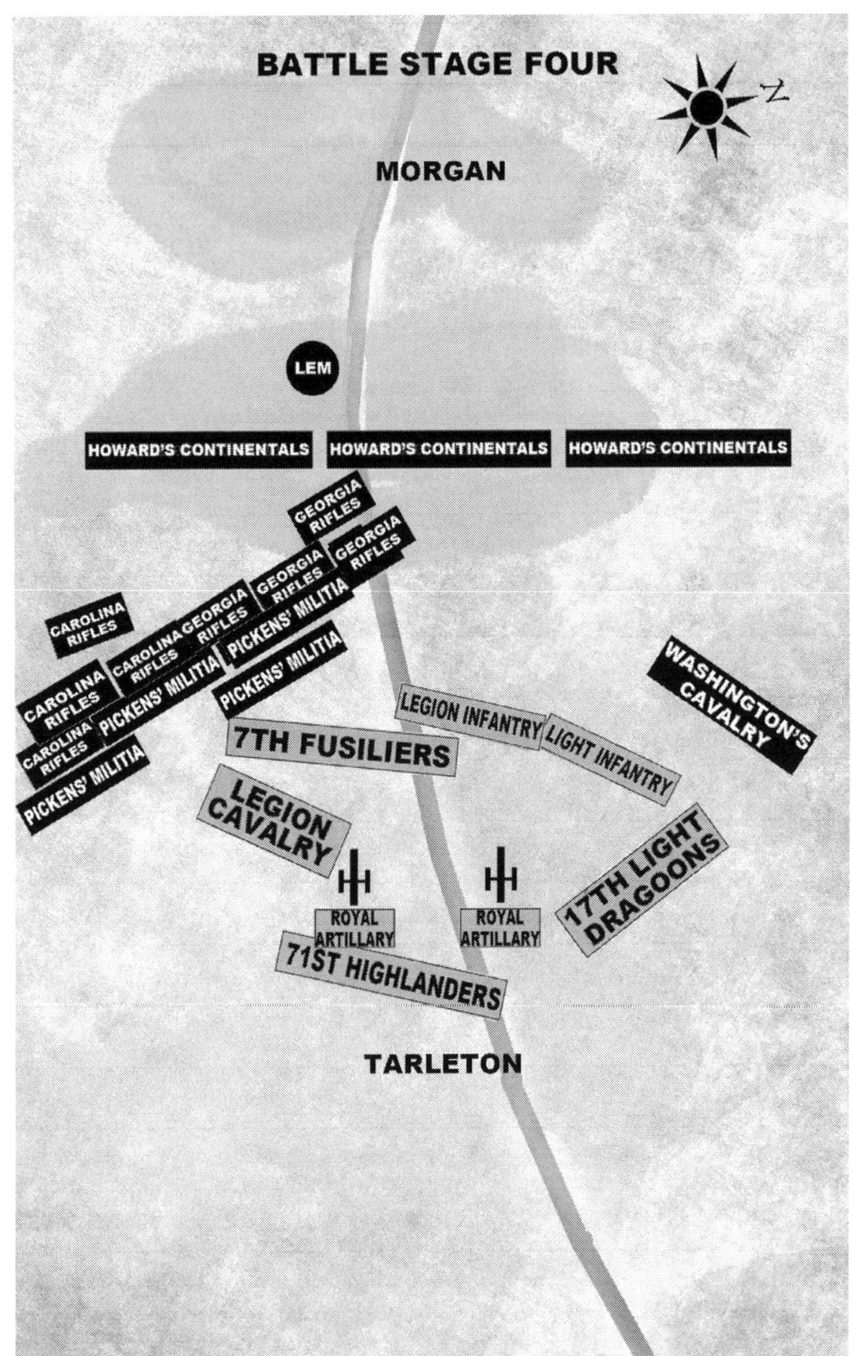
BATTLE STAGE FOUR
N
MORGAN
LEM
HOWARD'S CONTINENTALS
HOWARD'S CONTINENTALS
HOWARD'S CONTINENTALS
GEORGIA RIFLES
GEORGIA RIFLES
GEORGIA RIFLES
GEORGIA RIFLES
GEORGIA RIFLES
CAROLINA RIFLES
CAROLINA RIFLES
CAROLINA RIFLES
CAROLINA RIFLES
PICKENS' MILITIA
PICKENS' MILITIA
PICKENS' MILITIA
PICKENS' MILITIA
WASHINGTON'S CAVALRY
LEGION INFANTRY
LIGHT INFANTRY
7TH FUSILIERS
LEGION CAVALRY
17TH LIGHT DRAGOONS
ROYAL ARTILLARY
ROYAL ARTILLARY
71ST HIGHLANDERS
TARLETON

arms were gesturing and pointing. He peeled away, probably expecting more than a few of his cavalry to follow, but they must not have heard his call. Only a handful chased after him to overtake the three-pounders and the enemy foes. One amongst them was a negro boy, younger than Lem, probably Washington's manservant.

Tarleton and several of his officers heard Washington's approach and turned to meet his charge. To Lem's horror, one of the officers drove his horse at Washington and brought down a mighty thrust of his sword. Washington parried the stroke, but his blade shattered at the hilt. Tarleton noticed this, for he plowed into the duelers' midst to strike directly at Washington. The American colonel received the blow on the remainder of his sword's hilt. The negro boy, standing in his white steed's saddle, drew a pistol from his coat and fired at Tarleton from about ten paces. The shoulder of Tarleton's green jacket ripped, startling the Legion commander.

Mesmerized, Lem continued to watch as other American cavalrymen, at last, joined the fray. Upon seeing the oncoming danger, Tarleton drew his pistol and gave a parting shot at Washington. The bullet dropped the colonel's horse. For a moment, Lem could not see what had happened. Then, Washington leaped upon another riderless mount and took out after the departing enemy. His cavalry rallied and gave chase. The negro boy goaded his horse to follow. The last Lem saw of the infamous Colonel "Bloody Ban" Tarleton and his remaining Green Dragoons were their tails vanishing down Green River Road toward Grindall's. The bulk of Colonel Washington's cavalry and irregular horsemen were in close pursuit.

"Tis done and done." Jake sidled up to Lem. "We've made it through. Didn't take too long neither. Barely an hour, mind you." His crinkled features gazed out upon the gory aftermath.

Lem was incredulous. “Didst you say but a single hour? Tis all?” The affair seemed to have taken days. Individual acts played through his thoughts. Faces in the rictus of death. Limbs parted from their owners. Bodies blown to smithereens. His encounter with a young redcoat wearing a tricorn—head and hat split nearly twain by Lem’s own hand. He shuddered.

“Come along, now. There’s still much to be done. Pick up your drum.” Jake placed a withered hand upon his shoulder.

Slinging the instrument back into place against his hip, Lem caught movement out of the corner of his eye. He paused to look. General Morgan, radiant with joy, had raised up the little drummer boy to kiss him. Somehow, this blurred Lem’s vision.

“None of that, now,” said Chand. “I left Gilly back with Roebuck’s company and happened to overhear some preliminary totals.” He paused.

Lem wiped a sleeve across his eyes.

“Don’t keep us in suspense!” Jake kicked out as if to catch Chand in the shin.

“Hold yer horses! I’m telling. Twelve kilt, sixty-one wounded. No officers of rank in the bunch. Took near five hundred prisoners. At least eighty British kilt. Shy of two hundred wounded. Cotched twenty-seven commissioned officers. T’aint heard nothing about the trophies yet, but hundreds of muskets, the two three-pounders, and a bunch of wagons are all just standing on the field awaiting our pleasure!”

“I’d say having all that power don’t mean a thing if you ain’t got the discipline to use it wisely,” Jake said, scrunching his features as if to look clever. “Them British had everything they needed to win the day excepting one thing.” He left that statement hanging in the air.

“Do tell!” demanded Chand.

"Aye, Jake. Tell us." Lem saw the smirk on the oldster's lips despite the gray beard trying to engulf them and knew the answer had to be good.

"Modesty."

"Modesty?" both Lem and Chand asked together.

"Modesty! Haughty lunatics like Bloody Tarleton and his Lord Earl Cornwallis cannot believe that a bunch of uneducated backwoodsmen can stand against the British Empire. We've shown 'em time and again, but they taint never learnt! Twill be their undoing!"

23

The Aftermath

Lem allowed Jake and Chand to steer him down Green River Road toward the baggage carts. Already a steady stream of wagons and men were exiting the battlefield and cutting along a northeastward track toward Cherokee Ford on the Broad. At least a hundred downcast redcoats, in close two-by-two formation, were encircled by cavalry guards. Scattered amongst them were a few tall plumes of green. Lem supposed General Dan had ordered the army repair to the ford with the prisoners.

Against a backdrop of pine-clad foothills were two large beige tents. From within their flaps came moans of pain and cries of agony. Lem was unsuccessful at blocking out these visages of the recent battle. Even Jake, a veteran of many clashes, averted his gaze. Chand went pale.

"Now comes the gruesome part," Jake muttered.

Lem pondered the choice of words. "What mean you?"

"Burial of the honored dead, of course." When the old drummer continued, it was in a subdued tone, "From the looks of it, we'll need bury the enemy dead as well. Ye don't see none of them Britons hanging about to speed the process, do ye? Methinks them prisoners should do the dirty deed."

Lem had never considered disposal of the dead as an activity of war. Chand bent over abruptly, his drum giving off odd notes as it hit the ground. His demeanor was green-tinged when he finally straightened.

"Don't take it so hard, Chand. It'll be over before ye know it. Can't have our departed left to the buzzards. Best we say a proper word over 'em and let 'em rest in peace."

It almost seemed Jake had been overheard. The three signalers had to step from the road as a wagonload of redcoat bodies went past. Behind the wagon walked a dozen or so British infantry guarded by a small unit of Continental foot soldiers. It was a solemn affair. The musicians allowed the wagon and men to round the bend before following.

A few minutes later, the trio rounded the bend themselves and approached a long string of horses picketed beside the road. Many attendants were feeding, watering, grooming—even doctoring the beasts. Lem saw a man raise a crock canteen and pour a clear liquid into a gaping sword wound on the rump of a seventeen-hand bay. The horse squealed and bucked. The man's breath whooshed from his lungs as the distressed animal squashed him against the chestnut gelding next in line. Muttering curses, he staggered from between the horses, arms wrapped about his chest.

"I'm so naive," muttered Lem. "This day, I've seen suffering beyond imagining, both man and beast. How can war ever be justifiable?"

"Nary a one is ever more than naive when it comes to war, Lem," said Jake. "I've seen my share of battles, and none of 'em was the same. Every fight showed me new horrors of what man can and will do to his fellow man. There's no pride in being a veteran. All it truly means is I survived where many others fell. Justify war? There's no justifying war. When you can't stand by no longer and watch your friends and family suffer, then…hey…ain't that your wagon over yonder parked with all them others?"

Lem shielded his eyes against the sun to see where Jake was pointing. "Aye!" He quickened his pace, drum slamming against his thigh. Amadahy rounded the tailgate just as he arrived. She flung herself into his arms, sobbing.

"Oh, Lem. Sukey's dead!"

At first, he didn't register her words. "Dead?"

"She fell to stray ball. Glanced off tree. Caught her in temple. I'm so sorry, Lem." Her arms dropped helplessly to her sides. Chand and Jake, full of commiseration, were offering condolences to him and *Sallie.*

For a while, Lem was unable to speak. Finally, he managed, "Where is she now, Sallie?"

"They buried her during fight. Many of us with wagons—we dug trenches. She in one. Facing mountains. I take…I'll take you there."

Lem saw his two comrades exchange questioning glances over Sallie's oddly clipped phrases. He covered, "Please, Sallie. I know 'tis hard to speak of it, and there's no need. Simply take me to her." Containing his grief, he told Jake and Chand, "I must attend to Sukey, for no one else will. From there, I shall take Sallie home."

"Tis the lay of it, Lem. I don't blame ye for going. You've had a sore time and more ahead, I suspect. Me and Chand, we'll pay our respects at the grave of your servant woman. She was a good'un. Loyal. When we've done for her, we'll help ye find Colonel Brandon or Major McJunkin back at the camp, so's you can take your leave of them."

"Come, Sallie. Take us forth." Amadahy gripped Lem's elbow and led him off. The others trailed in silence. She kept to the road for about thirty yards, then steered them onto a newly worn footpath up through a sparse forest of long-needled pines.

When they crested the hill, the pines faded into a panoramic view of the Blue Ridge, just as Sallie had described. Halfway down the other side was a gaping furrow lined with red dirt. A mix of some forty-odd American soldiers and British prisoners were digging, laying bodies, and covering the remains. How would he find Sukey?

As if reading Lem's thoughts, Chand leaned down to say, "Tis not vital to discover her resting place. Her soul is of the matter now. Let us go down and speak words over her in general, and if a few of them spills onto others, so be it."

Amadahy brought them down to a freshly covered portion of the trench. She pointed.

Kneeling, Lem dropped his hat next to his knee and placed both hands in the loose dirt. "Oh Lord God, I beg you, see to the gentle soul of Sukey Farnandis, mother of her family and of mine. Ever faithful in her service, ever steadfast in her devotion to Thee." He paused, for his chest had constricted. Hands rested on his shoulders. When at last he could loosen his tongue, he said, "O' Great African Queen, I shan't forget you!" He took his hat in hand and struggled to his feet.

"Them's fine words, Lem. Mighty fine." Jake clapped him on the back.

Lem allowed himself to be guided to the wagon. Old Bo, tied off to a tree beside it, brayed at the sight of his master, shaking his great muzzle in delight. Lem rushed over, grasped the mule around the neck, and buried his face in coarse hair. The others gave him privacy whilst busying themselves around the wagon. They were preparing it for the return journey by offloading regimental sundries onto other carts.

Once done, Amadahy tapped his shoulder. He stepped back to allow Chand and Jake to tighten Bo's cinch. That done, the musicians stowed the drums aboard and sat on the backend with legs dangling. Lem and Amadahy seated themselves on the bench. Lem took the reins, gave them a shake, and coaxed Old Bo into the road. The mule must have realized the wagon was pointed toward home, for he stepped off at a sturdy pace. It seemed some things never changed.

The return to the Second Spartan encampment took only a few minutes despite going against a steady stream of soldiers, wagons, carts, and litters. Lem finally turned Bo across the battlefield, carefully rounding clumps of working legionnaires. He did not want to ponder their task at hand. Reaching the entrance to the camp, he saw that fires had been kicked out, tents struck, and equipment removed. Only a few officers' quarters remained at the end of the central path.

Sergeant Richard Brandon sat on a log in front of his tent, talking to a ring of other officers as Lem drove the wagon alongside. "Saints be praised! If it ain't Lem the Drummer! We wondered what became of ye, boy!"

"Lemuel and Sallie!" Major McJunkin extricated himself from the group and came over to assist them down from the wagon. He hugged them both.

Exuberant soldiers led by Jake and Chand surrounded the Farnandis siblings. Amadahy seemed taken aback by all the attention, for she seemed to fold in on herself. It was a celebration of victory for which Lem had no hankering.

McJunkin must have noticed something in the young man's demeanor to that effect. "So very sorry to hear of Park's demise," he ventured. "Witnesses were few as the engagement was hot at the time. Attention was spread thin. Though it pains you, honor us with your answer. Did James Park die well?" Silence descended as all awaited Lem's answer.

Lem surveyed the earnest faces, gleaning courage from them all. At last, he said, "Sergeant James Obadiah Park threw himself bodily upon the upthrust saber presented by a redcoat foe, thus saving me of that selfsame demise. I forthwith cleaved the skull of that red devil with me own tomahawk in just reprisal." A fair portion of bile had risen in Lem at the telling.

"Give them cups!" Colonel Brandon had apparently heard the witness, for he strode into the group with a small cask under his arm. Cups found their ways into all hands present, and the colonel himself poured rum rations for each. Once done, he sat the jug between his feet and raised a toast. "This day has seen many fall uponst the field in the name of Liberty, none of more passion than Sergeant Park. I declare his death a worthy sacrifice to that moral cause and implore Lem Farnandis to honor him by living well."

All present raised cups in accord, making comments of "...hear, hear...so be it...to Park...James Park...."

Once the toasting had finished, Lem asked, "Colonel Brandon, sir?"

"Aye?"

"I beg indulgence, sir. Must that I bring Sallie and myself home. Sergeant Park reported to me yesterday that my father and one of my brothers have been slain. He relayed no knowledge concerning the remainder of my family, only that our house had been burned and my father's store looted. May I take my leave, sir?"

"I heard tell of this also, young Lem. Godspeed in your journey, and may you find the remainder of your family in His succor."

What followed went by quickly. Lem's gear was retrieved from

Sergeant Brandon's tent. An officer he did not recognize reloaded the Brown Bess from a fresh paper cartridge. The rifle was stowed under the wagon bench within handy reach. A sack of victuals was loaded, enough to sustain him and Sallie for several days of travel. Blankets were spared on their behalf. A small bag of grain was laid in for Old Bo. In short order, the final goodbyes came.

Chand struggled to speak, but words would not come. He sufficed with giving Lem an honest hug. Lem gave him a wan smile.

Jake said, "For me own part, it's been a pleasure serving with ye. You're a man now—a veteran to boot. Don't let no one tell you different!"

Lem noticed that Major McJunkin had disappeared while the rest had their say. Now he returned, leading Bonnie. Lem had utterly forgotten the horse! McJunkin tethered her reins to the back of the wagon and pressed a man to retrieve her saddle and blankets. While that was being done, the major pushed a small leather pouch into Lem's palm. "A few coins to smooth the roughness to come, young Lemuel. Tis my fair hope you and your lovely sister, *Sallie,* will find your kin safe. If ever I make my way back through Grindall's, I'll expect to find a warm welcome at the Farnandis hearth." His countenance broke, and he gathered them into a firm hug.

Once released, Lem and Amadahy averted their eyes as they clambered aboard the wagon. It took no shaking or whistles or clucks for Old Bo to make a start this time. Upon his own cognizance, the mule turned toward Green River Road.

Lem called over his shoulder, "Major, sir, you and yours shall find more than a warm welcome at the Farnandis home!"

"Major Joseph *Caldwell* McJunkin at your service!" Lem hid a smile as he recollected the major's pride in his middle name.

Unexpectedly, a fife and drum tune struck up. Lem and Amadahy looked back to see Chand and Jake playing animatedly. All the militia officers were at unanimous salute.

24

The Road Home

Passing through the field, Lem noticed most of the grass had been churned under. Here and there were deep brown stains. Wagons in various shapes and sizes were scattered across the landscape, and soldiers performed grizzly tasks with the bodies in addition to retrieving munitions. Lem and Amadahy saw more than they wished, no matter which direction they looked. Already buzzards circled on high upon the midmorning.

Old Bo drew them near the Saunders cabin. The shutters to either side of the front door were flung open. The door itself was missing. It seemed the former home beheld the battlefield in wide-eyed horror. Lem shook the reins in hopes of coaxing the mule to move faster. It was a fruitless exercise. Even Bo sensed the musk of depression riding the air, plodding forlornly with head drooping low.

Once, they passed a wolf pit surrounded by forlorn Legion soldiers, again guarded by a contingent of Patriots. Lem had helped dig pits like this back home. They would place sharpened cane spears in the bottom, throw in offal from cow or pig butchering as bait, then cover the top of the hole with a flimsy mesh of limbs concealed by leaves and dirt. The smell of blood would attract wolves. If the beasts fell in, they would be impaled by the cane spears. This wolf pit was full of British deceased. Already the stench of death infused the area, so pungent Lem could almost taste it. He tried again to persuade the mule to a livelier pace, but Old Bo still had none of it. Whether slowly or naught, Lem was glad to leave the scene of horror behind.

Green River Road was much the same as the previous day. Dismal, hilly, gullied, and intersected by streams. Through it all, Bo plodded. Occasionally, they would pass an individual or small group of folks heading toward the cow pens. To the person, they were destitute, carrying all they owned upon their backs. Each time, Lem reached for the rifle and laid it out upon his knees in plain view. He had no intention of falling prey to needy robbers.

The day wore into late afternoon. A cold breeze wound through the forest. When they came to the stream where Lem saved Park's life, he related the story of firing at the green dragoon and shooting off his plume. Amadahy responded to the tale by favoring Lem with a prideful look. His chest swelled.

Bo's struggle to draw the wagon through the muddy tracks at the crick became a wearing battle. Lem's shoulders ached from the mule's testing of the reins. Amadahy, anxiety written on her features, strained to stay seated on the jostling bench. Once across, they reached Thicketty Fort without further mishap. They decided to pull off for the night, grateful for the respite.

The structure and surrounding woods were abandoned. Lem unhitched Bo, staking the mule to forage sweet blades around the fort's open foundation. He and Amadahy retired to the log structure's hearth and built a small fire, Indian style. They wanted to avoid the notice of anyone traveling the main thoroughfare.

After a small meal of corn mush laced with a few wild onions, they wrapped in their blankets and slept on the wooden floor. Their repose was unbroken until sunlight streamed through the shutters. Lem felt refreshed for the first time since his birthday.

Amadahy, however, wore an anxious air. She thrust a plate with the cold remains of the mush into Lem's hands and disappeared out the door. By the time Lem finished his meager fare, repacked his kit, and exited the fort, she had Old Bo hitched.

"Let us be gone, Lem!" She held the reins while he climbed up to join her. Once he sat, she released the brake and clucked Old Bo into a lively trot back toward the road.

"For Heaven's sake, Sallie! What bee's crawled under your bonnet?" Holding the reins in one hand, Amadahy jerked her bonnet from her head and beat it against the side of the wagon. Lem laughed. "You've not heard that expression?"

"Expression? What is this—expression?" She handed the reins off to Lem to restore her hat to her head.

"It means that something is bothering you."

"Aye, tis true." She silently gauged him, probably to see if he would take her next statement seriously. "I wish to return to Grindall's as soon as may be—to search for my family."

"I've been thinking upon this matter for some time now. James—" Lem's voice cracked. "—James received a report that my home was raised, and my father and oldest brother left for the worms." He paused, gathering fortitude to finish the telling. "The scouts that made the discovery buried their bodies where they lay. I dare not seek a tolerable situation upon our return for fear my hopes will be dashed."

Amadahy draped an arm over his shoulder. While no more than a sisterly act, her nearness was at once comforting and fearsome.

Neither spoke for several miles.

Through the last morning hour, their only company was the little blackbirds that hung around during the winter whilst most others of feather left for warmer regions in the south. Once, a rabbit sprang across the road setting Bo to braying. Lem struggled to calm him, not pleased that the mule's complaints announced their presence throughout the forest.

Midday passed without seeing another traveler, so Lem began to relax. This stretch of the road was three hundred yards of a gentle downgrade with a bend to the left at the bottom. Bo appreciated the ease of it and settled into a lively gait. Lem counted the hours and realized they would make it back to the store before nightfall. Amadahy leaned on him contentedly.

Thus, Lem was distracted as Bo rounded the bend in the road. The mule came to an unexpected halt, which nearly unseated both wagoners. In the middle of the track was a mound of destroyed carts. Their cargo of furniture, clothing, and victuals had been despoiled. Sprawled this way and that was a handful of dead redcoats, some face down in the mud, others staring emptily at the sky. A warhorse had died horribly of a massive gut wound, his thrashing having crushed his green-helmeted rider. Another dozen men lay dead in jumbled disarray upon the carts and in the road. Their homespun attire yielded not of affiliation, whether Loyalist or Patriot.

The foremost corpse was a man both Lem and Amadahy recognized. It was the bloated form of Major Patrick "Tyger" Moore!

Amadahy gasped.

"Stay here!" Lem leaped down from the wagon carrying his Brown Bess, new bayonet aimed forward as he crept near the corpse of their former captor. The man, tall and heavy as Lem remembered, lay on his side, staring at nothing. Wet blood stained his shirt and pooled in the dirt beneath his chest. It had leaked from around the handle of a large knife protruding from the pit of his stomach. Lem chanced to prod at the lapel of Tyger Moore's waistcoat with the bayonet tip. Moore's body suddenly drew a labored breath, and its eyes locked upon Lem with naked hatred.

Amadahy screamed!

Overtaken by terror, Lem could do nothing but stare into those baleful orbs.

The mule ignorantly chewed at his bit, taking respite from his labors.

"Well, well. Iffin it ain't my old friend, Lem," Moore gurgled. "Looks like yer wish is about to come true. I've been done fer by me own. They's still hanging about, mores the pity. Waiting fer me death rattle, they is." The ruined man coughed, bloody spittle dripping from his lips. "'Spect I'll see ye and yer squaw done fer before I meet me Maker." A ghastly leer spread across Moore's face…and…remained forevermore.

While Lem focused on Tyger's corpse, two silent forms had edged between the wrecked carts.

"LEM!" shrieked Amadahy. Bonnie whinnied.

Hearing his name rend the air revitalized his sluggish limbs. Backpedaling from Moore's truly dead body, he tried to place distance between himself and these new threats.

"Lemuel, me lad," the red-nosed man to the right sing-songed. "Where you be a-going?" He was disheveled, encrusted with all manner of filth, his canvas jacket all but shredded. Lem recognized the pale, round features of Leftenant Moon Face.

The other man was dark-visaged, scruffy, and wore the garb of a backwoodsman. He reached down and casually plucked the large hunting knife from Tyger Moore's body, wiping the blood from the blade on his pants leg. "Shame the Major had to be so finicky about his service to the Crown. Best leader we had, this brother o' mine. Bloody Tarleton's favorite, he was. Sergeant Major John Moore, at yer service! Wouldn't expect ye to notice the resemblance, stoat that he was in comparison." The man paused his slow advance to strut like a rooster.

Moon Face supplied, "COCK-a-doodle-DO!"

Old Bo took notice and tried to back away against the wagon's brake. Bonnie reared, bringing her hoofs down against the tailgate with a crash. Amadahy expertly snapped the reins as she released the brake with her foot. The mule surged forward headlong into Moon Face. The corpulent man fell backward over Moore's body, slamming his head into the nearest cart's wheel. He screamed as Bo's plate-sized hooves repeatedly stomped both his and Moore's torsos. Mercifully, Moon Face expired from the trauma. Silence descended as the mule spent his ire. The stench of ruptured bowels filled the air.

"My God!" erupted John Moore. "Methinks they smell worse in death than in life after all!"

Something in those callous words stirred Lem's wrath. He cocked the Brown Bess, took aim, and fired in one fluid motion. John Moore was blasted from his feet. His lifeless body fetched up against a large wooden trunk. One of the trunk's brass clasps could be seen through the hole in his chest.

Lem sank to his knees and, for some time, could do naught save wretch. Dimly he was aware of Amadahy calming Bonnie. A canteen was offered. He took a swig, rinsed, and spat. The Indian girl forced him to take several more swallows. Laced with rum or no, the water tasted of iron.

"Brother?"

Lem looked up.

"Let us be on our way. The day grows short."

Indeed, shadows were now lengthening down the road, a fair indication of midafternoon. There was still a chance of attaining Grindall's before nightfall.

Lem guided the mule through the pileup of ruined carts, luggage, debris, and bodies on foot. Bonnie was nervous, pulling sporadically against her tethers. The mule, at almost twice the mare's weight, felt none of it.

The road's left shoulder was a ravine, and the right was a hillside—the perfect setting for an ambush. Lem tried in earnest to keep his mind on the task at hand. Whether or naught he wanted, he saw enough carnage to fathom that a major skirmish had there occurred between Tarleton's supply wagons and Patrick Moore's traitorous scouts. It struck Lem how befitting it was for Bloody Ban to lose his precious baggage convoy to the very hands he had entrusted the ruination of Grindall's.

Amadahy walked behind, picking through the discards and bodies for anything that might be useful. She shoved whatever she found into the back of the wagon. For Lem's part, he was not curious. It was enough to successfully guide Bo through the debris and around the blind curve without further mishap.

Amadahy returned to the wagon. By unspoken agreement, they climbed aboard, watchful as they continued their journey. The girl's stoic nature did much to settle Lem's churning thoughts. Her warmth next to him was more than a small comfort. Lem laid his arm over her shoulder, and she responded by snuggling against him. It felt…right.

25

Crossroads

Eventually, Lem began to recognize landmarks. A bent tree here, a thicket there. At long last, the Asbury crossroad came into view. It was nearly dusk, the shadows now stretching long before them, and the warmth of the setting sun diminished upon their backs. The coming night would be cloudless and cold under a waning moon.

Old Bo had sensed the familiarity of the road and was tugging against the reins. Bonnie had long since wearied of resisting her tether and was unaware of any chance of recompense. She followed placidly. Bo wanted his reward of sweet feed for a hard day's labor, and he knew it was nearby. Since there was yet enough light to proceed, Lem was determined to make the last mile down to Farnandis Feed, Seed, and Flour. T'was his fervent hope to find peaceful rest in that familiar place.

The landscape and the crossroads appeared deserted except for a half-dozen sizable woodpiles in Adam Goudelock's front yard. Lem had delivered many items to the Goudelock farm and never had there been strange heaps. Adam and his wife were usually such tidy people. The scene was most curious, though Lem felt no desire to find out more at this time. Amadahy told him she felt the same, so he prepared to give Bo his head.

Just then, a stout figure appeared in the door of the cabin. A shrill tone preceded the crunch of hurried footsteps as the form bustled across the yard. "Lem! Lemuel Farnandis! Speak ye to me, boy!" It was Mistress Hannah, Goudelock's wife. She hove up to the wagon, flustered, her cheeks bobbing as she puffed from the exertion. Stray red curls sprang from under her bonnet, framing a piteous glint in her brown eyes. "Methought, I recognized ye. Shore as shooting, tis Lemuel Farnandis, I said, and his…sister?"

"Aye, tis Sallie. Been a while since she rode with me on deliveries." Lem thought it best to keep clear of details. The Mistress Hannah, being Irish, reminded Lem closely of his own mother. The thought brought on a yearning for home.

"There's a good name! Sallie. All fetching in the manner of youth as I once was to boot. Would that we had time to get acquainted, but grave doings have been stirring hereabouts this afternoon. Heard tell from George Washington's cousin, Bill, that yestermorn there was a fight up at the cow pens! Good old Dan Morgan's done gave them British a devil of a whipping at long last! Since you're a-coming from over yon direction, mayhap you know some particulars?" She laid it as a question, peering up hopefully.

Lem recollected Mistress Hannah to be quite a gossip, but there seemed to be more to it this time. He looked at Amadahy, and they silently agreed not to fuel her vice. They hankered to be on their way.

"Nary a whit can I tell you, Mistress Hannah. Been returning from Thicketty all the day, and nary a soul did we see beyond a few birds and squirrels." It was an out-and-out lie, of course.

Amadahy remained silent, which drew a wary eye from Mistress Goudelock.

"Strange, that. Mighty strange! Bill Washington and another colonel—Andy Pickens—flew through here several hours back with a sizable cavalry unit. They was chasing after that rat of a British commander, Tarleton—*Bloody* Ban—they called him. Paaaaah!" She spat on the road and milled it with her buckled shoe. "That evil popinjay done took my husband!" When Lem and Amadahy didn't rise to the revelation, she doggedly continued, "Anyhow, Adam's been forced to guide them British demons to safety! Left the girls and me home, thanks be to God, but I'm afeared for my poor Adam. He's leading them fugitives down to Hamilton's Ford at the Broad. Overheard 'em say they were trying to meet up with that Earl Cornwallis at Turkey Creek. Oh, my poor, poor Adam! When Colonel Bill asked me where they went, I pointed down toward Grindall's. Oh, Lem, I shouldn't have done it, 'cepting I didn't want my poor husband kilt in the crossfire iffin the dirty British was caught!" She buried her face in her hands, sobbing.

Lem was torn between stepping down or remaining in his seat. Amadahy, meanwhile, rounded the wagon to give the distraught matron a warm embrace. Taking solace from the young maiden quelled her tears. With a shuddering breath, Hannah launched into her story again.

"Tarleton's raiders set fire to the last of their supply wagons right here in my yard and took off with Adam. They dropped a horde of negro waggoners on my doorstep—slaves purloined from plantations hereabouts to carry freight. Left naught for 'em to eat! Thankfully, the colonels took pity on the girls and me. Bill ordered the fires put out. Then, he saw to the care of the abandoned slaves. They were herded to the old encampment yonder for feeding and bedding." She flung her arm out to point the way, nearly swiping Amadahy in the chin. "Lemuel, iffin you come uponst Colonel Bill's fine Patriots on the road, I beg you, send 'em to Hamilton's Ford."

"Aye, Mistress Hannah, that I will." Lem was getting anxious, for twilight was upon them, and these were ill tidings. "Best we away."

Amadahy had returned to her place on the wagon. "Fair well, Mistress!"

Not waiting for Mistress Hannah to start up again, Lem called, "Gee, Bo. Gee, big boy." The rattle of the wagon increased as the mule was given liberty to set his own pace. Lem only hoped enough feed would be left in a barrel to scrape a ration for the faithful beast.

The wagon climbed the gentle incline toward the store in little more than a quarter-hour. Lem had to keep a firm hand upon the reins now to hold Bo in check. The log structure was a black smudge against the backdrop of dark pines. Despite the shadowy darkness, Bo drew the wagon alongside the dock without a misstep. He watched Lem expectantly, breath steaming into the chill night.

Amadahy crawled over the seat to rummage in the cargo. Lem stepped down, intent on entering the dark edifice of the open dock doors. He heard a few clicks as flint struck steel, and a wick was lit.

Amadahy held forth a brass candle lantern. "Take this, Lem. I have another." He gratefully accepted the lantern, impressed by her competence. She continued, "I shall release Bo and Bonnie whilst you discover what grain may be had. There stands a bucket of water. Perhaps tis still fresh enough. If so, I'll give it to them. Where shall I find the stall?" She struck another lantern and clamored down from the back of the wagon.

"You'll find it behind the store next to the woods. It stands alone, a roof hung over poles. There should be enough room for both beasts. Beyond is a rivulet from whence we take water. I'll join you with whatever feed I can suss out. Mind to your welfare." He watched as she began to remove Bo's harness, then retrieved his rifle from the bench.

Dread at the thought of entering his father's store under such circumstance brought alive every sound and shadow. Standing in the dock entrance, he played the lantern's light across the storeroom. A disturbed field mouse scuttled over his boot, extracting a startled exclamation.

"What happened?" Amadahy called out.

"'Tis fine. Naught but a mouse." Lem stepped inside only to discover that few feed barrels remained; overall, the warehouse was empty. He propped the Brown Bess against the door frame to free his hands.

Next, he reached over Bo's sweet-feed barrel for the grooming brush and hoof pick still hanging on their pegs. Of a sudden, scratching noises arose from beneath his arm. He dropped the tools with a clatter and jumped back, the candle lantern guttering in his trembling hand. Now the scratching became an insistent scrabbling. Gathering his resolve, Lem held the lantern forth over the barrel's open head to peer cautiously inside.

Something big and gray hissed loudly. The hairs on Lem's nape stood on end. What the bloody devil was it? When the odd form did not move but only continued to let off a strange wheeze, Lem calmed enough to focus on the offending creature. Black eyes, razor-like teeth, fat body, hairless pink tale—naught but an opossum! Angrily, he kicked the barrel over to release the trapped animal.

Such was its corpulence the opossum could scarcely waddle out of the barrel. Perhaps it had climbed into the barrel four days ago, the day James Park mentioned the store had been raided. The animal had gorged itself until it grew so portly it could not crawl back out. Lem considered killing the beast to eat later but discounted the notion. Possum meat was awfully unctuous and gamey of flavor.

He found a single overlooked crock of sorghum under a discarded gunnysack and stuffed it in his jacket pocket. After a thorough search of every nook and cranny, nary a morsel of grain or flour remained. Besides the fright from the mouse and opossum, only a roach nest caused further discomfort. He despised roaches, endeavoring to crush as many as possible under his heel.

Lem collected the grooming brush and hoof pick from the floor and put them next to the sorghum. At least the mule would get his sweets.

Prudence told him to search the storefront next. Retrieving the rifle, he turned toward the central doorway. To pass through those doors meant negotiating overturned crates and barrels, stepping over broken crockery, and treading in sticky honey. As Lem stepped through the door and heard what sounded like a sniffle!

Ashamed to let fear get the better of him, Lem gathered his mettle. This was his family's property. No king, no soldier, no thief, no one outside of his family and trusted servants had a right to be here. Fury overrode the weariness in his bones—outrage over the deaths of his father, brother, Sukey, James, and all the rest! They had died at the hands of those who would take without having earned!

Lemuel Alston Farnandis, having recently turned thirteen on the thirteenth day of January in the year of our Lord seventeen-eighty-one, strode boldly with the bearing of a man to the center of his father's store and firmly rooted his feet. Placing the lantern on the floor, he readied his rifle.

"I heard you," he said in a clipped tone. "I know you are here." This announcement had not the effect he wished, so he added, "Show yourself! Iffin you don't, I'll run you through. One way or the other, on your back or on your feet, you are going to leave this place! I, Lemuel Farnandis, declare it so!"

There came a muffled shriek from behind the counter. Lem readied the rifle, cocked the hammer, and realized with sudden clarity that he had not reloaded the weapon since the encounter with Tyger. His knees went to water. Thoughts raced as he held his position to maintain the bluff. Sweat beaded on his forehead as he waited out the hidden robber.

A pallid face, wide-eyed, mouth open, stood up from behind the counter. "L-Lemuel? Lem? Can it be? Truly?"

"Mamma?" He couldn't believe his eyes! "MAMMA!

26

For Liberty

"AAAAEEEEEEEEEEE!!!"

Lem froze.

His mother's face dropped out of sight with a gasp.

There were sounds of mewling.

Lem, unsure whether to launch himself toward the intruder in the shadows, decided to retrieve the lantern. He held it aloft, placed the bayonet between himself and this new threat, and sought the source of the commotion. In the flickering yellow glow stood Amadahy, filled with Indian determination. She had produced a large hunting knife from he knew not where and was flashing it around as if to ward off evil spirits. A swell of pride filled his breast at seeing her ready to take on any attackers with such ferocity!

The wail of a distraught baby pierced the room.

"Shush, shush, Little Henry. Shush, child." Momma was trying to console Lem's youngest brother.

"Sallie," said Lem, "Tis all right. These ones are my family!"

"Sallie?" came a questioning voice. There was some rustling, and a large blanket was thrown over the counter. A bonneted head popped up, yielding the inquisitive glower of the genuine Sallie. When her eyes fell on Lem, she shrieked, "Tis Lemuel! Tis Lemuel!" She rounded the counter and launched herself at Lem, giving no thought to the Indian girl as she flew under the poised knife.

Since Papa's work surface ran the entire length of the central wall, those hiding behind it also had to pass Amadahy to get at Lem. One by one, they shuffled out, herded by Mamma's bulk only, for her arms were now filled with a squalling Baby Henry.

Lem was surrounded by stairstep children. Little "Caroline" Harriet, Jane "Emily," Sarah "Sallie," and finally, James "Grant" were all latched to his legs and waist. He struggled to remain upright with the lantern in one hand and the musket in the other, both a strain for his tired shoulders as he held them on high away from his siblings. Mamma stayed back, moisture glistening on her round cheeks, giving rein to her brood for this unexpected homecoming. Baby Henry quieted under her ministrations.

Until the room brightened as another lantern peeked in the doorway, everyone had forgotten "Sallie." In her disheveled apron, cap, and jacket, the Indian girl came forward, unarmed. The children instantly released Lem and shrank against their mother, dread etched in their bearings.

Lem said, "Tis no need to be afeared. She is a just and true friend." To his own ears, this sounded feeble, so he added, "My most faithful companion."

At these words, Mamma raked him with a beady eye. To her credit, she held her tongue, though she had puffed up like a mother hen protecting her young.

Amadahy looked to Lem gratefully, her features stoic.

Lem cleared his throat into the sudden void. "I present Amadahy, brave fighter of the mighty Cawtawbaw People. Of her, you need not hold trepidation. I warrant that Amadahy is the most honorable of all I chanced to meet during my recent trials."

This last statement sent a range of emotions playing across each brow to unanimously conclude that Lem's words should be accepted. All eyes turned to the Indian girl with curiosity and wonder.

Sallie, Lem's sibling in truth, spoke first. "Tis a great honor to meet a most noble warrior." She curtsied, spreading the folds of her gown as if to a queen.

Eyes wide with excitement, Grant came forward and stretched out his delicate hand. Amadahy stooped to grasp it and gave him a reverent nod. This seemed to break a barrier, for the children all rushed to her, voices raised in questions as only the young can bring forth. Astonished, the Indian girl tried to answer them all, resorting to clipped responses, "…aye…Indian…nay…moccasins…Christian. Maho'tcire himba'ri! To Heaven, I go!"

Lem came to Amadahy's rescue. "Hold! Heed my own words now. There's much to be said, but we are famished and weary. This long day has been arduous and vexing."

Mamma Farnandis drew herself up. "Children, attend! Fetch wood from the pile, lay the fire in the hearth! Sallie, bring out the victuals. We shall have tea. Those dirty brigands thought they took everything but failed mightily!" She gave Lem a wink, "Your father, God rest his soul, was a man prepared."

So, t'was true. Lem's father was dead. A hole opened in his chest, but tears would not come. So much had wrung passions from him of late that grief held no sway. Firmly he put it aside until came an appropriate time. Her attentions severely divided between the children, Lem's mother seemed unaware of having heralded ill tidings.

Lem silently blessed his father for that tiny hidden storage room at the mill. If it had not been well-stocked upon his urgent need, he couldn't imagine what would have happened to Amadahy and him. The location of this current stash of supplies was a mystery he would unravel later. Papa had clearly kept its very existence close to his breast.

Preparing to lay aside the Brown Bess on the counter, his grip tightened in shame. Prepared indeed. How could he have overlooked the servicing of the musket after its use? Papa would have sorely disapproved of Lem's neglect! He could almost hear Papa's scolding, "Take care of your tools lest they fail you in time of need!"

Mamma was in the proper form now, her homemaking authority in the fore. "Stop harassing Amadahy, children. It's like you've never seen an Indian! The poor child wants to sup and rest. T'will be time enough for plastering and pestering upon the morrow, to be sure!" It warmed Lem's heart to see a dimpled smile rise on Amadahy's cheeks.

Whilst Mamma and the children busied themselves, he attended to the security of the entryways. He handed off the crock of molasses to Amadahy. Finding a discarded pail and a wooden ladle, she mixed a portion of the grain Major McJunkin had so graciously supplied with a dollop of the sticky black substance. She then went into the cold night to give Old Bo and Bonnie their bonuses.

Lem saw to it that the front door's bar was securely latched. This left only the double doors at the dock. A whinny from the mule told him Amadahy had performed her task, and in moments, she reappeared out of the darkness. The two of them reset the skewed doors as best they could, dropping the main bar across in hopes of blocking them. Fortune did not favor them, however. The hinges had been badly damaged, so the latch was only partially successful in its job. To bolster the loose bar and sagging doors, they pushed seven of the empty barrels against them. Indeed, this weight would hinder any would-be thief long enough for Lem to obtain his gun.

From the front, Mamma called, "We've prepared a meager fare. Tis not the sumptuous meal of your birthday…(a strangled cry)…still…tis enough to fill your bellies."

When Lem and Amadahy returned to the front room, they set aside their weapons atop the counter—but not the Brown Bess. Lem reloaded the rifle before placing it alongside its brethren. At the hearth, they discovered several chairs arranged for their use. As they sat, bowls were thrust into their hands, and wooden spoons were presented. From the savory odor, Lem recognized his mother's venison stew. She habitually bolstered it with potatoes and onions. His head swam from repressed hunger. How long had it been since they last ate? He delved in.

Once Mamma ensured their bellies filled, bodies warmed at the lively hearth, and thirst slaked with warm tea, Lem and Amadahy found themselves entirely awake.

Despite Mamma's attempts to waylay the children's prying, the two young veterans had their long tale wrung from them like water from a wet rag. In a way, t'was fitting, for Lem felt that much weight lifted from his shoulders with the telling.

The high points were revealed by unspoken agreement whilst the low points remained buried for a more appropriate time and age. Mamma held her tongue, but Lem could tell she was fit to burst for more details. The children had spread out on a sizeable woolen blanket in front of the hearth. The excitement in their little voices was palpable but short-lived. One by one, each small body succumbed to dreams heroic. Mamma had placed Baby Henry in a crate next to her rickety spindle chair. It was lined with a mat of soft grasses covered in clean linen.

Eventually, only Lem, Amadahy, and Mamma were still awake. Flames from the hearth reflected in Mamma's eyes, and Lem saw that there burned a desire for answers that would not be denied. Reluctantly, he began to fill in the details unfit for younger ears.

"General Dan had a severe scar upon his cheek that I daren't ask over, so potent was his countenance. I couldn't work up the pluck, though I suspect he had taken a ball during some long-ago battle. The wound had healed rather badly. He was a right and true warhorse, General Dan was." Here Lem paused. Fatigue was finally overtaking his thoughts.

Mamma was not quite ready to let him go, however. "You're the man of the house now, Lemuel. Papa and John, me firstborn, they've gone to meet The Maker. Brother Walt joined up with militiamen that barreled through here earlier today, a-chasing some bigwig named Bloody Tarleton. Said t'was his duty to stand up for the family in the fight for Freedom. Would that I could've changed his heart, but tis right and fitting he stand against tyranny. Now, tell me, son. Is it your plan to stay and put to rights the family's holdings?"

Lem held back in the answer too long.

"I may be old and fat, but I have eyes, Lem. There's a spark between the two of ye. Injun or no, she has it written plain uponst her face. I want me answer. Out with it!"

Lem looked to Amadahy. He knew Mamma's words rang true. Yet, they still held their tongues.

"I'll tell ye a story whilst you consider me question. This past day, that old scalawag Jack Beckham come galloping through on his big black, Maw. Stopped, he did, in hopes of words with your father. Found only us in our desperate position. After a slug of rum, he imparted news of having seen a small band of Cawtawbaws down towards Musgrove's Mill on the road toward Tugaloo Town. These Injuns told the tale of having fled from a party of Loyalists somewhere near the ford. Their daughter got separated from them in the woods. Ye know Jack to be naught but a kindly old bear at heart. He promised to keep an eye out for the poor girl in his travels. The Injuns begged a pledge that if he happened uponst her, he would tell her to stay put at Grindall's. They would pass this way to ask of her on their homeward journey before summer. For his troubles, they gave him a wad of tobacco for his clay pipe, which pleased him exceedingly."

Amadahy burst into tears. She rose unsteadily to her feet. Mamma stood to grasp her in a tight hug. Lem knew that comfort well and longed for it himself.

"Hush, child. The moment I laid me eyes on you, I knew you were the lost Injun lassie. Somehow, I have the feeling that you'll see your family again, mayhap to only be visiting Cawtawbaw Town." Mamma gave Amadahy a bawdy wink.

This last shocked Amadahy into silence. She looked at Mamma Farnandis in astonishment.

Mamma, seeing her confusion, supplied, "Injun or no, I'd welcome another daughter. Ben Franklin says that a good wife lost is God's gift lost. All but one of me boys are grown to men now, and the oldest is walking with Our Lord. After the tribulations of this long week, I cannot deny my time in this world is passing swiftly."

Lemuel stood to wrap Amadahy and Mamma into his embrace, careful not to trod on any small hands or feet laying in repose. His vision was blurred, but he found his voice, "Methinks with the end of this dirty war a time will come when all men shall be seen as equals, and tyrants shall fade from history forever. God bless America!"

"Aye, tis true and right, my son."

"Niduks'or, niduks'or! Hear, hear!"

He kissed them, one on the cheek, the other…well…tis yet another story in the making. That be the lay of it!

Lemuel · Alston · Farnandis
Jauary 13, 1781

Glossary of Words and Terms

Adam's ale (slang) – water.

ale draper – barkeep or tavern master.

back up – angry or offended, like a cat raising its back.

bantling – a young child.

bacon-face – having a full, round face.

blackguard – a scoundrel or villain.

blue at the mizzen – Admiralty would fly a flag of blue covered in stars on the middle mast of a ship. Slang: haughty.

burr – another name for a millstone or grindstone. Burrs are raised edges cut into the stone's surface specifically to create abrasive action.

British Legion – the provincial regiment created of British Loyalist infantry and dragoons under the leadership of Lieutenant Colonel Banastre Tarleton. In America this legion was also called Tarleton's Raiders, the Green Devils, the Green Horse, and the Green Dragoons.

brook – tolerate.

cavalry – soldiers that fight from horseback. Also known as dragoons.

catch-fart – derogatory slang referring to how close a foot servant must follow his master or mistress.

chamber pot – a large crockery jug used as a toilet.

chaw bacon – a dullard or stupid person.

clockwatch – a pocket watch.

Continentals – soldiers fighting in the Continental Army against the British.

corn ditty – a negro spiritual, early Gospel music, sung by slaves.

dragoon – mounted cavalry.

Dutch comfort – relief over a bad situation not getting worse.

eternity box – coffin.

eventide – evening.

fellow – companion, compatriot, partner.

fetlock – the ankle of an equine such as a horse, mule, or donkey.

fie – disgust, distasted, contempt.

first-rate – largest Royal Navy sailing warships in the line.

flake – another name for cracked corn or maize.

flux – original name for dysentery, or extreme diarrhea, which can cause death.

flummoxed – confused, stumped.

Flying Army – nickname applied to General Daniel Morgan's contingent because of their ability to move swiftly.

furlong – one eighth of a mile, or two hundred twenty yards. Also known as forty rods.

gentleman – honorific reference applied to men of courteous conduct, a slightly elevated social rank above *Mr.* but not as great as *Master.*

Green Dragoons – Colonel Banastre Tarleton outfitted his cavalry in green jackets, thus the name. However, this elite group of horsemen earned another name, Tarleton's Raiders, for their scorched-earth tactics used throughout South Carolina.

Gullahs (also Geechees) – enslaved Africans brought to the Lowcountry of South Carolina, North Carolina, Georgia, and Florida to farm coastal rice fields in the eighteenth century. Descendants have maintained much of their African culture and speak a creole dialect of English.

happy hunting grounds – hunter's heaven, a Native American reference to the afterlife.

hominy – also called lye hominy grits, is made from kernels of dried maize or corn that has been soaked in lye (caustic potash) until the hulls and germ are removed. It was a common Colonial American food, usually prepared with a bit of salt pork and other vegetables.

husbandman – a farmer.

huzzah – a cheer or exclamation of support.

infantry – foot soldiers.

irregular – volunteer militia.

jackstones – the game of jacks, only played with stones or other small objects of similar size. To play, a larger round stone was tossed into the air. Using the same hand, one jack would be scooped up and then the tossed stone would then be caught before it hit the ground. The next turn, two jacks would be scooped, and then three, and so on. The winner is the one who could pick up the most jacks and catch the round stone without dropping any objects.

keep your powder dry – be ready for anything. Refers to the gunpowder used to fire a musket.

kin –to understand, relate.

leftenant – lieutenant.

linsey-woolsey – a coarse, homespun cloth made of linen and wool.

lustrum – five years.

macaroni – a fop, or vain man.

madam or ma'am – a respectful address to women, married or unmarried.

maize – Indian corn, a cereal grain domesticated by the ancient Mayans.

manstealing – enslaving.

master – in the 1700s not a reference to slave owners but referring to a skilled workman or one in business on his own. The connotation was of higher rank than simply *Mr.* Originally abbreviated as *Mr.*

mechanic – one who works at a trade or other occupation requiring manual labor.

merde – French for *darn*, a mild expletive.

Miss – during the eighteenth century this term would never be used for a woman unless she was a prostitute.

Mr. – a respectful reference applied to men regardless of marital status, and those who do not have professional or academic titles. Abbreviated as *Mr.*

Mistress – honorific prefix for both married and unmarried women, usually referring to the woman of the house. Abbreviated as *Mrs.*

noggin – the head; also, a pewter mug.

noddle – back of the head or neck.

offal – waste parts from a slaughtered animal.

offside – on a horse's right side, opposite the left side (near side).

Old Wagoner – General Daniel Morgan's nickname, earned for when drove wagons prior to the war. Wagoneering was a tough job.

Pearly Gates – the doorway to Heaven.

picnic – an outing with food and drink. The word began appearing in Colonial America just prior to 1800. It is a shortened version of the French phase pique-nique, which literally means to pick at your food rather than wolfing it down.

pilaster – the square column on either side of a fireplace that supports the mantel.

pippin – a slice of apple, one of unique and flavorful qualities.

post-haste – means, "Postman, move this message along the route quickly to the next post."

purse proud – rich man, afraid to get dirty.

pugilist – one who fights with fists, bare-knuckled boxer.

quarter – to spare the life of a captive.

rashers – sliced bacon, fried or boiled.

regulars – trained soldiers.

retainer – servant, attendant.

ring taw – the game of marbles, where the large marble, called a "shooter" or "taw" would be used to knock an opponent's marbles out of a circle drawn on the floor or ground.

ruckus – commotion.

sawbuck – a style of horse saddle featuring two wooden crossbars for supporting packs.

scallywag – a reprobate or rascal.

spark – a showoff or flashy man.

Scotch Irish (Scot Irish) – people of Scottish descent who lived in Northern Ireland. King Charles I tried to force these Presbyterians into the Church of England. Around 250,000 migrated to the American colonies between 1717 and 1775 to avoid falling under the control of the Church of England. They made up the backbone of settlers in the American frontier.

Scotch hoppers – Played both inside and out, this game is the same as modern-day hopscotch.

short gown – a short-skirted dress.

solar plexus – the pit of the stomach just below the ribs.

suffer – tolerate, endure, allow, permit.

take a gander – take a good look at something, like a goose craning its neck to see better.

tomb – a very large book.

Tory – Americans loyal to the British.

trepan – to cheat or swindle.

twig – understand.

tyger – a colonial name for the American cougar (*Puma concolor*). Colonists also called them panthers, catamounts, carcajous, mountain lions, pumas, leopards, swamp screamers, ghost cats, Indian devils, and tigers (tygers).

uncouth – rude, unmannerly, odd, unusual.

upstart – newly rich man.

vault – latrine.

vulgar – crude, not refined, simple, of humble birth. In 1781, applying the word to a situation would infer humorous connotations, not indecency.

water of life (slang) – whisky.

Whig – American colonists supporting the fight for liberty against the King of England.

Woden's Day – Wednesday, Day of Odin, the Norse god.

your servant – both "hello" and "goodbye." A polite way to greet and part.

zounds – a contraction of *God's wounds*, a swear word about as offensive in the late 1700s as is the modern use of *darn*.

Appendix

The following portrayals concern some of the prominent characters and locations in this book. Where possible, the age of the characters during the Battle of Cowpens has been posted. Information was gleaned from local family traditions, legends, historical records, and newspapers to present a realistic setting. Much effort was expended corroborating traditions with known facts. For certain, the Grindal Shoals community never recovered its former glory after the war, gradually shrinking from prominence into a mere footnote of our history. These portrayals are in order of appearance.

John Grindal's Shoals (Grandale, Grindle, Grendel, Grindall, Grindal, Grendale, Grendall, Grendle, Gryndall, Gryndel, Gryndale, and other spellings.)

Grindal Shoals, or Grindal's Ford, was named after the second owner of the adjacent land, John Grindal, who settled there around 1755. "The land that contains the shoals was part of the property first granted to Richard Carroll in 1752. He named the shoals, Carroll Shoals, but the name was changed to Grindal Shoals several years after John Grindal acquired the property. The shoals were first called Grindal Shoals in 1773." (Grindal Shoals Gazette, Ivey) Grindal's was a thriving frontier community prior to the Revolutionary War. Fords were critical for travelers and trade, as bridges were very expensive to build. Grindal's Ford offered a prime location for commerce, and the network of roads formed linked the area to Spartanburg, Union, Gaffney, Rock Hill, and the Lower Ninety-Six District.

Grindal Shoals settlers formed an armed patrol to push out Cherokee raiders in 1771. Lead by Capt. John Nuckolls, the group included young Ensign Patrick "Pad" Moore, soon to become an infamous Tory raider. These neighbors drove the Cherokee all the way to Tryon, North Carolina.

Traditionally, the Native Americans utilized Grindal's Ford as part of a network of trade routes along the ancient Lower Cherokee Trader's Path. Since prehistoric times, this path linked the Catawba and Cherokee Nations. According to ancient maps, Grindal's, along with several other fords of the Pacolet River were along this major trade route that cut across Spartanburg County. Thus, it is likely that in 1781, Grindal Shoals residents may have witnessed or participated in trade with Native Americans. By 1800, the Cherokees had been forcibly removed from the area. The Catawbas, who sided with the Americans, were confined to a reservation near Rock Hill known as Catawba Town. The Cherokees, who sided with the British, were confined in the northern mountains of Georgia in Tugaloo Town.

As with many thriving communities, Grindal's leading citizens cultivated area interest in their favorite pastimes. Among those diversions were horse breeding and racing. Captain Wade Hampton I was a renowned breeder, John Chisam owned a racetrack, and John "Jack" Beckham was a famous trainer. These men were friends, and it follows that they would be drawn together by their common love of quality horseflesh.

Another pastime was entertaining guests in the home. Since Grindal's was a hub of commerce, the plantation owners were wealthy. With wealth came leisure, especially with slaves being utilized as labor of the farms (plantations). Christie's Tavern, the

Sims-Marchbanks Meeting House, and a few private homes were recorded as holding dances and lively gatherings. This data is scattered among many source materials; however, it only makes sense. In a time before electronics, gatherings between friends and family would fill the evenings instead of radio or television shows.

Today, Grindal Shoals is only a footnote in history. Several hundred years of water erosion and sediment shift by the Pacholet River has covered this once notable ford. A few hundred yards below the ford, toward the Broad River junction, is a modern bridge leading from Jonesville to Gaffney. Grindal's Ford Road, recently renamed Meehan Road in remembrance of the author's father, is today only a broken, rutted path.

Lemuel Alston Farnandis (1803-1863)

The fictional character of Lem is based on a real person, the second son of Henry and Elizabeth "Betsy" Henderson Farnandis. Lem's maternal grandfather was Major John Lawson Henderson. His mother's brother, William Henderson, was brother-in-law to John "Jack" Beckham, the famous scout for Daniel Morgan. This means that Jack Beckham was Lem's uncle by marriage through his mother, Betsy. However, the real Lem Farnandis had not yet been born at the time of the Battle of Cowpens. It is unclear exactly when Lem's father, Henry, moved the family to Grindal Shoals, only that it was just prior to the turn of the century.

To find records on Lemuel's family one must understand that the spelling of a name was based on how it sounded to the scribe. Many people did not know how to write or spell their own names at that time. This explains the various spellings of the Farnandis name: Fernandez, Fernandis, and Farnandez. The spelling used throughout this book comes from the headstones in the Fernandez-Simms Cemetery, Jonesville, South Carolina.

Henry Farnandis and Family (1769-1823)

Henry Farnandis was born in 1769, Port Tobacco, Maryland, of mixed heritage. His mother was English, most likely Scotch-Irish, and probably a Protestant. His father was a Spaniard. Henry was described as having dark eyes, a dark complexion, and a foreign air about him. Henry moved to the Union District (present-day Union County), South Carolina, sometime between 1787 and 1799. He married Elizabeth "Betsy" Henderson, daughter of Major John Henderson.

Major Henderson was elected sheriff of the Union District near Grindal Shoals. He hired Henry as a deputy. After the war, during improved economic times, Henry built a plantation, started a grist mill, and opened a mercantile at the shoals. Once settled at the plantation, Henry increased his fortune through farming, milling, and distributing sundries.

The author posits that Henry grew his own grain to process at his mill. Further, since the area was a thriving farm community with horseracing as a local pastime, it is probable that Henry sold feed, seed, and sweet feed, in addition to flour. Sorghum molasses, popular as a colonial household sweetener, mixed with various grains like oats was (and is) used to bolster the diet of horses, cows, and other beasts of burden. As a former horse owner, the author can say that sweet feed has long been used as a special treat for large animals after a hard day's labor.

The Farnandis Family at Grindal Shoals:

Parents:

Henry Farnandis	1769-1823
Elizabeth Farnandis	1776-1844

Children:

John Henderson	1799-1831
Lemuel Alston	1803-1863
Walter F.	1812-1870
James Grant	1814-????
Henry II	1808-????
Sarah "Sallie" Elizabeth	1801-1880
Jane Emily	1804-1888
Caroline Harriet	1806-1886

Colonial life, especially on the frontier, was arduous. Children worked at whatever daily tasks they could handle. They fed farm animals, gathered eggs, cooked, cleaned, fetched water, and chopped firewood. Boys in their teens were treated as young men with adult responsibilities. Such would have been the case with Lemuel Alston Farnandis, Henry's second son. Most likely, Lemuel would have worked as a miller's boy, one who hauled grain to the grist mill.

While the Farnandis family was documented in several publications, and their family cemetery still exists near Grindal's Ford, it is unlikely they had settled there prior to the Revolutionary War. The author simply utilized this family in a fictional manner to present this story. However, maps and records show that at least two mills existed above the shoals during Revolutionary War times. Stories mention that a flood took out the Farnandis mill, leaving the Littlejohn mill untouched. The Farnandis family ventures must have turned sour after this mishap, for only a few gravestones remain to show they once lived at Grindal Shoals.

Angelica Mitchell Knot (1771-1849) Age: 10

Angelica's story began with the marriage of Judge "Major" Samuel Henderson's three eldest daughters. Elizabeth "Betty" married John "Jack" Beckham, a noted Whig scout for Daniel Morgan. Anna married Daniel Williams. Mary married Joab Mitchell,

Angelica's parents. Judge Henderson and his wife, Elizabeth, received a land grant at Grindal Shoals on the Sandy Run branch, which they apparently divided between their three married daughters. So, the Beckhams, the Williams', and the Mitchells all moved from Boonesborough, Kentucky to settle the grant at Grindal Shoals.

Angelica, the author of a book called *Traditions of the Revolution*, was described as well-spoken and scholarly. This publication has apparently been lost, but her reminisces were recorded later by the Reverend J. D. Bailey of Glendale Baptist Church, Spartanburg, South Carolina, in his book, A History of Grindal Shoals and Some Early Adjacent Families.

Angelica had fifteen siblings. As would sometimes occur, if a family met hard times, relatives might take up the duty of raising some of the children. This appears to have been the case with Angelica, as her parents moved back to Boonesborough leaving her behind at Grindal Shoals with Aunt Anna Williams. When Anna's husband died, she then married Adam Potter, a brick mason. Angelica became their adopted daughter, Angelica Henderson Williams Potter.

In 1794, Angelica married the Honorable Abram Nott. Nott was an attorney who hung his shingle at Grindal Shoals. He taught law to budding attorneys in his home. Eventually, he became a judge, and then a congressman. Angelica had eight children, all notables. Angelica, in her own right, was a major influence in the community.

Sandy Run Maidens Interrelated

Lily-Beth Beckham (12), Angelica Mitchell (10), and Phoebe Jasper (14) were all cousins living on the Sandy Run branch. Little Nancy Foster (8) was a neighbor and a friend. Her father, John Foster

(1750-1832) bought land from Lt. Nicholas Jasper (1744-1827), Phoebe's father. Jasper served under Col. Thomas Brandon in the Second Spartan Regiment of Militia. Nick's brother-in-law was John Foster. John also served in the Second Spartan. Foster's wife's sister, Susannah, married Nicholas's brother, John. It was a small community and these related families all had members who fought off the yoke of tyranny, helping to make this country free. They have descendants living near Grindal Shoals to this day.

Phoebe, at 14, was of marrying age. One must remember that for various reasons such as malnutrition, disease, congenital defects, and lack of proper medical care, people of this era did not live as long as we do now. This accounts for large families of up to twenty children. Deaths in childhood were expected and frequent. It was a novelty when adults lived into their sixties and beyond. Therefore, many colonials were married and had a family of their own by the age of nineteen. Girls were considered "old maids" if they were unmarried at twenty.

Monetary reasons also led to the prevalence of large families. Farms required laborers, and not all were slaves. Many families could not afford slaves. Slaves were not only expensive but required housing, clothing, medical care, and food. Parents wanted boys because they did farm labor starting at a young age. Girls could only handle household chores and lighter work, so it was best for them to marry quickly and move on, lightening the family's financial responsibilities.

Frontier children rarely had any formal education. Usually, schooling was at the father's knee. Any money for education would be invested in the eldest boy first. This, too, was almost unheard of in frontier families. They lived a hard life. Grindal families found times even harder when the likes of Tory Capt. Patrick Moore came around and plundered what little they could scrape together.

It is a wonder that Grindal Shoals produced several notable historic figures, having been ravaged first by natives, then by Royalists. Angelica Mitchell Nott was an exceptional woman of her era. Without her penchant for writing about what she witnessed during her long life, we would have very few records of Grindal's former glory.

Lt. Col. Wade Hampton I (1754-1835) Age: 27

Hampton was in the South Carolina Regiment of Light Dragoon cavalry during 1781. He was a known friend from childhood of John "Jack" Beckham, with whom he hunted and trapped during his frequent visits to Grindal. It is highly probable that horse breeder Wade Hampton, horse trainer Jack Beckham, and Grindal's racetrack owner John Chisam, were friends.

From 1795 to 1797, Hampton served in the U.S. House of Representatives. After a colorful military career, he amassed a large fortune in land speculation. He purchased properties along the Congaree River in Richland District, South Carolina, and later, several plantations in Louisiana. In South Carolina, he produced cotton at his estate, Woodlands. In Louisiana, his plantations produced sugarcane. He became one of the wealthiest planters in the country. Over three thousand slaves were on the books in his name.

John "Jack" Beckham (1735-1787) Age: 46

He was an expert horse trainer, friend of Wade Hampton, spy for General Daniel Morgan, active Whig, hunter, and trapper. He is buried in an unmarked grave in Hodge Cemetery at Grindal Shoals. He settled his large family of daughters on part of the Henderson grant along Sandy Run.

Jack was a friend of Laurence Easterwood, a Patriot soldier under Brandon's Regiment, and owner of the ford several miles above Grindal's. It was here that the bulk of Tarleton's forces crossed the Pacolet River on the evening of January 15, 1781. Easterwood's Ford was the upper limit of boat travel on the Pacolet. Both Easterwood's and Grindal's Fords were needed to quickly move more than a thousand men, several hundred horses, artillery, and baggage through the flooded Pacolet River.

M.C. Beckham, in his book, Colonial Spy, goes into detail concerning his ancestor. Jack was known to drink heavily at times and tended toward laziness. Despite his faults, he was a stalwart scout in the cause of Freedom.

Captain John "Blind John" Thomas Chisam (Chisholm, Chisham, Chisum, Chisam, Chism 1756-1829)

John was born in Amelia County, Virginia, son of James David Chisam and Barbary Estes Rogers. He married Sarah Harris in Spartanburg, S.C., in 1774. He had 15 children. When she died in 1848, he married Sarah Dabney, also from Spartanburg. He died in Marion, Alabama at age 73. He was rostered with Captain Taylor, Colonel Brandon Thomas, General Greene, General Pickens, and as a private in Roebuck's Regiment in 1776. He lived at Grindal's from 1786 through 1806, and his daughter, Nancy, was known to be the most beautiful maiden in the county.

Chisam moved onto a small tract that was once part of the Henderson grant. He built a house near a spring, which came to be known as Chisam Spring. An admiration of horseracing led him to construct several racetracks.

He lost his sight long after the war, reportedly from an old war wound. His home was known for dances and entertainment, probably because of Nancy. Angelica Mitchell's future husband,

Abram Nott, opened his first law office in the Chisam home. This house must have been quite a place.

Adam and Hannah Goudelock

The Goudelock cabin is two miles north of Grindal Shoals. According to the Gaffney Ledger, June 7, 1989, Gaffney, S.C., Adam received a one-hundred-acre grant from King George III. In 1769, he brought his family from Ireland to settle the land. Since the Goudelock story is portrayed faithfully in this book, it will not be repeated here. At least through 1989, Goudelock's decedents resided on the farm. At a ceremony hosted by the S. C. Food and Agriculture Council at Clemson College, U. S. Senator Strom Thurmond of South Carolina, recognized the family for having worked the land for more than two hundred years. Data on the Goudelocks may be found under many different spellings: Goudelock, Goudylock, Gudylock, Goudelocke, and Gaudilock, to name a few.

Captain John N. Nuckolls, Sr. (1732-1780)

John was a Patriot who lived near Thicketty Creek. In 1771, as captain of the group, he led Grindal neighbors in protecting the community from Cherokee raids. Among other neighbors listed in the armed unit were William Marchbanks, Patrick "Pad" Moore, John Goudelock, and William Coleman. He also became a captain in the Patriot militia when the war came.

The story goes that once the Cherokee were removed, he proceeded to build a plantation at Whig Hill, near Thicketty Creek. The plantation was so named because Nuckolls strongly supported the Whig cause. In 1843, his son, William, built the Nuckolls House, also known as Wagstop Plantation on family land. It remains to this day a beautiful Victorian home surrounded by a farm.

Nuckolls was murdered by Loyalist Davis and a group of Tories at McKown's Mill on December 11, 1780. William McKown was involved in the plot. When Nuckolls and his young son brought corn to the mill for grinding, McKown said he had not the time until the next day. He gave lodging to Nuckolls and his boy for the night. While they slept, McKown, also a Loyalist, betrayed Nuckolls to Davis and the Tory raiders. They spared the boy, letting him sleep while they took his father into the woods. The raiders shot John Nuckolls in the head. There is a historical marker set on his burial site at Whig Hill.

"Old High Key" Moseley (1756-1840) Age: 25

James Thomas "Hi-Ky" Moseley, Sr. was a private in the Continental Army, a Patriot scout for Daniel Morgan, Indian fighter, blacksmith, dentist (tooth-puller), backwoodsman, and childhood friend of Daniel Boone. He lived on Sandy Run Creek, tributary of the Pacholet River, just below Grindal's Ford. His nickname came from his high-pitched singing voice. During the Revolutionary War, he served in the Second South Carolina Militia under Col. Thomas Brandon.

His occupation meant sixty years of shoeing horses and pulling teeth, which paid for keeping his twelve children. He married Nancy Anna Jasper, another Grindal neighbor when he was nineteen.

The story told in this book concerning the wolves chasing Moseley up a tree over the deer he was carrying home is factual. Several sources relate this is how Moseley's Oak got its name. High-Key had a reputation as a talker. He is buried in the Moseley Family Plot on the Pacolet River near Grindal Shoals.

Gentleman William Thompson (1750-1823) Age: 31

Several accounts of the Battle of Cowpens refer to General Morgan choosing "Gentleman" Thompson's at Thicketty Creek as the location of a meeting on the night of January 15, 1781. Col. William Washington was among the commanders with whom Morgan discussed tactics—the purpose of the meeting. Thompson was known as an expert horseman and served in the cavalry of Col. Benjamin Roebuck. He may have fought at the Battle of Cowpens with this regiment, but no reference was found.

According to his obituary listed in the Yorkville Pioneer, Yorkville, South Carolina, September 27, 1823, he was "among the first who resisted the arbitrary measures of Great Britain. Under the celebrated Patrick Henry, he assisted in expelling Lord Dunmore from Virginia…." The City of Gaffney, S.C., honored him posthumously by bestowing his name on their oldest street.

A man referred to as "gentleman" was not of royal birth, but of good family, well-educated and well-mannered. According to English custom, he held the lowest rank of landed gentry. Records show that Thompson owned land contiguous to the street bearing his name. As a gentleman, he would not have worked the land himself, but most likely received rents from those who did.

William C. Hodge (1728-1820) Age: 53

William was the owner of Hodge Plantation at Grindal's. He was known as a "true Whig" and friend of John "Jack" Beckham. According to Major Joseph McJunkin in his memoir, Hodge was paid a visit by Tarleton directly after the Battle of Blackstock's Farm, November 20, 1780. Tarleton was pursuing Whigs from the battle. He chased them to Grindal Shoals and came to Hodge's house. The British commander "…took him [Hodge] prisoner, seized provisions and provender, killed up his stock, burned his fence and house, and carried him off, telling his wife as they started that he should be hung on the first crooked tree on the road." Hodge was jailed in Camden, S.C.

Lt. Col. Banastre Tarleton (1754-1833) Age: 27

Born to wealth, educated at Oxford, his officer's commission to the First Dragoon Guards was purchased by his family in 1775. He worked his way up to Lieutenant Colonel through ruthlessness displayed on the battlefield. He gained a reputation for arrogance and brashness. Cowpens was his first defeat. His British Legion contained regulars and Loyalist soldiers in the infantry, cavalry, and artillery. Colloquially, his command was known as Tarleton's Raiders, the Green Dragoons, the Green Devils, and the Green Horse. His elite cavalry wore green jackets, and their helmets were plumed.

On May 29, 1780, at the Battle of Waxhaws, also called Buford's Massacre, he earned the title "Bloody Ban." Whether justly deserved or not, the nickname stuck because his troops destroyed Abraham Buford's Continental forces under a flag of truce. It is possible the Loyalist and British fighters believed Tarleton killed during the truce by a stray shot, for his horse fell, trapping him underneath. While he was pinned beneath the dead animal, his command slaughtered the Continentals with bayonets. However, a Continental field surgeon claimed to have seen Tarleton, alongside his men, upon the field perpetrating the slaughter. Regardless of actual events, the cry "Remember Waxhaws!" and "Tarleton's Quarter!" became rallying chants to bolster Patriot soldiers.

Sukey, Big Tom, and Little Tom

These characters are fictitious, but their names were taken from

Union County, South Carolina slave roles of the period. As was customary, slaves were listed with the last name of their recorded owners; hence, Sukey Farnandis would have been proper. Although slavery was common across the world during the period, not all slaves were treated poorly. The quantity and quality of slave labor depended upon good health and some measure of contentment. It was in the slave owner's best interest to feed, clothe, house, and provide medical care. Additionally, to minimize flight risk, slave families were best kept together.

In a poor frontier community like Grindal's, slaves would have received better treatment simply because they represented a major investment to the backwoods farmers. Also, not all slaves were negroes, nor was slavery an American invention. Institutional slavery was common the world over.

Slavery began in America, not with the coming of the colonists, but with the Native Americans. It was a common practice to enslave the vanquished after tribal wars, in the Old World and the New. Colonials merely continued the practice. Roughly twenty percent of the colonial population, north, and south, at the time of Cowpens, were slaves. The American Revolution hastened the abolition of slavery by changing viewpoints with the words of the Declaration of Independence, "We hold these truths to be self-evident, that all men are created equal, that they are endowed by their Creator with certain unalienable Rights, that among these are Life, Liberty and the pursuit of Happiness."

Christopher Coleman (~1741-1784) Age: 40

Owner of Christie's Tavern, Coleman was considered a lukewarm Tory, probably because his establishment was known to serve Whigs and Tories alike. Playing both sides of the fence was probably the most profitable option for Coleman. An article in

Union County Heritage declares, "It was said that he would turn no man away, even during the American Revolution. If the Tories were coming to rest and water their horses, the Whigs would scamper down a ramp built over the creek and hide in the woods." The ruin of Christie's is located about two-and-a-half miles southwest of the ford on Park Farm Road, Jonesville, South Carolina. According to the Union Times, the structure existed until 1991 when it burned to the ground.

Coleman was born in Amelia, Virginia. He married Mary Marshall, in Lunenburg, Virginia in 1759. They had seven children. Coleman received a land grant for a 600-acre plot at Grindal on April 29, 1768. He brought his family to the Grindal community and settled. Then, he established Christie's Tavern, which was also the family home. The tavern offered food, lodging, and of course, alcoholic beverages such as beer, rum, and whiskey.

Colonial taverns were meeting places where one could boast and toast with friends, hold dances, and occasionally listen to musical entertainment. Traditionally, toasting was a contest to see who could come up with the most outrageous toast. Mary Coleman was known to be a stout Tory. Considering that Christopher wanted to serve both factions, wouldn't it have been interesting to see her face when the Whigs were whooping it up downstairs? Or better yet—to hear the arguments between the two over serving their clientele?

Capt. Patrick "Pad" Moore (~1754-1781) Age: 27

According to descriptions, Patrick was of "great height," a shade over six-and-a-half-feet tall. The average height of a man in those days was five-and-a-half-feet. He was known as "fierce and intimidating." Born in Virginia of Scot Irish parents, Patrick and his brother, Hugh, settled on land next to Thicketty Creek, South

Carolina.

Both brothers served under Capt. John Nuckolls and Lt. William Marchbanks for nine days against the Cherokees beginning February 9, 1771. As the Revolutionary War caught them up, they became Loyalists and set out with various units to disrupt the livelihoods of their Whig neighbors. They even served under their oldest brother, Col. John Moore, on a foray down through Georgia against the Whigs.

After a series of engagements and defeats with lucky, harrowing escapes, Patrick and Hugh returned to commandeer Thicketty Fort (also called Anderson's Fort), originally garrisoned against the Cherokees, as a Tory stronghold. From there, with over a hundred Loyalists, they plundered Whig residences from the Catawba River down to the Tyger River. They took anything and everything, leaving families destitute. Finally, a combined militia force of over six hundred Patriots secured the fort's surrender on July 13, 1780. Col. Isaac Shelby, one of the Patriot commanders, imparted to Moore under a flag of truce, that if he didn't surrender, he and his men would receive Tarleton's Quarter. Moore returned from the truce to surprise his men by surrendering the fort without a battle. The Tory force was paroled per an agreement that they would no longer serve the British.

After this defeat, Patrick dropped from sight until July 1781. Reports came from Patriots, who were scouring out Loyalists, that an unusually tall man was captured and killed near Ninety-Six. Moore's remains were recognized only because of his unusual height.

Alexander Chesney (1756-1843) Age: 25

Alexander Chesney had received a land grant from King George III. His tract, on which he built a plantation, was rich land of mixed forests and glades. It was about half a mile northeast of Grindal Shoals. Chesney appreciated the king's gift enough to have become a Loyalist. His neighbors were mostly Whigs, and they must have made life arduous for him.

General Daniel Morgan and his "flying army" arrived to encamp on Chesney's land, on December 25, 1780. At that point, Morgan's Continental forces numbered about five hundred, and they were hungry. Morgan ordered his men to secure Chesney, raze Chesney's fenceposts for firewood, and confiscate his livestock. These tasks probably fell to the Little River militia under command of Col. Joseph Hayes. It was known that Tories had been plundering the Grindal populace for some time, so Morgan's treatment of Chesney must have served as both retaliation and warning. His property was utilized by his enemy, his plantation destroyed, Chesney fled to Charleston, and from there returned to England.

Major Joseph C. McJunkin (1755-1846) Age: 26

McJunkin's military career began with fighting the Cherokees. He was a veteran of many actions including the Battles of King's Mountain, Cedar Springs (Spartanburg), Hanging Rock, Musgrove's Mill, Hammond's Store, Blackstock's Farm, the Siege of Ninety-Six, and the Battle of Cowpens. At Cowpens, he served in Colonel Brandon's Second Spartan Regiment of Militia. His tale is an exciting adventure, well-chronicled by Rev. James Hodge Saye, Memoirs of Major Joseph McJunkin.

James Park (unknown) Age: ???

Little is known about James Park. He traveled with Joseph McJunkin to Hammond's Store and back to General Morgan at Grindal Shoals by way of Colonel Pickens' camp between the

Fairforest and Tyger Rivers. Park was listed as serving in Col. Brandon's Second Spartan Regiment. It seems he was an aide to the major; however, one account mentions him riding with McJunkin to warn General Morgan of Tarleton's approach on January 15, 1781.

Laurence Easterwood (Owner of Easterwood's Shoals)

A known Patriot soldier, records from the South Carolina Archives show that he served under Capt. John Thompson in Col. Thomas Brandon's Regiment of Militia. Between 1780-1781, he was attached to the Spartan Regiment. Eastwood was a friend of John "Jack" Beckham, noted Patriot scout.

Laurence Easterwood was the owner of Easterwood's Shoals, located about two miles upriver from Grindal Shoals. Prior to Easterwood's acquisition, the ford was known as Lukeroy's Shoal. Easterwood was a runner of fish traps who sold his catch to locals. On the night of January 15, 1781, Tarleton's Legion used both Easterwood's and Grindal's to ford the Pacolet River.

Amadahy (~1767-18??) Age: 14

Amadahy, pronounced Ah-mah-dah-high, is a Catawba (Cawtawbaw) name. She is the fictitious character who told Daniel Morgan she was, "Ye iswa'here," which means "of the People of the River." To this day, the Catawbas live on tribal lands alongside the Catawba River near Rock Hill, South Carolina.

Catawbas have always been known for their fine clay pottery. In ancient times, they traded furs, natural dyes, baskets, pottery, and mica with coastal tribes for fish and salt. From European colonists, they exchanged for firearms, cloth, beads, and other sundries. They would travel to trade with the Cherokees for stone pipes for smoking tobacco.

During the Revolutionary War, the Catawbas served on the side of the Americans as skillful backwoods guides. According to Michael Scoggins, historian for York County Cultural and Heritage Museum, York, South Carolina, there was a Catawba fighting unit under the command of Gen. Thomas Sumter's Patriot militia.

Private John Foster (~1750-1832) Age: 31

John was a resident of the Sandy Run branch, neighbor to John "Jack" Beckham and James "High Key" Moseley. Mary McElfresh (1755-1832) was his wife. He served under Col. Thomas Brandon in the Second Spartan Regiment of Militia alongside his brother-in-law, Nicholas Jasper. Foster bought land from Jasper and built a farm.

Lt. Col. William Washington (1752-1810) Age: 29

A cavalry officer in the Continental Army, he was a Virginian and second cousin to George Washington, first President of the United States. He created the Stafford County Militia, Third Virginia Regiment. His prowess as a dragoon led to the victory at Cowpens. Washington personally pursued Tarleton from the field in hopes of capturing the British commander but failed due to misleading information given by Hannah Goudelock at the Asbury crossroad. For his services at Cowpens, he received a silver medal from the Continental Congress.

Capt. Dennis Trammell, Sr. (1759-1849) Age: 22

As corroborated by the captain's military pension record, he served in the First Spartan Regiment, Col. Roebuck's Battalion of horsemen in January 1781. He lived two miles from Saunder's Cow Pens and knew the area very well. A day before the battle,

Trammell met with General Morgan, Morgan's bodyguards, and aide-de-camp, to select the battleground site and make plans to surprise Tarleton's forces.

Prior to the opening volley, Morgan reportedly said, "Captain, here is Morgan's grave or victory." After the battle, Trammell was left behind with his command to see to the burial of the dead on both sides. Morgan also tasked him with guarding the Patriot graves against desecration by roving Tories. His service during the Revolutionary War was extensive.

Hiram Saunders

Tory plantation owner Hiram Saunders was known for his fine herd of cattle. Periodically, he would ship cows down the Broad River to the Charleston market. His stockyard was described as having multiple barns surrounded by stacked log corrals. Locally, the farm was called Saunders' Cow Pens.

For the purposes of this story, the character of Hiram Saunders is fictional, as no record could be found describing his home or whether he was present at his farm during the Battle of Cowpens. From sketchy records, it seems that Hiram and his family may have resided in a manor house a few miles from his stockyards.

However, tradition has it that on October 6, 1790, Saunders was visited at his home by the Overmountain Men under Colonel Joseph McDowell. They were searching for Major Patrick Ferguson and his Tory forces the day prior to the Battle of King's Mountain. McDowell's eight hundred men were hungry and helped themselves to Saunders' cattle. Saunders was questioned as to Ferguson's whereabouts, apparently in a rough manner. Information obtained, Ferguson was discovered and defeated at King's Mountain the next day. No record was found concerning Saunders after that date.

The Pacolet (Pacholet, Packolate) River

The Pacolet River originates in two locations. The North Pacolet flows from the Blue Ridge Mountains in the northwest section of South Carolina. The South Pacolet flows from Greenville County to Spartanburg County, South Carolina. The forks come together in Spartanburg County and continue to the Broad River toward the east near Winnsboro, South Carolina. Lawson's Fork Creek, location of the famous Wofford's Iron Works, flows through the City of Spartanburg and joins the Pacolet River in the town of Pacolet.

The word "Pacolet" is pronounced "packolate," and is thought to have French origins. Only the account of Angelica Mitchell Nott says the river got its name from a person with the last name Pacolet.

Wofford's Iron Works

The site of Wofford's Iron Works is in the current town of Glendale, South Carolina, on Lawson's Fork Creek. Colonel William Wofford, a stout Whig, opened the business in 1773 to produce war materials for the Continental Army and Patriot militia. For a short time, it was the only ironworks in the state. It came under siege several times by Loyalists. Evidently the ironworks buildings were used as a fortified position; hence, the name Wofford's Fort became attached to the site.

Most of the Wofford family were Whigs, but Benjamin Wofford, one of Col. William's brothers, was a Loyalist living on the Tyger River. Ben's son, also named Benjamin, was the founder of Wofford College, Spartanburg, South Carolina.

The author has visited the site of the Iron Works several times throughout his life. It is a unique location in that Lawson's Fork flows through a manmade slough cut deeply into a wide expanse of solid, smooth river rock. It would have made a powerful flow for a waterwheel.

List of Sources

A History of Gilead Baptist Church. (2011, August 5). Grindal Shoals Gazette. https://grindalshoalsgazette.wordpress.com/2011/08/05/a-history-of-the-gilead-baptist-church/

Adair, J. (2013). The History of the American Indians: Particularly Those Nations Adjoining to the Mississippi, East and West Florida, Georgia, South and North Carolina, and Virginia. Cambridge University Press.

American Revolution Sites, Events, and Troop Movements. (n.d.). Retrieved February 24, 2021, from http://www.elehistory.com/amrev/SitesEventsTroopMovements.htm

Bailey, J. D. (1927). History of Grindal Shoals and Some Early Adjacent Families. Ledger Print.

Bailey, J. D. (1924). Some Heroes Of The American Revolution In The South Carolina Upper Country. Band & White, printers. https://www.google.com/books/edition/_/3wIRAQAAMAAJ?hl=en&sa=X&ved=2ahUKEwjIxOeM1IfuAhWKjlkKHf5eCSMQ7_IDMBF6BAgTEAQ

Bailey, L. (n.d.). Catawba Indians sided with colonists in Revolutionary War. Rock Hill Herald. Retrieved January 13, 2021, from https://www.heraldonline.com/news/local/article26418919.html

Banastre Tarleton—Wikipedia. (n.d.). Retrieved January 6, 2021, from https://en.wikipedia.org/wiki/Banastre_Tarleton

Battle of Cowpens. (2021). In Wikipedia. https://en.wikipedia.org/w/index.php?title=Battle_of_Cowpens&oldid=1000295104

Beckham, M. C. (2007). Colonial Spy. BookSurge Publishing.

Big Cats of the Southeast (Part 1): The Panther in American History. (2017, June 6). The History Bandits. https://thehistorybandits.com/2017/06/06/big-cats-of-the-southeast-part-1-the-panther-in-american-history/

Brooks, J. S. (n.d.). The Iron Works of Lawson's Fork. Retrieved September 30, 2021, from https://glendalesc.com/ironworks.pdf.

Campbell Co Tn Military—Revolutionary War—Dennis Trammell. (n.d.). Retrieved January 17, 2022, from http://www.usgennet.org/usa/tn/county/campbell/_sgg/mbmi_1.htm

Cann, K. (2014). Turning Point: The American Revolution in the Spartan District. Hub City Press.

Catawba | people. (n.d.). Encyclopedia Britannica. Retrieved January 13, 2021, from https://www.britannica.com/topic/Catawba-people

Catawba | Encyclopedia.com. (n.d.). Retrieved January 13, 2021, from https://www.encyclopedia.com/history/united-states-and-canada/north-american-indigenous-peoples/catawba

Catawba Language and the Catawba Indian Tribe (Katapu). (n.d.). Retrieved January 13, 2021, from http://www.native-languages.org/catawba.htm

Catawba people. (2020). In Wikipedia. https://en.wikipedia.org/w/index.php?title=Catawba_people&oldid=995846180

Chores of Colonial Children. (n.d.). Daily Lives of Colonists in the 1700s. Retrieved January 13, 2021, from http://colonistsdailylives.weebly.com/chores-of-colonial-children.html

Colonial Vocabulary—Colonialtimes. (n.d.). Retrieved February 16, 2021, from https://sites.google.com/site/colonialpassport/colonial-vocabulary

Connell, S. (2018, January 18). The Forgotten Battle That Changed the Tide of the War For Independence. The Federalist Papers. https://thefederalistpapers.org/history/forgotten-battle-changed-tide-war-independence

Cook, J. (1773). A Map of the Province of South Carolina with all the Rivers, Creeks, Bays, Inletts, Islands, Inland Navigation, Soundings, Time of High Water on the Sea Coast, Roads, Marshes, Ferrys, Bridges, Swamps, Parishes Churches, Towns, Townships; Country Parish District and Provincial Lines. https://commons.wikimedia.org/wiki/File:Cook,_James_%E2%80%94_Map_of_the_Province_of_South_Carolina_1773.jpg

Culper Ring—Wikipedia. (n.d.). Retrieved January 6, 2021, from https://en.wikipedia.org/wiki/Culper_Ring

Fleming, T. J. (2020). "Downright Fighting": The Story of Cowpens.

https://www.gutenberg.org/ebooks/62413

Gaffney, M. A. C. N. B. 338 N. P. R., & Us, S. 29341 P.-2828 C. (n.d.). Forty-eight Hours Following the Battle of Cowpens—Cowpens National Battlefield (U.S. National Park Service). Retrieved February 24, 2021, from https://www.nps.gov/cowp/learn/historyculture/forty-eight-hours-following-the-battle-of-cowpens.htm

Galbraith Robinson House, Horseshoe Bridge Road, Westminster, Oconee County, SC | Library of Congress. (n.d.). Library of Congress. Retrieved January 6, 2021, from https://www.loc.gov/item/sc0044/

Geni—Henry Fernandis (1769-1823). (n.d.). Retrieved January 22, 2021, from https://www.geni.com/people/Henry-Fernandis/6000000034627088249

Geni—James Adair, Indian trader (c.1709-1783). (n.d.). Retrieved January 19, 2021, from https://www.geni.com/people/James-Adair-Indian-trader/6000000012681494324#/tab/revision

Geni—Maj. John Lawson Henderson (1744-1824). (n.d.). Retrieved January 22, 2021, from https://www.geni.com/people/Maj-John-Henderson/6000000005414488455#/tab/overview

Great Wagon Road. (2021). In Wikipedia. https://en.wikipedia.org/w/index.php?title=Great_Wagon_Road&oldid=1007767480

Grindal Shoals map. (n.d.). Retrieved February 17, 2021, from https://www.zeemaps.com/view?group=500961&x=-81.659743&y=34.851926&z=3

Grindal Shoals Was Important Crossing. (1954). https://dspace.ychistory.org/handle/11030/71435

Grose, F. (2004). 1811 Dictionary of the Vulgar Tongue. https://www.gutenberg.org/cache/epub/5402/pg5402.html

Hammond's Store Raid of William Washington | Encyclopedia.com. (n.d.). Retrieved January 20, 2021, from https://www.encyclopedia.com/history/encyclopedias-almanacs-transcripts-and-maps/hammonds-store-raid-william-washington

Hammond's Store: The "Dirty War's" Prelude to Cowpens. (2018, December 10). Journal of the American Revolution. https://allthingsliberty.com/2018/12/hammonds-store-the-dirty-wars-prelude-to-cowpens/

Henry Farnandis (1769-1823)—Find A Grave... (n.d.). Retrieved January 22, 2021, from https://www.findagrave.com/memorial/13055495/henry-farnandis

Hope, W. (2003). The Spartanburg area in the American Revolution: A narrative, interpretive and illustrated history of the hitherto grossly underestimated role of the ... thoroughly changed the history of the world (2nd edition). W. Hope.

Hudson, J. (1998, January 28). Molasses' Bittersweet History. SFGATE. https://www.sfgate.com/recipes/article/Molasses-Bittersweet-History-3014292.php

Index of Patrick Moore. (n.d.). Retrieved February 18, 2021, from http://www.carolinaspartan.com/PatrickMoore/

Indian Trading Paths | NCpedia. (n.d.). Retrieved January 13, 2021, from https://www.ncpedia.org/indian-trading-paths

Individual Page. (n.d.). Retrieved February 17, 2021, from https://worldconnect.rootsweb.com/trees/219950/I150776/-/individual

Ingle, S. (2020, July 1). Patriots in Petticoats. Sheila Ingle. https://sheilaingle.com/2020/07/01/patriots-in-petticoats/

Ivey, R. A. (n.d.). Grindal Shoals Gazette. Retrieved January 6, 2021, from http://grindalshoalsgazette.com/

James "Horseshoe" Robertson. (n.d.). Gaffney Ledger.

John Beckham. (n.d.). Geni_family_tree. Retrieved January 11, 2021, from https://www.geni.com/people/John-Beckham/6000000025985246680

John "Jack" Beckham Sr. (1736-1789)—Find A... (n.d.). Retrieved January 11, 2021, from https://www.findagrave.com/memorial/84701934/john-beckham

John Fernandis—Historical records and family trees—MyHeritage. (n.d.). Retrieved January 22, 2021, from https://www.myheritage.com/names/john_fernandis

John Nuckolls. (n.d.). Retrieved January 12, 2021, from https://sc_tories.tripod.com/john_nuckolls.htm

Johnson, W. (1822). Sketches of the Life and Correspondence of Nathanael Greene: Major General of the Armies of the United States, in the War of the Revolution. author.

Joseph McJunkin. (2020). In Wikipedia. https://en.wikipedia.org/w/index.php?title=Joseph_McJunkin&oldid=942605821

Journal of the American Revolution: History, culture, politics, war. (n.d.). Journal of the American Revolution. Retrieved January 11, 2021, from http://allthingsliberty.com/

Johnson, W. (1822). Sketches of the Life and Correspondence of Nathanael Greene: Major General of the Armies of the United States, in the War of the Revolution. author.

Kennedy, J. P. (1835). Horse Shoe Robinson: A Tale of the Tory Ascendency. Carey, Lea & Blanchard.

Landrum, J. B. O. [from old. (2015). Colonial and Revolutionary History of Upper South Carolina. Andesite Press, Chapter XIX, p.131.

Landrum, J. B. O. (1900). History of Spartanburg County: Embracing an Account of Many Important Events, and Biographical Sketches of Statesmen, Divines and Other Public Men. United States: Reprint Company.
Lemuel Alston Farnandis (1803-1863)—Find A... (n.d.). Retrieved January 22, 2021, from https://www.findagrave.com/memorial/13059297/lemuel-alston-farnandis

Logan, J. H. (2009). A history of the upper country of South Carolina, from the earliest periods to the close of the war of independence: Volumes I & II. Reprint Co., Publishers.

Lower Cherokee Traders' Path. (n.d.). FamilySearch Wiki. Retrieved January 13, 2021, from https://www.familysearch.org/wiki/en/Lower_Cherokee_Traders%27_Path

Lynch, J. (n.d.). A Guide to Eighteenth-Century English Vocabulary. 21.

Maj. General Nathanael Greene (Continental Army). (n.d.). Geni_family_tree. Retrieved January 19, 2021, from https://www.geni.com/people/Maj-General-Nathanael-Greene-Continental-Army/6000000010111324564

Maj James Galbraith "Horseshoe" Robertson (1759-1838)—Find A Grave Memorial. (n.d.). Retrieved January 6, 2021, from https://www.findagrave.com/memorial/27235310/james-galbraith-robertson

Marty. (2019, January 15). January 15, 1781 – This Day During The American Revolution – On the Road to Burr's Mill, Spartanburg County, South Carolina. U S Military History. https://mwh52.wordpress.com/2019/01/15/january-15-1781-this-day-during-the-american-revolution-on-the-road-to-burrs-mill-spartanburg-county-south-carolina/

Moncure, J. (1996). The Cowpens Staff Ride and Battlefield Tour. ARMY COMMAND AND GENERAL STAFF COLL FORT LEAVENWORTH KS COMBAT STUDIES INST. https://apps.dtic.mil/sti/citations/ADA530379

Mooney, J. (1894). The Siouan Tribes of the East, pp. 67-74. Johnson Reprint Corporation.

Myers, T. B. (1881). One hundred years ago. The story of the battle of Cowpens. [Charleston]. https://ia800308.us.archive.org/32/items/onehundredyearsa00myer/onehundredyearsa00myer.pdf

Nicholas Jasper | WikiTree FREE Family Tree. (n.d.). Retrieved February 25, 2021, from https://www.wikitree.com/wiki/Jasper-94

Norfleet, P. (n.d.). Battle Sites. Retrieved January 7, 2021, from https://screvwarsites.tripod.com/battle_sites.htm

Old Colonial era idioms & sayings we use today. (2013, December 23). Williamsburg Tours. https://williamsburgprivatetours.com/old-colonial-era-idioms-sayings-we-use-today/

Pacolet. (n.d.). Retrieved January 12, 2021, from https://www.sciway3.net/2001/spartanburg-schools/Pacolet.htm

Pacolet Memories Home Page.html. (n.d.). Retrieved January 6, 2021, from https://pacoletmemories.com/

Person:Adam Goudelock (1)—Genealogy. (n.d.). Retrieved January 11, 2021, from https://www.werelate.org/wiki/Person:Adam_Goudelock_(1)

Phillips, D. (1922). Horse Raising in Colonial New England. Cornell University.

Pvt James Thomas "High Key" Moseley Sr.... (n.d.). Retrieved January 13,

2021, from https://www.findagrave.com/memorial/5619238/james-thomas-moseley

Ramblin—Pafg293—Generated by Personal Ancestral File. (n.d.). Retrieved January 22, 2021, from http://freepages.rootsweb.com/~ramblin/genealogy/pafg293.htm

Ramsay, D. (1858). History of South Carolina From Its First Settlement in 1670 to the Year 1808. W. J. Duffie.

Rev Daniel Asbury (1762-1825)—Find A Grave... (n.d.). Retrieved January 13, 2021, from https://www.findagrave.com/memorial/33744476/daniel-asbury

Revolutionary War Battles for the Year 1781. (n.d.). Retrieved February 15, 2021, from https://www.myrevolutionarywar.com/battles/1781-battles/

Revolutionary War Raids & Skirmishes in 1780. (n.d.). Retrieved February 15, 2021, from https://www.myrevolutionarywar.com/battles/1780-skirmish/

Robertson, J. A. (n.d.). Global Gazetteer of the American Revolution. Retrieved January 6, 2021, from https://web.archive.org/web/20070911030541/http://gaz.jrshelby.com/

Robertson, J. A. (2005, December). Burr's Mill Found? Southern Campaigns of the American Revolution, 2(12). http://southerncampaign.org/newsletter/v2n12.pdf

Saye, J. H. (1847). Memoirs of Major Joseph McJunkin: Revolutionary Patriot. Watchman and Observer.

SC Historic Properties Record: National Register Listing: Nuckolls-Jefferies House [S108177110211]. (n.d.). Retrieved February 17, 2021, from http://schpr.sc.gov/index.php/Detail/properties/12052

SC Mills. (n.d.). [Historical]. South Carolina Mills. Retrieved January 8, 2021, from http://www.scmills.com/history.php

Slave Narratives, Union County, South Carolina Genealogy Trails. (n.d.). Retrieved February 17, 2021, from http://www.genealogytrails.com/scar/union/slave_narratives.htm

South Carolina Legislature resolution to place a roadmarker for James Moseley | These Fosters. (n.d.). Retrieved January 13, 2021, from https://www.myfosters.com/2009/south-carolina-legislature-resolution-to-place-a-roadmarker-for-james-moseley/

List of Sources

Slave Narratives, Union County, South Carolina Genealogy Trails. (n.d.). Retrieved February 17, 2021, from http://www.genealogytrails.com/scar/union/slave_narratives.htm

Sullivan, B. (2015, July 27). Well Said, Old Fellow! How To Speak Like A Colonial Virginian [Travel]. Colonial Williamsburg.

Tarleton, B. (1787). A History of the Campaigns of 1780 and 1781 in the Southern Provinces of North America. Reprint Company.

Tarleton In Ugly Mood. (n.d.). Battle of Cowpens. Retrieved January 11, 2021, from http://www.battleofcowpens.com/memoirs-journals/memoirs-major-joseph-mcjunkin/tarleton-ugly-mood/

Taxes in the Colonies. (n.d.). Retrieved January 28, 2021, from https://www.landofthebrave.info/taxes-in-the-colonies.htm

The American Revolution in South Carolina—The Miscellaneous Players in the Military. (n.d.). Retrieved January 19, 2021, from https://www.carolana.com/SC/Revolution/patriot_military_sc_miscellaneous.htm

The Battle of Cowpens. (n.d.). Battle of Cowpens. Retrieved January 11, 2021, from http://www.battleofcowpens.com/

The Battle of Hammond's Store and the Burning of William's Fort. (2021, January 12). Buk's Historical Ad Hockery. https://bukowo.com/2021/01/12/the-battle-of-hammonds-store-and-the-burning-of-williams-fort/

The Catawba Indians. (n.d.). Access Genealogy. Retrieved January 13, 2021, from https://accessgenealogy.com/north-carolina/the-catawba-indians.htm

The Capture of Thicketty Fort. (2020, August 4). Buk's Historical Ad Hockery. https://bukowo.com/2020/08/04/the-capture-of-thicketty-fort/

The Differences Between a Puma, a Cougar and a Mountain Lion. (n.d.). Sciencing. Retrieved January 11, 2021, from https://sciencing.com/differences-puma-cougar-mountain-lion-8514376.html

THE FOWLER FAMILIES OF UNION COUNTY, SC – A Study of the Henry Ellis Fowler, John Fowler, and Israel Fowler lines. (n.d.). Retrieved January 6, 2021, from https://henry-ellis-fowler.com/

The Iron Works. (n.d.). Retrieved January 20, 2021, from http://glendalesc.com/ironworks.html

The Orion: A Monthly Magazine of Literature and Art. (1843). W. Richards.

The Patriot Resource: Battle of Cowpens. (n.d.). Retrieved January 11, 2021, from http://www.patriotresource.com/amerrev/battles/cowpens/page3.html

The Royal Colony of South Carolina—The Scots-Irish Settlers. (n.d.). Retrieved January 18, 2021, from https://www.carolana.com/SC/Royal_Colony/sc_royal_colony_scots_irish.html

These Fosters | John Foster ~1750 – 1832. (n.d.). Retrieved January 6, 2021, from http://www.myfosters.com/a-foster-saga/john-foster-1752-1832/

Thicketty Fort – EKBarnes. (n.d.). Retrieved February 15, 2021, from https://ekbarnes.com/thicketty-fort/

Union Daily Times. (2018, July 25). The story of an American patriot. https://www.uniondailytimes.com/features/lifestyle/17152/the-story-of-an-american-patriot

University, O. S. (1921). Contributions in History and Political Science. Ohio State University.

Waccamawcharlieblue. (2017, June 9). The Ruins of Christie's Tavern. https://www.youtube.com/watch?v=V5eNCiWoNx0&lc=UgyhCW7jn5a0AIFCl2x4AaABAg

Wade Hampton I. (2021). In Wikipedia. https://en.wikipedia.org/w/index.php?title=Wade_Hampton_I&oldid=1003434730

Wagner, J. R. (2005). Native Americans of Upstate South Carolina. 18. http://cecas.clemson.edu/geolk12/scstudies/files/NativeAmericanFinal%20-%20Copy.pdf

Whig Hill Historical Marker. (n.d.). Retrieved February 17, 2021, from https://www.hmdb.org/m.asp?m=39046

Whig Hill—Gaffney—SC - US. (n.d.). Historical Marker Project. Retrieved February 15, 2021, from https://historicalmarkerproject.com/markers/HMQ4X_whig-hill_Gaffney-SC.html

Windsby, C. (n.d.). Colonial Soap Making. Soap-Making-Essentials.Com. Retrieved January 8, 2021, from http://www.soap-making-essentials.com/colonial-soap-making.html

Who Exactly Were the Scot Irish Ethnically? (n.d.). Retrieved January 25, 2021, from https://www.sjsu.edu/faculty/watkins/scotirish.htm

7 Jun 1989, Page 20—The Gaffney Ledger at Newspapers.com. (n.d.). Newspapers.Com. Retrieved February 17, 2021, from http://www.newspapers.com/image/?clipping_id=9251054&fcfToken=eyJhbGciOiJIUzI1NiIsInR5cCI6IkpXVCJ9.eyJmcmVlLXZpZXctaWQiOjc5NDY1NTcxLCJpYXQiOjE2MTM1ODExMzgsImV4cCI6MTYxMzY2NzUzOH0.Z2YulNCplVi-CMP-94KN5i-EibEaHBMxOFiyJeQqrc0

Tribute to John Robertson

John was born in Tallassee, Alabama, in 1935, where he was raised in the country. His interest in history came from exploring the woods with his three siblings. They would find arrowheads just by looking down. John was the first in his family to complete college, scraping up money for the first year from his savings. He graduated from Auburn University on an ROTC Navy scholarship. Afterward, he served three years as a naval officer.

His civilian career was in the textile industry, including periods in management. However, his passion was for solving technical problems. He was an early adapter of computer and electronic technology, using these promising tools to solve intractable problems.

After retirement from textiles, John found the perfect job at Cowpens National Battlefield, eventually becoming a Park Ranger. In this role, he frequently conducted tours of the battlefield, sharing his insights into the topographical layout of the battle. He always pointed out how local militias and their intimate knowledge of the terrain were essential to winning the day.

John's craving for revolutionary war history extended beyond the Battle of Cowpens. His interest in seeing where history happened and studying the stories of the historical figures drove him to specialize in making detailed maps of Revolutionary War events and campaigns. He spent extensive time visiting historic sites across South Carolina, rediscovering old forts, skirmish locations, and forgotten homeplaces. He used GPS to mark these locales for posterity. He extended his mapping of Revolutionary War sites worldwide, incorporating land and sea military actions. By utilizing layman's tools such as Google Maps, he created many detailed specialized maps. John has provided some of the most comprehensive visualizations of numerous campaigns. Many of John's maps are available for viewing at Cowpens National Battlefield.

Richard C. Meehan, Jr. (left), Mr. John Robertson (right)

About the Author

Richard C. Meehan, Jr. was born on July 18, 1960, near the end of the Baby Boom. He grew up in Spartanburg, an upstate South Carolina town rich in Colonial American history. Richard, Dick Meehan (Richard's father), Dr. Alva S. Pack, III (Optometrist), and James Anderson (Realtor), became partners in Grindal Shoals Sportsman's Club. The club owns the property adjacent to Grindal's Ford, a parcel of Tory Alexander Chesney's original king's grant. It contains several duck swamps and teems with wildlife, just as in the olden days.

In 1982, after graduating from Wofford, his hometown college, Richard became a full-time employee of Marko Janitorial Supply, his parents' business. Over the next thirty-eight years, he performed all jobs at the company but was primarily a marketing expert. Richard's writing appears in fiction and nonfiction magazines, e-zines, newspaper columns, and novels. In addition, he enjoys singing, playing the saxophone and the piano. He lives in Spartanburg with his wife, Renee, his most demanding critic who happens to be a teacher.

Other Books by This Author

These books may be found on Amazon, Barnes and Noble, and many other websites.

Duck Tale: A Quacking Good Trek to Manhood! – a coming of age adventure memoir.

Tales From Omega Station – a science fiction shared world anthology featuring Charlie Manus, intrepid envirosuit salesman.

The Janitor's Closet: How to Get into the Janitorial Business and Stay There! – A quirky look at the whys and hows of the cleaning industry for those wishing to succeed in the World of Clean.

For further information, please visit www.rcmeehan.com.

SAUNDERS'
WASHINGTON'S CAVALRY
HOWARD'S CONTINENTALS
LEM
X
MORGAN
PICKINS' MILITIA
SHARPSHOOTERS
N. CAROLINA
BATTLE OF COWPENS
JANUARY, 17, 1981
MAP BY RICHARD C. MEEHAN, JR.

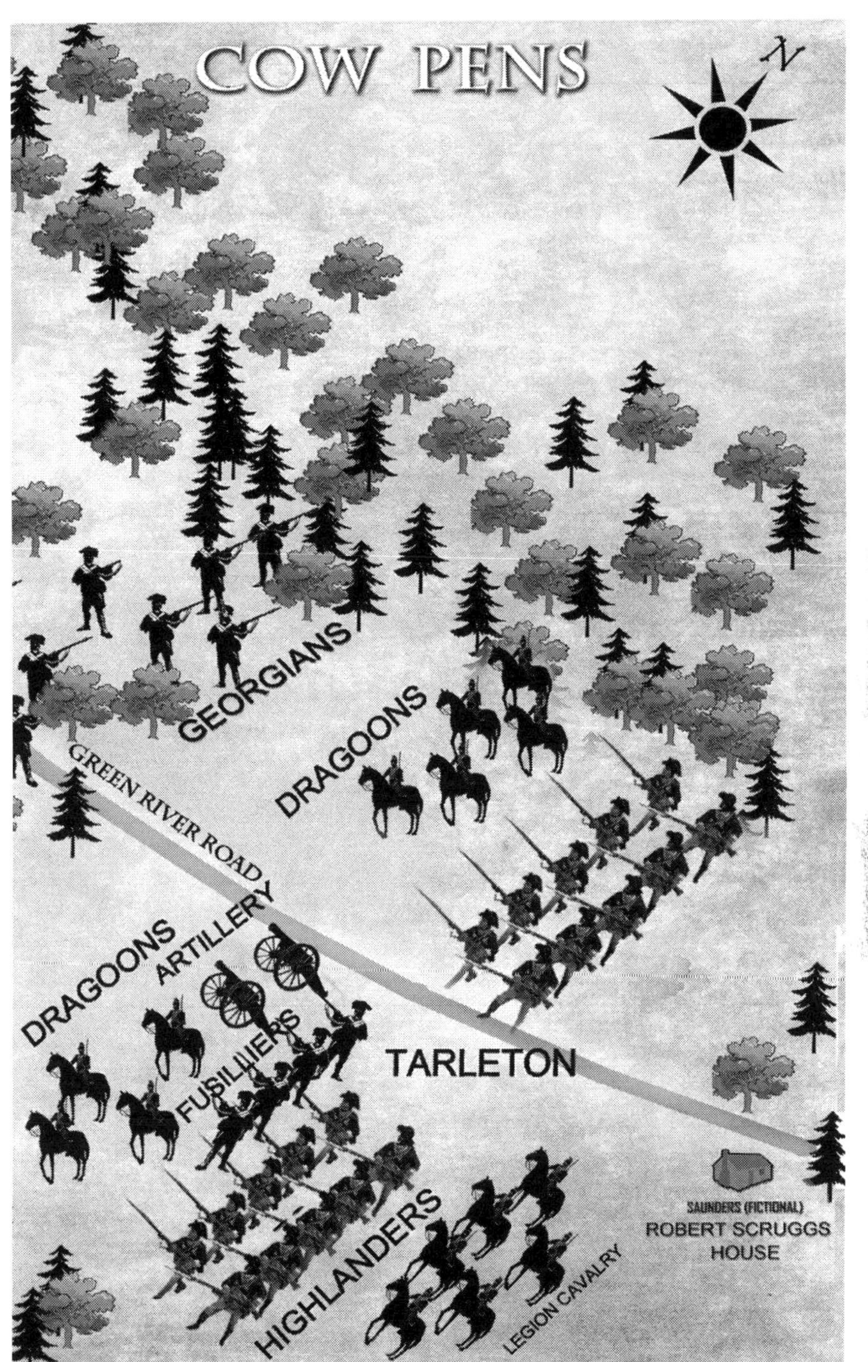
COW PENS
N
GEORGIANS
DRAGOONS
GREEN RIVER ROAD
ARTILLERY
DRAGOONS
FUSILLIERS
TARLETON
HIGHLANDERS
LEGION CAVALRY
SAUNDERS (FICTIONAL)
ROBERT SCRUGGS
HOUSE

SAUNDERS COWPENS
N
WASHINGTON'S CAVALRY
HOWARD'S CONTINENTALS
LEM
MORGAN
PICKINS' MILITIA
SHARPSHOOTERS
GEORGIANS
DRAGOONS
N. CAROLINA
ARTILLERY
DRAGOONS
FUSILIERS
INFANTRY
TARLETON
HIGHLANDERS
GREEN RIVER ROAD
LEGION CAVALRY
ROBERT SCRUGGS
HOUSE
BATTLE OF COWPENS
JANUARY, 17, 1981
MAP BY RICHARD C. MEEHAN, JR.

Made in the USA
Monee, IL
02 May 2022

10580787-fc9d-42d2-be66-e214891ab6c1R01